MW00761325

THE CUSTER
CONSPIRACY

Dennis Koller

PEN
BOOKS

California

Pen Books
A Division of Pen Communication
Pleasant Hill, CA

This book is a work of fiction. Names, characters, places and incidents either are products of the author's imagination or are used fictitiously. Any resemblance to persons living or dead is entirely coincidental.

Second Pen Books paperback edition October 2016

Edited by: Patricia Leslie; Ed Addeo and David Almeida

Cover Design: Ruth Schwartz, The Wonderlady

Visit Pen Books on the World Wide Web at
www.PenBooks.biz

Manufactured in the United States of America

ISBN-13: 9780998080802

ISBN-10: 0998080802

Thank you for purchasing this Pen Books paperback.
Please remember to leave a Review
at your favorite retailer.

To Sarah—
my Muse, my best friend,
and the love of my life.
With her, everything is possible.

CHAPTER 1

Arnaud Winery
Chinon, France

Alain Arnaud followed the faint plume of dust the vehicle made as it climbed the unpaved road from the highway to his vineyard. He had no doubt the men inside that vehicle were coming to kill him. And after him, his son. They couldn't afford to leave any family member alive.

He picked up the phone. "The men, Marcel ... the ones we knew might come someday?" Arnaud paused, swallowing hard. "They're here." The gasp he heard in his ear was not unexpected. "Yes ... exactly Marcel. Now listen to me. We don't have much time. Carefully check to see if everything you need is still in the trunk. Put the trunk in the van, then call me back. I'll alert Christophe you're coming."

He hung up and placed a call to Canada. His eyes filled at the sound of his son's voice. "Christophe," he said, not allowing the overwhelming sorrow he felt to be heard in his voice, "I have bad news. The secret is out." He paused to let that sink in. "Now listen to me carefully. Men will be coming for you. Dangerous men. Maybe tonight. Maybe tomorrow. But they will come. I want you to leave your apartment immediately." Arnaud shook his head vigorously as he listened to his son's reply. "Christophe, stop!" he said. "Don't argue with me!" He grimaced, then took a deep breath, calming himself. "There are men on the way to the winery as we speak. What will happen when they get here is anybody's guess. And even if I knew, there is nothing I could do about it now. What's

1

done is done. It's the future I have to protect. Your future, Christophe. Marcel is coming for you. He will arrive tomorrow morning and meet you at the agreed upon spot. You remember where that is, don't you?" Hearing Christophe's reply, he continued. "Good. Now listen to me carefully. When we hang up, I want you to take all the money you have, put it in your pocket and simply walk out the door. From now on remember – you will use only cash. Leave your keys; credit cards; wallet; anything that would identify you as Christophe Arnaud. Destroy your phone or, better yet, dump it down a sewer. Just walk away. Don't look back. Go to the spot where Marcel will meet you. He has your new identity papers with him."

There was a moment of awkward silence as Arnaud remembered the last time he was with Christophe. Ten months ago. In this very room. The morning sunlight streaming through the window. Like now. He remembered tousling Christophe's hair as they sat waiting for Marcel to take him to the airport. Choking back a sob, he said, "I love you, Christophe. More than you will ever know. May God be with you." And hung up.

Arnaud walked over to the table and poured himself the last of the Domaine Arnaud, the red that won him the *2008 European Winemaker of the Year* award. Staring at his reflection in the mirror above the fireplace, he cursed the day the American professor found him. Sighing in resignation, he raised his glass in a final salute. "To the secret," he whispered in a final toast. "May my son survive its revelation."

~~~~

The American had arrived unannounced the week before. His business card identified him as Matthew Conroy, a professor of history at St. John's University in New York. He asked the assistant if he could speak with Alain Arnaud. He told her a colleague of his at the University of

Laval in Quebec stumbled upon some startling historical information. Information that only Arnaud could confirm or deny.

Arnaud agreed to meet him. His son was a student at Laval. As soon as he heard Conroy mention the Laval connection, his heart thudded like a fist against his ribs. The family's secret, the one so carefully guarded for the past five generations, had been compromised. The genie was out of the bottle.

While Arnaud denied all Conroy's assertions, he knew Conroy didn't believe him. He also knew it was just a matter of time before others found out. Those *others* would also come to his winery. Those *others* would be ruthless men who would do everything in their power to make sure the family's secret never saw the light of day. Those *others* were here.

~~~~

Marcel Toussaint called ten minutes later. "Everything we need is in the car, my friend. I am ready to depart.

"The passports, U.S. driver's licenses, financial records? Are you sure?" Arnaud asked.

"Yes. And the two FedEx packages as well. I will be sure they get to Professor Conroy. I'll send the first package as soon as I get to Paris. The second after Christophe and I settle in New York."

"Excellent. Now promise me, Marcel, that by the time you leave Canada, Christophe will have completely immersed himself in his new persona. You know how young people are – they haven't lived long enough to appreciate how precious life is." He paused, then said, "Or how quickly it can end."

"I will, *mon ami*. You can count on me to keep him safe until you join us."

"You know I'll try my best," Arnaud said, "but with these men …" He shrugged and let the thought drift away into the early afternoon air. "Tell Christophe …" He felt his eyes starting to burn again. "Tell him I love him dearly." He paused, wiping his eyes with the back of his hand. "And you, dear friend, I love you dearly as well. May God be with you."

"And with you, Alain," Toussaint said. "Know I will protect Christophe with my life."

~~~~

Arnaud watched from the window as the vehicle finally came into view. He felt at peace – confident that as of twenty minutes ago, the names Marcel Toussaint and Christophe Arnaud had vanished from the face of the earth. He smiled as he watched three men get out of the car. *Too late, gentlemen*, he thought. Walking back to his desk, he picked up the .45 automatic, put it under his chin and pulled the trigger.

CHAPTER 2

San Francisco
Three Days Later

I stepped out of the shower and reached for the towel just as the phone rang. *How annoying*, I thought. *No way I'm going to drip my way back into the bedroom to answer the damn phone.* Just then, the ringing stopped. I smiled into the mirror. *See? There is a God.*

But, unfortunately, it wasn't God. It was my ex-wife, Maureen. Without warning, the bathroom door flew open. And there she was, scowl on her face and phone in hand.

I jumped a foot. "Geez, Mo, you scared the crap out of me," I said, quickly wrapping the towel around my waist. An odd reaction, I know. I'd been married to this woman for twelve years. We even had a child together. You'd think her seeing me in the nude wouldn't embarrass me. But oddly enough, it did.

"You've added a few pounds," she said with a smirk.

"Thanks," I said. "Nice of you to notice."

She pushed the phone at me. "It's for you." I took it from her, covering the receiver with my hand. A habit born from experience. In case we ended up in a shouting match.

"What the hell you doing here?" I snapped. "And how'd you get in?"

She took a key ring from her pocket and shook it in my face. "I got the keys to your damn house from TJ. Your son, in case you've forgotten. From the last time he stayed here." She took two steps back, probably to give her more room to jab a finger at me. Which she did. "And don't you dare use that tone of voice on me ever again."

This conversation was reminiscent of old times. A big fight was coming; I could feel it. I raised my free hand like a stop sign. "Hold on, okay? Let me get rid of this call. Then we can talk." I put the phone to my ear. "Yes?"

"Is this Tom McGuire?"

A freaking sales call, I thought. I was about to hang up, but something in the voice stopped me. "It is," I said tentatively.

"San Francisco PD homicide inspector extraordinaire?"

"Some would say," I answered, now intrigued as to who it might be.

"Ex-coach of the best damn high school football team in Northern Cal a few years back?"

I smiled, all the anger and frustration of the last few minutes melting away. One of my *guys*. "You got *that* right," I said.

"Coach Mac? This is Matt Conroy."

I felt the smile flood my face. Maureen took notice, too, and scowled. "Matt? Son-of-a-bitch. Hold on for a sec, okay? I've got a visitor here. She's just about to leave." I pressed the phone to my chest. "Gotta take this," I said, shrugging my shoulders like there was nothing I could do about it.

She knew she was being dismissed, and wasn't a happy camper. She retreated a step, clenching and unclenching her fists. "We're not done yet," she stammered. "This is about TJ. His future."

"You're wrong, Mo. We *are* done. At least for now. I'll call you later."

With a glare that would make hell freeze over, she turned and stomped out of the room.

"Hey," I yelled after her. "Leave the damn keys to the house on the table on your way out."

I put the phone to my ear. "Sorry about that, Matt. The ex showed up unexpectedly."

"Didn't mean to interrupt, Coach. Want me to call back?" Just then the front door slammed shut. The perfect exclamation point to Mo's visit.

"Nah, don't worry about it. She just left," I said. "God, it's good to hear your voice, Matt. You in the City?"

"No. Still back east."

"How long has it been? I've lost all track of time."

"A sign of old age, Coach." He laughed. "Let's see. I moved back after the accident."

Accident. The very word made the hairs on the back of my neck stand at attention. I was there that day. Matt's last collegiate football game. Being talked about as a second- or third-round NFL draft pick. I'm on the sidelines as his special guest. Then the hit from behind. His piercing scream. The ambulance rushing him and his shattered leg to the emergency hospital.

"I moved to New York in early 2006," he continued. "So, yeah, it's been ten years already. I'm sorry I haven't kept in touch as well as I should have. Been really busy. Teaching and writing."

"I know. I get your Christmas cards."

Conroy laughed. "You mean Cindy's 'year-in-review' missive? You're probably the only person in the world who reads the damn thing. I tell her she writes too much. No one has the time, nor probably the interest," he chuckled again, "to read her five page epistles."

"Well, I do. Tell her that. If it wasn't for her, I would never have known you won a silver medal in the Paralympics," I said. "Congrats."

"Thanks, Coach. Shot Put. And let me tell you, it's hard to *put* the *shot* with only one leg." He laughed.

"I can only imagine."

"But … yeah … after having my leg amputated, I needed something to keep me from feeling sorry for myself. So I started working out again. Hard. I really pushed myself. Just like I would've had to do to make the NFL.

Anyway, Paralympics gave me the motivation. Winning that medal was really special. Got me noticed by prosthetic manufacturers. They started sending me their latest devices to try out. Talk about being a guinea pig – I tried 'em all. Rated them from best to worst. I've been told my ratings helped put the right prosthetic on our Vets coming back from Iraq and Afghanistan. Quite fulfilling."

"I'm really proud of you, Matt. You're a tough son-of-a-bitch to bounce back like you have."

"Thanks, Coach. But, listen, that's not why I called. I'm coming out West and hoped you could get a few days off and we could visit."

"Well, hell yeah, Matt. Are you kidding me? When?"

"Day after tomorrow," he answered.

"Hmm. Kinda short notice," I said, mentally clicking through my schedule. "But, yeah. I think I can arrange the time. Let's see – have a dentist appointment tomorrow morning, but I could cancel. No problem there. Probably talk my supervisor into giving me a few vacation days."

"Sorry for the short notice, Coach. I didn't even know until late yesterday that I'd be coming."

"You're coming to San Francisco?"

"No. That's the other thing, Coach. I'm flying to Montana."

"Montana?"

"Yeah. Let me explain. You may not know it, but I've published three historical biographies in the past five years."

"Thanks to Cindy's Christmas *missives*, I knew that," I said with a laugh. "Even bought the one you wrote on President Grant. Nice job. Impressive."

"Thanks. But you're going to be even more impressed with the one I'm working on now." He stopped, waiting for me to ask.

"Okay. You got me hooked. Tell me."

"I'm writing a book on General George Custer. One of your favorites, if I remember correctly."

"You do remember correctly," I said with a chuckle. Conroy took my history class as a senior. I spent a lot of time on Custer and the opening of the American West.

"So, Coach, that's why Montana. I'm coming out to the battlefield to do final research for the book, and thought you might want to join me."

"Son-of-a-bitch, Matt. Going to the Little Bighorn has been on my bucket list forever," I said, thinking of different ways to maneuver my supervisor into granting me the time off.

"It gets better, Coach," he said. "We'll be there on June twenty-fifth. The anniversary of the battle. Thought that might be an added incentive."

"How cool is that? But, truthfully, Custer and the *Con* are the only incentives I need."

"I'm bringing Cindy with me, by the way. You'll get a chance to meet each other. She's heard a lot about you over the years."

"Uh-oh," I said. I heard Conroy laugh.

"And one more thing, Coach. The most *important* thing. In the past few days I've corroborated some startling information on Custer and the battle at the Little Bighorn. Seriously, it will knock your jock off."

"Okay. You've managed to pique my curiosity. Whatcha got?"

"Can't say over the phone. Tell you when I see you. It's big, Coach. And I mean *big*. Could possibly rewrite the past hundred and forty years of world history."

"Whoa. Hold on, my man," I said. "Sure you're not exaggerating just a wee bit? The Battle of the Little Bighorn is one of the most written about, most studied, battles in all of American history."

"True. That and Gettysburg," Conroy said.

"Yeah, and Gettysburg," I said. "But I have to tell you, I've read most every book written on Custer and the Little Bighorn battle. Far as I know, just about everything's been said."

"Not everything, Coach. Not *everything*."

CHAPTER 3

Conroy and I talked another thirty minutes while I tried to cajole him into telling me his damn secret. No luck. I'd just have to wait.

After hanging up, I walked into the kitchen and found the keys Maureen left on the table – along with a scribbled note. *TJ told me he's thinking of majoring in criminal justice. If he does, he'll turn out to be a cop. Like you. I won't stand for that. You've got to talk him out of it. Call me.*

No way I was going to call her. Ours had been a contentious divorce. *I was a terrible father. A crappy husband. I spent more time with my damn high school football team than her. Didn't make enough money to support her in the style to which she aspired.* If I'd heard those complaints once, I'd heard 'em a thousand times. I was in no mood to hear them again.

About the crappy husband part? She was probably right. I did spend more time with my football team than her. Given the choice, who wouldn't? They were a hell of a lot more fun. The year TJ turned seven, Maureen forced me, under penalty of divorce, to quit my high school teaching job and get a *real job*, as she called it. Tore me up. But I did it for her and TJ. To save our marriage. Signed up and was accepted into the SFPD. My dad had been a decorated San Francisco PD homicide inspector. He was killed in the line of duty six years ago. *Line of duty*, my ass. I'd been in the department for eight years by then. I knew the real story. But I never pushed back. What was done, was done. Nothing I could do or say was ever going to change the "official" cause of his death. Probably the reason why the higher ups in the Department felt safe when Lt. Bristow took me from Robbery to Homicide. But it didn't save the marriage. She hated me being a cop more than she did a coach. No mystery there. I smiled at the thought. Even though I was making more money, I had gone from one primarily male environment to another. Lots of swagger. Lots of testosterone. Lots of late nights. Not what she had in mind.

Mo divorced me when TJ was ten years old. Shortly afterward, she moved to Los Angeles. Shortly after that, she remarried. Her new husband was, no surprise, a complete jerk. They both kept me away from TJ as much as they could, making it difficult to keep a good relationship with him.

Eight years later, Maureen returned to the Bay Area. Unmarried. By that time, TJ had graduated from high school and been accepted to UCLA.

Her coming north turned out to be a blessing. Having both his parents in northern California meant I got to see TJ more often. And the more I saw him, the closer we became. He started staying with me during the summers, and before long our relationship was back to how it had been prior to the divorce. Even though TJ felt duty bound to root for the Dodgers, we started going to Giants games together. Just like old times. Happier times. He started hanging out with me in the squad room. Unlike when he visited a decade before, there were now women in the department. Being a good-looking kid, the female officers flirted with him unmercifully. He loved it. So it didn't surprise me that he wanted to become a police officer. I loved life again.

A terrible father? Screw you, Maureen. I picked up the phone and punched in a number.

"Hey, TJ. It's your old man."

"Hey, Dad. How's it going?"

"Couldn't be better. You?"

"Doin' okay, Dad. Glad you called. I was going to call you later this afternoon. Guess what?"

"Surprise me," I said.

"Got a job for the summer. Riverside PD."

"Whoa. Good for you. How'd you score that?"

"UCLA Criminal Justice Department. One of my profs called last night and said they had an internship for a junior majoring in Criminal Justice. They chose me."

"That's a real honor. I'm proud of you."

"I'm pretty stoked, too. Can't wait. It's only going to be for a month. That's all they have the funds for."

"Have you told your mom yet?"

"Not yet. You know she is trying to talk me out of this major?"

"I know. She came over today and insisted I talk you out of it. Fat chance. When do you start?"

"Wednesday. They want me right away. Even though it's just a month internship, I'll be getting paid for it."

"Hey, paid or not, makes no difference. It's all about résumé building. Besides, you don't need the money when you have a father who's shelling out the big bucks for tuition and booze." I laughed. So did he. "Too damn bad, though, you have to start so soon. I'm taking a trip to Montana on Wednesday. Came up suddenly. Like your internship. Goin' to the Little Bighorn. Calling to see if you wanted to come with me."

"Dad, you know I'd love to, but ... the job and all."

"Hey, I understand. No need to apologize. We'll have a chance to do it again. Maybe I can come see you when I get back. You got room for me?"

"Got that ratty pull-out sofa. It's all yours. I think you've been the only person to ever sleep on it. My friends won't. But Dad, can you do me a favor?"

"Anything."

"Can you keep Mom away from me for a while. I hate to disappoint her, but I really do want to pursue this justice thing."

"I'll try, TJ. But you know how headstrong your mom can be at times."

"Yeah, I know." He paused, and then said, "Dad, I'm glad you're back in my life. I know I never told you, but I really missed all the things we had. Thanks for sticking with me."

An indescribable feeling of warmth came over me. All the hurt, over all the years, had just been washed away.

CHAPTER 4

Little Bighorn Battlefield
Montana

I turned the rental car into the entrance of the Little Big-horn Battlefield National Monument just past eight in the morning. It was late June. The sun was out, the sky an early summer blue, and the soft breeze coming through the open car window smelled of newly mowed lawn.

My flight was delayed an hour in Portland due to mechanical problems. I called Conroy and told him to expect me sometime around eight. He said it would be no problem. To meet him at the Visitor Center.

Even with my late arrival, the park would still be closed at this hour. Somehow Conroy had finagled a way to show me around before it opened.

A long time coming, I thought, as I drove through the open gates. It was June twenty-fifth. On this day, one hundred and forty years before, two hundred and ten troopers of the U.S. 7th Cavalry, under the command of Lt. Colonel George Armstrong Custer, fought and died in the valley now spread out before me.

Goose bumps dotted my forearms. A bucket list two-fer. Reconnecting with the *Con* and walking Custer's battlefield. It didn't get any better than this.

I read my first book on Custer and the Battle of the Little Bighorn while I was at Annapolis. I was immediately hooked. Some claimed that the battle illustrated the bravery of two hundred and ten men led by a flamboyant, gallant and heroic former Civil War general who never gave up despite being outgunned and outmanned. Others claimed that the Cavalry, and especially their arrogant commander Custer, got what they deserved for trying to end the Plains Indians' way of life only because they had become an inconvenient obstacle to America's westward expansion. Truthfully, I wasn't interested in either view. As I told Conroy on the phone, all I really wanted was to put myself in Custer's boots. To see what he saw. To understand his tactical options. To understand why he died that day.

I followed the signs directing me to the Visitor Center. It was on the high side of a slope overlooking a field of crosses. Cemetery Ridge. Custer's E Company regrouped on this ridge in a desperate attempt to reach his surrounded command. What became known as Last Stand Hill was about one hundred yards to the east. Most of E Company was cut down before they got there.

I parked, bowed my head in respect to the men buried under those crosses, and walked toward the Visitor Center. No Conroy. The door was locked and there was not a light on anywhere in the building. The sign on the door said it opened at nine-thirty. A sidewalk led from the Visitor Center to Last Stand Hill where Custer and fifty or so of his remaining troopers clustered together to fight and die. Tombstones marked the spot where each fell. At the crest of the hill stood a large obelisk memorializing the area where Custer himself was killed.

I decided I might as well explore Last Stand Hill. Since there was no one else in the park that early morning, I knew Conroy wouldn't have any trouble finding me.

I was mistaken about being the only person in the park. As I cleared the Visitor Center and started up the incline toward the memorial, I saw someone seated at a funny angle with his back against the obelisk. From this distance I couldn't tell if it was Conroy, but I couldn't imagine who else it would be.

"Matt?" I shouted.

Whoever was sitting there didn't move a muscle. My cop instincts went into the red zone. I broke into a jog. At twenty feet I saw a prosthesis sticking out from a pant leg, and I knew it was Matt. At fifteen feet I noticed a swarm of flies around him. At ten feet I saw the back of his head was missing.

CHAPTER 5

Even though I hadn't seen Matt Conroy in more than fifteen years, seeing him like this felt like a kick in the groin. But the cop in me quickly overcame the shock. I knelt beside him, bending sideways to see his face. It showed no sign of *rigor mortis*, which meant he was probably shot within the last hour. *I'm so sorry, Matt,* I thought. *That damn airplane. If I had been on time, I might have been able to prevent this.* I took off my jacket, wanting to put it over his head. At the least, it would keep the flies off him.

As I bent to cover him, two things happened simultaneously. First, a bullet buzzed past my ear and hammered into the obelisk behind me. Second, the dull sound of a distant rifle shot registered in my brain. Instinct immediately took over. I flattened myself on the ground next to Conroy's body and reached for my P7. It wasn't there. *What the fuck,* I thought. Then I remembered. After parking the rental car by the Visitor Center, I placed the weapon out of sight under the driver's seat. Not that it would have done me much good out here. In an urban environment, my HK P7 9mm was my best friend. In the open prairie like this and facing an enemy with a long gun, it would have been virtually useless. With no weapon, I did the next best thing. I pulled out my cell and hit 9-1-1.

The shot had come from the Deep Ravine, about five hundred yards down the hill and to my right. While waiting for the call to connect, I elbow-pulled myself behind a headstone that told me that an unknown trooper of the 7th

Cavalry died on that spot on June 25, 1876. It offered me good cover. I silently thanked him for his service.

"9-1-1." A woman's voice. Calm and reassuring. It didn't work on me. I was anything but calm and reassured. I gave her my name and SFPD badge number. "I'm unarmed and taking fire. We have a casualty." I could hear her keyboard clicking away, verifying my *bona fides*. I knew that her screen's GPS would tell her where I was calling from.

"Do you need an ambulance?"

"No," I said as calmly as I could. "It's a fatality. But if you don't get someone here ASAP," I continued, my voice rising, "you're going to have another fucking fatality here. Me." I took a deep breath, forcing myself to calm down.

"I'm sorry, sir. I have a highway patrol vehicle on its way. ETA five minutes."

"Tell them there's an active shooter with a rifle in the Deep Ravine. I'm sure they'll know where that is."

"Copy that." She left me for a few moments. Coming back online, she said, "I've alerted the county coroner's office along with the local law enforcement agencies. Both ETAs within ten to fifteen minutes."

"Thank you," I said. "One more thing. Could you alert the Billings office of the FBI? This is going to end up on their desk. Might as well give them a heads-up."

"Copy that," she replied.

By that time, the highway patrol car had entered the Monument's parking lot. Siren screaming. Announcing to the shooter it was probably time to adios. I breathed a sigh of relief. Unlike the trooper whose headstone I was hiding behind, *my* reinforcements had arrived on time. I made a note to be sure to thank them.

"Billings FBI will arrive in forty-five minutes," the 9-1-1 dispatcher said. "I heard the highway patrol arrive. You're in good hands now. Anything more I can do for you?"

"I appreciate everything you've done. I'll let the right people know," I said. And I meant it. "And I'm sorry if I yelled at you. Wasn't professional of me."

"Not to worry, sir," she replied. "I've heard a lot worse. Good luck to you." Then she was gone.

CHAPTER 6

Leesburg, Virginia

Nineteen hundred miles east, in a stately Victorian on the outskirts of Leesburg, Virginia, a phone rang. A neatly dressed middle-aged man walked across the Kashan Oriental rug that covered the middle part of what, in those homes, was called the *Study*. He unlocked the bottom drawer of an ornate mahogany desk. From the selection of eight identical cell phones, he picked up the one that was ringing.

"Yes," he said in a controlled voice.

"It's done," said the caller.

"You're certain?"

"I am," the caller answered. "A head shot."

"From the Springfield or the Winchester?"

"I used a Winchester. I only needed one shot. You told me you wanted to be as authentic and efficient as possible."

"Yes. Thank you." The man paused, and then said, "Did his friend arrive?"

"He's here. I'm looking at him now through the scope. I pumped one by his ear. A warning to stay away. He's flat out on the ground now. Behind a tombstone. No weapon that I can see. He's on his cell phone. Probably calling 9-1-1." The caller pulled his own cell phone from his ear and listened. "In fact I think I hear a siren now. Probably should get going."

"I'm glad you didn't kill him," the man said. "Conroy's death won't raise much of a fuss. You take out a cop and the shit will hit the fan. We certainly don't need that." He paused again. "Can you get out easily?"

"Yes. I'm in the Deep Ravine. I'll re-cross the river. My car is not far from here."

The man in Leesburg closed his eyes so he could visualize clearly where the shooter was. Deep Ravine was a long, steep-sided gully filled with brush and trees at the bottom of Cemetery Ridge. Twenty-six bodies of Custer's E Company were found in that ravine. Speculations as to why they didn't stay and help defend Last Stand Hill range from sheer panic to a deliberate order from Custer. Apparently, in all the confusion, Custer sent five mounted troopers east to fetch Captain Benteen's command to come rescue him. Ordering E Company to rush the ravine could have been a diversionary measure. No one knows for sure. What they do know was that E Company and the five troopers he sent to find Benteen were all slaughtered. Custer and those with him on the hill were next.

"And you will visit the wife?"

"That's my next stop. Don't worry. We'll have everything wrapped up by nightfall."

Satisfied, the man in the study hung up. He erased the phone's number by clicking the "burn" button. Knowing that was nothing more than cosmetic, he walked to his garage, put the phone into his commercial grade trash compactor and pushed "pulverize."

CHAPTER 7

Little Bighorn Battlefield

There were two highway patrol officers. One carried a shotgun, the other an AR-15. They took up positions behind the Visitor Center and acknowledged my presence with a wave. All business. Good for them. "Shooter," I yelled. "Deep Ravine." I pointed down the slope. They give me a thumbs up. After conversing for a few moments, the one with the AR-15 crawled around the side of the Center and took up a position behind a stone barbeque pit facing the Ravine. The other took off in the opposite direction, circling around Cemetery Ridge in a flanking maneuver.

In the distance, I could hear the whine of more approaching sirens. Six minutes later, the parking lot was teaming with police and county medical staff cars.

Different jurisdictions had different procedures in homicide cases. The way they went about business here reminded me a lot of how we did it in San Francisco. The coroner had complete authority over the crime scene. Before any police officer was allowed on an active homicide scene, the coroner and his or her staff had already bagged, tagged and photographed all relevant evidence. As the county coroner trudged up the hill, I knelt beside Conroy's body and said a prayer. Standing, I murmured to myself, "I'll find the son-of-a-bitch who did this to you, Matt. I promise. And when I do, he'll pay."

While the coroner and his staff were doing their ghoulish work, I joined the local law in the Visitor Center drinking coffee and eating donuts, both supplied by the last car to arrive. Standard operating procedure. We did the same in San Francisco, except our donuts were better. To the uninitiated, stopping on the way to a murder scene to pick up coffee and donuts might seem cynical and callous, but the reality was crime scenes involving homicides were mind-numbingly dull. Even factoring in the time the coroner needed to finish his investigation, the officers standing around eating donuts in the Visitor Center understood this was a National Park. Federal jurisdiction. No matter what, none were going to be involved in any part of this investigation. For them, speeding to the scene was just a way to get out of the office, kill time and eat donuts.

Twenty minutes later the two highway patrolmen came back. They made eye contact with me, motioning with their heads that I should follow them. We all grabbed coffee and a donut and went to an inner office.

After introducing themselves, the officer named Carl said, "You're right, Inspector. Shooter was in the Deep Ravine. I was careful not to disturb the area in case he left shoe prints or somethin'. But the guy knew what he was doin'. Hardly a grass blade disturbed. But …" He paused to sip his coffee.

"But …?" I said.

"But, he made a mistake," Carl said, taking a bite from his donut. "A biggie, too."

"Come on, Carl. Stop with the drama. What mistake?"

"Left a shell casing. At the bottom of Deep Ravine."

"You're kidding," I said. "A shell casing? Geez, we dealing with an amateur? I just lost a lot of respect for this guy."

"Don't be too quick passin' judgment on that boy just yet, Hoss," said Carl. "You been in that ravine?" I shook my head. "Steep sum-bitch. I'm thinkin' he ejected the shell when he was going to zing one by your ear. Maybe it kicked off a rock or somethin' and went over the side. I'm thinkin' when we came roaring into the Park, he decided it was time to vanish. Didn't have time to go after it. Let us find it. Probably figured it didn't make any difference, one way or the other. Fact is, if it were just any ol' casing, he'd a probably been right."

"So you're telling me he made a mistake? Or didn't make a mistake. Which one?" I asked.

"Oh, there was a mistake, alright," Carl said. "The casing is from a 44.40 Winchester cartridge."

"And what's so magical about a 44.40?" I asked.

"Not magical. Just curious is all. You don't see it 'round much anymore, 'cept maybe in specialty catalogues. It was originally made for the Winchester Model 1873. The so-called 'Gun That Won the West.' Lot of those rifles, by the way, found their way to the Custer battlefield in the hands of Sioux and Cheyenne warriors." He took a sip of his coffee. "Just sayin'."

"Don't tell me you think …"

"Hey, boss," he interrupted. "I ain't telling you nothin'. It's just curious. The 44.40 fell out of favor a long time ago. Last few years, though, made a comeback in a competitive contest known as Cowboy Action Shooting. The rules require shooters use firearms from the mid-to-late eighteen hundreds. Your shooter made a damn difficult shot. Four, five hundred yards. Uphill. If I were you, I'd make it a point to talk to the national CAS folks. Perp could have just left you a clue to his identity."

CHAPTER 8

Both highway patrolmen left. I was talking to the sheriff from Harding, a small town ten miles north of the Monument, when Jeff Meeks, the Special Agent in Charge of the FBI Montana office, arrived with three of his agents.

"You're the one who called this in?" he asked. I nodded and started to reach for my credentials. He waved off my effort. "You don't need those," he said. "9-1-1 dispatch gave me your creds. I called San Francisco PD. Spoke to your supervisor, Lt. Bristow."

I nodded. As if reading my thoughts, Meeks said, "He vouched for you. You're a homicide inspector, huh?"

"I am," I replied. "And I'm glad you guys are here. The murder victim was a friend of mine. I'm offering you my services. I want to find the prick who did this."

"I hear you," Meeks said. "But just to be clear – even though this is federal land, this isn't our jurisdiction."

"I wondered about that." I said. "US Park Police?" Meeks nodded. "I've worked with them a few times in San Francisco. Good people."

"After I called SFPD to check you out, I called Chief Jenkins at the Park Police office in San Francisco. I just wanted to alert him that we'd baby-sit the scene until he arrived. He said he knows you. Said to say *hi*."

"I've worked with him on a few cases," I said. "Jenkins is a good man."

"Strange thing happened on the way down here, though. Jenkins called me back. Said when he requested authorization to travel to Billings to take over this case, he was denied. He was told his office had too much of a case-load in the Bay Area to handle this one. That's from his people in D.C. Told him it was going to be turned over to the FBI."

"Never heard of anything like that happening. Strange," I said.

"Tell me about it," Meeks replied. "I haven't heard from my people in D.C. about this." He waved his hand in the air. "In any case, you're stuck with me, even if only for a little while. So, tell me, what the hell happened here to-day?"

I told him everything. Letting it spill out in as much detail as I could. From how I knew Conroy; to the initial conversation where he told me he was working on some-thing so big it would rewrite the history books; to my plane being delayed in Portland even though I knew it had zip to do with what happened; to arriving at the Park and finding him dead on Last Stand Hill; to the shot that had whistled past my ear; to my calling 9-1-1, and finally about the two highway patrol officers who were the first to arrive. I told him about the shell casing they saw at the bottom of Deep Ravine.

Meeks made a few notes on a scratchpad he took from his inside jacket pocket, but otherwise didn't interrupt my stream of consciousness. When I finished my tale, Meeks told two of his agents to secure the Deep Ravine as a crime scene, and to find the shell casing that was reported to be lying at the bottom of it.

"So," Meeks said, turning back to me. "Rewrite histo-ry, huh? You think someone killed him because of that?"

"I know it sounds far-fetched," I said, "but I can't help but believe it's related somehow. That's how I read the shot that was fired at me. The shooter could have hit me. Hell, he took Conroy under the left eye at five hundred yards. Standing up like I was, I'd have been an easy kill. But he chose not to. Obviously a warning shot. Telling me to stay away. Mind my own business. That it's not worth getting killed over."

"Hmmm," he said, jotting down a few more notes on his pad. When finished, he changed direction. "Was Conroy married?"

"Yeah. About ten years. Woman named Cindy. Never met her, but know what she looks like from pictures he posted on his Facebook page. I even talked to her on the phone about this Montana trip. He used her as his *de facto* trip planner, and she was coordinating with me." I paused, knowing where he was going with his question. "And no, didn't seem like they were having marital problems."

"Whoa. You're way ahead of me," he said. "Did they have children?" Before I could answer, one of the agents he'd sent to the Deep Ravine was at the door requesting a word. Meeks excused himself and went out.

I sat there thinking about Cindy. Who was going to tell her about Matt? Unfortunately, it was probably going to be me. I wasn't looking forward to that. I wondered where she was.

"Son-of-a-bitch," I whispered to myself, my hand flashing to my jacket pocket and jerking out my cell. "What the hell have I been thinking?" Cindy told me she would be here with Matt. She texted me last week with their rental address. I found her phone number in my contact list.

Seemed like forever before it even connected, and then just rang and rang. Dammit, I murmured as I disconnected. I checked to see I had the right number then punched it again. Still no response.

I could see Meeks out front in an animated conversation with his agent. I called Cindy's number one more time. *Nada*.

I disconnected and sprinted out the door.

CHAPTER 9

"Something's come up," I said as I ran past Meeks. "Gotta go."

Being younger and faster, he caught up with me halfway through the parking lot. Grabbing my shoulder, he spun me around.

"Whoa. Slow down, McGuire. Where you think you're off to? We're not finished here yet."

"Conroy's wife." I panted, ashamed I was out of breath from such a short run. "They rented a house. She's there alone."

"You think she's in danger?"

"I have no fucking way of knowing," I said. "All I know is less than three hours ago someone, for reasons that neither of us know, ambushed and blew the head off her husband. I forgot his wife was with him. I've been calling her. No answer. You got any reason to think she *wouldn't* be in danger?"

"Point taken," he said, holding up his hand to stop me. "Come on. I'll go with you." He didn't give me an option. "We'll take my truck." Again, no option. "Give me the keys to your piece-of-shit rental. I'll have my guys drive it back for you." While he sprinted back to the Visitor Center with the keys, I went to the rental and retrieved my P7.

Six minutes later we were on I-90 headed northwest toward Billings. "Got an address, Inspector?" he asked as he pushed his fully loaded Ford F-150 to eighty.

"Yeah, hold on." I checked the text message Cindy had sent. I passed the phone to Meeks. He read the address.

"I know exactly where the house is," he said. "Southeast corner of the city. Fairly rural. It's closer to where we are, though. Will cut about ten minutes off our drive time."

He called his office, telling them the address. "Call Billings Police and request a squad car to that address ASAP. Tell 'em it's urgent. Possible B & E. Suspect is armed and dangerous." He disconnected.

"How far are we from Billings?" I asked.

Meeks took a moment to key the address into his GPS. "From this spot, about thirty-five miles. We'll be there in twenty-five minutes." He pushed the truck effortlessly up to ninety. "Maybe sooner."

Thirteen minutes later Meeks's cell phone chirped. He listened for a few minutes, grimaced, thanked whoever had called, and took his foot off the accelerator.

"My office heard from Billings PD. We're too late. When the squad car arrived, the only thing they found was the smoldering ruins of a house. Billings Fire was there. Neighbor called in an alarm about an hour and a half ago. By the time they arrived, the house was engulfed in flames. Not much they could do but watch. While they haven't been able to pinpoint the exact cause of the blaze as of yet, they have determined it was arson. And they can confirm there was a fatality inside the home."

CHAPTER 10

The phone in Leesburg rang eight times before it was answered. "Took long enough," the caller said. "You had me worried."

"Sorry," came the reply. "Visitors. Dropped in unexpectedly. Wanted to know if everything was taken care of on your end." Static filled the pause, then, "Has it?"

"It's finished here," the caller said.

"All of it?"

"All of it. I'm sitting in my car on a freeway overpass about four miles from the house. Or what's left of it. Watching the fire crews trying to beat down the flames. I don't think they're going to be successful."

"Did you find anything?" the man in Virginia asked.

"Nothing useful. The wife said she had no clue what her husband was working on."

"And you believed her?"

"After I cut off two of her fingers and she still didn't tell me anything? Yeah, I believed her. Then I shot her. Went through the house thoroughly. Found a few files, but nothing that would give us a problem."

"You left her body there?"

"Of course. Turned on the gas stove. Hauled in a propane tank from the back yard BBQ and opened its valve. Threw some gasoline around for good measure. Left a dime packet of C-4 on a timer switch. Incinerated her and the files.

"Excellent. Anything else?"

The man hesitated for just an instant. He decided not to say anything about the shell casing. No need to worry these people. They were paranoid enough. Besides, the probability of that casing being found was close to zero. Even if they did find it, so what? There were no prints or DNA samples on the damn thing. And the rifle from which it was fired would be laying in pieces in the Missouri river by the time he boarded the airplane tonight.

"No," he said. "Nothing else."

The man in Virginia noticed the slight hesitation in the shooter's voice. It worried him. Was this man becoming sloppy? Or even worse, secretive? He made a mental note to alert his contact. Maybe they would have someone pay him a visit when he returned from Montana.

"What's next on your agenda?" he asked.

"Me? Driving up to Helena for my flight home. Takes off in four and a half hours."

"You've done a good job, as usual. Our friends will be happy."

Our friends. The shooter smiled. This guy had no idea whose sandbox he was playing in. Why should he? He was just a Congressman. Probably one of twenty or thirty in the Corporation's employ. Just because he was head of some House Committee or subcommittee on something-or-other, he thought he was hot shit. In the scheme of things, this guy was a nobody. A *useful idiot*. The Congressman also had never put together that the man whose Corporation he worked for, the man responsible for everything the Congressman had – his seat, his big mansion in Leesburg, his trophy wife – was the shooter's grandfather.

CHAPTER 11

McGuire and Meeks arrived at Conroy's rental just as the man, whose driver's license identified him as James Burns, turned in his rental car at the Helena airport, went through security and boarded the five o'clock commuter flight to Denver. Burns arrived in Billings three days earlier on a flight from Portland, Oregon, and stayed at the downtown Holiday Inn under the name of William Hocking. Having multiple aliases for operations such as this was a precaution the shooter always took. He knew from experience it was only a matter of time before the FBI got around to checking hotels for anyone who booked himself in a day or two before the murder and fire. They would then try to match that name with anyone who had flown either in or out the day of, or the day after, the crimes were committed. They would check every airport in the state, but, he thought with a smile, they wouldn't find a match. Or if they did, it wouldn't be him.

Two hours later, the same man took his seat in the first class cabin on a United non-stop from Denver to New York's JFK. The credit card used to purchase this ticket identified him by his real name, Thaddeus Mosby.

Tad Mosby pushed his seat back as far as it would go and ordered a gin and tonic. It had been a long day and he was tired. Mosby was in his mid-forties, of medium height and weight. His thick, dark hair was just beginning to show silver strands, giving him a sophisticated look that attracted stares from the opposite sex. His tanned face was evidence of a life spent either out-of-doors under the sun or indoors under a sun lamp.

Reflecting back on the day, his only regret was the necessity of having to dump the rifle. He would love to have brought it home with him. He remembered the *Cowboy Action Shooting* contest coming up in the next few weeks. Would've been nice to have that model '73 with him. He couldn't, of course. That damn shell casing he dropped in Deep Ravine precluded that. He didn't think anyone would find it, but just in case, he disassembled it and, on the way to Helena, threw the pieces into various sections of the Missouri River that paralleled the road. It pained him to throw away such a fine piece of workmanship. And it was a fine piece. He should know. Having been a Marine sniper for thirteen years, he considered himself a weapons expert.

After finishing dinner, Mosby asked for a blanket and pillow, turned off the light above his seat, and closed his eyes. Before falling asleep, he thought of the $1.5 million that would be deposited into his Cayman Islands account in the morning. *A lot of money to keep secret something that happened on that battlefield one hundred and forty years ago,* he thought. *Must be damn important, though. A few days ago that guy in France blew his head off rather than talk to me.*

~~~~

It was the importance of that secret that had the shooter's grandfather awake that night, also. The secret, it turned out, wasn't about what happened *on* the battlefield, the secret was about what *didn't* happen on that battlefield.

CHAPTER 12

Meeks and I parked outside the perimeter set up by the local police. He recognized the chief and called him over.

"We heard there was a fatality here."

"You heard right. This is now officially a homicide scene," he said. "Homicide and Arson. Body found in the house was female. Burned beyond recognition. The ME found a bullet hole in her skull, and two fingers missing. We'll have to do dental records to get the vic's identity."

"Her name's Cindy Conroy," I said.

The chief looked at me quizzically, then over at Meeks with a *who's this joker?* look that only seasoned police officers can pull off. I smiled. Meeks introduced me to Chief Brian Newton and told him what had transpired at the Custer battlefield.

"Since this has now taken on *interstate* characteristics, I guess the investigation will fall under your jurisdiction," he said with just a hint of indignation. "You guys seem to get all the interesting cases." Meeks gave a shrug of apology.

"Any witnesses?" I asked.

"One, but won't help much," Newton said. "You can see this is prairie land. Homes pretty far apart. Guy down there …" he motioned to a house about half a mile away, "… thinks he saw a car pull into the driveway about nine this morning. That fits pretty much with our timeline. We estimate the fire started about nine forty-five, ten o'clock." He turned and pointed to a blackened cement pad. "Parked back there. The witness didn't give it much thought and couldn't ID the make or model."

"Who called it in?" Meeks asked.

"Same guy," Newton said. "He was in his house and heard an explosion. Followed real close by another one. He came running out and saw the house was, his words, *swallowed up with fire*."

"Did he see the guy leave?" I asked.

"No, he didn't. The perp must have used a timed fuse of some type. Otherwise, we'd be finding pieces of him in there, too. The first explosion was caused by gas. No doubt the stove. We found pieces of it, unburned by the fire, about a hundred yards away. The second explosion was caused by a propane tank the perp must have brought into the house. We found remnants of the tank in the rubble. We also found parts of a gasoline can. We think he must have doused the house, too. No other way the house was so quickly engulfed. Guy knew what he was doing."

Newton gave us a moment to digest what we were seeing, then said, "It's all yours, now, Special Agent Meeks. Good luck." With that, he turned and walked back to his men.

"What do you think the perp was doing?" Meeks asked as we walked back to the car. "Why the overkill? He had to know we'd identify Conroy's wife. Why go to such extremes to obliterate her like that?"

"Another message, maybe? But this one probably unintended. He cut off Cindy's fingers. What does that tell you?"

"He was looking for something?"

"Precisely. Thought Cindy might know where it was. Maybe she did, and told him before he killed her. In which case, this is the end of it. But I'm guessing not. In the same way Conroy wouldn't tell me what he had found, I doubt he would have told her, either. For no other reason than he knew its value and that other people would be after it. I'll bet you that whatever Conroy had, it's hidden somewhere deep. In either scenario, we'll know soon enough. If more dead bodies start to surface, then we'll have our answer."

CHAPTER 13

Meeks dropped me off at my hotel at three thirty. I got to my room and flopped on the bed, utterly exhausted. Closing my eyes, I just started drifting off to sleep when my cell chirped. I reached for it, looked at the number and smiled. TJ.

"Hey, pardner," I said. "How's my favorite junior cop?"

"God, Dad," he said breathlessly. "I'm glad you answered. You okay? What happened up there today? A terrorist attack?"

"Wait a minute, TJ. Wait a minute. Slow down. I'm fine. Terrorist attack? Where the hell did you get that?"

"The police department, Dad. It's my first day, remember? My first squad meeting. I'm on the third shift. We meet every day before going on duty. The lieutenant goes through everything of importance that happened during the day. Starts with global, then national, and ends with local. When he got to the national, he says there was a killing today at the Little Bighorn National Monument. Possible terrorist. I knew you were there. It scared the shit out of me. I had to wait for the meeting to be over before I could call."

I smiled. It was nice to be loved. Especially by your kid. "I'm fine, TJ. Honest. But my friend, Matt Conroy, the fellow I was meeting, isn't. He was murdered. In fact, I found him. And it wasn't a terrorist attack. Actually, it was an assassination." I spent the next fifteen minutes telling him what happened and how I was going to force myself on whatever federal agency was assigned to the case. "I'll take you along if you want," I said. "You can experience how a murder investigation proceeds, beginning to end."

"Thanks, Dad. It's probably a wee bit premature for me at this point, don't you think?"

"Yeah. Probably. Just thought it would be cool to be with you."

"I feel the same, Dad. Let's be sure to get together as soon as you get back. I'll be an experienced police officer by then." He laughed. "Same as you. Mom will be so thrilled." We both had a good laugh at that one. "Love ya, Dad."

"Ditto, TJ. Take care. Talk to you when I get back."

Now I was wide-awake, my mind weighing options. The flight back to San Francisco wasn't until Friday, two days from now. No way I was going to stay in Billings that long. And no way I was going back to San Francisco and simply wait while someone else investigated Conroy's murder. To hell with that. Whichever federal agency was finally given jurisdiction, I was going to be part of their task force, invited or not. And if not, I knew a *quasi*-federal agency that just might be of some help to me.

Grabbing my phone, I scrolled through my contact list looking for the name "Rob Kincaid." Rob played football for me. In fact, he was on Conroy's team. We had sporadic connections over the years, but I wasn't sure I'd kept his information. I said a silent prayer of thanks when I found him. Reno area code. Perfect. I dialed his number.

"Rob Kincaid."

"Rob, this is Tom McGuire. A voice from your past."

There was a brief moment of silence. I could hear Kincaid's memory banks clicking through his internal address book. "Well, son-of-a-bitch," he exclaimed. "Coach Mac. What a surprise. How the hell ya' been? Where are you?"

"I'm calling from Billings, Montana." I had already decided not to waste time bullshitting about the past. At least not yet. "I need your help," I said simply.

Kincaid's voice immediately changed in tone. Serious now. "What can I do for you, Coach?"

"You remember Matt Conroy?" I asked.

"Absolutely. Who could ever forget the Con? Played ball with him for two years. And I've heard snippets of what he's accomplished after losing his leg. Heroic. What's up with him?"

"He's been murdered. Both he and his wife. It's a long story how I got involved, but I'm going to find the son-of-a-bitch who did it."

There was a moment of silence on the other end, then, "Coach, whatever you need from me, you got. My men and I are at your disposal. You're still a cop, right? Homicide inspector? Just so you know, Red Squadron Agency isn't particularly skilled in murder investigations."

"I know that, Rob," I said. "I'm thinking mostly of your contacts."

"Those I've got. I was twelve years a SEAL, so I know everyone in that community."

"I was thinking more governmental. Maybe FBI? Hell, Rob. I'm not even sure what I'm looking for."

"First off, what are you trying to accomplish? We'll start there. Better yet – you're in Billings? Why not just fly here to Reno? We can talk, figure out how we can work together, and then you can hop a plane back to SF."

"Thanks, Rob. I'll get the flights and call you back. Shitty we have to renew acquaintances on a note like this."

"Roger that, Coach," he said. "In any case, it'll be good to see you. If you need government contacts, we can help you. My Agency takes on government jobs that may not pass congressional oversight. We are in the *find-it and fix-it* business. We'll help you *find* Conroy's murderer, and when we do, we'll help you *fix* it."

CHAPTER 14

Reno, Nevada

I arrived at the Reno airport at nine fifteen the next morning. If I had any doubts about recognizing Kincaid after all these years, they were put to rest as soon as I walked into baggage claim. He was standing near the back wall. You couldn't miss him. Just the way he carried himself.

Kincaid made eye contact, waved and walked toward me. He still had his boyish good looks and enough of a swagger to attract the glances of every female in the area under the age of ninety. He shook my hand warmly. "Welcome to Reno, Coach," he said, flashing a smile that was both rich and genuine. He picked up my suitcase, and before I had a chance to protest, said, "Follow me."

As we walked to his SUV, we caught up on our lives. My divorce. TJ. Did I enjoy my job? Things like that. He told me about how he became a SEAL, his deployments in Iraq and Afghanistan, and what had happened there since he left. He told me about the company he started and how they had been hired to go back to Iraq to help train Sunni tribesmen to fight ISIS. But the President, for some reason, pulled the plug.

"Good thing, too, it turns out," he said as we had buckled our seatbelts. "If the president had allowed the deployment, we'd be there now and not in a position to help you."

"I appreciate you even talking to me about this, Rob. But before we go any further – I never got a chance to say this, but I want you to know I really admired what you did after 9-11."

He waved his hand in dismissal. "For all this country has given to me – given to all of us? Least I could do."

"Well, you went beyond, Rob. Come on, you were an All-American football player in a major college program. A Heisman Trophy candidate. The guys told me that the day after 9-11 you quit the program, walked to the nearest recruiting office and enlisted."

"Best damn decision I ever made, too. And let me tell you – it wasn't just me signing up. I had to stand in line, for God's sake."

As we drove out of the parking lot, Rob turned to me and said, "Okay, so tell me what happened to Conroy."

I gave him a version that lasted the entire thirty-minute ride to his house, starting with Conroy's phone call to standing over his body on Last Stand Hill.

"Tell me why you think he was murdered?"

"I thought about it all last night, Rob. Never got to sleep. Could only think it had something to do with what Conroy discovered about Custer and the battle. Nothing else makes sense."

"But who would care what happened a hundred and forty years ago?" he asked "What difference could it make now?"

"I thought of that, too. And, honestly, I have no answer. But *somebody* killed Matt. And *somebody* took a shot at me. And deliberately missed. What's up with that?" I shook my head. "And what about Cindy Conroy, with two fingers cut off. Incinerated. Somebody went to a lot of trouble to bring in an accelerant to make that fire into an inferno. Plus, they used a timer, for God's sake. A professional. *Somebody's* after *something*, Rob. Or trying to hide *something*. Or both. Doesn't make any sense otherwise. At least not to me."

"I hear you, Coach," Kincaid said. "Where do we find answers?"

"I'm thinking of going back to New York. Where Conroy was from. Talk to people at St. John's, where he taught. In my experience, murders are about motive. Always! This case might be as easy as finding a history professor who murdered Conroy because he or she wanted the glory of publishing what he found. Or maybe Conroy stole it from somebody, and that somebody wanted it back, or was seeking revenge. Or maybe this has nothing to do with Custer. Maybe Conroy was boffing somebody's wife, and the cuckold husband took it upon himself to eliminate the rival. Or – hell, Rob, there could be a gazillion reasons.

"All I know is I have to go back there. This is what I do. Investigate murders. And I'm damn good at it. It's getting *back* to New York that's going to be the problem. Getting out of SFPD to pursue a case that's not mine. The Department is provincial about those kinds of things. They'll say 'no'."

"So how can I help?" asked Kincaid.

"Same as we discussed on the phone last night. Your contacts. Either in the military or in D.C. itself. You've got to know people that could call my boss and have enough juice to get me off work for a week or two. Maybe the excuse could be that Conroy was working on some military history issue. They could tell my boss that since I was close to him, and the last person to see him alive, they needed me to assist in the investigation."

Kincaid was silent for a minute, then a big grin crossed his face. "Your lucky day, Coach. I know just the guy. Admiral Roy Thompson. Director of JSOC. In my early days as a SEAL, he was my mentor. He's become a personal friend. Red Squadron gets a lot of work from him. I'll call him. I'm sure he can get you off work."

"JSOC? Joint Special Operations Command?"

"Yep. The people who work for me are all AFO guys."
He noticed me looking at him quizzically. "Yeah. I know.
Acronyms. Sorry. *Advanced Force Operators.* Mostly
former Team 6 personnel like me. Admiral Thompson is
our biggest employer."

CHAPTER 15

San Francisco

Two days after I got back from Reno, Admiral Thompson called SFPD's Chief of Police. Kincaid called later that morning and told me that Thompson had squared my absence with the Chief. In the early afternoon, I received a phone call from Matt Bristow, head of SFPD Homicide Division. Lt. Bristow and I go back a long way. He had been my father's supervisor, also. When my dad was "killed in the line of duty," Bristow essentially hired me from Robbery to take his place. Pretty sure it was his way of honoring my dad's memory. He even calls me "junior."

"Shit, Junior, you got some powerful friends," he said over the phone.

I decided to play along. Pretending I didn't know what was coming. "How so, L-T?" I asked.

"The Chief received a call this morning from an Admiral Thompson. I think that was his name. You know him?"

I could tell he was fishing. Wanting to know why a powerful, connected military guy would be calling about my services. I loved it. "Thompson – hmmm. Doesn't ring a bell. But over the years I've met a lot of people."

"Yeah? Well, this guy is the head of the Joint Special Operations Command at Ft. Bragg, for God's sake. You know who they are?"

"Of course, L-T. You forget – I'm an Annapolis grad. Had lots of friends that were SEAL and Delta Force operators. So I know who they are, but I'm at a loss as to why they were calling the Chief about me." I had to suppress a chuckle.

"Your friend who was killed in Montana? This Admiral said he was working on some hush-hush operation. He was asking for your help with the investigation into who killed that professor." He emphasized the word *your*, as if there had to be a mistake here somewhere.

"You're kidding!" I said, trying to sound surprised. "I'm flattered, I guess. Where do they want me and when?"

"Don't know," Bristow said. "The Chief gave his blessing, though, so you'll probably be hearing from them soon. My job was to give you the heads up."

"Thanks, L-T. I'll keep you informed." I hung up and called Kincaid.

CHAPTER 16

The next day I found myself on the tarmac of Oakland International's North Field admiring the sleek lines of the Legacy 650 executive jet that was to take me to New York.

"Hell of an aircraft," I yelled to Kincaid who stood under the rear fuselage talking with the guy fueling the plane.

He waved in acknowledgement and yelled back, "Leave your bags by the front passenger stairs. The baggage handlers will pick them up and put them on the plane." I dropped my two bags, saluted and walked up the stairs.

The cockpit door was open. I peeked in at the two pilots going through their pre-flight checklist. They looked up as I passed, gave me a polite nod and went back to work. I parted the curtain on my right, expecting to find the main cabin. Instead, I found myself in the forward galley. I also found myself face-to-face with a very pretty 30-something woman fussing through her own pre-flight checklist. She wore a chic pleated burgundy skirt that did not quite reach her knees, and a cream-colored, high-necked blouse. A perfect complement to her lively blue eyes and black glossy hair pulled back in a ponytail. She looked up as I entered, put down her clipboard and offered her hand.

"Hello," she said. "My name is Katelyn. Katelyn Murray. I'll be your flight attendant on this flight."

"Nice to meet you, Katelyn," I said. Her hand was feminine, but not fragile. "My name is Tom McGuire, but most people simply call me Mac."

"Your first flight with Red Squadron?"

"It is. Are you their regular attendant?"

"Only for the last two flights. Can I get you something to drink before we take off?" She brought her left hand up to look at her watch. I checked it out. No ring. *Good*, I thought, not that I planned to do anything about it. "We have about thirty minutes," she said.

"Coffee would be …" There was a clunk of something hitting the floor directly behind me followed immediately by a gravelly voice saying, "Give my Bro here a Sapphire tonic, Katelyn."

We both turned. "You're Mr. Delgado, I presume?" she said.

"That I am," he said. "My reputation, I see, precedes me."

"Mr. Kincaid has already warned me about you, if that's what you mean," she said, flashing a practiced, but absolutely dazzling, smile.

"When Rob showed me your picture, I literally begged him to bring me along," Delgado said with a wink. Katelyn smiled and rolled her eyes at me. I shrugged my shoulders in a *sorry, but I can't do anything about this guy* motion. "And you can call me Vinnie in front of Mr. McGuire, here. He's not going to tell our little secret." Another wink.

"See what I have to put up with on these flights?" she said to me.

"They better pay you well," I replied with a smile.

Katelyn shook her head in mock disgust and returned to her checklist.

Delgado turned to me and put out his hand. "Hey, Brah, my name, as you heard, is Vinnie Delgado. I work for Rob. He told me about what happened to your friend.

I'm here to make sure that what happened to him doesn't happen to you."

Delgado came up to my shoulders. Short, but wiry. My dad, who boxed in the Navy, would have said he resembled a middleweight. With his shaved head and dark brown eyes, he was just the kind of guy you didn't want to run into in a dark alley at 3 a.m. At least unarmed.

"Did I get your drink right, Bro?" Delgado said as he took my arm and escorted me into the main cabin. I took a quick look back at Katelyn. She acknowledged my look with a nod and went back to work.

"Actually, you did. How'd you know?"

"I'd love to blow smoke and tell you I have extrasensory perception, but the truth is Rob told me right before I boarded."

Walking into the main cabin, I let out a soft whistle. The Legacy 650 was about half the size of a 737, but elegantly designed. Delgado and I took a seat in one of the six white leather chairs configured around a dark wooden circular table. Embedded in the armrests of each chair were enough knobs and switches to launch a small spacecraft. Except for the on-off switch to the pop-up television screen attached to my seat, I was way out of my league. The back end of the cabin was outfitted with two eight-foot white leather sofas, one affixed to each side of the aircraft. Between them ran a table of the same dark wood.

No sooner had Vinnie and I taken our seats than Rob joined us. "Nice plane, huh?" he said with a smile.

"Well, hell yeah. I'm impressed. Didn't know you were doing so well."

Kincaid laughed. "We time-share the aircraft with a tech start-up out of Silicon Valley. They employ more people than we do. The plane holds up to fourteen, not including the pilots and the flight attendant. It looks spacious now, but you put fourteen passengers in here and you tend to get claustrophobic."

"Glad it's not that way today," I said. "Wouldn't feel right talking about what happened to Conroy in front of strangers."

"You bet," Kincaid replied. "And we've got a lot to talk about. The fewer the distractions, the better."

As if on cue, Katelyn walked in with our drinks. She had fixed a Bloody Mary for Rob. She set down a coffee and a gin and tonic on my tray. "Didn't know which one you wanted more," she said, a ghost of a smile creasing her lips.

"Captain has informed me we'll be taking off in twenty minutes," she announced. "I'll collect your glasses before that, so drink up. I'll be back in a few minutes for breakfast orders so I can serve you once we're airborne."

"You gonna sit with me during take-off?" Delgado asked, patting his thigh.

"Against regulations," she answered. Looking at him directly, she said, "According to FAA rules, I can only sit on a passenger's lap during take-off if he is taller than me."

Kincaid laughed so hard he nearly choked on his drink. "Good one, lady," he sputtered, wiping his mouth on the back of his hand.

"Hey," Delgado said in a petulant voice. "I'm as tall as Tom Cruise."

"He's richer, and ..." She stopped mid-sentence, executing the perfect pregnant pause, then said, "uh, probably should leave it there." As she walked back to the galley, she stopped, turned and blew him a kiss. "Just kidding. And don't forget to stow that duffel in the overhead before take-off."

Once she was out of sight, Kincaid leaned over and said to me, "I'm afraid I'm gonna have to apologize for Vinnie's manners. He's usually not this bad. Probably off his meds."

I laughed, waving his words away. "No need to apologize, Rob," I said. "I don't blame him for hitting on her. She's a nice lady. Cute *and* funny. A good combination. And can obviously take care of herself."

"True enough," said Delgado. "Hey – if you like her, dude, go for it. She's not my kind of woman. Too stuck up to succumb to any of my lines." He smiled. "Good luck, Bro."

"Yeah. Good luck." I said. "I've been divorced for twelve years. I'm purposely out of the *good luck* business. I'm definitely content with my *almost* celibate love life."

Delgado laughed. "You ain't gettin' any, dude? That what you're sayin'?"

"Well, I didn't mean it *quite* like that," I said. "Let's just say I'm content. That famous philosopher Chuck Berry once said, romance is just *too much monkey business for me to be involved in.* And I believe him."

"I hear you, Bro. That's why I'm giving Katelyn to you."

"*Giving* her to me? Kind of you – *Bro*," I said. "Can't wait to tell her. I'm sure she'll be thrilled."

Just then the warning light came on in the cabin and we heard the engines come to life. Katelyn peeked through the curtain. "Seat belts fastened for take-off," she said. "And, Vinnie, stow the duffel please."

When Delgado didn't move, I nodded my head at the duffel. "You gonna stow that?"

He patted it with his hand. "Too heavy. Think I'll just keep it here."

"What's in it?" I asked.

"Take a look?" He shoved it towards me.

I bent over, grabbed the shoulder strap, and pulled it to my seat. Delgado was right. It was heavy. I unzipped it and looked inside. "Holy shit." I said. It was full of weapons.

"I never leave home without them," he said. "They're like my kids. Especially when I'm on assignment."

"How many you got in there?"

"Two of everything, Bro. Just like Noah." He laughed. "Well, close, anyway. There's a broke down HK 417. Got the twenty-inch barrel and a sniper scope for longer-range targets. Then there's the MP7 with the 556 suppressor, for closer targets. You ever handled one?"

I took it out. "The MP7 I have," I said, turning it over in my hand. "Practiced with it. Sweet little weapon. Never with the suppressor, though."

"The nice thing about that particular suppressor? It's so quiet you can shoot a guy in one room and never wake his buddy in the next. Isn't that right, Rob?"

Kincaid laughed. "Vinnie's right. He and I were in a number of fire-fights where that puppy saved our ass."

I rummaged through the rest of the duffel. A few knives; two Glocks, one in a .45 caliber and one in a .40, and boxes of ammo.

"These are too much gun for me. I carry the HK P7," I said.

"Good little weapon," Kincaid said. "Only problem is it's a 9mm."

"I like the P7 precisely *because* it's a 9," I said. "Good in an urban setting. Those cannons you got in here rip through doors, cars, maybe even tanks, for all I know. Could end up killing a lot of innocent people. Too prone to collateral damage."

"Reason I brought all these weapons," Delgado said, "is because Rob filled me in on your shooter. Head shot from 500 yards? Gotta be good. Missed you from the same distance. Probably on purpose. Lookin' at that, I'm think-ing *professional*. More than likely ex-military. He's not going to care about collateral damage. Neither am I. We're going to be in New York in roughly six hours. My words to him? *Come to us, my man. Come and get us. Let's see who's the best."*

CHAPTER 17

Twenty minutes after take-off, Katelyn returned to serve us breakfast. It was airline food, but *first class* airline food. I could count on the fingers of one hand the number of times I'd flown first class. I could get use to this. When we finished, she cleared the plates, left a carafe of coffee and a pitcher of water and disappeared, allowing us to conduct business.

We poured ourselves coffee. "Let's start with some background on us," Kincaid said. "Red Squadron Security Agency is comprised of myself, Vinnie and, at present, three of our teammates from Naval Special Warfare Development Group. DEVGRU is divided into four color-coded squadrons. When active, we were assigned to Red Squadron. So we used that name for our business.

"I purposely designed Red Squadron to be a team of people with unique talents." He took a sip of his coffee. "I'm sure you are aware that our getting involved in what is essentially a routine murder case is a departure from the norm. It's a fact that no one on the RS team has your particular skill set, Coach. What we really do well is watch each other's back. And that's why we're here. To watch your back while you find who murdered Conroy and his wife."

We sat making small talk for another half hour. When Vinnie got up and went to the lavatory, Rob took the opportunity to say to me, "You may think Vinnie Delgado is a strange bird, but let me tell you, he's the toughest SOB you'll ever meet. Be thankful you have him watching your back."

Just then my cell phone rang. Didn't even know I had it on. Probably against federal aviation rules. I answered anyway.

"Mac? Special Agent Jeff Meeks."

"Jeff. Hey, pardner, good to hear your voice. I was going to call you. I'm on my way to New York to start a parallel investigation into Conroy's murder. Wanted to coordinate with you."

"Not me," he said. "I'm afraid you're on your own with this one."

"On my own? What happened? Did they give the New York office jurisdiction or something?"

"Worse. They've taken the FBI out of it completely. Stand down. It's not ours."

"Not yours," I said, my voice rising. Kincaid looked over at me. "You mean the FBI? It's not a FBI case?"

"That's what I was told from HQ just twenty minutes ago."

"Whose case *is* it?"

"I was told the locals have it. The way it's being spun is that the murder of Mrs. Conroy is the primary crime. Matt Conroy's murder is being labeled an *associated* crime, therefore allowing local law enforcement jurisdiction."

"That's absurd," I said.

"You know it. I know it. But the people in charge see it differently."

"Has this ever happened to you before? Being pulled from a case?"

"Never."

"What the hell's going on here, Jeff? Somebody get to somebody?"

"Looks like from where I'm standing," Meeks said. "But from now on, you're on your own. I just work here."

CHAPTER 18

"What the *hell* is going on?" I shouted in frustration, slamming the cell into my leg.

Katelyn peeked through the galley curtain. "Everything okay out here?"

"Everything's fine," answered Kincaid. "Thanks." He looked at me. "Hey, take it easy. What happened?" By this time, Delgado had come back into the cabin and was listening to the conversation. "The guy who called told you they've pulled the FBI off the Conroy case?"

"He wasn't just a *guy*. He was Special Agent in Charge of the Billings FBI office. That makes two federal agencies that have been told to back off. It doesn't make any sense."

"*Two* agencies?" Delgado asked.

"Yeah." I nodded to him. "The US Park Police, the law enforcement agency that *should* have the jurisdiction for Conroy's murder, was pulled off it right from the get-go. *You have too big a backload to take on anything new,* they were told. I happened to be okay with that because the USPP don't do a lot of murder cases. I knew if they were the lead agency, Conroy's murder wouldn't get the resources it deserved."

"And now the FBI has been told to back away, too, huh?" Kincaid asked.

"In all my dealings with issues related to crime," I said, "especially violent crime, I've never seen anything like this." I looked at the floor and shook my head. "Strings are being pulled, Rob. Has to be. Can your people

56

look into that? At least find out who's calling the shots on this."

"I'll try," he said.

"And speaking of shots," I said, remembering the shell casing that was found at the scene. "I have something else you could do for me, Rob."

I told him that the two Montana Highway Patrol officers who were the first on-scene saw a shell casing at the bottom of Deep Ravine. How they thought the shooter left it inadvertently. They think it was the casing from the bullet that killed Conroy."

"No shit. That's helpful. Do you have it with you?" Delgado asked.

"No. I'm assuming the Billings FBI has it now. I'll call Meeks back and ask him. But in any case, the Montana Highway Patrol officer, a good ol' boy named Carl something-or-other, is a hunter. The kind that reloads his own shells. Knew a lot about this particular caliber. Identified it as a Winchester 44.40 cartridge."

"And the significance is?" Kincaid asked.

"I asked that same question," I said. "Carl said it was a cartridge fired by the famous Winchester '73, a rifle many Indians had at the battle. He told me the actual caliber fell out of favor in the twenties and thirties. No one used it. But then, about twenty years ago, it made a comeback in a national competition known as Cowboy Action Shooting. During the event, contestants have to use firearms that were in use from the mid-to-late eighteen hundreds."

"Never heard of 'em, but I can find out. Shouldn't be too hard," Kincaid said.

"That's what the Highway Patrol guy told me. He said leaving the shell could be a fatal error. May be a way to track the guy."

"Let me know if your FBI contact will release it to us. If we can get it from him, we can put it through a ballistic scrub. See where it leads us. Leave that one to me," Kincaid said.

CHAPTER 19

I felt the plane start to descend. A moment later Katelyn walked into the cabin to collect the empty cups and bottles. "We've started our descent into Teterboro," she said. "We'll be landing in about forty minutes. Where are the other guys?"

"They're in the back catching a few winks. The beer made them sleepy. The wimps."

She laughed. "You want another beer?"

"Sure," I said. "Why not."

She left and reappeared with two Dos Equis. "I've got about thirty minutes before I have to start securing the cabin. Mind if I join you?"

"Not at all. Be my guest."

She took the seat across from me. I couldn't help but notice how her burgundy skirt inched up her thighs. She caught me looking and smiled. Heard *Too Much Monkey Business* playing in my head.

"Couldn't help overhearing about your friend. I'm really sorry."

"Thanks. I appreciate it."

We sat in silence for a minute or two, sipping our beers. Then she said, "I've never known anyone who solved murders. Except for your friend being the victim, it must be exciting work."

"When you catch the perp," I said, "the job is really kick-ass. But until you do, the time spent chasing down all the leads tends to be tedious and dull."

"How long will it take you? To find out who shot your friend?"

"Could take forever. You really never know. I've allotted two weeks to poke around out here."

"Must be hard on your family," she said. "Being gone for such long stretches."

"I'm divorced," I said. "Have a son. Twenty-two. Lives in Los Angeles. Gonna be a senior at UCLA. Most of the time he doesn't even know I'm gone."

"Have you been to New York before?" she asked.

"About twenty-five years ago."

"It's changed a lot in those twenty-five years, I can assure you," she said. "I'd be happy to show you around if you want."

Whoa, I thought. *Wherever this conversation was headed, I never expected it to head this way.* "Eh ..." I stammered, taking a quick look again at her left hand. She caught me and smiled.

"No. Not married," she said.

"I'm sorry. I ... I ...I didn't mean to be so obvious. It's kind of you to offer."

"That's okay. I'm glad you checked out the ring. Tells me something about you." She put her beer down. "I was in a long-term relationship with a guy. Going on four years. But he got tired of me flying all over the country without him. Gave me the choice. Choose him or flying." She laughed softly and held up her ring finger. "You can see who won." She paused again, and then asked, "Where are you staying?"

"The Four Seasons," I said.

"Nice digs."

"Rob made the arrangements. I'm more used to a Travelodge or Sleep Inn, I'm afraid. Shows you what a high flyer I am."

"Take my word for it. It's a nice hotel. 57th and Lexington, if I'm not mistaken. And just so you know, I'm not a snob. Travelodge or whatever – they're all good for sleeping." She paused and looked to the back of the plane. "Is Mr. Delgado staying with you?"

"Same hotel. Different rooms."

"Good," she said with a smile. "I live in Peter Cooper Village, about twenty blocks south of where you're staying. Mr. Kincaid told me he has a car and driver to take us from the airport into the city. Because of the relative locations, the driver will drop you off first, then me." She looked out the plane's window. "Time for me to go to work." She looked back at me. "Would you like to go to a play with me tonight? I know that came way out of the blue, but there's one on Theater Row. Close to where you're staying. It's called *Delirium's Daughters*. A comedy. Gotten great reviews. I've wanted to see it for the past two months but have been in and out of town. It's closing next week."

"Sure I'd like to go. I think that would be fun," I said. "I hate to brag, but I was the lead in my high school play. *Billy Budd*. Melville."

"I'm impressed," she said with a crooked grin.

"I didn't get any offers," I laughed.

"Maybe they're just slow to recognize talent." Again that grin. *Mac*, I thought. *Get a grip, pardner. It's only a smile.* I'd been out of this man/woman thing for so long, I didn't even know the rules anymore.

"Okay. Play starts at eight. I'll grab a cab. Be at your hotel by seven-thirty. Meet me in the lobby. We'll cab it to the theater. There's a great Vietnamese restaurant nearby we can go to afterward. All this and I'll get you home early." She took our two bottles and started to leave. Right before she reached the galley, she turned to me and winked, "Buckle up."

I fell back on the seat – exhausted. *Spend some time with this woman*, I thought, *and I'll be dead in a month. On the other hand,* I muttered to myself, *what a way to go.*

CHAPTER 20

Manhattan

The alarm went off at 6 a.m. I rolled on my back and propped the pillow under my head. I knew I had to meet Delgado for breakfast at seven-thirty. Normally, I'd use this time to plan the day ahead. But not this morning. This morning all I could think about was last night – and Katelyn.

Not being used to female companionship, I had a surprisingly good time. Except for those few awkward moments as we stood in front of the hotel after returning from the play and dinner. She had gotten me back by midnight, as promised. *Now what?* I asked myself. I couldn't remember the dating etiquette. First of all, I wasn't even sure this would be classified as a *date*. But if it was, should I invite her in for a drink? Up to my room? What?

She was kind enough to rescue me. "I had a great time tonight," she said. "I'll take a cab from here." She pointed to the taxis lined up in front of the hotel. "You told me you'd be in the area for the next two weeks. If that's true, be sure to include me in at least one of those evenings. I'd like to see you again. You're an interesting man, Tom McGuire." With that, she leaned in and kissed me. Full on the lips. It wasn't like a passionate kiss. I mean, there was no tongue involved or anything. But it was unexpectedly intimate. With that she turned and got in the first cab in line. I stood there watching her taxi fight its way into the traffic.

A half block away, she took a quick glance back and blew me a kiss.

CHAPTER 21

Long Island, NY

Delgado rented a blue Toyota Highlander for our trip to Long Island. I drove. Delgado was my GPS navigator.

"So, where're we going, Bro – and why?" Delgado asked.

"First stop is a place called Lloyd Harbor." I gave him the address that he keyed into the GPS. "We have an appointment to meet Francis X. McNamara. More precisely, *Doctor* Francis X. McNamara. President of St. John's University. Where Conroy taught."

"Tell me again, *why*?" he asked.

"Come on. We've already gone through this. Remember I told you the key to solving murders is motive? You find the motive; you narrow down the list of suspects by a factor of four."

"And you think this dude might have motive?"

"No, I don't. But I think he might lead us to who did."

"Maybe a fellow professor?" Delgado said.

"Exactly. Or maybe a grad student. And if not one of them, the list narrows to family and friends. Family, by the way, are always the prime suspects."

"Does Conroy have family in New York?" Delgado asked.

"Not in New York. Matter of fact, not anywhere. I checked. The Con became a Mormon in his sophomore year in college. As you know, the Mormons have big-time genealogy records. Conroy was listed in the records as one of the *elect*."

"Lucky man."

I chuckled. "Yeah. He was born in California thirty-four years ago. No brothers or sisters. Father and mother both deceased. No living kin. This particular strain of the Conroy family ended with his death."

"So right now you've narrowed it down to faculty dudes, and maybe friends?" Delgado said.

"Precisely. McNamara is also important because he either authorized Conroy's sabbatical, or can point us to who did. Whoever authorized the sabbatical had to know what he was looking for in Montana. Conroy told me it was so big it would rewrite history."

"Forgive me," Delgado said. "I know I ain't got the sharpest teeth in the woodpile, but something big enough to rewrite history? Dude, come on. Doesn't that sound a little far-fetched to you? It does to me." He paused, looked at the GPS, then told me to get off the next exit.

"Have you ever considered that all this could be about Conroy's wife?" Delgado continued. "Maybe she's lettin' dudes, or even ladies, in her berry patch? Then she gets all religious about it, or somethin'? Tries to break it off? Some jealous dude says no way, and takes her out? Guy then does Conroy because he perceives him as the dude that gave her religion? I don't know. Maybe even the wife of the guy she was doin' found out and had her offed."

"I've considered it as a possibility. But it just doesn't *feel* right. Why would they kill Conroy if it was his wife that was messing around?"

"Who knows? Maybe they thought the dude would finger them."

"Anything's possible, I guess. We'll ask Conroy's colleagues about their marital relationship. If we even get sniff there was trouble, we'll sift through *her* life, too."

"But I'm hearin' you're bettin' on another professor."

"I'm not ruling anybody out," I said. "But the professor thing is not as far-fetched as you make it sound.

There's been violence in colleges before. Six or seven years ago a professor shot and killed a colleague and wounded three others. In a faculty meeting, of all places. All because she was denied tenure. Money? Job security? People do strange things for those two commodities. In Conroy's case? You never know. The prospect of fame and fortune are powerful incentives. What if we were talking about a huge book deal? Or a prestigious national or even international award? Or a lucrative professorial contract? Shit like that?"

"Dude!" Delgado exclaimed, shaking his head. "I just never thought of college professors as that mercenary."

"Yeah? Well, welcome to the real world."

CHAPTER 22

The mid-morning sun hung heavily in the sapphire blue sky as we pulled the Highlander into McNamara's driveway.

Dr. Francis X. McNamara lived in a substantial two-story colonial on a narrow lane one block south of Long Island Sound. He heard the car coming up the driveway and was standing at the front door waiting. He was a small man, dressed in white shorts, a freshly ironed green and white striped short-sleeve shirt, and sandals. No socks. We introduced ourselves and he escorted us into a large, rectangular, air-conditioned study whose walls were lined, floor to ceiling, with shelves full of books.

"May I offer you tea or coffee?" he asked. Both Vinnie and I opted for coffee. Both black. "Please make yourselves comfortable," he said, sweeping his hand toward the large leather sofa that anchored the corner sitting area. McNamara excused himself, and Vinnie and I ensconced ourselves on opposite ends of the sofa. A few minutes later McNamara reappeared carrying a sterling silver tray filled with petit fours in an array of pastel colors and three cups of coffee. He placed the tray on the table in front of us.

"Bon appétit," he said.

We made small talk for a few minutes as we sipped our coffee and downed a few petit fours.

"You've been a gracious host," I said, wanting him to know we appreciated his hospitality, "but we have a lot to cover today, Doctor, and we don't want to take up your whole day. You know why we are here?"

"Of course. That terrible tragedy that befell one of our distinguished faculty members. He was also a dear friend."

"He was a dear friend of mine, as well," I said. "And let's be clear, Doctor. This wasn't just a *terrible tragedy*. This was a cold-blooded murder."

"Of course," he said. "Forgive me. I didn't mean to be dismissive of the heinous nature of his death. And, please, call me Frank."

"We might as well cut to the chase, Frank," Delgado said, choosing to leave behind his *dude* and Bro slang in the company of the Frank who had the PhD letters after his name. I smiled inwardly. "Can you think of anyone who might have known in detail what Conroy was working on, and what got him killed?"

"I'm not sure I can add anything to what I already told the two FBI agents who visited a few days ago."

I choked my coffee onto the floor. "Say again?" I sputtered. "FBI?"

"Well, yes," he responded. "You sound surprised."

"Uh, yeah. A little, I guess. I was told the FBI had decided not to involve itself in this case." I put my cup down, pulled the hankie from my back pocket, and wiped my mouth.

"Well, they were here," he said. "Sat just about where you are now."

"Were they local?" Delgado asked.

"If you mean were they from the New York office as opposed to the D.C. office? I assumed they were, yes," McNamara said.

"Did they show you any identification?"

"Well, of course they did," he answered. "I wouldn't have let them in, let alone spoken to them, otherwise. They both had badges. And they brought me the news of Matthew's death. And they even mentioned you. They told me you were the person that found him."

"I was, unfortunately."

"I feel for you," he said with a slight shiver. "That had to be particularly gruesome."

I nodded.

"Did either of the agents give you a business card?" Delgado asked.

"No, they didn't. They said they don't give out cards anymore. For security reasons." I looked at Delgado. The irony was not lost on either of us. "But they did give me a phone number to call if I thought of something that might be of assistance in their case. Do you want me to get it?"

"Please," I said. "If you have it handy."

McNamara went behind the desk on the far side of the room and opened the top drawer. Pulling on a pair of wire rim glasses from his shirt pocket, he moved some papers around and returned, handing me a small notebook-size piece of paper upon which was written the names of the two FBI agents and a phone number with a 212 area code. Manhattan. I thanked him and handed it to Delgado who folded it once and put it in his shirt pocket. "I just have a few more questions, and then we'll be out of your hair."

"Of course," McNamara replied.

"Did Matt come to you for his sabbatical?"

"That's one of the questions the FBI agents asked, too. I'll tell you what I told them. Technically, I don't grant sabbaticals. All of those kinds of requests are filtered through their own department chairs. No university president, as far as I know, handles sabbatical requests. We give final approval, but, in reality, the approval is merely a formality. The decision is made at the department level."

"But you did give your approval?"

"The truth is Matthew never even asked his department chair for a sabbatical. I knew he was doing research for a book he was writing on General Custer. He didn't request a sabbatical because he didn't need to. He was going to Montana in the summer. He checked to see if we had him scheduled for summer classes. We didn't, so he was free to go."

"Did he talk to you about why he was going to the Little Bighorn?"

"Not a word. I assumed he was headed to the battlefield to substantiate something or other he had found in his research. A few weeks ago, he went to France. I don't have any idea why, but I assumed it had to do with his book. It was a quick trip. Three days. Never had to get permission because he never missed a class."

"Do you know where he went in France?" I asked.

"A town called Chinon, as I recall. I think it's in the Loire Valley. That's all I know." He paused, his forehead wrinkled quizzically. "Now that I think about it, the *where* in France was a question the FBI people *didn't* ask." He shrugged his shoulders.

"Frank, it's important that we find out what Matt was working on. It got him killed. I know it. I can feel it in every fiber of me. But no one we've met so far knows what the hell he was after." I took the final sip of coffee in my cup. "How about friends and colleagues of Matt's that might have known what he was working on. Can you give us their names and how to get in touch with them?"

"I can give you the names I gave the FBI when they asked for the same information," he said. "A list of the professors in his department, and his department chair. Hold on."

McNamara walked back to his desk, pulled open the bottom drawer and returned with a manila folder that he passed to me. "In there is a copy of the names I gave to the FBI agents. Only six, including the chair. Matthew didn't seem particularly close to any of them. That's not unusual in college faculties. These six professors were not necessarily friends, just colleagues. And, as far as I know, were the closest people to him on the campus."

"You gave this list to the FBI people?"

"I did. All the folks on that list are, or were, professors at St. John's. Oh, wait. I forgot. There's one more professor. He's not on that list because he left the college years ago. Before I became president. Even before Matthew was hired, as a matter of fact. His name is Kyle Escher. I'd never have thought of him in connection with Matthew except those FBI agents mentioned they had heard about a recent connection between the two. They told me that Conroy visited Escher's home a couple of times in the past few weeks."

"Did they give a reason?"

"The agents had already interviewed Escher. They told me he said Matthew had some old papers he wanted authenticated. Wanted to know when they were written, I think. They asked me if I heard the same thing? About his having papers. I hadn't."

"And why would Conroy think this guy Escher could help?" Delgado asked.

"Good question. I had to look myself. Escher has a PhD in chemistry. Not sure where, or even if, he taught anywhere after leaving St. John's. Heard his rich wife died and left him a ton of money. If I was that lucky, I wouldn't be teaching anymore, either. In any case, I could look up his address if you want. Not sure it would do you any good, though."

"What was the FBI agents' take on him?" I asked.

"Escher told them he couldn't help Matthew. Even if he had wanted to, he'd been out of the profession for so long that he wouldn't even know where to begin. Didn't have any machines that would help in that kind of analysis."

"Did they believe him?"

"Apparently. But maybe you should talk to him, too. I've met him. He's a different sort of man. A brilliant fellow, though. Did his undergrad at MIT. But before pursuing his doctorate, he joined the Marine Corps. Served eight years."

"Not the usual path," Delgado said. "And a long time in the service."

"An unusual path to a doctorate in chemistry, for sure," McNamara said. "Colleagues of his told me that after his wife died, and he inherited her fortune, he couldn't wait to quit teaching. Wanted to get out into the field, again. Supposedly, he took up hunting."

I looked over at Delgado. By his faint smile I could tell he was thinking the same thing I was. "Might be good if you gave us his contact information," I said. "We probably should talk to him."

"No problem," he answered. "Would you mind if I called first to get permission to give out his address?"

"Not at all. More than likely we'll visit tomorrow, if that's alright with him. Tell Dr. Escher that we'll call before we leave the city." I paused, lifting myself off the sofa. "This list of his teaching colleagues you gave us?" I passed him back his folder. "We'll be seeing these people today."

"Good," McNamara said.

"One more favor? We don't know our way around New York City. Could you look at your list and tell us the most efficient way to get to these folks' homes?"

"Sure, no problem," he said. While he was outlining the most efficient route for us to take, Delgado and I walked around the study looking at the professor's bookshelves. All the books were in alphabetical order by author. I looked at Delgado. "Anal," I mouthed. He smiled.

"Here's the list," McNamara said. "I've numbered them by proximity to the campus. One being closest, then two, and so on. Get to house number one, and your GPS will show you the way from there." He folded the list and handed it to me. "The professors live fairly close to one another. Shouldn't be too hard."

"That's kind of you, Frank. I hate to burden you any more than we have, but could I ask you to call each of them to see if they would be available to meet with us?"

"Absolutely," he replied, returning to his desk.

Eight minutes later he was escorting us to the door. "Ms. Schaeffer won't be home, but the other five are expecting you. I also called Professor Escher. He'll see you tomorrow morning. Ten thirty. Here's his address. It's east of here about forty minutes."

"Doctor," I said, taking his hand. "Sorry to have taken so much of your time. We thank you."

"Nonsense. Find Matthew's killer, Inspector. That's all the thanks I'll need."

~~~~

As McGuire and Delgado walked down McNamara's driveway, the bald-headed man parked a block away in his Mercedes S550 put his cell phone to his ear and started the engine.

CHAPTER 23

As soon as we got in the car, I told Delgado to call the FBI number McNamara gave us. "Let's see if these assholes are for real."

While he dialed, I turned on the air conditioner and punched the first address into the GPS. Just as I pulled into the street, Delgado turned to me, nodded and pointed at the phone on his ear. "Got 'em," he mouthed. "FBI."

He introduced himself as a Vincent Tarantino, a stockbroker from Cooper Trading on Cuthbert Street in Lower Manhattan. He was making this up on the fly. Being a cop my whole life, I've listened to a whole hell of a lot of made up stories. Delgado's was not only plausible but, it turned out, quite entertaining. I started to understand why Rob Kincaid held him in such high esteem.

"I was visited by two of your agents about a ..." he paused and closed his eyes. I could hear the wheels of his imagination turning. "... about an insider trading deal that supposedly happened in my office." He stopped talking to listen, rolling his eyes at me and nodding his head. "Last week." Pause. "Yes. Cooper Trading." Pause. "Well, yes. They asked questions I found personal and intrusive. Frankly, I was offended and want to make a formal complaint." Another pause. He looked at me and smiled, shaking his head. "Yes, I do have their names." He picked up the paper from his lap. "Agent Raymond Decker and Agent William Townes." He put his hand over the receiver and whispered "*Ms. Raycraft* is checking on these guys," then smiled. Silence engulfed the car for what seemed like forever before Delgado jerked to attention. He nodded his head a few times, politely said "thank you" and hung up.

He looked at me. "They have no record of a Decker or Townes currently working for the FBI," he said. "You were right. The guys who visited McNamara? Them were the bad dudes."

~~~~

"They're on the move again," the bald-headed man said into his iPhone as he pulled away from the curb. A soft buzzing sound ensued. The man imagined his voice traveling at least once around the world through a series of cut-outs before it reached the ear of the man for whom it was intended. He leaned back in the luxurious seat of his Mercedes and waited. *I'm a lucky man*, he thought. *Bought and paid for by a fictitious company named Global Affinity Partners.* He smiled, knowing they probably knew that he knew they were not who they claimed to be. *They may be fictitious, but that six-thousand-dollar retainer check deposited in my bank account every month is real enough. Who am I to complain?* Before Global Affinity Partners had entered his life, the bald-headed man was a competent, albeit starving, private detective. Leaning forward, he patted the dashboard and inhaled the smell of sun-warmed leather. *And this here Mercedes sure beats the living hell out of that Ford Fusion I was driving a year ago.*

"Are they going back to the city?" the voice asked, bringing him back to the present.

"Yes. I'm about a quarter mile behind them."

There was a pause on the line. The bald-headed man could hear papers rustling. "Okay," the voice replied. "I know where they're headed. Silence again, then, "Stay with them. We'll need the addresses of the people they visit. Just in case it's someone new. Just don't be seen. Can't afford a fuck-up on this."

An icy finger sliced down the middle of the bald-headed man's back, making him shiver. He knew these were men that didn't accept failure. "Hey, don't worry. Have I ever let you down? These amateurs couldn't make me in a million years." A few moments later the voice returned. The bald-headed man nodded. "You got it. I'll call again with the addresses."

CHAPTER 24

We were back at the hotel by five and, after a quick shower and change of clothes, in the bar ordering a Sapphire tonic by six-thirty.

"Well, dude. Wasn't a completely wasted day," said Delgado, smiling as he watched the waitress place the drinks in front of us.

"Elimination day," I said with as much enthusiasm as I could muster. I took a sip. "Good drink at least." Delgado raised his glass in agreement. "But seriously, six – no, seven, people down."

"And replaced by how many more?" Delgado asked.

"Yeah. Forgot about those new people. But I can tell you, in an investigation, this is par for the course. And between the six, they only gave us three names. So we're still three to the good."

"Dude," was all Delgado said.

"We did learn some things, though," I said. "While no great revelations, we learned a lot about Conroy."

"That we did. He was one quiet son-of-a-bitch. Didn't have what you'd call a lot of friends."

"True," I said. "And his wife. No hints that any of this had anything to do with her. So it's another possible motive we can probably eliminate."

Delgado motioned to the waitress to bring us another round. "Agreed. But, dude – I don't know about you, but their marriage wasn't what you'd describe as the white picket fence variety."

I laughed. "Reminded me of mine. Though I at least got a divorce."

"Speaking of divorce," Delgado said. "You never mentioned how it went with Katelyn last night. You get any?"

"I never kiss and tell," I said with a purposely misleading grin. "And that reminds me. I'm thinking of calling her. Seeing if she's busy later tonight."

"You did get some, you son-of-a-bitch," Delgado said with a laugh. "First piece of ass you've had in what? Months? And you fall in love. You are one easy MF'er."

"Hey, nothing even close to that." I smiled. "I was even thinking of asking you to come with us. Probably just go shopping. Stuff like that. Girl stuff."

"Dude," Delgado said with a look of disgust.

"Thought so," I said, as I took out my phone.

~~~~

The bald-headed man sat in a booth across the hotel bar, talking on his cell phone. "No. Just sitting having a few cocktails. Want me to stick on them? I will, but it doesn't look like a lot is going to happen tonight."

There was a long pause, then the voice said, "No. What hotel are they in?"

"The Four Seasons," the man answered.

"Damn." Then, "Oh well. Get a room. We'll reimburse you. Just be there in the morning when they leave. They will have more people to visit."

CHAPTER 25

K atelyn sounded surprised to hear from me. She had plans to meet some friends in the Village, she told me, but could get out of it with a better offer. By this time Delgado had finished his drink, mouthed me *good luck* and left.

"Do you have anything in mind?" she asked.

"Nothing special," I answered. "Hoped that *just hanging out* would be considered a better offer."

She laughed. "The truth is you're bored and lonely with nothing to do. So you called me."

"Bored? Probably. But how could I be lonely? I have you." I said smoothly. Getting back in the "game."

"I hope that's not your best line," she said.

"They improve with good company and a few drinks," I said, trying to recover my swag.

"Okay. You're so smooth, you've talked me into it." I could hear the smile in her voice. "Let's meet at a place called Pegu. Heard of it?"

"No."

"It's the best bar in New York. Classy. I know you'll like it."

"I'll be on my best behavior, then. Won't embarrass you. Promise."

"Whew. That's a relief," she said with a laugh. "I can meet you there in an hour." She gave me the address. "It's not that far from you. Take a cab. Will that work for you?"

"Sure."

"I'd have you come here, but my place is a mess."

"No worries," I said. "I'm not taking it personally –
yet."

I went back to my room, changed into a pair of khakis
and the most unwrinkled shirt I had in the closet. A long-
sleeved, light-blue button down. Hoping I wasn't going to
look too outdated, I put on a blue blazer and checked myself out in the mirror one last time before leaving. Hadn't
thought this much about my wardrobe in years.

I arrived about ten minutes early. Even at that, she beat
me. I entered Pegu and saw her standing at the bar. Wearing jeans. *Dammit*, I muttered under my breath. If I had
only known. I had a pair of jeans in the closet. Course hers
looked a whole hell of a lot better on her than mine would
have looked on me.

She was right about the bar. Not crowded. Classy and
fairly quiet. Definitely a younger crowd, though. Most
wearing some version of denim. *What did I expect*? I
thought. *They're Katelyn's age, for God's sake.*

Smiling at the thought, I walked toward her. I had to
admit, the jeans did her justice. Black. Complementing her
hair. Tight. Complementing her ass. With spiky heels. I
could now appreciate her dig at Delgado about being too
short. In those heels, she would have towered over him.
The jeans were paired with a red silk shirt that draped just,
well – just perfectly. She looked stunning.

She saw me in the mirror behind the bar as I walked
toward her. "You cleaned up," she said, giving me an ap-
praising look.

"I kinda feel out of place here, tell you the truth." I
tugged at the lapels of the blazer.

"Don't be silly. You look great. In New York, anything works as long as you wear it with confidence."

I immediately felt better. She's right. *Grow some co-
jones, McGuire*, I thought. *I'm a fifty-two-year-old SFPD
homicide cop. Why should I give a shit about what these
kids think?* I stood up straighter. Caught my reflection in

the bar mirror. Gave myself a wink. She caught me, smiled and shook her head.

We ordered some bar food and sat there for the next four hours sampling Pegu's delightful array of specialty cocktails. And talking. Mostly small talk. Getting to know one another better. And with that knowledge, whether we wanted to take this further. She spoke of her budding interest in wine, spawned by what happened to her at a dinner party over a year ago.

"I was at an upscale restaurant with my roomie-boyfriend," she said, "and three other couples. Friends of his from California. When the waiter arrived for drink orders, I asked him if they carried a white zinfandel." I winced, knowing what was coming.

"Well, the table went completely silent. In fact, it felt like the entire restaurant had gone quiet. Every customer looking at me. I didn't know until later what a terrible *faux pas* I'd made."

"I feel your pain," I said, patting her leg. She looked down at my hand, then back up at me. Then smiled. I quickly removed my hand. "Sorry," I said. "Talk about a *faux pas*."

"Not at all," she said. "I liked the spontaneity of it."

I took a sip of my drink, thinking up a clever comeback. "It wasn't spontaneous," I finally said. "I've wanted to touch your leg all night." *Congrats, Mac*, I thought. *Hell of a line*. "And was just waiting for the opportunity. Thank you white zin." I raised my glass in a salute to her.

She laughed, patting my knee now. "You're funny. I think I'll keep you around for a while."

We talked more about her interest in wine, and California, and about my life in San Francisco. The dance had begun.

Then she asked about my day. Not thinking it was at all interesting, I gave her the short version. But she wanted more. I was flattered. For the next hour I showed off.

Wanting her to think I was some bad-ass detective from San Francisco who inevitably got his man. I told her about the supposed FBI agents that had visited McNamara's house asking questions. And then the story Delgado made up when he called the FBI's Manhattan headquarters to find out whether those agents were real. She laughed at that. And about the guy we were going to see tomorrow – the ex-Marine, turned chemistry professor, turned hunter.

By this time, we were on our sixth cocktail, and I started to feel tired. I hated to admit it. Didn't want her to think I was a wimp. Or even worse, old. Then I thought of the day ahead of me. I could just see myself falling asleep in the middle of an interview.

"I hate to do this," I said, "but I have a big day tomorrow. Maybe we should start heading back, huh?"

"It's only twelve-thirty, for goodness sake," she said. "I'm gonna have to toughen you up, McGuire." She laughed, put her arm through mine and said, "Lead the way."

I asked her if she wanted to walk home. "Sounds romantic to me," I said with a purposeful leer.

"It sounds stupid to me," she replied. "Do you know how far we are from my place? About thirty-five blocks. If you were thinkin' about getting any tonight, you definitely do not want me walking thirty-five blocks." She laughed.

"Taxi," I yelled. She laughed harder. I was starting to enjoy the *dance*.

Katelyn fell asleep on my shoulder during the cab ride back to her place. As we pulled up in front of her building, she slowly raised her head and looked around. "We're here already?" she asked.

"And I thought I was the tired one," I said. "Guess that means I'm not getting any tonight, huh?"

She smiled. "I think you're gonna have to wait. Sorry. Must be the drinks."

"Let's do this again tomorrow night. Just dinner. I won't be buying you any drinks." I laughed.

"Can't tomorrow night. How 'bout the next night?"

"You're on." I said, helping her out of the back seat. She smiled, pressing her body against me. She brushed her lips to mine and then whispered in my ear. "I'll be sure to clean up my place, too."

CHAPTER 26

I met Delgado for breakfast at seven fifteen the next morning. He never mentioned Katelyn. Neither did I. Didn't have the energy to walk through and examine every nuance of every sentence we spoke to one another last night. I certainly didn't mention that I was meeting her day after tomorrow.

We left the hotel at eight twenty-five. The GPS told us it was a two-hour drive to Stony Brook. It was ten thirty exactly when I took the Holland Road exit into Stony Brook.

"Nice town," Delgado said looking at the passenger side mirror. They were the first words he had spoken since we passed through the little town of Hauppauge about fifteen minutes before. He loosened his seat belt and reached into the back for his duffel bag.

"How far to Escher's place?" he asked, pulling the duffel onto his lap.

I looked at the GPS. "Half a mile down this road we'll turn left on Dogwood Street. He lives about a quarter-mile up Dogwood. Why? You got to go to the bathroom?"

"Not quite," he said with a scowl. "When you make the turn on Dogwood, I'll hop out." He reached into his duffel and rummaged around. "You keep going to Escher's. I'll meet you there later." A moment later he pulled out his Glock, attached the 40 Osprey suppressor, and jacked a shell into the chamber. "We got a tail."

"You sure?"

"Been watching him since Hauppauge," he said. "Hung back about a quarter mile. Big black Mercedes. Never varying. That's what caught my attention. So when he turned off the same exit back there, I knew he was shadowing us. When he comes by here, I'll ask him." He smiled, put the Glock in his waistband, strapped an M-48 Tanto knife to his leg, and patted me on the shoulder. "I'm gonna have some fun with this asshole."

I left him at the corner and drove down Dogwood to Escher's house. Dogwood was a quiet street of stately homes, most of them barely visible behind a forest of oaks and red maples. In the rearview mirror, I saw Delgado quickly look back down Holland Road, then duck into the dense woodlands surrounding this neighborhood.

I turned right into Escher's driveway; a meandering, cobblestone lane bordered by well-tended laurel and azaleas. As I parked, the front door opened and out stepped a man of medium height with a high and tight cut of salt and pepper hair. "Hello," he said from the doorway. "I'm Kyle Escher. You are?"

"Tom McGuire," I replied.

"The San Francisco homicide inspector. Nice to meet you. Where's your friend?"

"Running an errand. He'll be here later."

Escher walked down the front steps to greet me. "You came all the way from Manhattan?" He extended his hand. "Must have left early. Getting here in the morning from New York can be a nightmare."

"No problem at all," I said, shaking his hand. "Probably because I learned to drive in California."

He smiled. "Come in, please. Can I get you something?" We walked up the stairs. "Was just preparing lunch," he said. "Hope you like ..." No sooner had Escher closed the front door than my olfactory nerves were assaulted by the overpowering smell of ...

"… garlic. Sorry for the smell. Made garlic chicken. Probably put in a few too many cloves."

"No problem," I said, trying to blink away the tears already forming in my eyes without him noticing.

"Had to learn how to cook when my wife died. I've always loved garlic, and since I live by myself, I don't mind the smell at all. I forget that some people don't share my guilty pleasures."

I took out my handkerchief and dabbed at my eyes. "Maybe we could just move to a different room?" I said. "Not to be difficult, but …"

"You don't have to say another word, Thomas."

"Mac," I said, putting my hankie away as we walked toward the back of the house. "You can call me Mac."

"Sure, Mac. Just wanted you to know I understand your reaction completely. I started out as a professor of chemistry. This house has experienced its share of different odors. My poor wife. When she was alive, she made me build an add-on room where she could go and not have her eyes water like yours are now because of my chemicals." He smiled at the thought. "After she died, I figured I could use the same room for my getaway space. Made it into my own man cave. Of course, I picked out the manly furniture and, oh yeah, put in air conditioning." He laughed. "Here we are." He opened a door and, with an exaggerated sweep of his hand, invited me in.

The room was larger than I expected. It was furnished in dark wood and leather, and smelled of gun oil. It was a man's room filled with man artifacts. A large stone fireplace dominated the back wall. Framing the fireplace were the heads of three trophy animals. Escher saw me looking. "On the far side is a wildebeest from South Africa. Bagged him in aught-three." He paused. "A beautiful, elegant animal," he said, with just a hint of regret in his voice. "On this side is a leopard. Got him the next year in Tanzania. But this guy…" he pointed to the mounted head directly over the fireplace. "… he charged our Jeep. Fifteen hundred and forty-two pounds of pissed off animal. Took me two shots to bring him down. Another sixteen feet, four inches and he would have smashed into the Jeep. There were three of us sitting there. We all would have been toast. Our heads would have been mounted on *his* fireplace." He laughed at his little joke.

Under the buffalo's head was a gun mounted on an open rack. I walked over and stood looking at it. "Nice weapon," I said.

"Thanks, Mac. A Browning BAR Mk II. Safari grade. That's the gun that brought down the buffalo. Shoots a .338 Win Mag cartridge. Cost me a fortune, but well worth it."

"Expensive hobby," I said. "You're a chemist. What's with the hunting?"

"I was a chemist only for a short time," he said. "Here, let's sit." He pointed to two high-backed leather chairs. "Let me be more exact. I was a professor of chemistry exactly one year. Then I married Margaret. Didn't have to work after that. Benefits of marrying rich. I recommend it to everyone." He laughed.

"Dr. McNamara told me you were in the Marines for a while."

"Ten years, two months," he replied. "Loved it."

"So, let's see," I said. "MIT undergrad then to the Corps and then a PhD. Unusual career path."

"Are you interrogating me, Inspector?"

"In a manner of speaking. But don't think you're special. I do this with everyone when I'm on a case. Habit. Surprised you even picked up on it."

"Well, interrogate away," he said. "I've got nothing to hide." He paused, then smiled and said, "Well, a few things. But you'll never know them."

"Because you won't tell me?"

"Precisely."

"Then let's go over what you will tell me. Marines? What's with that?"

Escher bent over in his chair, put his elbows on his knees and looked at me. I could see in his eyes he was weighing what he should or shouldn't tell me. "Like a lot of kids that age," he began, "I really didn't know what I wanted to do with my life. The difference between the others? I really liked school. And I especially liked chemistry. Weird, I know. But you know what got me interested in chemistry?"

"I give up," I replied. "What?"

"Gunpowder."

I wondered how many times he had told that story, and how many times he got the look I just gave him. His answer, "I can see by your expression that surprises you," answered my question. "Did you realize that the advent of gunpowder, and its effects on artillery and naval power, changed the face of the world? Forever?"

"Never thought about it," I answered, feeling like the dumb kid in the back of the room.

"It was my epiphany moment," he said. "I saw clearly that discoveries in laboratories, chemistry or physics or you name 'em, are what really change the world. I wanted to be a part of that."

"And what does all this have to do with you joining the Marines?" I asked.

"Before I gave my life to science, I wanted to experience first hand the consequences of the advent of gunpowder. What better way than to enlist?"

"And did you learn the effects of gunpowder?"

"Not only learned the effects. Saw the effects. The Marines made me a sniper."

CHAPTER 27

After leaving the car, Delgado melted back into the tree-line. About forty seconds later, the black Mercedes turned onto Holland Drive and came slowly toward him. *My, my, my said the spider to the fly,* he thought. *Jump right ahead in my web.* He patted his waistband. Feeling the comfort of the Glock, he smiled.

He watched the car approach the intersection where he crouched hidden in the brush. He saw the indecision in the bald-headed man's eyes when he looked down Dogwood and didn't see the Highlander. He didn't see the Highlander down the next street, either, so he rolled to the side of the road and made a call on his cell phone. A few minutes later, he put the phone down, made a u-turn and drove back toward Dogwood. Delgado watched as the driver, without hesitation, turned up Dogwood, slowed down in front of Escher's driveway, then drove to the next corner. There he pulled another u-turn and parked facing Escher's house.

Interesting, Delgado thought. *The driver got Escher's address from the person on the phone.* It would be something he would ask about when he met the guy face-to-face.

Delgado surveyed the terrain. No easy way to get to the Mercedes without being detected, unless he hiked through the forested property that lined Dogwood. He unsheathed the M-48 Tanto. *Hope there are no fucking dogs guarding property along here,* he thought as he started to move slowly through the tree-line. *I'd hate to have to kill someone's pet.* Even if the dogs ignored him, the M-48 would come in handy if he encountered heavy brush.

It took Delgado ten minutes to go the quarter-mile that separated him from the Mercedes. The dogs left him alone, so the knife went back in its sheath. He purposely ended up behind the car so he could read the license plate. Sinking deeper into the brush, he placed a call to Kincaid at Ft. Bragg. Ten minutes later he had the name of the driver. Mitchell Randolph from New Jersey. Former private detective. No information on current employment status.

Delgado pulled the Glock from his waistband, "press checked" to make sure there was one in the chamber, and broke cover fifty feet behind and to the right of the Mercedes. *No worries*, he thought. *To the guy in the car I could be any local resident out for an afternoon stroll.* He approached the car slowly. Even though the windows were tinted, he could see the outline of the guy's bald head. It was facing down toward his lap. *Catching a few winks or playing a game on his cell phone*, Delgado thought. *Either way, not very observant. In for a big surprise.*

Delgado easily walked to the car unnoticed and tapped on the passenger side window with the tip of the suppressor. The driver looked up in surprise, his right hand reflexively reaching for the handgun lying next to him on the seat. Delgado took a step back, pointed the Glock at the driver's head, pursed his lips and slowly shook his head. The driver obediently pulled his hand away and raised it in the air. *Unlock the doors*, Delgado mouthed. When he heard the click of the locks releasing, he opened the rear door and slid into the back seat.

"Dude," he said, pushing the Glock against Randolph's forehead. "You're fucking with the wrong people."

CHAPTER 28

" A sniper?" I said, flashing back to Conroy lying on Last Stand Hill with half his skull missing. "You're kidding."

"No, I'm not kidding. That's where I developed such a love for hunting, I think."

"Different kind of game," I said.

"Definitely. They don't shoot back." He paused, then said, "But you didn't come all this way to talk about hunting or being a sniper. You're investigating the murder of Matthew Conroy and his wife. I want to help in any way I can."

"I appreciate that." I said. "He was a friend of mine."

"I didn't know him as well as you, but I considered him a friend as well," he answered. "So we both have skin in this game."

"How well *did* you know him?"

"Funny. That was the same question those *poseur* FBI agents asked me."

"You knew they were fake?"

"Shit. I've been around law enforcement types all my life. Guys just like you, Mac. I don't want to insult you, but I knew you were a policeman the moment I saw you. You walk like one. You talk like one. You even smell like one. At least you did before you came into my house." He smiled broadly. "Anyway, I know dozens of FBI agents. I knew in my gut those guys who came to see me were imposters."

"Did you ask to check their IDs?"

"Of course. The *IDs* were authentic. The men carrying them weren't. I took their names. Decker and Townes. After they left, I called a friend of mine at the FBI crime lab at Quantico. He searched the complete FBI data bank. *Nada* on either of them."

"What kinds of questions did they ask?"

"Just about what you'd expect. About Matthew and what he was working on. They asked if I had any idea who or why anyone would want to murder him. I told them jack shit. Said I didn't know anything. Which actually is the truth. Or close to it."

"And when they asked you the question as to why he was murdered, you said?"

"Nothing. I told you, I didn't give them jack."

"But you know why he was murdered, don't you?"

"Why do you say that?" he asked.

"Because I've been a cop for close to fourteen years, and I can read *you* like a book," I replied with a smile.

"Touché", he said, grinning back. "Hell yes, I know why. It's obvious, isn't it? Somebody didn't want him to publish what he found about the Custer battle."

I sat in silence for a few minutes staring at him. So much of my job as a cop is simple intuition, and at that moment, I was being overwhelmed by intuition. "And you know what he found out, too, don't you!"

Escher turned silent. He stared at me for what seemed like an eternity. His expression neutral, but his jaw muscles working. I felt him openly take my measure. A test. Deciding how much he could trust me. When I saw his face soften, I knew I'd passed. "Come with me, I've got something to show you," he said in a quiet voice. "I helped him authenticate his damn document."

CHAPTER 29

Adrenaline. God's greatest gift to us earthlings. Hard to compare the intensity of the high I was feeling. Winning the lottery? Having the sexiest lady at the bar ask you up to her room? Neither of those things ever happened to me, unfortunately, but if I had to guess, Escher having Conroy's document had to be close.

I followed him out of his man cave and into the back yard. At the far end of his house a pair of large shutter doors announced an underground storm cellar. He unlocked them, and I helped wrestle them open. A flight of stairs led down under the house. At one time this space may have been a storm cellar, but when the lights went on I found myself standing at the outer edge of a full-size rifle range.

"Son-of-a-bitch," I uttered. "I've never seen anything like this in someone's freaking basement before. You really take this shit seriously."

"Where I practice," Escher said. "I find it fun." He reached to his neck and pulled out a braided piece of rawhide. Hanging on it was an animal's tooth. "I'm proud to wear this."

I recognized his piece of *jewelry* immediately. "You knew I went to Annapolis, right?" I asked. Escher nodded. "Then you know *I* know what that is."

"I was hoping," he said with a smile.

"In my eight years in the Navy, I never met anyone who had qualified to wear the hog's tooth. HOG. Hunter of Gunmen. Not many snipers reach that level. I'm impressed."

"Yeah. Not to brag – though that's exactly what I'm doing – getting this tooth hung around my neck was the equivalent of winning the Medal of Honor. At least for me. Took me four years to earn it." Sweeping his hand left-to-right, he said, "This is just the way I have of keeping my skill-set up to date."

"Delgado will have an orgasm when he sees this layout. You'll never get rid of him. How many people know you have this range under your house?"

"None of my neighbors, that's for sure," he said with a laugh. "But a few of the local police. I do a lot of work for the police departments around here. Even the FBI, as I told you. Mostly on the forensic side. My chemical knowledge can be of assistance." He paused and looked around. "But really, other than wanting to show you what a hard-ass I am, the real reason I brought you down here was this."

He walked me to a closet at the far end of the room. Opening it, he spread his hands out, and like a proud papa, said. "My gas chromatography-mass spectrometry machine."

I was looking at what reminded me of a large copier that you might see at Staples or Kinko's.

"MIT was about to retire this puppy," he said. "I conned them into giving it to me."

"Guess a guy can't have too many gas chromatography-mass spectrometry machines, huh?" I teased.

"Smart ass. You should consider yourself fortunate just to be invited down here."

"I actually do," I said. "I find this stuff fascinating. But you're going to have to go slow with me on this. "First of all, what did you mean you *authenticated* his document? And did you do that on this machine?"

"It was the dating I did for him," Escher said. I looked quizzically at him. He took my cue and continued.

"Conroy showed up at my house one day. Maybe two or three weeks ago. Out of the blue. I'd already heard about him from some friends of mine. That he was doing research on General Custer, so it wasn't a complete surprise when he knocked on my door with some papers he wanted analyzed. Said he had heard from a colleague that I had a machine like this, and asked if I could authenticate some source material he had. He needed an approximation of the historical time-frame in which it was written. You know what carbon dating is?" I nodded. "This machine can do the *dating* part. It can chemically analyze the resins used in ink and give a pretty accurate time signature as to when the document was written."

"And *pretty accurate* means what?"

"Within a decade or so."

"You did the tests?"

"I did. Only one at first. He asked me to swear, if it proved authentic, not to tell anyone until he published the findings."

"He must have trusted the hell out of you," I said.

Escher nodded. "I was both honored and flattered. I put it through my machine here. Took less than two minutes to give him an answer."

"And?"

"The ink sample he brought to me was consistent with the inks used between 1870 and 1888 in this country."

"Which certainly was within Custer's lifetime." I felt the adrenaline kick in again.

"Correct."

"Did you see him again?"

"Hell, ya. We became pretty good friends. I mean, as good a friend as coming over the house four or five times in a two week period just to shoot the shit can allow you to become."

"When was the last time he was here," I asked.

"Just four days ago," Escher replied. "Brought me another ink fragment, a small one. Asked if I could analyze it. I knew he was on his way to Montana, so I didn't think there was a rush. I did the analysis of that fragment two days ago. Right before I found out he was murdered. Never got to tell him my finding."

"Which was?"

"The second sample he gave me was from a source of much later lineage. The ink on the fragment was consistent with those used in the first two decades of the twentieth century. The inks were European in origin, strangely enough."

"I'm guessing he didn't let you keep what he gave you."

"No. The second one was just a scrap. Not big enough to keep. I burned it. The first one I gave back to him. I had no use for it."

"Would the one you gave back to him be at his house? Would he have kept it there?"

"If he did," said Escher, "it's long gone by now. Be assured that our friends Decker and Townes have already been through his house with a fine tooth comb. No, not there. I'm gonna guess he kept it at his girlfriend's house."

"His girlfriend?" I said. "You're telling me Conroy had a girlfriend? That's gotta be bullshit. I don't believe it."

"Well, I'm not sure if they played house together, but he spent a lot of time there," Escher replied. "At least in the past two weeks. When he wasn't spending time with me, he said he was with her. Said she was just a *friend*. I knew he was married, so I never went any further." He paused. "Her name is Rachel Skinner. I have her address if you want."

CHAPTER 30

I called Delgado. "You doing okay?" I asked when he answered.

"Couldn't be better," Delgado replied.

"Need you back here, pronto. We gotta go. Escher gave us the name and address of Conroy's girlfriend."

"His girlfriend?" Delgado said, not sounding too surprised. "Well – yeah. Okay. Give me ten minutes. I've got some things to work out with the dude who was following us."

Delgado reached Escher's house thirty minutes later. "Sorry I took so long," he said. "Had a few things to clear up with that dude." His nose twitched and he took a step backward. "Shit, Bro, is that garlic?"

"Yeah. You'll get used it," I said with a laugh. "Don't mention it to Escher. He's embarrassed enough." Delgado screwed up his face and dabbed at his eyes.

"The guy in the Mercedes – he was tailing us, huh?" I asked.

"Yeah. We met. Sat in his car. Had a good ol' fashioned man-to-man talk. Where's Escher, by the way?"

"Right here," came Escher's reply as he walked in from the kitchen. "Nice to meet you, Mr. Delgado." The two shook hands. "Sorry about the smell."

Delgado waved it away. "You're in deep shit, Professor," he said. "They know where you live."

"The bad guys?" replied Escher, with no hesitation. "The one your friend and I talked about? The ones posing as FBI agents? Hell, they've already been here."

Delgado looked at me and cocked his head. I nodded. "Yeah, same guys, Vin. They visited Mr. Escher. You don't have to call him professor anymore. He hasn't been one for a long time. You can call him doctor, though. He does have a PhD."

"Well, watch yourself, anyway," Vinnie said to Escher. "These dudes are wired in. Guy following us? I'm watching him from the bushes back there." He pointed back toward Holland Street. "He loses the Highlander because Mac has already parked in your driveway. So he pulls over to the side of the road and makes a call. Two minutes later he turns around, drives up this street, stops in front of your house. Making sure the Highlander's there. Then he drives to the next corner, turns around and parks facing the house." Delgado paused, then said, "Guys he talked to on the phone? Had *your* address on their speed dial."

"What'd the guy have to say for himself, Vinnie?"

"The driver's name is Mitch Randolph. I got that from calling Kincaid with the dude's license plate number. A private detective. Dude told me he contracts exclusively with a company called *Global Affinity Partners*. Mostly just surveillance.

"I called Kincaid about that *Global* group, too." Delgado continued. "Didn't get even one hit. A super shadowy operation. He said he'll try other resources and get back to me."

"Glad you got Rob involved early on," I said.

"Yeah. I took the dude's cell phone, wallet, bank account numbers and gun. I told Kincaid I'd give it all to him next time we're together. Hoping his contacts can put places and faces on all Randolph's incoming and outgoing calls. Maybe get lucky on who's been funding his bank account. At the very least, Admiral Thompson's people at JSOC confirmed Randolph's name and address. And that he's a licensed PI. Now we know where he lives."

"I'm not all that worried about these guys," said Escher.

"Maybe you should be. Randolph's scared shitless of them."

"You don't know Dr. Escher yet, Vinnie," I said. "He's a former Marine sniper. Ten years. A HOG."

"No shit? Well I guess that levels the playing field somewhat. Sorry, dude. Didn't know."

"No problem. I got something to show you before you leave. Think you may like it." Escher replied. "But before that, did Randolph tell you why this *company* is on you guys?"

"He says he has no clue. His instructions were to follow us, not get made, and keep *Global Affinity Partners* informed of our movements."

"And after your *talk*, you just let Randolph go?" Escher asked. "You're not afraid he'll pick up another gun and come after us? To show his boss or bosses that he didn't fuck up?"

"Him? Nah. Before we parted company, I broke both his thumbs. I figured he could always get himself another gun, but he wouldn't be able to hold it without thumbs. Dude won't be able to fire a gun until we're safely back home."

"Gotta tell you, Vinnie," I said. "Leaving the part about the thumbs out, I was thinking you got the makings of a pretty good cop. Thinking maybe of recommending you to the police academy."

"Don't think," he replied. "I probably wouldn't pay as much attention to the so-called *civil rights* of the bad guys as they'd want. Because personally, I don't think them dudes are entitled to any."

I chuckled. "You're right. I'm thinking the police academy may not be right for you."

CHAPTER 31

Delgado was properly impressed with Escher's basement firing range. The three of us spent an hour blasting away at targets from the myriad of weaponry that Escher had available. Vinnie and I left with a keen appreciation of Escher's shooting accuracy. Practice does, indeed, make perfect.

~~~~

Rachel Skinner lived in Manhasset. Took us fifty minutes to get there. Delgado spent the whole trip looking out the rear window. That was all right by me. The more paranoid he was, the safer I felt.

Escher called ahead and told Rachel we were on our way. She had received the news of Conroy's death yesterday and was devastated. Had taken the week off work.

Rachel Skinner lived in a modest home in one of the better neighborhoods in the north side of Manhasset. The house sat back on a broad flat lawn, shaded by a variety of birch, hickory and white ash trees. Tiny yellowish-white flowers surrounded the paved path to the front door.

We rang the bell and heard footsteps slowly approaching. We heard the security chain being deliberately pulled back, and slowly the door opened. Rachel Skinner's swollen eyes spoke volumes. She led us to the living room and invited us to sit. The floor was strewn with jeans, hoodies and shoes of various styles and shapes. She caught our looks. "I told Dr. Escher to tell you not to expect a clean house," she said.

"He told us," I said with a warm smile. "And I want you to know we respect your privacy and your pain. My name is Tom McGuire. I'm a policeman from San Francisco, and an old friend of Matt's." I took out my identification and passed it to her. She did a cursory check and returned it. "I knew Matt when he was a teenager. This is my associate Vince Delgado. We both share your sorrow."

Rachel was not what you'd call a stunning beauty but was pretty in a fresh, uncalculating way. She had high cheekbones and just the faint hint of a mid-summer tan. Her butter blonde hair was stacked messily atop her head and held in place by a long, scarlet ribbon. She wore rimless glasses that magnified the puffiness of her eyes.

"I know Professor Escher told you, but we're in New York investigating Matt's death. We think he was killed because of the work he was doing on General George Custer and the Battle of the Little Bighorn. Professor Escher said you might have some information on what Matt might have found."

She nodded, her eyes tearing up. She dabbed at them with a tissue. "He shared with me most of what he was working on," she said. "But not everything. He said there might be things that could put me in danger, and I'd be safer if I didn't know."

"Have you told anyone about what he was doing? A friend? A neighbor?"

"Not a soul," she said. "Matt and I kept our friendship quiet. I'm sure you knew he was married." I nodded. "I didn't want our relationship to come to light and ruin his life."

"Were you in love with him?" I asked. I knew I was being blunt, but I didn't have the time or the patience to dance around the issue.

She shivered in discomfort, the sobs becoming more pronounced. Tears cascaded freely down her cheeks. She removed her glasses, put them on her lap and covered her cheeks with her hands. "I was," she finally said. "But we were never intimate, if that's what you mean." She quieted herself. "That was a threshold I didn't want to cross," she continued. "And neither did Matt. We're both Catholic. At least Matt was at one time, and still believed that getting divorced and remarried wasn't right." The floodgates then opened. Delgado and I waited a full five minutes as she struggled to calm her emotions.

"I wish sometimes I wasn't so damn religious." She smiled, but her eyes continued to drip. "Matt warned me not to tell anyone about his work. When he was ready, he wanted to be the one to announce his discovery. He told me there could be some serious blowback."

"We want to find out what he was working on so we can narrow down the search for his killer," I said. "Dr. Escher had a fragment of a document and a letter that Matt told him was the key to his puzzle. Would you know where the originals are?"

"I ..." she hesitated. I didn't blame her. I'd be wary, too, before giving away secrets to virtual strangers. "I have them," she said. "They're all here. And more, actually. I received a package two days before Matt left for Montana." The flow of tears resumed. She brought herself under control, and said, "From France. Matt was excited when it arrived."

I tried my homicide cop best to keep my voice even. I felt on the cusp of breaking this case wide open. I don't care if you do crack, meth, H – whatever. There's no greater high than this. The rush is life-defining. "Would it be possible for you to share them with us?"

"I'll give you everything," she said, standing up. "Especially if it helps find his killer. There's a small house on the back of this property. It's where Matt actually slept if he stayed overnight." She noticed Delgado's reaction, and said, "I told you I'm Catholic. And he's married. Enough said." She paused and laughed softly. "This way."

We followed her to the cabin. "Used to be a gazebo that was built in the middle of the last century," she said. "They're so hopelessly old-fashioned, I just had to tear it out and build something useful."

I wanted to tell her I was born in the middle of the last century. Or close to it. And it wasn't *that* long ago. But I kept quiet. My dignity intact.

"Matt and I got rid of the gazebo, doubled the cement foundation, and built this room for overnight guests. Little did I know that Matt would be the primary beneficiary." She started to cry again. As much as I wanted, I didn't think comforting her would be appropriate. Delgado had no such compunction. He folded her into his embrace and patted her back.

She cried for a good five minutes, then unlocked the door. We followed her inside. A large Persian rug covered the entire floor. A double bed was nestled into the right corner, while an ancient five-drawer dresser stood on the opposite wall. Rachel bit her lip, squeezing her eyes tightly, trying to avoid another faucet of tears. It worked – partially. Delgado walked over to her, but she waved him off. "That dresser," she said. "Move it out to the middle of the room, please." We complied. "Now pull the rug back from the wall." We again complied. She walked over and tapped the floor with her foot. The hollow sound told us what she didn't have to say aloud. I walked over and knelt down, feeling with my hands for a hold I knew was there. Rachel, in the meantime, sat on the bed. "Pull the floorboard up," she instructed.

I found the hold and pulled. Sure enough, four hardwood planks rose silently in my hand. "The documents are in there," she said, pointing to the two-foot square combination safe staring up at me.

"Combination?" I asked.

She gave me four numbers. My fingers could barely keep steady as I moved the dial right, then left, then right, then left. I felt like a kid at his birthday party. Moving the dial right and left was like ripping off the brightly colored paper covering the box that held your surprise gift. The anticipatory feeling was euphoric. Like that child at his birthday party, I just knew the safe contained my heart's desire.

I heard the satisfying click as the tumblers fell into place. I lifted the safe's lid and peered inside. At the bottom lay a small FedEx box sitting on top of a plastic sleeve holding some kind of paper. *A present within a present*, I thought, as I lifted the box and plastic sleeve out and placed them on the carpet. Rachel and Delgado moved closer, flanking me. I looked back at them and smiled.

"Are you going to open the damn thing or sit there all day with that stupid grin on your face," Delgado said.

"Savoring the moment, my man," I said. "Savoring the moment."

"You might want to read what's on the paper in the plastic sleeve first," Rachel said. "It was from this paper that Matt cut the piece to give to Dr. Escher."

I nodded to her and retrieved it.

The letterhead said *New York Life Insurance Company*. Under it was a typed message. A signature was scrawled under the message. It all looked official. I noticed the bottom right hand corner of the letterhead was cut off. Conroy's gift to Professor Escher. I turned the plastic sleeve toward the window so I could read it better.

NEW YORK LIFE INSURANCE COMPANY

This is to certify that the New York Life Insurance Company, hereafter known as "The Company", has received from Mr. George Armstrong Custer, hereafter known as "The Insured," the amount of $1,000 in the form of gold bullion to purchase a Life Insurance Policy from "The Company" that would pay Elizabeth Bacon Custer, here-

*after known as The Beneficiary, the sum of $5,000 upon
the death of "The Insured."*

It went on for another two paragraphs and then was
signed and dated by a Henry A. Bogert, President and Attorney.

Okay, I thought, *so Custer had a life insurance policy*.
Not a particularly historic find. Lots of military people,
even in those years, took out life insurance policies. But
then I looked at the date the policy was issued and saw
immediately what grabbed Conroy's attention. *April 28,
1876*. Custer had taken out the policy less than two months
before the battle. *Big time coincidence*, I thought, feeling
the excitement start to churn in my stomach.

"Damn," I said. "Take a look at this." I passed the
plastic sleeve to Delgado. Rachel stood reading it over his
shoulder. "A copy of an insurance policy Custer took out
on his life. Notice the date it was issued."

"Dude." Delgado said. "Like he knew this battle
would be his last. Maybe a gesture to the old lady? Saying
no matter what happens to me, babe, I'm taking care of
you?"

"That's one way to read it," I said, picking up the
FedEx package. "Let's see what other goodies are in here."
I put the box on my lap. "When did you say this arrived?"

"It arrived at my house on Sunday," she replied. "The
day before Matt left for Montana." She brought her fist to
her mouth, stifling back a sob. "It came from France. The
sender had paid extra for the Sunday delivery. I received a
call at two thirty Sunday morning telling me to expect a
package and to let Matt know immediately when it arrived.
Probably from the man Matt met in France two weeks ago.
Matt went through the box pretty carefully. You'll see.
There are a lot of papers in there. Some letters, but mostly
loose pages like a journal."

"And from that pile Matt took a letter to Dr. Escher, correct? For authentication purposes?"

"Yes," she replied. "Late Sunday afternoon. Mr. Escher never got back to Matt."

"We know. He told us this afternoon that Matt mentioned he was going to Montana, so he felt no urgency to do the analysis. By the time he finished the work, Matt was already dead. Escher told us his findings showed the ink samplings to be consistent with those used in the first two decades of the twentieth century. And, curiously enough, were of European origin. The paper Matt had given him was just a scrap containing the letters *esper*, obviously torn from a larger note. Escher told us to look for the page these letters were ripped from. If we found it in the box from France, we should assume everything in the box is from the same time period."

"Hurry up, then, and open the damn box." Delgado said.

"I'm on it," I said, lifting the flap and peering inside. Rachel was right. A lot of paper, but now neatly arranged in stacks perpendicular to one another. "Did Matt arrange them like this?" I asked Rachel.

"Yes," she said. "He didn't get to read through everything, but arranged the ones he did read according to language. Some are in English, some in French. The ones in English are on top. He also filed them by date. The last letter written should be on top.

"Well," I said, picking up the first paper on the stack. "Let's see what got Matt so excited."

It didn't take long. The answer was in the first letter I picked off the pile. The paper was thin and brittle, like an old man's skin. The envelope was still attached. A letter never sent. The letter was dated *September 6, 1914,* and addressed to *My Dear Bill.* I picked up the envelope to see who *Bill* was. It was addressed to *William F. Cody* in Golden, Colorado. I could feel my head inadvertently lowering, getting closer to the page as I started to comprehend what I was reading. The writer's *Dear Bill* could be none other than *Buffalo Bill Cody,* Indian scout, buffalo hunter and showman supreme.

His Wild West Show was so famous it even toured in Europe. I didn't bother with the contents of the letter. The anticipation was killing me. I flipped it over and went right to the signature.

Your friend,
Geo. A. Custer

"Son of a bitch," I whispered. I looked up at Delgado and Rachel. They were both staring at me, bent in anticipation. I couldn't contain the grin that took over my face. "Son – Of – A – Bitch," I yelled, bouncing to my feet. "Look at this." I held the letter out in front of me. They both came around behind me so they could see what I was referring to. "Look." I pointed to the date. Even read it for them. "September 6, 1914." I let that sink in. "And look who it's written to." I showed them the envelope and pointed to the addressee. "Damn, man. Is that something? To Buffalo Bill Cody. Can you believe it?" I paused, letting my brain catch up with my mouth. "And best of all, look *who* wrote it." I turned the letter over, pointing to the signature. "G-E-O dot A dot Custer," I articulated grandly.

Rachel let out a sharp gasp. Delgado leaned in and looked closely at the signature. Studying it, like maybe it was a forgery.

I sat back down, bringing my emotions more under control. "Do you know what all this means?" I asked quietly. "It means that Lt. Colonel George A. Custer did not die in 1876 at the Battle of the Little Bighorn. That was Conroy's earthshaking discovery. Custer didn't die. He took out that life insurance policy and then faked his own fucking death."

CHAPTER 32

We spent the next hour at Rachel's reading what we now called *The Custer Papers*. We were about a quarter of the way through when Delgado pointed to his watch and then at Rachel. *Time to go*, he mouthed. He was right. She was fading fast. The psychological pressure of Matt's death was overwhelming her. I should have been more sensitive to her need for grieving time. I asked if we could take the papers with us. She nodded, and said, "Just find Matt's murderer. Bring him to justice. That's all I ask."

As soon as we pulled away from her house, Delgado said, "I didn't want to bring this up in front of her, Bro, but tell me why you think this find is such hot shit. I mean, I know you *historians...*" he said it like we were carriers of the bubonic plague "... will all be having wet dreams over this, but except for you and a few professors, who cares? You talk about motive. Correct me if I'm wrong, but this happened one hundred forty years ago, for God's sake. You think Conroy got snuffed because Custer lived? Except for those few wet dreamers here and there, tell me who the hell would give a shit?"

I laughed. "Well, forgive the pun, but while I'll 'cop' to having wet dreams, I can honestly say I've never had one dreaming about George Custer."

"Thank goodness, Bro. You had me worried."

"Seriously, though – somebody gave a shit. Question is who? The answer has to be in those papers. Names. Didn't you find it curious that Custer started his journal the year of the battle? If he intended it to be a simple memoir, he would have started it earlier in his life. Like maybe when he entered West Point. But he didn't. He began with a dinner he had at the Willard Hotel in Washington with General Sheridan in March of 1876. Three months before the battle. He did that with a purpose in mind."

"Dude. I read that part, too. You're talking about where Sheridan tells him there are rich and powerful men plotting to kill him? Oh, wait … *they* weren't going to kill him. They were plotting to get the Indians to kill him." He looked over at me. "You actually believe that shit?"

"If it was good enough for Sheridan, then it's good enough for me. You read the papers, Vinnie. Sheridan thought it was a foregone conclusion that Custer was a dead man. So he knew those "rich and powerful men" had enough juice to pull it off. Not even Sheridan could stop them."

"So what happened? Turns out those rich dudes weren't very good 'plotters' after all. Custer didn't die," Delgado countered.

"You obviously didn't read far enough, Vinnie. In the conversation, Sheridan tells Custer that *someone* named George Armstrong Custer had to die in the upcoming battle. It just doesn't have to be him."

"So you're telling me that's why Custer is still alive. Somehow he faked his death and escaped to France? A cover-up to end all cover-ups? Give me a break. Couldn't happen."

"But apparently it did," I said. "Custer lived."

Delgado took a deep breath and exhaled slowly. And noisily, just in case I didn't get his dramatic gesture. "Okay, back to the rich and powerful men. Sheridan said those guys thought that by having Custer die at the hands of the Indians, the country would be so enraged they would demand the Army crush the Plains Indians. And once the Indians were dealt with, all the lands west of the Missouri River would be opened to settlers. Is that what you're saying?"

"It's not me saying that," I responded. "It's what George Custer is saying. And, by the way, isn't that exactly what happened? Talk about motive. Can you imagine the enormous wealth that was generated when those pesky Indians finally went away?"

"Okay. So those guys would have had motive," said Delgado. "I get that. But I keep coming back to the same question I've had from the very beginning. Why would anyone care now? Why would they care enough to kill Conroy? To go to war with Red Squadron Security Agency? Or go to war with anyone, for that matter? Just doesn't compute."

"Depends," I said, "on who those rich and powerful men were, don't you think? What if their names were Dupont or Vanderbilt? You wouldn't have to be a wet dream historian to know what kind of shit that would cause. If it were guys like that, I think we may have just answered your question."

"That's a big-ass leap, dude," Delgado said. "May I remind you that no names were mentioned in those papers?"

"You may. But let me remind you we haven't read through them all yet?"

CHAPTER 33

We arrived at the hotel a little after seven. "I don't know about you, Bro, but I'm exhausted," said Delgado, as I handed the car keys to the valet. "If you don't mind, can we tackle the rest of *The Custer Papers* tomorrow? I'm up for a drink at the bar, but otherwise this dude wants nothing more than to get a good night's sleep."

"I'm really disappointed," I said with a laugh. "I got paired up with a wimp."

Delgado, true to his word, had one drink and was gone.

I had another drink at the bar, and started to think about what Katelyn might be doing. I looked at my watch. Eight twenty. I knew she said she wouldn't be available tonight, but –

Shit, Mac, an interior voice said. *What the hell you doing, man? You want female company? There are plenty of women around this hotel.* But then another voice took over. *But what the hell,* it said, *she might be home. You never know. In any case, why not call and leave her a voice mail. Let her know you were thinking of her.* This was freaking crazy. Having an argument with myself.

One of me won the argument. Not sure it was the wise me or the stupid me. All I know is I pulled out my cell and dialed. She answered on the third ring.

"What a surprise," she said. "I was just thinking about you."

"Good things, I hope."

"What else could there be?" I took a deep breath. If I didn't know better, I'd swear she was intentionally flirting with me. Started feeling pretty good about myself.

"Well, uh – I know you said you had plans tonight. Didn't expect you to be home. Just thought I'd call and leave a message," expecting any minute to be struck dead for telling such a bald-faced lie. I wasn't, thank God. Just the opposite. Rewarded.

"I was supposed to be at a fundraising dinner tonight," she said. "My date got sick and had to cancel. Now I'm all dressed up with no place to go." She paused. "If you're not doing anything, why not grab a cab and give me that voice mail message in person."

She didn't have to ask twice. I hurried to my room, took a quick shower, changed and ran down to catch a cab. Just off the concierge stand was a florist. Pays to stay at classy hotels, I thought. I bought a single long-stem red rose. *Mac*, I thought as the bellman hailed me a cab, *for better or worse, you are back in the game.* Exactly sixteen minutes later, I was knocking on her door.

It opened. She stood framed in the doorway like a photograph. Her hair fell in a lush tumble across bare shoulders, outlining her face. The soft light spilling out from behind her filtered through a wayward strand which she absentmindedly brushed back into place.

She wore a short black slip dress, just barely secured to her body by tiny spaghetti straps. It clung to her like green on grass. You didn't have to be the best homicide inspector in San Francisco to see she wasn't wearing a bra. Aside from a black choker and milky-white opal earrings, she wore no jewelry. In this muted half-light, her smoky blue eyes were violet. I felt myself being drawn into them. Into her. The spider and the fly. I was the fly! And loving every minute of it.

"I hope I pass muster," she said with a shy grin. "But if you don't come in soon, I'm going to freeze to death."

"Sorry. It's hard not to stare. You look beautiful."

"You're sweet," she replied, and pecked me on the cheek as I walked by her into the living room.

"Here. This is for you." I handed her the rose.

"Oh, you are more than sweet." She raised it to her nose. "I *love* roses. Thank you. Let me put it in a vase and then we can go."

I followed her into the kitchen. Opening a cabinet, she stretched to reach a slender glass bud vase. Her dress rode high up her thighs. I felt myself becoming aroused. A warning voice sounded in my brain. *Do you want to become involved? Be careful. Relationships are a lot of work. Especially long distance ones. This woman is uncharted emotional terrain.*

I refocused when she said, "I made reservations at a place called Ramponi's. In the Village. Ten-minute cab ride."

She draped a shimmery gray scarf over her shoulders and took a quick peek in the mirror. With a satisfied nod, she grabbed my arm and steered me to the door.

CHAPTER 34

Ramponi's was an intimate and romantic restaurant. The main dining room was turn-of-the-century Italian Renaissance with ornate dark wood, sky-high ceilings, cleverly placed mirrors and fake Italian waiters.

The restaurant was half full when we arrived. I swear, though, every eye in the house followed Katelyn as we were escorted to our table. I've many times marveled at how beautiful women seem oblivious to the stares they get. Maybe it happens so often they become inured to it. Expect it, even. Me? Hell, I *count* the number of women who look at me as I pass. If I get up to three, my day is made. Walking in with Katelyn, though, definitely didn't damage my ego.

We had cocktails and made small talk over a dinner of baby-artichoke salad with roasted walnuts and sheets of Parmigiano Reggiano, and Calamari Steaks. Getting to know one another. Revealing just enough of our insecurities to invite the other into our life without completely stripping away carefully constructed masks. Baby steps. Intimate without being threatening. We talked about our jobs, our families, growing up. Skirting the edges of each other. Probing for likes and dislikes. Filing them away for future reference. This was a time for discovery. Not once did we even mention what our day was like.

When the meal was finished, she suggested we go to a place called Johnny's. "It's just down the street," she said. "It's a hangout for the twenty-something crowd. I think you'll like it." She smiled.

"Won't we be a bit overdressed?" I asked, hoping to at least talk her into someplace with a thirty-something crowd. Even a forty-something crowd would have been cool.

"Come on, Mac. Don't be so uptight about your age. Nobody will even notice that you're an old guy." She smiled and took my arm, leading me to the street. "You'll see."

Uptight? Shit. That stung. Implied premature senility. Arthritis of attitude. *I'm going to have to get out more*, I thought to myself as we walked the three blocks to Johnny's.

It was a retro bar. *Early to mid-nineties*, I thought as we made our way past the bar and found a table on the corner of the small dance floor. I'd been in plenty of these when I was – well, when I was in my twenties. The music drowned out all conversation. We ordered drinks and surveyed the scene. On the dance floor, guys were dancing with guys, girls with girls, a few heteros were thrown into the mix. A girl jumped up on the bar and started swaying sensuously to the music. At least I thought it was a girl. Her hair was shorn in an irregular way so she appeared boyish. A necktie was loosely knotted at her throat. A leather vest zippered halfway up her chest was all she had on top. Bellybutton rings flashed on her bare navel. I had to admit she was pretty in an androgynous sort of way.

A slow song started and Katelyn leaned over and asked if I wanted to dance. We bullied our way through bodies to the dance floor. She moved toward me. I held her close, but not tightly. I loved the feel of her body as it folded into mine. The music wrapped around us. Her face brushed mine and I tingled at the softness of her skin. We moved slowly within the tight confines of the bodies surrounding us. I buried my face in her hair, inhaling its fresh, soapy, female scent. I was disappointed when the song ended. Wanting more. Wanting her. We made our way back to the table. My hands holding her hips. Guiding and following at the same time. She moved with a dancer's grace, a complete lack of self-consciousness. I could feel myself teetering on the edge of a deep precipice. A bright, shimmering light at the bottom beckoned me.

It was past midnight when we left. I was clammy with perspiration and welcomed the cool night air. I hailed a cab. Katelyn pulled her scarf tightly around her and burrowed into my chest. I held her close. No resistance from either of us.

"Have a drink before you go?" she said as the taxi pulled up to her building.

"Coffee would be great." I didn't particularly want coffee, but I didn't want to leave, either.

I listened to her rattling around in the kitchen as I sat on the couch glancing through some of the magazines she had scattered around the coffee table. She came out carrying two steaming mugs and sat beside me, tucking her bare feet under her. We sat in silence. Tension high. Palpable. Getting up the courage, I set my mug down and turned towards her. She sensed my intent and put hers down, too. Taking her face in my hands, I gently kissed her mouth. She responded immediately, her hand sliding around my neck, pulling me closer, crushing my lips to hers. She opened her mouth. Our breath commingled, as did our tongues. My fingers traced the bareness of her shoulders, and then slid down her back. Felt her ribs through the silk of her dress. The slimness of her waist contrasting with the flare of her hips. Positions changed without breaking contact.

Her body twisted until it reclined fully on the couch. Mine slid off the couch until I was on my knees leaning over her. My free hand slowly traveled up her body.

The reverie was broken when she pushed me back and moved her lips away from mine. "You didn't bring your toothbrush," she whispered in my ear. Confused, I pulled back and looked at her. "I never ask a man to stay with me if he didn't bring his toothbrush. House Rules." Smiling at me playfully, she sat up and kissed the tip of my nose, tugging at the hem of her dress that had climbed half way up her thighs. "It's late. You probably have to go to work tomorrow. Your murder case, remember? Besides, your shirt is all wet. I swear, Tom McGuire, you're in awful shape. Sweating like a horse from just a few dances. I'm going to have to do something about that." She smiled again, trying to deflect the passion that still curled around us like wisps of incense. "I like you a lot. Maybe too much. Going to bed with you would be so easy right now. And I really want to. But I don't want to cheapen whatever it is we have by jumping your bones on our first date. Okay, *second* date, maybe *third*, even, but who's counting? You understand, don't you?"

I didn't, but said I did. Women's logic was unfathomable, but you learned over the years you had no choice but to accept it.

"Sorry," I said. For what I wasn't sure, but it sounded like the right thing to say. "It's what you do to me. It wasn't the dancing that made me sweat." Making a joke of it. Getting her out of a difficult situation. Acting like leaving was exactly what I had in mind, too.

She walked me to the door and kissed me. "I had a great, great time. Call me tomorrow, okay?" Sweet. Almost pleading.

The first thing I did when I got back to my room was call her. "Is it tomorrow yet?" She laughed, gave me a sloppy, through the phone kiss, and hung up.

Chapter 35

I was in the middle of one of the most erotic dreams I'd had in years when I was awakened by my suite's doorbell. Since I don't usually stay at hotels with doorbells, I was momentarily disoriented. I looked at the clock beside the bed. Seven thirty-five.

Dammit, I thought. *Forgot to put out the do not disturb card.* "I'm still here," I yelled from my bedroom. The doorbell rang again.

I got up, put on a robe, and stomped through the living room to the front door. I was not a happy camper. "I told you I'm still here. Come back later." I peeked through the peephole expecting to see the cleaning staff drill sergeant, clipboard in hand, impatiently waiting for me to open the damn door. Instead I was greeted by a much more pleasant sight.

There, with her hair in a braid down her back, wearing black and purple spandex leggings, a lycra short-sleeved pull-over shirt and carrying a gym bag, stood Katelyn Murray. I quickly breathed into my cupped hand, checking my breath. *Passable*. I opened the door.

She gracefully brushed past me into the living room. Taking in the surroundings, she said, "Got to admit, McGuire, you *do* know how to live. I'm gonna enjoy getting to know you better." She smiled. "This hotel happens to have an awesome spa and fitness center. While I'd rather be there getting their famous *oxygen infused facial*, I'm giving that up to run with you. Treadmills. For an hour and a half. You game?"

"An hour and a half? That's all?" Macho me. "Hell, yeah. Let's do it." There were a hundred things I'd rather do besides running a treadmill, but if it meant being with her, I *was* game. "You teased me last night about not being in shape. Want you to know, my partner and I run two miles every day. Minimum. At least the days when we're not swamped."

She flashed me a heartbreak smile. "Come on, Mac. I was kidding you. I could feel the muscles through your sweaty shirt. Just gave me an excuse to come bother you today." We both laughed.

I changed into sweat clothes and followed Katelyn out the door. Five minutes later a buffed dude in a blue Under Armour t-shirt handed us towels and pointed the way to the treadmills.

"I can't figure out how this damn machine works," I said, pointing to all the blinking lights telling me to press this and press that.

"What? You don't have gyms in San Francisco?" she said with a laugh.

"I hang at Walt's gym on 34th and Noriega," I said. "It doesn't have machines. Just a boxing ring and lots of free weights."

"Doesn't sound like a place where you're likely to pick up many women," Katelyn said as her machine kicked into high gear and she started running. "You're missing a lot of opportunities, McGuire."

"I'll have to remember that when I get back to SF." By this time, I had deciphered the machine and settled into a comfortable jog. "In San Francisco, my partner and I run the beach."

"The sandy part?" she asked. "I'm impressed."

I laughed. "No, not the sandy part. Used to do that thirty years ago when I was in the Navy, but not now. Now we run on the street that *fronts* the beach. Close enough to say we run the beach."

"Thirty years ago? God dang, McGuire, you *are* an old guy."

"Thanks."

"Come on. I was just teasing." She lightly punched my arm. "Flirting, actually."

I looked over at her. She flashed me a crooked grin and winked.

We were quiet for a few minutes as we both adjusted our speed and incline. I snuck a quick peek at the number of calories she had already burned. Forty-two. Mine said fifty-seven. I smiled inwardly.

"So, tell me what's going on with your investigation? I didn't get a chance to ask last night. Anything new and exciting?"

"Well, no. Not much." Matter of principle. I never talk about an active investigation with *outsiders*. No matter how pretty or how good a friend. If you weren't a fellow officer, I didn't want to talk about the particulars of my job. It was one of the things that pissed off Maureen about me being a cop. Actually turned out to be one of the things that poisoned our relationship. *One of the many things*, I corrected myself. But I couldn't do anything about it. If Katelyn and I were to become serious, she was going to have to put up with the cop part of me.

She caught my non-responsive reply. "I'm sorry. I didn't mean to pry."

"No. I'm the one who's sorry. It's that we're trained to be just a little bit suspicious of everything – and everybody." I really didn't want to get into this with her. Especially so early in our relationship. I backtracked immediately. "But not you. I trust you one hundred percent."

"That's sweet of you to say, but I understand. I'm just curious about you and what makes you tick. That's why I was asking about your investigation. Not that I want to know the particulars, but more about you. Your job. What you like and don't like. And I must admit, I watch enough cop shows on television to be interested in a real-life murder case."

I thought about Maureen. About my job. About the poison. About how I didn't want to jeopardize what I had going here with Katelyn. What could I tell her that she would think interesting, but her knowing wouldn't hurt the investigation? Screw it. "Well, we did have an interesting find yesterday."

"Can you tell me?" she said. Her voice excited. "But only if it doesn't violate your principles."

"I think I can tell you this. It's more a historical find than anything." We had started the cool-down part of the program. Since we were now in a fast walk as opposed to a full-on run, it was easier to carry on a conversation. "Remember I told you we had visited Conroy's girlfriend? He left some of his research at her house. One of the things he left was a packet of papers Custer wrote." I wasn't going to tell her these papers were written thirty-five years after he had supposedly died, and probably contained at least some link to why Conroy was murdered. "I didn't get to read all the material yet. Let me just say it was a healthy bundle."

"Do you have it with you?" I nodded. "How exciting. Would you let me see it?"

"Can't do that. Sorry. Fact is I shouldn't even have it myself. First thing I'm going to do today when you leave is take the *Custer Papers* to the nearest NYPD office and have them lock it up. All has to do with what we call *chain of custody*. Lawyer speak for *don't taint the evidence*."

"I understand," she said. "No problem." This girl was the anti-Maureen. The girl I wish I had found twenty years ago. But then if I had, I'd be in jail for child molestation.

We were back in the room, both hot and sweaty, by mid-morning.

"Want to take a shower?" I asked.

"You go take one," she said. "But don't be too long. I'll order up breakfast." She gave me a peck on the cheek.

Fastest shower, shave and teeth brushing that ever was. I put on a fresh pair of warm-ups and was back in the living room just as room service arrived. Ham and eggs for me. She sat next to me with coffee.

"You're not eating?"

"I'm not a big breakfast person. Would you mind if I showered while you ate?"

"Absolutely not. There are fresh towels on the rack."

I finished my breakfast and was having coffee when the shower turned off and I heard her walking around the bedroom. A moment later she padded into the kitchen wearing a Four Season's blue terry robe, while tugging at her wet hair with a towel. She came around behind me, tilted my head back and kissed me. Wet, stringy hair tickled my cheek. "Come with me," she said with that smile. "I found your toothbrush."

She took my hand and led me into the bedroom. Standing by the side of the bed, I unwrapped her from the robe. She closed her eyes and took one step back, allowing me to witness her beauty in the privacy of my own arousal. A voyeur's fantasy. All white and pink and dark blended in the most delicate of shades. I drew her to me, our bodies intertwined in an intricate pattern of peaks and valleys.

I never considered myself clumsy in this lovemaking business. Rusty? Maybe. But definitely not clumsy. But with Katelyn, it was different. I felt clumsy. Like a teenager. Trying too hard. Part of it was the unexpectedness of her coming to me so suddenly. Maybe it was because I wasn't the controlling factor.

Once on the bed, my hands actually shook as I traced the outlines of her body. If my clumsiness showed, Katelyn didn't let on. Even in my eagerness, I took my time. Memorizing her curves. The softness of her secret places.

We made love for what seemed like hours, alternating between quiet tenderness and unrestrained frenzy. I tried to hold off as long as I could, partly because I didn't want it to end, partly because I wanted her to think I was some kind of stud interested only in her pleasure. I had this weird image of the hotel guests on either side of us, ears pressed against the walls, listening to the rhythms of our bodies moving together.

We finished exhausted and wet – the physical evidence of the intense intimacy that no other human activity can provide.

Her skin was like perfumed silk as she lay cradled against my chest. Looking down at her, I was filled with awe. The reality of having the very core of my being touched and renewed.

Or maybe it had just been too long between sexual adventures. I was too tired to think about the magnitude of it all. *Just enjoy the moment*, I told myself. *Whatever happens, happens.*

"The breath of the present," she whispered into the hairs on my chest.

"Huh?"

She raised her head to me, hair cascading forward, cloaking her face. "Making love. It's the breath of existence."

"I never thought about it quite like that," I confessed. "What does it mean?"

"I don't know. Really, I don't," she giggled, brushing her hair away. "It just came to me. I *feel* what it means, but can't explain it. Does that make sense?"

"Sure." It didn't, but who was I to argue at a time like this?

The reverie of the moment was broken by the ring of the hotel phone. I reached across Katelyn and answered.

"Hold on," I said to the caller, putting my hand over the receiver. "Delgado," I whispered.

"How long?" she whispered back.

I shrugged my shoulders. "No telling."

"Okay," she said, getting out of bed. "Don't mind me. I'll get dressed."

CHAPTER 36

"Things heating up fast and furious," Delgado said. *If he only knew*, I thought, looking at Katelyn at the foot of the bed. She had pulled some jeans out of her gym bag and was making a big deal of tugging them up her over her hips. I got captured by the dance and lost track of what Delgado was saying.

"You still there, Bro?" he said, irritation in his voice.

"Yeah. Still here. Sorry."

Katelyn heard me and looked over. She grabbed her shoes and pretended to tip-toe out. I put my hand over the phone. "I'll let you talk," she whispered. "I'll be out here waiting." She threw me a kiss, smiled and walked into the living room, closing the bedroom door behind her.

"What's up?" I said into the phone.

"Remember our boy Randolph?" Delgado said. "The tail from over near Escher's house?"

"Yeah. Is he coming back in the picture?"

"Only way *he's* coming back is from the dead," Delgado said. "He was found this morning inside his New Jersey home. Back of his head blown off. Probably happened last night. He lives alone. Daughter came to visit him around seven thirty this morning and found him. Cops are there now. No sign of forced entry. No sign of a fight. Neighbors didn't hear anything. The only thing that didn't belong was the neat hole in the front room window with the attendant spider veins trailing down the glass. Shot from afar. Remind you of anyone?"

I sat on the edge of the bed, a warning bell going off in my brain. "Vinnie – you gotta call Escher. These guys are starting to clean up. Tell him to ask his cop friends to put him in some kind of temporary witness protection program 'til all this blows over. He's gotta get out of sight – pronto."

"Will do. Something else equally important. Just got off the phone with Rob. He's at Ft. Bragg seeing his friend, Admiral Thompson. Kincaid filled him in on your case and how weird things have gotten. The guy tailing us is now dead; the FBI and Park Police pulled from the murder investigation; the phony FBI guys visiting anyone who knew Conroy professionally; Global Affinity Partners; Randolph's phone – hell, you know. Just all the shit that's been piling up."

"Can Thompson help?" I asked, pulling on the bottom of my sweats.

"In a lot of ways. While Rob was there, Thompson called the Director of the FBI. Apparently they're friends. He asked him about the FBI suddenly standing down."

"And?"

"He told Thompson that the *stand down* order came straight from the Department of Defense. Get this! Conroy's murder has been classified a Level 2 national security concern."

"Son-of-a-bitch. *National security*? How the hell did Conroy get himself in the middle of a national security issue?"

"Good question. Admiral Thompson is hiring Red Squadron to help the DoD find the answer. Congrats, dude. You've just become a paid member of the team."

"Wait a minute! This is all going too fast," I responded. "I'm honored; I want you to know. But hired for how long? I still have a job in San Francisco, in case everyone has forgotten. Will I still have that job when you guys cut me loose?"

"Rob is handling all that as we speak. You'll just be on temporary leave from your department. Don't want to burst your bubble, but we've done this before. When your supervisor hears "national security," he'll roll over. They all do.

"By the way, Rob wants us in D.C. tonight. He's scheduled a meeting tomorrow with a small, elite CIA unit that handles these kinds of problems. We'll actually be working with them. Their unit goes by the acronym AFF."

"Adult Friend Finder?" I laughed.

"Yeah. Right. According to Kincaid, it means – Analyze, Find and Fix."

"Sounds like a tech agency."

"Close. Has something to do with automobiles. That's their cover, anyway. With this group, *Find and Fix* has a completely different meaning than most people would expect. *Find* the bad guys. Then *Fix* the bad guys. Rob tells me it's a group that handles *target specific* national security issues."

"Target specific?" I asked. "They already have a target?"

"Guess we'll find out tomorrow, Bro. In the meantime, I'll make the plane reservations and let you know the time."

Damn poor timing, I thought as I hung up. How was I going to tell Katelyn that I have to leave town tonight? I'm so hopelessly old-fashioned. Even though I know she is a full-grown woman, I worried she might think I took advantage of her or something. Like *how convenient – he leaves town right after he gets into my pants*.

It was a needless worry. I opened the bedroom door and walked into the living room. It was empty. I noticed all the drawers of the large mahogany desk under the front window were pulled out. I was only concerned about the bottom one. I walked over. It was empty. Katelyn had gone and the *Custer Papers* had gone with her.

CHAPTER 37

Leesburg, VA

"What the hell!" said the angry voice of Mitchell Perry into the burner phone he held in his hand. "It's after nine. About time you called."

"Hey, screw you," replied Tad Mosby. "You're probably still lounging around in your jammies while I'm here freezing my ass off in Paramus, New Jersey."

"Don't be a wise-ass. I expected to hear from you by seven, at the latest. Had to postpone an important congressional hearing this morning because of you."

"I probably did the country a big favor," Mosby said with a chuckle. "All you ass-holes do on the Hill is have meetings. What a great job. While I'm staying up all night, living out of my car and cleaning up your messes, you're churning out the bullshit that actually causes the messes."

"You're not paid to be funny."

"No. I'm also not paid to call your ass at seven in the morning, either," Mosby said. "You could have gone to your fucking meeting. You didn't have to wait for me."

"Unfortunately I did. We have another job for you."

"In a minute. First things first. Randolph's out of play."

"I know. I'm watching it live on TV. They're saying he was killed sometime in the early morning hours. After his daughter left."

"At 2:06 a.m. to be exact. Never thought his damn daughter would leave. Was beginning to think she would end up staying. That I'd have to come back another night."

"The local news is reporting she found him."

"Yeah, that's why I'm late getting back to you. I wanted to wait until someone found him before I called. You never know. Maybe no one would come visit him. In that case, I'd have had to call in an anonymous tip. Can't leave things to chance in this business. In any case, she came back about seven thirty this morning."

"Where are you now?"

"I'm with the rest of the nosy neighbors outside the police perimeter. Probably a hundred or so people here. I'm on the west side. Twenty or so feet behind the mob."

Perry laughed. "I can see the mob. Can't pick you out, though. Why not wave to me?"

"Just what I want," Mosby said. "To make myself stand out." *What an asshole*, he thought. "Okay, tell me who else ya' got for me."

"You know the guy that met Conroy at the Little Bighorn?"

"The cop?"

"Exactly. Name is Thomas McGuire. Too bad you didn't just waste him when you had the chance."

"You expressly told me not to. Bad news killing a cop. *Would bring way too much attention*, you told me."

"Well, he's becoming a real pain in the ass. Going all over New York talking to Conroy's friends and acquaintances. Corporation thinks there's too much of a chance he'll find something. He's a loose end. They want him eliminated, once and for all."

"How do I find him, and how much time do I have? Oh, and how much will they pay me?"

"They think he's in D.C., but I'll know more later today. We'll let you know. Not sure about the money. You'll have to work that out with them. I'm just delivering the message."

"Shit! Okay, I understand. I hate loose ends, too."

CHAPTER 38

Mitchell Perry pushed the pulverize button on the industrial compactor. He stepped back and closed his eyes, tantalized by the sound of the machine vaporizing another burner phone.

It reminded him of the line in *Apocalypse Now*: "Napalm son. I love the smell of napalm in the morning." *I must be one sick puppy,* he thought with a satisfied smile as he walked back into his house.

He checked the time as he passed the Emperor grandfather clock in the hallway. A twenty-five-thousand-dollar gift to his wife. Eleven minutes past ten. He walked back to his study knowing he had another four hours before he absolutely had to be back at the Rayburn Building to chair the sub-committee hearing on military appropriations.

At his desk, he opened the bottom drawer and carefully counted the number of the untraceable, one-time use phones he still had. Twelve. *Good thing we did away with Randolph.* He smiled at the thought. *That damn guy alone cost us fifteen of these puppies.*

He fired up the laptop. The order for another four-dozen had to be placed through *Global Affinity Partners.* This was the only computer in the house that he used to contact headquarters. He spent the next six minutes burrowing deep into the web's underbelly.

After finishing, he closed the computer and walked to the window overlooking his estate. What he saw didn't displease him. An elaborate garden that covered an acre, more than one-third of the entire property. He often described it to friends as his mini-Versailles.

Another present to his wife. His trophy wife, as people called her. She was thirty-five years old. Twenty-two years his junior. Their marriage five years ago was the talk of gossip-hungry D.C. He was into his third congressional term, so he wasn't afraid of the political backlash, confident that his primary employer wouldn't let anything happen to him. His position in the Congressional pecking order was far too valuable. It would take them years to duplicate what he could do for them. But he wasn't naïve. When he was no longer an asset, they would cut his ass loose in a heartbeat. In fact, he wondered if they were grooming his wife to take over his power-space in their organization. She was in Aspen exploring the possibility of becoming the chief of staff of a current senator thinking of running for president in four years. Even though Perry didn't know the names, he knew there must be other congressional people beside himself who took orders from Global Affinity Partners. It wouldn't even surprise him if his wife were being groomed to be GAP's direct conduit to the future president of the United States.

A twinge of jealousy, mixed with a jolt of fear, coursed through him. Were they thinking of replacing him? With his wife? *No fucking way*, he told himself. He was a survivor, always landing on his feet.

Most people knew his story. Hell, he'd used it often enough on the campaign trail. He wanted to show his constituency he was one of them. Just ordinary folk. That he could feel their pain.

The story about his delinquent dad was true, as was the part about his mother having the fortitude to kick her drug habit and hold down two jobs so the both of them could eat. From those stories, he crafted the campaign pitch he used to get elected the first time. He told them he learned from his mother the value of hard work. That if you worked hard, good things happened. God bless America. It was all bullshit, but the voters bought it hook, line and sinker.

What actually happened had nothing to do with how hard his mother worked. Or how many jobs she held. It mostly had to do with what happened to him after being sent to a juvenile detention camp in the Blue Ridge Mountains for selling drugs on the street corner. While there, a counselor, who happened to be on the payroll of whatever name the Corporation used back then, approached him. His job was to identify hardscrabble kids like himself who had the smarts and moxie to understand the great rewards to be had by simply following directions. Perry *did* follow orders, and great rewards *did* start coming his way.

Seven months into his twelve-month sentence, the detention camp released him into the custody of his mother. On the day he was released, the Corporation deeded her the house she rented. The day after that, her salary doubled. When the school year started, he went off to a boarding school in upstate New York. His education paid for; his criminal record expunged. Is this a great country, or what?

Perry felt the buzz of the special pager embedded in his watch signaling a call coming in on one of the twelve burner phones in his desk drawer. He walked downstairs and answered. It was Corporate, instructing him to inform Mosby that the loose end they wanted tied up had arrived in Gaithersburg, Maryland. Mosby was to drive to D.C., check into the Westin in Georgetown, and await further instructions.

CHAPTER 39

New York City

I looked at my watch. *What the hell*! I'd only been on the phone with Delgado for fifteen minutes. How long ago had she left? I hadn't heard the door open or close. She could've been gone but a few minutes, or the whole quarter of an hour. But where?

There had to be some reasonable explanation for why she left. In my desire not to confront the fact that she may have just played me for the biggest fool in the history of the world, I started fumbling for excuses. Maybe she had just taken the *Papers* to the lobby bar to read. Or to the nearest Starbucks. Something. Anything. I refused to be the poster child for the cliché of the horny male thinking only with his dick. I got my phone from the bedroom and called her cell. It rang until going to voice mail. I left a message for her to call me back. "Urgent," it said.

I called Delgado and told him about Katelyn. "What the fuck, dude," he said.

"Yeah, I know. But there has to be a good explanation. She just wouldn't steal those papers. Impossible."

"You know her better than I do," he answered.

"For what purpose? Doesn't make any sense."

"I hope to hell you're right, Bro." He didn't sound like he thought I was. "What do you want me to do?"

"I'm going to find her." I almost said *to find the bitch*, but I didn't want to let myself go there. Just yet. "Can you call Kincaid? Tell him what happened and that we can't make plane reservations to D.C. until this is resolved."

"You got it."

"This could all be completely innocent," I said, my heart hoping that was true. "She could have just wanted a cup of coffee and taken the *Papers* with her to read." Even I could hear how lame that sounded, but I still wanted to give her every benefit of doubt. More to save myself embarrassment, I had to admit, than to save her. "If I have to, I'll even go to her apartment. In any case, I'll give you a call. Should be back within the hour."

She wasn't in the lobby bar or in any of the hotel's eating establishments. The concierge told me there was a Starbucks a block from the hotel. I jogged down. No luck there, either.

Delgado called on my way back to the hotel. "Just got off the phone with Kincaid. He isn't a happy camper about any of this. Doesn't blame you, but …" He let that hang in the air, leaving little doubt Kincaid *did* think I was to blame. "In any case," he continued, "there's a flight out of La Guardia to Reagan National at five thirty. Wants us on it. I already made reservations."

As soon as he hung up, I hailed a taxi to take me to Peter Cooper Village. I felt like shit. Letting everyone down, including myself. *Katelyn*, I pleaded internally, *please – you can't do this to me*.

Telling the cabbie not to wait, I walked into the lobby. "The woman who lives in Apartment 3B," I said to the doorman. "She come in recently?"

"Lots of people comin' and goin'" he replied, shrugging his shoulders.

"Pretty lady? Dark hair. About five foot six. Early thirties. You couldn't miss her."

"Lot's of pretty ladies live here," he said. His condescending attitude started to annoy me. "Hey…" I started to say *asshole* but his phone rang. He held up his hand to shut me up, answered and turned his back.

I wasn't about to wait for the son-of-a-bitch to get off the phone. I quickly walked to the bank of elevators and punched the third floor. Walked straight to 3B and rang the buzzer. I couldn't hear any movement in the apartment. I buzzed again, letting it ring longer this time. Still no movement or sound.

Dammit, Katelyn. Be here. Just open the goddamn door. No answer. I knocked, waited a few minutes, and knocked again. Harder this time. The door of the apartment next door opened. A guy about my age stuck his head out.

"Can I help you?" he asked.

"I'm looking for the lady who lives in this apartment. Have you seen her today?"

"Must have the wrong apartment, bud," he said. "No one lives in 3B."

"You're wrong about that, *bud*," I said. "I was here last night. Picked her up about nine, brought her back about one. Left close to two. I wasn't hallucinating."

"You musta been on a different floor then," he said. "That apartment's been vacant for over a month. If you don't believe me, call the Super. Or the owners, for all I care. Just stop that pounding on the door. I work at night. I'm trying to sleep in here."

I had a hollow feeling in my stomach. This couldn't be happening. Katelyn Murray wasn't a fraud. No way I could have been so wrong. Where the hell was she?

I went back to the lobby. I told myself to try and play nice with the doorman, but I was in no mood to screw around. If he gave me even the least bit of shit, I'd pull my cop card and charge his ass with aggravated something-or-other. NYPD would back a fellow officer. Professional courtesy. At least I hoped.

I got lucky. Only had to show him my credentials once. As soon as he saw I was a cop, even one from San Francisco, he became my best friend. Score one for the respect New Yorkers had toward their police department. I asked him to call the doorman who was on duty last night.

He made the call. "Name's Jimmy," he said, handing me the phone.

"Jimmy," I said into the receiver. "You don't know me, but I came last night about nine to see a woman named Katelyn Murray. In 3B. We went out and I brought her back at one. I'm a guy in my early fifties. Medium build. Do you remember me?"

"Last night? Sure do. Don't remember you too well. Remember her *real* well. Remember thinking what a lucky bastard you were scoring with such a young chick. Thought you must be rich or somethin'."

I smiled at the irony of it all. "Well I'm a cop, so I'm not rich. Anyway, she lived in Apartment 3B, right?"

"Can't confirm that, sir. Not allowed to give out apartment numbers. Privacy rules. You understand. You'll have to call the property managers to confirm the apartment number. Richard, the guy who called me, can get you their number. Not sure even *they* can give that information out over the phone. Might be a legal thing. Might be you'll have to go see them in person."

"Thanks, Jimmy. We'll see." Richard gave me the property manager's number. I called. I identified myself and the reason for the call.

"I'm sorry, sir; we can't give out any private information."

"I understand. But I'm a San Francisco homicide inspector here on a case. I can give you my badge and a phone number if you want to call my supervisor. Seems like a lot to go through just to find out who lives in Apartment 3B, though. But I understand how the bureaucracy works. I'll hold until you can get back to me."

"If all you want is who lives in 3B, I can tell you that right now." He paused. "No one. It's been vacant for over a month."

"That's impossible," I said. "I was in that apartment last night. With the woman who rents it."

"I'm telling you, sir, it's been vacant for a month."

"Bullshit." I handed the phone back to Richard and pulled out my cell. I punched in Katelyn's number. She didn't answer, but this time I didn't get her voice mail. I got a message saying the phone was disconnected.

CHAPTER 40

Washington, D.C.

Kincaid met us curbside at Reagan National. The rain that accompanied our flight from New York had stopped, but the evening was still thick with mist.

Delgado threw his duffel into the front passenger seat and followed it in. I slipped into the back.

"We're going to Gaithersburg, Maryland," Kincaid said. "About an hour away. I already got us hotel rooms. We've got an appointment with these people tomorrow at 0900."

"Who exactly are *these* people?" I asked.

"First of all, welcome aboard," Kincaid said, making eye contact with me through the rear-view mirror. "Don't know if Vinnie told you, but I talked to your Lt. Bristow at SFPD. Not only took care of you being away for the next week or so, I even talked him into giving you a *paid* leave. As of now, you are officially double-dipping."

I laughed. "Couldn't happen to a more deserving fellow, if you ask me."

"Yeah, maybe. We'll see" he replied. "Tell me, Coach, what the hell happened between you and that Katelyn woman?"

"I screwed up royally, Rob. I'm really sorry. She played me for a freaking fool. I'm obviously way outta my league here. Big time embarrassed, to say the least. She wormed her way into my trust and then walked off with the primary evidence in a murder investigation."

I caught Kincaid looking at me in the rear view mirror, his blue eyes flashing in the reflection of the headlights behind us. "I'm sorry, too, Coach," he said, managing a smile. "Don't kick yourself over it, though. I can see why you would trust her. Hell, she crewed on our plane. But, truthfully, that's all. We vetted her, of course, but her background came back clean. Just hired crew."

"She came from some agency that Chris Fuller found," Delgado volunteered. "Chris, by the way, is one of our teammates in RSSA. I talked to him this afternoon. He called the agency, and they told him she had quit as soon as she flew into New York with us. They tried to get in touch with her, but no luck."

"I'm not surprised," I said. "Same M.O. she used with me. Her cell phone had been disconnected within an hour of leaving the hotel. This whole operation had to be planned. We were set up." I paused, rethinking that last sentence. "Take that back. It was me. I got set up. She had me over to her apartment in Peter Cooper Village last night. A damn big complex, by the way. I found out this afternoon from the property manager that the apartment she lived in, the apartment that I visited last night, has been vacant for over a month. Go figure. Someone with clout had to arrange that shit."

"What's the damage?" Kincaid asked.

"Severe, as far as I'm concerned," I replied. "First of all, without those papers to guide us, we'll probably never know who murdered Conroy or why. I think we can assume it had something to do with Custer and that damn battle, but that's it. Whoever that woman worked for told her to get those papers. It's obvious now that there's something in them somebody wants buried. Enough so, they were willing to kill to keep it buried." I leaned back in the seat. "Damage you asked? As far as I'm concerned, my whole fucking investigation just went south. I'll stay with you guys as long as I can be of some help, but right now, I'm not holding out much hope."

"Well, shit," Kincaid cursed. "But let's not give up hope just yet. You asked about the people we're scheduled to meet tomorrow?"

"Yeah," I replied. "Who are these people, and what the hell is *their* interest in this case?"

"All I can tell you is what I've been told, "Kincaid said. "AFF is an ..."

"Hold on," I said. "Delgado already told me about this group. *Analyze, Find* and *Fix,* right*?*"

"Correct," Kincaid replied. "One of many small, secret CIA units running around. They play in the same sandbox as the National Security Agency. Both monitor the web, picking up intelligence on anything that sounds like it might be a threat to the country. What sets AFF apart from NSA is the people we are seeing tomorrow are allowed to play *outside* the sandbox. They have authority to act on what they find. They have the authority, for example, to hire people like *us* to *act* on what they find. I told you when I first saw you in Reno. RSSA is in the *Fix* business."

CHAPTER 41

Gaithersburg, Maryland

We were out of the motel in Gaithersburg by eight thirty the following morning, heading northeast. Following GPS instructions, we left the freeway at Industrial Parkway East. A mile later we came upon the industrial park the road was apparently named after.

The park was comprised of seventeen auto specialty shops. A veritable cornucopia of small businesses dedicated to fixing everything having to do with automobiles, from auto-detailing to a shop that advertised itself as an "auto hospital." Including, by the way, its own "auto ER." We spotted AFF at the end of a small cul-de- sac. The sign above its entrance said: *Does your car have an electronic illness? Let our expert technicians Analyze, Find and Fix it.*

We drove into a large barn-like structure. A man in his fifties, dressed in jeans and a green camo shirt, came out of the office on our right and guided us to a parking spot. He introduced himself as David Sullivan. Kincaid introduced us as well, and told Sullivan a friend at Ft. Bragg had recommended his shop. Sullivan gave him a thumbs-up and invited us into the office. He closed the door, told us to sit, and asked for our papers. Kincaid gave him a sealed manila envelope fastened with a waxed seal in the shape of the ST-6 Trident. The man looked us over, nodded, broke the seal and pulled out our credentials. He spent more time reading mine than the other two.

"Not a team member?" he asked, looking at Kincaid, but pointing at me.

"A member on *my* team," said Kincaid. "He's good enough for me, he's good enough for you."

Sullivan took one final inquisitive look, punched a few numbers on his desk phone, talked to someone, and then said, "this way." He walked to the back of the office and opened what looked like a wall thermostat but in reality was an iris recognition system. After a few seconds of staring, a section of the wall in front and to his left opened on silent runners.

"If you have any firearms, knives, Chinese stars?" he smiled. "You get the picture. There are sensors of all kinds lining the rooms you are about to enter; x-ray, laser, olfactory, and others I can't even pronounce. Think airport screening on steroids. If any sensor detects what it's identified as a weapon, it will not ask any questions. You will be shot immediately. Understood?"

We all nodded and walked into the corridor. Long and narrow, it sloped steeply downward, enough to force us to hold onto the handrails affixed to the side walls.

"I wonder if we are underground yet?" whispered Delgado as we kept descending.

"Have to be," I said. "The building outside wasn't this large."

After another fifteen or so feet, the corridor leveled out. "You know, Bro," Delgado said as we stopped at another sentry station. "Whoever planned and built this? You got to admire their work. If someone tried to overwhelm this place with force, they wouldn't stand a chance."

Two men in BDU's carrying M-4s led us into a larger room where two more armed men stood. David Sullivan, who'd been following behind us, came forward. "We are going to enter our office space. Please follow me." After walking through another narrow passageway, we entered a window-less, medium-sized, no frills office with a conference table in the middle surrounded by four desks.

Two of the desks were occupied. A man, so pale it looked like his skin had never seen the sun, stared at us anxiously, like maybe we had come to rescue him from his underground prison. "James Holmquist," Sullivan said. "So good at web analysis we call him *Master Alomar of the Dark Web*." Holmquist smiled, came forward and shook our hands. "And Emily Wyatt," he said, pointing to the person occupying the second desk. "She, too, has her own handle. *Mistress Torgand, Shadow of the Night*." She smiled sweetly and waved her fingers. "Gamers," Sullivan said by way of explanation. "It's a sub-culture. They all carry an alias. Difference is, James and Emily are *professional* gamers."

Before asking us to sit, Sullivan pointed to the empty desk, and said, "We have one other person who is not here yet, but will join us soon." He looked around and scratched his head. "Okay, who'd like some coffee?" All hands went up. Sullivan asked Holmquist to make a pot. While Holmquist fussed with the coffee in the alcove, Sullivan invited us to sit at the conference table.

Holmquist served the coffee as Sullivan called the group to order. "Let's get right to it, shall we?" We nodded in agreement. "Good. First some housekeeping. AFF's job, as you probably know, is to comb the Internet looking for deep, dark secrets. We have some of the most sophisticated electronic equipment in the world in this facility. The room next to us is ten times this size; an eighteen-foot ceiling, racks and racks of servers – three hundred and twenty-two to be exact, and is air-conditioned." He paused. "And just so you know we aren't playing around, every word spoken in this room is recorded and then encrypted before being sent to Headquarters." Sullivan looked at us, then said, "We are all here to find out who murdered Professor Matthew Conroy and his wife, and why."

CHAPTER 42

W e all sat in silence. Finally, Kincaid said, "I hope you don't think us naïve, Mr. Sullivan. Red Squadron Security Agency is made up of people who spent most of their military lives gathering intelligence. It's how we stayed alive. So believe me when I tell you we respect what you do. But it's a mystery to us why a small unit of the CIA wants to find who killed …"

"Assassinated," Sullivan interjected.

"Point taken," Kincaid said. "*Assassinated* a college professor, and how that death became a national security issue. What the hell do you know about Conroy that we don't?"

"Until recently, not nearly enough," Sullivan said. "Don't know how much you know about us, but we work closely with the National Security Agency."

"We were told that."

"NSA's original charter was passive electronic collection," Sullivan continued. "Because of the massive amounts of secret information Snowden leaked, everyone now knows that NSA's reach has gone far beyond *passive electronic collection*."

"That Snowden dude was a traitor, you ask me," Delgado said.

"You won't get any argument from me," Sullivan said.

"Or me," Holmquist interjected.

"Ditto that from me," intoned Emily Wyatt.

"Now that we know the feeling about Mr. Snowden is unanimous," Sullivan said with a smile, "let's move forward." He half-sat against one of the desks. "Have any of you heard of the Tor browser, or the Tor network, as it's sometimes called?"

The three of us sat in silence for a few moments, not knowing who should go first. Finally, I said, "I heard about it a few years ago when a fellow in San Francisco got busted by the Feds for running a highly sophisticated, hugely profitable drug operation on the web."

"Silk Road," Sullivan said, nodding in recognition of the event.

"Yeah. That's it. Guy's making like half a mil a month. Pure profit. I got involved because we became concerned he was running a murder-for-hire operation as well. And all on the web. All underground. Run on that Tor network you mentioned."

"Underground is right," Holmquist chimed in. "In fact, *under* – underground."

"I happened to be there when they took him down," I continued. "The most surprised perp I'd ever seen. We put him in the back of the squad car to take him downtown. The whole way he kept muttering – *how'd they find me? How'd they find me?*"

"And he had ample reason to ask that question, too," said Sullivan. "I remember that trial. How we *found* him were secrets we couldn't divulge in open court. We finally had to get the bastard on money laundering and tax evasion. Everything else we had on him turned out to come from highly classified source information."

"Vinnie and I have experience with Tor as well," Kincaid said. "Worked on it with some of your spook friends in Afghanistan a few years back. We actually watched an auto race – live – on a network that didn't exist, coming from satellites that weren't there."

"Well then, you understand it, too," Sullivan said. "The bad guys love it because it assures them anonymity.

Untraceable Internet activity. Extremely sophisticated shit."

"Should be," said Delgado. "Hell, our Navy designed the damn thing. To protect their classified, top-secret data transfers."

"That's precisely why the bad guys use it," Sullivan said. "Secrecy."

"Dude. Secret is right. They could send and receive messages that we couldn't read. Unreadable and untraceable."

"Unfortunately, the Navy guys who designed it thought it would be cool to take it public. And they did. At the beginning, only geek heads used it. Like the people in this room."

"That be us," Holmquist said as he and Emily smiled and raised their hands. "Proud geek heads."

"It had an extraordinarily sophisticated encryption system," continued Sullivan. "And, as our enemies became more and more involved, the system became more and more sophisticated. We named it the Dark Web. And, believe me, the deeper you go, the darker it becomes."

"It's also a place where the scumbags go to purchase child porn," I said. "Conroy wasn't involved in that shit, I hope."

"Nothing of the sort, Inspector," Sullivan said. "Let me explain how all this ..." he swept his hand across the room, "... came about." He took a sip of coffee from the cup Holmquist had placed next to him. "No matter what power the Patriot Act gave the National Security Agency, they simply couldn't keep track of the sheer volume of electronic intercepts they collected every day."

"Favor? In the interest of time, could we just stay with Conroy and the Dark Web?" I said. "We don't have to know the history of NSA and the Patriot Act."

"Hold on," Sullivan said, obviously in no hurry. He took another sip of his coffee, made a face and asked

Holmquist to reheat it. Turning back to us, he said, "because of the volume of intercepts, they decided their time and resources could better be spent playing exclusively in the same sandbox as the bad guys – the Dark Web. But since they had no investigative authority, everything they found they handed over to the FBI. Didn't take long before the FBI became overwhelmed, too. And here we are. More importantly, here *you* are.

"We're a thin unit. Only one of us has any operational experience. The rest are nothing more than narrowly focused NSA types. You've been brought aboard to put teeth into the final *F* our AFF acronym. The *Fixer* part."

"I hate to be a one-trick pony," I said, "but could you please just tell us how Conroy got involved in all of this?"

"Yes, of course. Forgive me, but I thought it important for you to know how and why we became involved. The Dark Net, as you've heard, presents some particularly interesting challenges. NSA has overcome some of those challenges. Not fully, but discovered some cracks in the structure."

"So it's not so anonymous anymore?" I asked.

"It's still anonymous, yes," Sullivan replied. "But not as much. How they came across Conroy's name, I can't tell you. It's classified. But I can tell you his name was mentioned a number of times by someone NSA considers a *person of interest*. They gave it to us to pursue."

"And what did you find?" I asked.

"We found a college professor in the process of writing a book about General Custer. A certain group of bad guys were interested in his research for that book. Just seemed odd to us. Not something we see everyday. We hoped he might know why. Maybe help us out. Maybe even work undercover for us. So, we had an operative approach him a few weeks back. A guy who could give Conroy some valuable assistance on his research if he would help us find out why the bad guys were interested in him. But before the operative could ask Conroy to join us, the bad guys got to him."

Holmquist poured Sullivan more coffee. He took a sip nodded appreciatively, and continued. "The fact is if he hadn't been assassinated on Federal property, we probably wouldn't be having this conversation. As fate would have it…" he turned to me, "… the FBI alerted us that you, Inspector, had an interest in the case. That's how *you* showed up on our radar screen. And through you, your Red Squadron friends. I told my superiors from the get-go that we could use your help in finding who assassinated Conroy and why."

"And you have a suspicion that his murder was orchestrated by the same people NSA is interested in?" Kincaid said.

"We didn't know for certain, but if they *were* responsible, we now had a way to bring them down."

"Who was your operative that gave Conroy assistance?" I asked.

"Ordinarily we wouldn't give you his name. It's classified. But since you've already met him," Sullivan said with a shrug, "his name is Kyle Escher."

"Dude!" Delgado exclaimed.

"Kyle Escher?" I said, not masking the surprise in my voice. "The guy with the rifle range in his basement? The guy I had Vinnie call to suggest getting into the witness protection program? He's gotta be laughing his ass off right about now."

"It's a long story. He's never been a full-time employee. Though he has been a valuable asset of ours over many years," Sullivan replied.

"Since Escher works for you guys," I said, "you already know about the papers Conroy discovered."

"Yes we do. But, unfortunately, he never had a chance to read them," Sullivan said. "All he knew, and therefore all *we* knew, was they were written in and around Custer's time. When Conroy returned from Montana, Escher was going to ask if he could read them. But Conroy never returned from Montana. Alive, anyway."

"Delgado and I had a chance to read some of those papers last night," I said. "I can tell you they contain a historical blockbuster. If Custer actually wrote them, and I know your boy Escher hasn't authenticated that for certain yet, but if he did, then George Custer wasn't killed at the Little Bighorn. Those papers we read were dated September 6, 1914. Thirty-eight years after he supposedly died."

I expected a big gasp from the AFF people. Instead, complete silence. *Okay*, I thought. *Maybe it's the geek in them. Or maybe they're thinking what Delgado thought. One hundred and forty years ago? Dude – who cares?"*

Looking at the blank eyes staring back at me, I sighed, then continued. "I'm a homicide cop. All I look for is motive. With that in mind, in one of the Custer papers I read, he mentioned six rich and powerful men that would benefit from his death.

"It's early, I know, but I'm thinking that keeping those names a secret could be a powerful motivation for murder. I admit I don't know why anyone in this day and age would want to keep them secret, but until somebody can come up with a better theory, I'm sticking with that one. Unfortunately, Custer didn't mention any of the six by name. So it's gonna be hard to prove my theory because those papers were stolen from me yesterday."

"Not stolen," a female voice said from behind me. "Only borrowed. And there weren't six names. Only two."

Son of a bitch! I jerked around. Katelyn Murray dropped the *Custer Papers* on the empty desk, looked at me and nodded.

CHAPTER 43

"**W**hat's *she* doing here?" I banged my fist on the table. "She works for you guys? This is bullshit." I kicked my chair aside as I stood. If I could have found my way out of that rat's maze, I'd have been long gone. I swept my arm back in Katelyn's direction. "This…" I wanted to say *bitch*, but thought better of it in front of her colleagues. "This female wormed her way into my trust and then stole evidence germane to a murder investigation. I'm talking *felony* here. I'm talking eight-to-twelve in Soledad." I felt myself slowing down. Losing steam. My anger, dare I say *pride*, slipping away. Must have been that "felony" bullshit I spouted. I knew it wasn't true when I said it. So did Sullivan. And he called me on it.

"Hard to prove a felony, Inspector. This material hasn't yet been placed into evidence for *any* murder trial. In fact, if anyone *is* looking at eight-to-twelve, it would be you for not immediately turning this *evidence*, as you call it, over to the courts. By now, this *evidence* would be inadmissible. You know it. I know it."

"Stealing personal property, then," I said, sounding stupid, but not willing to give it up. I heard Katelyn laugh behind me.

"Damn. I'm probably looking at a whole week of washing dishes at some homeless shelter," she said. Her colleagues laughed with her, adding to the sting.

Delgado reached over and patted me on the arm. "Steady, boy," he said. I jerked away from his touch and raised my arms in mock surrender.

"I know you're angry, Inspector," Sullivan said. "And I'm sorry. But we had no choice." He stopped. I could tell he was recalibrating. "Let's just say we're in national security territory here, and we have every right under the law to do what we think necessary for the greater good of the country. Katelyn is our only member with operational experience. We needed answers, so we turned to her. She got them.

"We heard Professor Conroy's name mentioned a number of times on the Dark Web. It made us curious. We did our homework. We found out what he did and where he lived. And then he gets himself murdered. We figured we better start getting serious about this." He pointed to the three of us. "You gave us the perfect opportunity. Inspector McGuire planned to investigate Conroy's assassination. Traveling in a private jet. We found out what agency RSSA used to hire flight attendants, and persuaded them to hire and send Katelyn. Her initial reports to us were not encouraging. We began thinking that having her attached to you full-time was a waste of resources. Then she heard you mention the *Custer Papers*. She asked to stay for at least one more day. We agreed. That should teach you a lesson, Inspector." He didn't smile when he said it. He had it right. Too big a mouth. *My Bad*.

"She convinced us to at least see what you had. Even though we knew by then that you and your group would be coming to assist us, I didn't want to take any chances. You were just being too careless with those papers. I told her to *borrow* them and bring them here. She did. Simply following orders."

Sullivan nodded and Katelyn stood in front of us. In front of me. I couldn't believe this woman and I had made love yesterday morning. *Made love?* My first big mistake. There was no *love* involved. On her part, at least. To her, this was all a game. To me? To me she had become nothing more than a one-eyed jack in a deck of cards, and I was in no hurry to see the other side of that face.

"We had the same question as you," she began. "What did Conroy find that our persons of interest considered a threat? A threat great enough to kill both Conroy and his wife?"

She turned to me. "Inspector McGuire said …" mentioning me as if I were just another face in the crowd. Not the guy who twenty-four hours earlier had been told that our making love was *the breath of existence*. I squirmed in my chair, realizing I wasn't feeling anger, but embarrassment! Embarrassment at having been taken in so completely. Embarrassment for being played for such a fool. Embarrassment for having everyone in this room know it. The classic jilted lover's lament.

"… there were men who plotted to have Custer killed at the Battle of the Little Bighorn, but said their names were never mentioned. He just hadn't read far enough."

"Bullshit," I said through pursed lips. "I just didn't have the damn papers long enough."

"Whatever," she said, waving her hand dismissively. She turned and walked back to her desk, retrieved her computer from its case and gave it to Emily Wyatt.

"While she sets up, let me fill you in on what the *Custer Papers* actually said. General Sheridan told Custer about two months before the battle that, quote, *rich and powerful men,* unquote, were plotting his death. These men, Sheridan said, lusted after the riches to be had by opening up the land west of the Missouri River to settlement. But the Indians had to be gone. Either dead or stuck on a reservation somewhere. The government had some success getting them on reservations but were moving too slowly for these men. Custer's death would jump start that process. Get the government to act forcefully. Sheridan didn't say a word about this to anyone. Who knows? Maybe they promised him a piece of the pie. In any case, he essentially told Custer that if he didn't want to die, better get a stand-in." She stopped and turned to Wyatt. "You ready yet?" she asked.

"Give me a minute more," Wyatt replied.

"Okay." She said, turning back to us. "Let me wrap this part up. You would have thought that the men behind this plot would be names we knew from our history books. Names like John Rockefeller, or Leland Stanford, or Cornelius Vanderbilt. Names of people who did, in fact, became rich and powerful because the West opened up. But no. Custer named only two men. No one you've ever heard of. Both Brits. And their agenda had nothing to do with opening the West. Custer, in his old age, finally had it figured out."

She hesitated, looked directly at me and said, "Inspector McGuire told you it's the motive you have to find. The *Papers*, as I've read them, supply us with a real motive why certain people today would do anything to prevent the secrets in those papers from becoming public. These two Brits had been sent here by higher ups to test a theory, and Lt. Colonel George Armstrong Custer had been chosen to be their guinea pig."

CHAPTER 44

Katelyn had Wyatt project her report on the screen. Wasn't all that long. Richard Neville and his family had been in the gun manufacturing business since the fifteen hundreds. Made a decent living supplying guns to the Confederates during the Civil War. All through brokers in Bermuda. George Clark Allan, the second guy, sold arms to the Union army during the war. She went into their family history quite a bit, but on the surface it didn't look like a promising thread to me. Except for making a few bucks selling guns to the US Army to fight the Indians, what did they have to gain?

"If you stole my papers to find these guys," I said, "you wasted your time." There, I said it. Not real classy, I know. Purposely being a prick. But made me feel a whole hell of a lot better. But not for long.

"You don't know that yet," said James Holmquist, pushing back in defense of Katelyn. "There's a lot to her report she hasn't mentioned, and can't mention, until we finish our analysis. We're following those men into and through World War I. Seeing where the connections are, if any, with people today. Custer certainly saw connections."

"Great," I said, again being satisfyingly petulant. "He couldn't have seen *that* many connections. He died in September of 1914. The damn war was barely a month old."

"If there are any connections," Holmquist rebutted, "we'll find them. Remember the line about Custer being the guinea pig. That can lead us in a whole new direction."

I started to reply, but Delgado interrupted. "Dude," he said, looking directly at me. "Let it go, Bro. Let them do their work." He didn't lose eye contact with me until I responded. Nodding to him, I slouched down in my chair. Surrendering – again.

"Good," Delgado said, patting me on the back. Turning his attention to the others, he said, "Okay. I have a few questions. Have you looked into the connections we gave to you regarding Randolph? You have his phone. That should give you *something*. Global Affinity Partners? His employer? Him getting his head blown off yesterday I hope put some urgency into your analysis."

"Of course it has," Sullivan said. "We've already analyzed Randolph's phone. Most of his calls were to family and friends. In the past thirty days, however, there were a number of calls made to various phones around the country. Random phone numbers. One call per number. All in different area codes. When we called those numbers, they were no longer in service. Burners, no doubt. Which made us curious as to who answered them. We're in the process of triangulating the calls. What cell towers were involved, that kind of thing. Not easy, but hopefully can lead us to the neighborhood of the person holding those phones. It's going to take us a few days, though.

"Randolph had an app for a VOIP connection. You know, like Skype. It's password protected. That caught our attention big time. Won't take us long to crack it, I'm sure. But as of right now, we haven't. We'll let you know what we find out."

"I have a question for you," Kincaid said. "Did you know that Mac came home from Montana with a shell casing? A casing from one of the shots fired by the shooter that day? You want to tell them about that, Coach?"

I gave them the shorthand version.

"Tell them what the cop told you," Kincaid said.

"He was a good ol' boy and knew weapons. He told me the caliber was a 44.40 Winchester. I have it with me in case you want to put it through tests. It's back at the hotel."

"Couldn't do any harm, Inspector," Sullivan said. "If you could bring it back sometime today would be great."

"He told me you don't see 44.40 around much any more," I said. "Mostly found in specialty catalogs. Made a comeback recently in a nationwide sport contest known as *Cowboy Action Shooting*."

"And that's precisely where I want to go with this," Kincaid said. "I'm hoping it wasn't an accident that the shooter used that caliber. A kind of *catch me if you can* attitude. That we're not smart enough to make the connection between the 44.40 caliber and modern day shooters."

"You want to – what? Infiltrate CAS events? See if you can find him?"

"Not infiltrate," Kincaid said. "Well – let me take that back. Now that I think of it, *infiltrate* might be the right word. A few of my former SEAL teammates are active in those contests. Said they'd be happy to show me around. Since you are now our employer, I wanted to run the idea by you. See if you think it's worth a shot." He laughed. "No pun intended."

Sullivan laughed, too. "Sounds like a perfect avenue to pursue."

CHAPTER 45

We started filing out of the office into the narrow corridor leading to the first of the checkpoints when I felt a tap on my shoulder.

"Got a minute?" Katelyn whispered.

I turned toward her, blocking the doorway. She pulled me back into the office. Delgado passed me, leaned over and squeezed my shoulder. "Meet you up top, Bro," he said. I acknowledged with a nod of my head.

Conflicting emotions started battling one another. On the one hand, the anger bubbling up from my bruised ego wanted to fight. On the other, I wanted to hear her story. Hoping to hear her say she didn't think me a fool. That she had feelings for me even though they couldn't lead to anything permanent. In short, to hear her give me back my manhood. Childish, I know. But aren't we all. I stepped back into the office.

"I want to personally apologize to you. I didn't mean to play with you. You understand command and control." She paused and looked me straight in the eye. "I followed orders. That's all."

"*The breath of existence*? Really?" I couldn't help myself.

The long face I hoped would appear as she finally realized the enormity of her deception – didn't. But I did get a smile and a touch on my arm. Somewhat ashamedly, I had to acknowledge the goose bumps that were spawned by that gesture.

"I made that up on the fly," she said. "I told you at the time that I didn't know what it meant, remember? I told you I *felt* what it meant, but couldn't put it into words."

"Who the hell *are* you?" I asked, becoming petulant again. I hated myself for getting like this, but quickly rationalized it away by blaming it all on her.

"That is a good question and a long story," she uttered softly. She still hadn't let go of my arm. I could feel the equilibrium shifting. Slowly rebalancing. From the previous parent/child relationship, where Katelyn, the parent held all the cards, to something more akin to a sibling relationship. Even though she still had the upper hand, I started feeling less delicate. Less beat-up.

"You have a dinner date?" she asked, flashing that heartbreak smile of hers.

Damn her! No matter how hard I tried, I found it hard to stay mad. That smile could melt the iciest of hearts. And mine was already thawing quickly.

We entered the narrow corridor. By the time we got to the top level, the rest of the group had already gone. Katelyn went through her iris scan and the door slid silently open. Rob and Vinnie were waiting for me in AFF's car repair reception area. No words were necessary. They looked at us, just nodded and said they'd meet me back at the hotel.

Katelyn made dinner reservations as she drove us into Gaithersburg. Except for the phone call to the restaurant, silence dominated the fifteen-minute ride into the city. I couldn't think of anything to say, and apparently neither could she. I smiled inwardly. *Playing a new game with one another*, I thought. *This one about power.* Bringing the relationship back into equilibrium.

She gave her keys to the valet and we walked into the restaurant. It wasn't until we were seated that the silence between us finally broke. Katelyn spoke first. I considered it a win for me, but by this time I couldn't have cared less.

"What are you going to do now?" she asked. "Will you go back to San Francisco or stay in the area to see what happens next?"

"I'm not going back home. I've got a murder case to solve."

Silence again. Then I said, "You?"

"Well, when it comes to solving murder cases that border on National Security," she said, "I want to be as close to the streets as possible – and that, I think, means tying up with you."

"Do I have a choice?"

"Everyone has choices," she said. "Yours and mine happen to dovetail. We either choose to work together, or we choose to go after it alone."

"Not saying I will, but if I do decide to work with you, who is the *you* I'd be working with? Do you officially work for the CIA? A contract agent? What?"

"I'm officially an agent. And operational," she answered. "That's what separates me from my colleagues back there. That's why I was the one in New York and not Emily. She and James, and even Tom Sullivan, are strictly analysts."

"How long have you been doing this?" I asked. "Working for the CIA."

Before she could answer, the waiter appeared and we ordered dinner. Left alone again, she took a sip of water, pressed back into the faux leather booth, and said, "Does the name James Tucker ring a bell?"

I thought for a moment. The bell rang. "The Ambassador to Lebanon? The one assassinated by Hezbollah in what – 2000-something?"

She nodded. "2002, as a matter of fact. November 10th. He was my father."

Stunned, I reached over and took her hand in mine. "Son of a bitch," I said. "I'm sorry." I found myself savoring the hand touching too much, so I pulled back and said, "So your last name is not Murray?"

"No. It's Tucker. But my CIA name is Murray. So the bad guys don't make the connection with my dad and me. CIA's call, not mine. Keeping Tucker would have put a target on my back, they said. I chose the name Murray because my mom's family answers to Murray." She paused, took another sip of water and said, "You asked how long I've been working for the CIA? Since 2003."

I nodded. "Were you with him in Lebanon when it happened?"

"No. Living in the States. A junior at Georgetown University. Majoring in International Politics. Looking back, I was pretty naïve. Thought learning all that stuff would make a difference. Make the world a better place."

"How'd you make it to the CIA from Georgetown?"

"They recruited me," she said. "After my father was killed, I dropped out of school. November of 2002. In February, the CIA knocked on my door."

"And you became a spy?" I snapped my fingers. "Just like that?"

"Hell, no, it wasn't *just like that*," she protested. "I worked my ass off. Spent ten months at a boot camp in the Adirondack Mountains. Twenty-seven of us. Only seven graduated. I was determined to make it through. And I did."

"I met some CIA grads at Annapolis," I said. "They took language classes with us. Also trained with us. I can attest to their – your – toughness."

"We took pride in that," she replied. "At least I did. But when I turned operational, all I wanted to do was find the bastard that had murdered my father. The CIA brass gave me that chance. In 2006. I'll be forever indebted."

"They captured him?"

"They did. In Khartoum. The CIA had known his name since 2004. They got word through an informant that he'd be attending the African Union summit held in Khartoum in January of 2006. Our operatives captured and held him until I arrived."

"Then you actually got to meet him?"

"I did," she replied. "In a little room above a barber shop in the western 'burbs of the city. They left me alone with him. Hassan Al-I'man. I'll never forget that name."

"Did he speak English?"

"No. I speak Arabic. Learned it when my father was stationed in Israel. From a Palestinian boy about my age. I'd sit with him for hours practicing."

"Did the Hassan guy admit to killing your father?"

"He did. They had him tied to a chair in the middle of the room. They left me alone. I pulled up a chair and sat in front of him. Face to face. I unholstered my pistol and put it in my lap. As soon as I introduced myself, I knew from the look in his eyes that he remembered the name.

"We stared at each other for a few minutes. Then he smirked and said, 'I killed your father. I suppose you know that and have come here for revenge.' I said nothing. Just kept staring at him."

'You don't know what you are up against,' he continued. 'Islam will conquer and destroy you. The *West*.'

"I remember how he spit out that word. 'Allah has granted us funding from all over the world. Funding mostly from the infidels. From your own country. People high up. People who take no sides. People who for whatever reason just love the violence. They gave me your father. They honored me by allowing me to pull the trigger.'"

"*Gave them your father*," I said. "What the hell did that mean?"

"A lie. Just another slice of the knife trying to cut me up. At least I thought so then."

"Not now?"

"Now I'm not so sure."

"Did you ask him?"

"We spoke for another five minutes or so. I simply couldn't take his smug and condescending attitude. Like Allah had ordered him to kill my father. I finally just brought the pistol up from my lap and shot him in the face."

I sat there in stunned silence.

"My first kill," she said. "But not my last."

CHAPTER 46

Washington, D.C.

As McGuire and Murray were about to order dessert, Mosby arrived at the Westin in Georgetown. Congressman Perry had called to tell him to call Corporate at eight fifteen. Perry didn't know what they wanted, but gave the sequence of numbers Mosby needed to connect with them. There were five strings with eight numbers in each string. He pulled over to the shoulder and wrote them all down, making certain to copy them in the exact sequence and order that Perry gave him.

At exactly eight fifteen, Tad Mosby sat on the edge of his hotel room bed with cell phone in hand. He dialed the first string. Static entertained him for what seemed like minutes, then a disembodied voice asked for another number. He dutifully punched in the second string of numbers. Mosby had communicated with Corporate before, so he knew what to expect. This routine would go on until he had dialed all the strings Perry had dictated. He looked in the mirror across from him and smiled. *Must be what it would be like phoning Hell*, he thought. The vision amused him. Extension after extension after extension until you finally reached Da' Man. Although he knew the final voice he would hear on this call wouldn't be Da' Man. In fact, it wouldn't be a man at all. It would be a machine. An intelligent machine, but a machine nonetheless.

Mosby knew how all this worked, if only through a glass darkly. They told him to purchase a VOIP app for his smart phone so he could make calls over the Internet. All the extension strings were nothing more than a series of passwords. Once you were identified through the pass-words, you entered the encrypted world of the Tor Hidden Services, the darkest of the Dark Net. Mosby knew this call would never hit his Verizon bill.

"Hello, Mr. Mosby," the voice said. "I've been expect-ing your call." From past experience, Mosby knew he had to respond to this greeting.

"I'm glad you answered," Mosby replied. He could have said, "screw you," and knew the voice would have continued in a cheerful manner. *The machine was smart*, Mosby thought with a knowing smile, but not *that* smart.

"Headquarters has a job for you," the voice continued.

Mosby shook his head. *This is the new DAC all the techies are talking about*, he thought. *The **decentralized autonomous corporation**. Welcome to the brave new world. Talking to a machine. Taking orders from a fucking machine. The whole damn world is going to end up like this. God help us. I hope I'm not around to see where all this is going to end up.*

"I thought I was to eliminate the police officer," he said. The machine didn't answer for a few moments. Mos-by imagined his words being stored briefly in the ma-chine's short-term memory while it flashed electronically through all the words in the English language to put to-gether a meaningful sentence. *Just like a human brain does*, he thought with a shiver.

"A new job," the machine said.

"Tell me," he said.

"Do you have something to write with?" the machine asked. "I'm only going to say it once." Mosby smiled. "I do," he said. One time, when all this was new, he had pur-posely screwed with the machine by saying he didn't need a pen and paper because he was recording this. Just to hear the machine's reaction. It immediately hung up. The next day Mosby received a slap-on-the-wrist phone call from Perry.

This message actually surprised him, but he didn't want the machine to search its memory banks for the answer, so he didn't question it.

Per the machine's instructions, tomorrow at ten in the morning he would take a cab over to the Rayburn Building and have a conversation with Congressman Perry. The machine told him what to say. He didn't understand any of it, but then he really didn't care.

In any case, the trip across town to meet with Perry was going to be it for a while. Come Friday, he'd be in Cleburne, Texas for the **Wild Bunch Championship. The Super Bowl of the Cowboy Action Shooting** season. He couldn't wait.

CHAPTER 47

Unbeknownst to Mosby, another man was on his cell phone, also making plans to visit Cleburne.

"Jimmy?"

"That be me, pardner," the voice said in a syrupy southern drawl. "Who's this?"

When Kincaid heard the voice he smiled, remembering it well. "Rob Kincaid," he said. "Remember me?"

There was a pause on the line, then, "Well sheee-it. Hell yes, I remember. What a surprise, L-T."

"I'm sitting in a hotel room in Maryland with Vinnie Delgado. Watch what you say. We have the phone on speaker."

"Well, then, let me take back what I just said. Sheee-it. This isn't just a *surprise*; this is a *great* surprise. How long has it been?"

Jimmy Cartwright was a former Team-6 teammate of both Kincaid and Delgado. Over the course of three years, they had four deployments together, two each in Iraq and Afghanistan.

"I retired two-and-a-half years ago. So it's been at least that long," Kincaid replied. "And don't give me that Southern shit. You're from New Jersey."

"Been down South since I retired. It's a great accent. Women just love it." He laughed. "And how 'bout you, Vinnie? How long you been out?"

"I jumped ship, so to speak, a month before Rob," Delgado said.

"I figured you two left around that time," Cartwright said. "Been just over two years. How's life been treating y'all? I heard through the grapevine y'all *Blackwatered* yourselves."

"Yeah. Red Squadron Security Agency."

"Great name. Old times."

"Fits, doesn't it?" Kincaid said with a laugh. "Been in operation a year and a half already. So how about you?"

"Sneakin' by."

"Oh, come on, Jimmy. It's better than that. Heard you're involved in a shooting club. Cowboy Action Shooting?"

"You heard right, Rob. But tell ya' what, it's way more than just a club. Practically a way of life. I'm lovin' it. Guns, girls and glory. What's not to love?"

Kincaid laughed, then said, "Glad to hear you haven't changed any. Hey, Vinnie and I are comin' down your way. Besides catching up with an old teammate, obviously, we're working a job. We want to find a guy. Hopin' you could help. We know he's a shooter. Think he may be a member of your organization."

"I'll do whatever I can to help, L-T, you know that. What's the dude's name?"

"That's our problem, Jimmy. We don't know. But hopin' to find out. Maybe you and Vinnie and I could meet sometime soon? We've put together a profile, but no name."

"Would love to meet. Whatcha up to this weekend? I happen to be the Board's Southwest Regional Director of CAS. Startin' Friday, we're hosting what we're billing as the CAS Super Bowl. If the guy you're looking for is one of us, I guarantee he'll be there."

"Music to our ears, Jimmy. Where you holding this event?"

"In a small town about thirty miles south of Ft. Worth. Name of Cleburne. Starts Friday. One or both of you could even take part in the contest if you want. We only shoot weapons real cowboys used. But hell, as I remember it, you guys were always real cowboys." He laughed. "I can lend y'all the weapons y'all need."

"We'll see about that, Jimmy," Kincaid said. "Tell me about your contest, though. What's the goal? You win on getting closest to the bullseye?"

"It's all about speed and accuracy, Rob. There's an array of weapons you've got to use. Vintage rifle. Shotgun. Single action pistol. Weapons like that. Contestants bring their own rigs. We only supply the venue and judges. The venue includes a table where they lay out their weapons. We put up targets at varying distances. Nothing too far. Twenty – thirty yards, max. Targets are about the size of a dinner plate. Made out of metal so they make a *clunk* or *ping* when hit. Pepper poppers, we call 'em. Can you picture it?"

"Pretty much," Kincaid said.

"Like I said, it's just a matter of speed and accuracy. When the timer says *Go*, you pick up the rifle and take five shots at the most distant targets. Then you pick up the shotgun. You fire the two in the magazine, then reload and fire off another two. The same with the pistols – fire six, reload and fire another six. Winner is determined on how many hits he has in how many seconds."

"Dude, sounds like fun," Delgado said. "Sign me up."

"See what you got yourself into, Jimmy?" Kincaid said. "Anyway, the shooter we're looking for isn't too concerned about speed. Accuracy, for sure. Killed a friend-of-a-friend of ours from four to five hundred yards out. We're guessing he thinks of himself more as a sniper than a quick draw artist. And if that's the case, then there's a good chance he's ex-military. Only reason we think our guy might be part of your group is because he shot our friend's friend with a 44.40 cartridge."

"Lots of shooters here use that cartridge."

"That's why we're hopin' he'll be there," Kincaid said.

"And we do have a lot of ex-military people in our organization," Cartwright said. "Like me, for example. Guys who miss the shooting range camaraderie plus the testosterone rush of competition. Again, like me. And you two." He laughed. "You want to smoke him out, right? That what I'm hearin'?"

"Loud and clear," Kincaid replied.

"Let me give it some thought. I'll come up with some kind of special contest. Maybe one shooting a modern rifle over a long distance?"

"Interesting," said Kincaid. "If you come up with something like that, I have just the guy for your contestants to beat."

"Not you or Delgado, I hope?"

"No way," Delgado said laughing.

"Okay. Let me think about it. Can you come down Thursday? Bring your shooter. And anyone else you want. Just let me know and I'll make hotel reservations for you. By the time you get here I'll have run a few scenarios by our board. I think it's doable. This agency of yours – they got a plane they fly you around in?"

"Well, hell yeah. We won't be walking to Texas."

"Just askin' because Cleburne has its own airport. Can handle anything smaller than a 737."

"I can assure you our plane is smaller than that, Jimmy," Kincaid said. "I'll make the arrangements. Let you know when we'll arrive. It's gonna be great to see you again."

"You bet. Get plenty of rest. You're gonna need it." He laughed. "And Lieutenant?"

"Yeah?" Kincaid replied.

"We'll find this shooter for you."

"Thanks, Jimmy." Kincaid hung up and gave the phone to Delgado. "Call Kyle Escher. Tell him to get his ass down here by tomorrow morning. We have a job for him."

CHAPTER 48

Botanic Garden
Washington, D.C

Congressman Mitchell Perry exited the Rayburn House Office Building and turned right on First Street. He checked his watch. Nine fifty. Corporate had scheduled the meeting for ten, but Perry wanted to be early. Check out the lay of the land. Perry recognized his paranoia, but he had a reason. He simply didn't trust any of them. Why did they send Mosby? Their assassin, for God's sake. Was their plan to assassinate him? Hell, Mosby could have the crosshairs on him right now. But they wouldn't do that to him, would they? Assassinate him in broad daylight? A block from the Capitol? For what purpose? He'd always been a loyal soldier. And a highly placed one, at that. It would take them years to replace him. Unless, of course, they already had a replacement in mind. His palms felt sweaty and he wiped them on his pants as he walked. *Stop this paranoia shit,* he commanded himself. *Put the game face on. Show fear to this asshole and he'll own me.*

Crossing Independence Avenue, he turned left as instructed and followed the path that skirted the main Botanic Garden complex. It led to a comfortable patio, complete with a gurgling fountain. Tad Mosby was already there, sitting at a small picnic table in the back corner.

"This better be good," Perry said, trying to show strength from the get-go. "I've got two important committee meetings today."

"Hey, chill out," said Mosby. "Didn't I pick out a nice setting? Relax and enjoy it. Hell, you can even see the Capitol Dome from here."

"Don't go all touristy on me, okay? I work right across the street. I see this shit every damn day."

"I know that," Mosby said with a smirk. "But this …" he emphasized the word *this* with a sweep of his hand, indicating the gardens, "… as a taxpayer, I enjoy the view. One of the few things I've seen that's actually *worth* the money the taxpayers ponied up."

"Funny," Perry said. "But I'll tell you what the taxpayers are going to wonder - why is the ranking member of the House Armed Services Committee wasting *their* money sitting in the Botanic Garden talking to a nobody like you?"

"Because that's what the ranking member's real employers told him to do." Mosby sat back, letting that fact sink in. He waited a beat, then said, "Look, let's just get this damn meeting over with. I'm going out of town for a few days. I have a lot of things to do, and last I checked, lippin' with you wasn't one of 'em."

"Then why are you here?" Perry asked.

"Got a call from Corporate last night. Through the network. They wanted me to deliver this message. Tell him *your wife has gone off the reservation.*"

"Bullshit!"

"I'm just carrying the message. You can believe it or not. But if I were you? My being here today should be a warning in and of itself."

Perry sat in silence. His fingers steepled. Like he was praying. *If I were in his shoes*, Mosby thought, *dealing with my grandfather? I'd be praying, too.*

"What did they tell you?" Perry asked quietly. "What do they want me to do?"

"You know she's interviewing for the Chief of Staff position on Senator David's reelection committee."

"Yes."

"And it's probably no surprise that the Corporation set that interview up for her."

"I'm aware they did. It's no surprise."

"And she's aware of that fact, also, right?"

"I suppose. It's not something we talk about. I don't think she has a clue about their power and reach. What has she done?"

"The FBI contacted her."

"Oh, shit," Perry said. "For what?"

"No one knows – yet. But she can't be talking to them at all. You have to impress that fact on her. She *can't* talk to the FBI. The Corporation absolutely won't stand for it. She knows too much and has never been trained in the art of evasive answering. They'll have her drained of everything she knows within two hours."

"What do they want me to do about it?"

"Get her lawyered up. That would be a start."

"What if she won't do that?"

"Let me tell you a story, Congressman. The Corporation had a similar upset about five years ago in Bulgaria. The wife of one of their ministers found herself in generally the same position your wife finds herself in."

"And that situation resolved itself?"

"Yes. Yes, it did."

"Did she retain an attorney?"

"No. She wouldn't do that."

"Then how did the Corporation resolve it?"

"They brought me in to help."

"Did you?"

"Yes."

"How?"

A smile spread across his face. "Like I've always helped the Corporation, Congressman. I shot her."

CHAPTER 49

Katelyn dropped me off at my hotel around ten. The phone in my room was blinking red. A message from Rob to call him as soon as I arrived.

He told me of his conversation with his SEAL buddy Cartwright. That he and Delgado were flying to Texas tomorrow to see if they could get a bead on Conroy's killer. They had already invited Escher and wanted me to come, too.

At noon the next day, the four of us were seated in Kincaid's Legacy 650 as it rose gracefully from Reagan National on its way to Texas.

We sat in relative silence for a long time before Kincaid looked over at Escher and said, "Last time Vinnie, Mac and I flew together, a colleague of yours flew with us. Pretending to be a flight attendant."

"I heard," Escher said. "Too bad she's not here now."

Both Rob and Vinnie stole a quick glance my way. Escher saw them and immediately recognized his *faux pas*. "Sorry. Just meant I could use a drink."

The others laughed. I didn't. Feeling myself slipping back into a snarky mood, I said, "Probably should've invited her to come along today. You two guys play the dual roles so well. Hell, she could be in the galley making us drinks right about now. Laughing at us for being so gullible, while you're out here regaling us with sniper or big game hunting stories."

"All of which were true, by the way," Escher replied. "You know, McGuire, I don't blame you for being pissed.

Living a lie has its consequences. Especially when you have to lie to loved ones. Or at least people you care about. But for me? When I first met you folks, I could've cared less about playing straight with you. But now that I know you, I'm glad I didn't have to carry it any further than I did. I'm guessing Katelyn feels the same way. Glad to have it behind her."

"Funny how easily the landscape shifts, though, isn't it?" I said.

"Come on, Coach," Kincaid said. "Enough. This isn't getting us anywhere."

"Hold on for a minute, okay?" I said, my mood still enveloped in darkness. "A week ago you were a simple chemist analyzing Conroy's samples. Now you're a Marine sniper and CIA operative."

"*Former* Marine sniper," Escher said, the tone of his voice telling me his mood had started to match mine. "Tell me, Inspector. You ever work undercover on your job?"

"Some," I answered, knowing where he was going with this. Waiting for my chance to push back.

"There you go, then. You're no different than me *or* Katelyn."

I looked at him for a moment, then slowly said, "Difference is I didn't *fuck* my marks."

Escher looked at me with hooded eyes. "Don't kid yourself, Inspector. If fucking your marks were what you had to do to complete your assignment, you would have. And you know it. Maybe hated yourself afterward, but you would have done it. If it makes you feel any better, I'm sure Katelyn feels as badly about it as you do."

Just then I felt the plane start to descend. Delgado, taking the opportunity to diffuse the tension in the cabin, pointed out the window. In the distance, a small town was clearly visible. "Welcome to Cleburne, everyone." Escher leaned over me to get a better view.

"Looks hot down there," he said. "See that lake yonder?" We all looked and nodded. "Lake Patrick Cleburne. Hear it's a great fishing spot. Have to try it out before we leave. You game, Mac? No better way to clear the air than in a boat with a few fishing lines hanging from it."

I took a deep breath, appreciating his trying to dial down the rhetoric. "Thanks for the offer," I said. "Probably not the guy you'd want to go with. I'm not what you'd call an accomplished fisherman. Maybe Vinnie or Rob. I'm not saying no, but – let's see what happens here first, okay?"

"Fair enough," he said. He leaned in close, pretending to look out the window as we descended, and whispered, "Just so you know, I've known Katelyn Murray for close to six years. Seen her in action a hundred times. She has plenty of ways to get what she wants from people without having to get physical. First time I've known her to do it. Just remember that."

He turned away. I didn't move, hoping he couldn't hear the sounds of demons being released from my soul.

Cleburne, Texas

"This Cleburne dude musta had somethin' going for him here, huh?" Delgado said as the plane flattened out into its glide path. "Dude not only gets a town named after him, but a lake, too." He laughed.

"Cleburne was a general in the Confederate army," Escher replied. "A real FBI." He noticed Delgado's quizzical look. "Foreign Born Irish," he said.

"Dude," Delgado said with a smile.

"It's an old one," Escher replied, returning the smile. "Anyway, Cleburne sided with the Confederacy. Rose to the rank of major general. Got himself killed in Tennessee near the end of the war. The irony is the guy never stepped foot in the state of Texas all during the war, and yet gets a damn town named after him. Go figure."

"And now his town is the host for the Super Bowl of Cowboy Action Shooting," Delgado said. "Ol' Cleburne is gettin' to be big time."

The plane landed smoothly, and the four of us stepped out into the heat of central Texas. The pilot said he'd get our bags, so we wasted no time in getting into the air-conditioned comfort of the small terminal.

Rob spotted Jimmy Cartwright slouching against a support column talking on the phone. As soon as he made eye contact, Cartwright shut the call down and sauntered over.

Going about six four, two twenty, Cartwright was Clint Eastwood thirty years ago. Even walked like him. "Well, sheee-it," he said, wrapping Kincaid in a bear hug.

"And lookie here. You brought the little guy." He laughed and turned toward Delgado, arms outstretched.

"Whoa, dude," Delgado said, putting his hand out to stop him. He even took a step backward. "Last time you did that to me, you damn near broke my shoulder."

"Pussy," Cartwright said. "Must not be the Vinnie Delgado I once knew. The man who held the record for the most barehanded combat kills of anyone who ever wore the Trident. *That* VD was a tough hombre."

"I'm the older, wiser VD," Delgado replied, laughing. "The younger VD got his Trident revoked for being such a tough hombre."

"That – and a few other things, I hear," Cartwright said with a big grin. He draped his arm over Delgado's shoulder and said, "Good to see you, again, man."

"Ditto, brah," Delgado replied.

"Hey, Vinnie," I said. "*Trident revoked?* That's a story I haven't heard yet. Time to share?"

"I don't think so. It's a story you'll never hear, if I can help it," he replied in a voice that said he meant it.

"Hey, Jimmy," Kincaid said quickly, recognizing the tone in Delgado's voice. "Got two guys I want you to meet. This here is Tom McGuire, my old football coach from high school days. He's now *Inspector* Tom McGuire, San Francisco PD. And this is Kyle Escher. Our resident sniper." He laughed.

"Nice to meet you both," Cartwright said, shaking our hands. "Rob told me a lot about the both of you." He turned to Escher. "I told him it was a stroke of pure genius bringing you along," he said. "We've got to talk about how to catch this piece of shit shooter of yours." Then turning to me, he said, "If the guy who shot your friend shows up, we'll find him. Take his ass out."

"Thanks," I said. "Appreciate your help."

"We probably should get going, Rob," Cartwright said.

We retrieved our gear, threw them in the back of Cartwright's pickup and climbed in.

CHAPTER 51

We quickly found out how lucky we were to have Jimmy Cartwright fronting for us. Even though every hotel in Cleburne had been rented out for the CAS event, his contacts were good enough to score rooms for us in one of the nicer establishments in town. His contacts weren't good enough, however, to save us from the hundred or so middle-aged men in cowboy hats and chaps who beat us to the registration line.

"Have we entered the Twilight Zone?" I asked Cartwright who was standing in line with us. He had checked in two days before.

"Part of the fun," Cartwright said. "Everyone at this event has to dress up as a cowboy, circa mid-to-late 1800s."

"Well, certainly could be that century here," I said, looking over those in line with us. "Damn. A few guys here actually wearing spurs on their boots, for goodness sake. They must be thinking it's Tombstone. Gunfight at the O.K. Corral comin' up tomorrow."

"Guess I forgot to tell y'all, huh?" Cartwright said with a smile. "Most of the people who come to CAS events dress up as their favorite movie cowboy. Or cowgirl, as the case may be."

"Dude," said Delgado. "You mean I coulda come as Josey Wales?"

"Still can," said Cartwright. "In any case, y'all have to do something about what you're wearing. Cowboy garb, or nothing. Them's the rules. Otherwise you don't get in.

Even if they let you in dressed as you are now, wouldn't do y'all any good in catching the dude you're after. You'd stick out like a sore thumb. I can just hear him. *What the hell they doin' here? Cops, no doubt.* Your shooter would go underground, for sure."

"Yeah, I can see that," Kincaid said. "Might actually be fun to be Josey Wales."

"Right on, Bro," Delgado said. "Where can we buy shit like that?"

"There's a place just a few blocks down. *Hole in the Wall Western Wear.* Or just go to Macy's over on 6th street. The one piece of gear, though, that is gonna be absolutely essential is a hat. A cowboy hat. Going to be hot as hell at the event. I highly recommend you to get a Stetson or something similar. Not only fit in better at the contest, you won't get heat stroke. Y'all can buy Stetsons at *Hole in the Wall.* Other than that, Macy's has everything you'll need. Jeans. Cowboy shirts. Boots would help, too. Make you look more like real cowboys. Tennies, though, are allowed and will get y'all in the gate."

The line inched along. "You know what we should do?" Cartwright said. "After y'all get to your rooms and unpack, change, go to the can, why not come up to my room? We can talk there. Too damn noisy in the bar, and we've got a lot to go over before tomorrow." He gave us his room number. "I'll order up a bottle of Jack and Sapphire, some mixes and snacks. I'll also make reservations for dinner at nine. Should give us plenty of time. Sound good?"

Everyone agreed, and an hour and a half later we were sitting in Cartwright's suite having a drink and starting to discuss how we were going to recognize Conroy's killer in this sea of gun-totin' cowboys.

"Just so we're all on the same page, here's what you'll be lookin' at tomorrow," Cartwright began. "We're expecting somewhere between four to five hundred people. Three hundred and seventy-eight are active contestants."

"How long does the event last?" I asked.

"The Opening Ceremonies are tomorrow afternoon at five," Cartwright said. "Much ado about nothin', though. I'll give the opening remarks. Welcome everyone. Tell 'em how we expect 'em to act. You know, *be respectful. Don't shoot anyone.* Where the various events will be held. Vendor stands are already set up so people can get food and drinks, chotskies – stuff like that. All shooting events start Saturday morning. Park opens at nine. Events start at ten. Last event on Sunday will begin at eleven. Then it's over."

Silence filled the room. Delgado was the first to articulate what I'm sure everyone thought. "Finding our shooter will be like finding that proverbial needle in a haystack."

More silence, then Escher said, "This guy shot Mac's friend from five hundred yards?" He looked at me. I nodded. "In my experience, hitting a target from that distance is an acquired skill."

"Yeah. Ex-military. That's what Rob told me when we first spoke," Cartwright said. "Knowing that, though, won't move the needle much. Of the three hundred and some active contestants, I'm guessing maybe half are ex-military."

"Good to know," Escher said. "If the shooter is here, I think we can make him break cover."

"How?" Cartwright asked. "Not through the CAS shooting contest I hope. I'm tellin' you, we could have fifty trained snipers here. But the way our contest is structured, there's no way you'll be able to tell who is and who isn't."

"Tell him what you came up with," I said to Escher.

"I thought you could advertise you're hosting a special long-distance shooting contest pitting the people who sign up against a retired Marine sniper. Personally, I think just that challenge alone would smoke the prick out."

"Challenge is said in many ways," Cartwright said. "For one, none of the contestants brought that kind of long-gun with them."

"I'm providing the rifle," Escher said. "I brought along my Remington Mk 21. That will get their attention real quick."

"Well, hell yeah," Cartwright said. "Getting a chance to fire the newest precision sniper rifle will be a draw, no doubt about it. They'll know you're a pro." He thought for a minute. "We'll have to do it Sunday. After the CAS event is over."

"Perfect," I said. "We were hoping you could offer it as an add-on to the CAS contest. A *Thanks for Coming* kind of thing. But only for the most qualified."

"Nothing in our charter prevents us from having such a contest," Cartwright said. "But there are other issues. Like where you set up. You'll need a hell of a long field."

"Twelve hundred meters minimum," Escher replied. "I'm thinking it would be kick-ass to take the targets out to fifteen hundred meters. That's the effective range of the Mk. It's going to be a really long shot for all but the best."

"Shit. Okay, I'll look into it first thing in the morning," Cartwright said. "Time?"

"What time will your contest wrap up?" Escher asked.

"Last shooting contest will be held at eleven. Then lunch and the awards ceremony. The day should wrap up no later than two."

"Good," said Escher. "We can start at three-thirty."

"How many shooters can you handle?" Cartwright asked. "Not sure, but we could have maybe fifty people sign up."

"Way too many," said Escher, shaking his head. "The way I'm looking at this, I think five would be the max number. Five who are the most qualified."

"Five? How will you determine who's the most qualified? And what if your guy doesn't make the cut?"

"I'll determine who makes the cut. Mostly by their experience," Escher said. "And don't worry. Guy we're looking for is a professional. I know the type. He'll sign up just to challenge me mano-a-mano. And he'll be the last to sign up, so he gets my full attention."

CHAPTER 52

The next day we got up late and walked down to *Hole in the Wall Western Wear*. We each found a Stetson that fit. We stopped in at Macy's, but nothing there excited us. Figuring our Stetson's would suffice, we drove to the Fairgrounds and found Cartwright at the registration table.

"Well, hell," he said, giving us the once over. "Iffin' I didn't know any better, I'd say you gents were real cowboys." He laughed. "Except this here dude." He pointed at Escher. "Looks more like a Marine. Which ain't all bad." He laughed again and walked over to Escher, patting him on the back.

Escher had refused to dress in western gear. Instead, he wore an olive green skivvie shirt and desert camo pants. "Thought I'd dress up in my own persona. No one's gonna believe they're facing a Marine sniper if he shows up lookin' like a character outta *Blazing Saddles*."

"Good point," Cartwright said with a smile. Looking at the gathering crowds, he motioned us to follow him. About fifty yards from the registration area, he turned to Escher and said, "You'll be glad to hear I got permission from the CAS Board to hold what I'm calling *The Sniper Challenge*. Our last event on Sunday. They thought it was a great idea. Something our constituency would really enjoy. I didn't tell them our real motive."

Escher nodded. "So what are you going to tell the contestants? About the sniper they're challenging?"

"We have to tell them something about your service. So they know you are, or were, a real sniper. Hard to have

The Sniper Challenge without a real sniper." Cartwright said, with a soft chuckle. "Are you okay with that? I was thinking a short bio, maybe on the length of time you were in the Marines, medals earned, number of recorded kills. That kind of thing."

"Let me think about that, okay? I'm not real anxious to be a celebrity. Having people poring over my background. Can I use an alias?"

"Of course. We want to respect your privacy. How 'bout an alias *and* a small bio? Maybe your first deployment? Something to lend credibility?"

"My shooting would be my credibility," Escher said.

"I realize that. But I've got to give the audience something in advance."

Escher thought for a minute. "Okay. Short bio. Enough to give me credibility, but nothing to where they could find me on Google. And not my real name. Good enough?"

"Good enough," Cartwright said. "And before I forget." He reached into his pants pocket and pulled out three plastic clip-on nametags. "These are for you." He handed one to me, Rob and Vinnie. Had only our first names.

"Did you find a suitable range?" Escher asked.

"I hope," Cartwright replied. "It's a vacant field on the adjacent farm. Talked to the owner this morning. He thinks it will suit your purpose. Wanna go take a look? It's just down the road a piece."

"You bet," Escher said.

Cartwright commandeered a dune buggy from one of the vendors. Escher got in. "Room for one more," Cartwright said. "Mac! Why don't you come with us? I'm guessing you'll be helping Kyle set up, right?" I nodded, climbed in, and off we went.

We left the fairgrounds and followed a one-lane country road until we came to the farm. Turning onto the property, we followed a dirt path that took us to the field.

"We're going to start this at three thirty, correct?" Escher asked as we bumped along.

"Correct. I asked the rancher about that. He said as long as we're shooting away from his house, and we don't stay past dark, we're good to go."

"The way I have this set up in my mind," Escher said, "with five contestants, we should have this wrapped up by six. You okay with that?"

"Good by me," Cartwright said as he pulled up on a small rise and stopped.

Escher jumped off the dune buggy and looked around. "Close to perfect." He pulled out a small laser rangefinder. "The field measures 1720 meters. We'd shoot this way." He pointed left to right. "Targets would be down there. Shooting positions would be up on that small hill. Notice there's a slight drop from the shooters to the targets. Exactly what you'd want. An extra challenge. The sun's behind us that time of day, so at least we won't have that to contend with." He turned to Cartwright. "How many people do you expect to come watch?"

"Hard to say. Maybe three hundred. But that's just a *SWAG*."

"If you're expecting that many," Escher said, "I'd go with bleachers. Set them up behind the shooters. It'll cut down the possibility of anyone walking around unsupervised and getting their fool ass shot off."

"How many targets will you shoot at?" I asked.

"Let's see. Maybe fourteen targets total." he answered. "I'm seeing two shooting corridors." He pointed directly in front of him. "Corridor one. Eight targets. First one at nine hundred meters, and one each for every hundred meters thereafter out to sixteen hundred. Seeing as how they'll have to figure out their own dope on the fly, they'll be tested big time."

"Dope?" I asked.

"*Data on personal equipment*. Snipers are used to firing their own weapon. It's like their baby. They clean it, dress it, feed it with ammo, protect it from the elements, and even sleep with it. Using my rifle will be like making it with a strange woman. She's got all the same parts, but they just don't work exactly as the one you are used to."

Escher pointed to the swale on his right. "Corridor two. Notice there's more brush. We'll place six targets at varying distances in the brush, starting at four hundred meters. Shooters will need to acquire the target, shoot, eject; acquire, shoot, eject. Six times. They'll have two minutes."

"What will you use for targets?" I asked.

"I have them in my hotel room," Escher said. "Brought twenty with me. We'll bring them over and set them up Sunday. They're made out of tungsten carbide. Each one is about the size of a human torso. Not real heavy, but not light, either." He turned to Cartwright. "We'll have to get one of those dune buggies of yours to cart them around."

"No problem," Cartwright said. "I'll have one for you on Sunday. You have the next two days to figure out where you want to place them."

CHAPTER 53

On Sunday morning, Kincaid and Delgado worked the CAS event while Escher and I positioned the targets on the range. It took me an extra two hours to set up the wind flags exactly where Escher wanted. When I got back to the firing line, he had just finished setting up the spotter station.

"Most important piece of equipment on the battle-field," he said, pointing to the Leupold Mark-4 spotting scope. "After the contestants are chosen, I'll be the first to fire. You can be my spotter if you want, but you probably won't be of much help."

"Thanks a lot," I said.

"Seriously, on a real sniper team, the shooter is just the gun monkey. The spotter is the balls of the operation. He tells the shooter the target distance and wind direction. If the shot is missed, he tells the shooter where he missed and how to get back on target. Information like that. Critical information. Doubt you could tell me those things."

I laughed. "Sure. I could say stuff like … *a little low. Or … a smidgen off to the left.*"

"You'd be a great addition to any team," Escher said, also laughing. "In any case, I don't plan on missing."

"What happens if one of the shooters misses the target?" I asked.

"He gets another shot. In real life, shooters actually miss a fair amount of their first shots. In combat, you can miss that first one, but you better not miss the second. That's where the spotter comes in. You'll see a lot of missed first shots today. Mostly because the shooters don't have the dope for my rifle. The spotter's job is to get them back on track."

When he finished screwing the Leupold to the tripod, he said, "The targets, when they're hit, will ping loudly. That's why we're using the tungsten ones. No matter how far away they are, we should always be able to hear the hit. Sometimes, depending on the wind or other environmental factors, we may not hear it. That's another reason we have a spotter. The spotter will see the target move if hit, and will make the call. Every time the target is hit, spotter's job is to yell out *hit.*"

"Even though everyone heard the bullet hit the target?"

"Yes. Because it's only a hit if the spotter says it's hit. The spotter is also responsible for telling the windage. But don't worry, I'll handle that myself." He looked downrange. "Hey, wanna have a quick shooting contest? We got time."

"Against you?" I asked. "Hah."

"Wimp," he said, smiling. "I'll be blindfolded if that makes you feel better. But I think I could win blindfolded, too."

"And I'm supposed to rely on you to be a good spotter?"

He grinned again. "Coward." He passed me the gun. "You first."

Escher had fitted his Mk 21 with its long barrel for today's contest. It totally surprised me how light the weapon was. "Cartwright seemed pretty excited you had a Mk 21. Something new?"

"Well – this here weapon is one of the most modern in the arsenal. About two years old. But, truth is, guns are all the same. You point them. You shoot them."

"Sounds easy," I said as I lay on my stomach, resting the Mk on the bipod that Escher unfolded from the barrel.

I looked through the scope. "Son-of-a-bitch," I muttered. Looking back at Escher, I said, "This is a freakin' unreal scope, man. I feel I could reach out and touch that damn target."

"Yeah. I bought all this equipment myself. The best. Expensive, too, let me tell you. That reminds me – hand over the rifle for a few minutes. I want to give you a fighting chance in this contest. At least for the first target." He took it from me, then looked downrange through the scope. After turning the little knob on the side, he gave it back. "Here. That'll help."

"And what did you just do?"

"I had the BZO set for three hundred yards. Just reset it for nine hundred yards."

"Enough with the acronyms," I said. "Bee-zoh?"

"Sorry. Stands for *battlesight zero*. My scope is naturally set for a shot three hundred meters down range. Three hundred meters is my *zero*. You are about to shoot at a target nine hundred meters away. If I hadn't reset the *zero* setting, your shot would have come up about five hundred meters short. So low even your spotter wouldn't have seen it hit the ground."

"Thanks," I said, as I lay prone and brought the Mk up to my shoulder. "Okay, let's have silence here as I kill that target." I remembered sniper practice from my days at the Academy. All the midshipmen had to at least be familiar with the practice. Keep both eyes open. Acquire the target. Take a deep breath and slowly let it out. When your lungs are close to empty and you feel utterly relaxed, slowly squeeze the trigger. That's exactly what I did. I saw the target sway a little before I heard that satisfying *ping*.

"Hit," yelled Escher. "A little low and to the right. But not bad. You hit approximately where the eighth circle would be on a paper target."

"Must be the damn wind out there. Knocked my kick-ass shot off just a tad."

"The *eighth* circle is not a kill shot. Sorry about that." Escher said as he took the rifle from my hands.

"Hey," I said. "He didn't shoot back, did he?"

Escher looked at me, nodded his head and smiled. "Here, stand over there behind the scope," he said. "Tell me where I hit."

Escher lay prone and adjusted the scope. It seemed like forever before he fired. "Hit," I yelled. Before I could tell him where, his second shot rang out. I heard another *ping* and moved the scope up to see the next target in line. "Hit," I yelled again.

Escher stood up. "There's no wind out there, Mac. Your shot? You just missed."

CHAPTER 54

At noon, the shooting from the CAS event mercifully stopped. A few minutes later, Kincaid and Delgado showed up. I described to them what we had done and how we laid out the course.

An hour later, ten or so people came to the ranch to inquire about the contest and whether or not they would qualify. Escher sat in the stands with them. After listening to their qualifications, all but one left. Over the next half hour, thirty more individuals spoke with Escher. By now he had four of the five contestants chosen. Escher took a break and walked over. "Not looking good," he said. "I know in my gut none of them is our guy."

At three-ten another possible contestant showed up. A female. Escher nodded, shook her hand, looked over to us and shrugged. We had our five.

At three-twenty, Jimmy Cartwright, microphone in hand, started to address the crowd. I estimated it as somewhere between one hundred and one fifty. Not as many as expected, but still decent. He told them a made-up story about how Escher approached him asking if he thought the CAS group would like to try out their skills against a retired Marine sniper. "I checked his bona fides," he told the audience. "The guy checked out, so I invited him to join us. He's doing all this at his own expense, by the way. Pretty special, if you ask me."

Cartwright then introduced Escher under his chosen alias, Bob Lee Swagger. Most people present smiled, knowing Bob Lee was the name of the Marine in the movie *Sniper*, played by Mark Wahlberg.

Cartwright then read the short bio Escher provided. It said he had been in the Corps for ten years. His first deployment was with the 1st Battalion, 8th Marines in Beirut, Lebanon in 1983. While on a sniper mission the evening of October 23rd, a Hezbollah suicide bomber drove a truck full of explosives into the Marine barracks. "Killing two hundred and twenty of his comrades," said Cartwright into the microphone. An audible gasp was heard from the crowd, then applause. He waited until the applause quieted down, then said, "I'd like you to meet him."

Escher, dressed in desert cammies and a boonie cover, stood and waved.

~~~~

Cartwright introduced the five contestants. Two were former SEALs; one a former Marine sniper who lost a leg to an IED in Iraq in 2011; one a former Army Ranger, and the last, Maggie Kerns, a retired Marine Gunnery Sergeant. Under the rules, Escher would shoot first and then be the spotter for the others. He asked Gunny Sergeant Kerns to be his spotter.

Each contestant was allowed two shots to hit the target. A hit on the first shot scored a five. A hit after a miss scored a three. Escher led off.

Just as he laid flat and lined up the first target, I noticed movement behind me. I turned and saw a man carrying a military drag bag walk behind the stands and start to approach the firing line. I caught up with him just as the first shot rang out.

"Hit," yelled Gunny Kerns. I put up my hand to stop the man while at the same time putting a finger to my lips requesting silence. The man stopped and nodded as the second shot fired. By this time, sensing potential trouble, Delgado sauntered over to me.

"Hit" yelled Kerns again. The man started to whisper something, but I shook my head and mouthed *wait*. "Hit" Kerns yelled as the third shot found the target. I looked back at the man. He had put his drag bag down and was standing attentively watching Escher shoot.

"Hit." Four shots, four hits. On the next shot, the spotter remained silent. A miss. I counted the targets on my fingers. Escher had missed his first shot on the target at thirteen hundred meters. *Thirteen football fields*, I thought. *Nothing to feel bad about missing a shot that far*.

But Escher apparently didn't agree. "Wind," he yelled.

"Sorry," Kerns yelled back. "Southwest. Approximately six knots."

I could see Escher make a few adjustments on his scope and then fire. "Hit," she yelled. Escher also hit his next shot, but did a miss and hit on the second-to-last target.

After missing the target at sixteen hundred meters twice, he scowled, refilled his magazine, and turned his attention to the hidden targets in corridor two. He hit all six targets on his first shot. Took him one minute, forty seconds.

"Bob Lee Swagger's total score is sixty-one," Cartwright said to applause from both the stands and the five contestants. Escher stood, waved and relieved Kerns as spotter.

Delgado and I turned to the man. "Can we help you?" I said.

The man read our nametags. "Thomas and Vincent," he said, looking both of us in the eye as he spoke our names. "I brought my own rifle to this contest." He pointed to the drag bag at his feet. "I'm hoping I'd be allowed to shoot."

I didn't know what to say. My heart started to race. This was unfolding just as Escher had described. The shooter would come late and want a *mano a mano* shootout with him. Could I actually be face-to-face with our guy?

Delgado recognized my uneasiness and rescued me. "You'll have to ask the organizer," I heard him say, noticing he didn't mention Escher's name. And the use of the word *organizer* was brilliant. Like neither Delgado nor myself was part of Escher's entourage. "We've been told he won't be available until this particular contest is over. You can ask him then if you want. Not sure what he'll say."

"I'll wait," the man said.

CHAPTER 55

At the end of the day, Escher had simply out-shot all of them. His total score of sixty-one beat his closest competitor, Gunny Sergeant Christine Kerns, by five points.

The crowd had thinned out considerably by the time the contest ended. I joined Escher as he was talking to Gunny Kerns. He introduced me, and I shook her hand.

"I hate to interrupt," I said, "but I need to have a word with Bob Lee."

"Of course." She smiled politely. "I have to run anyway. Nice shooting with you, Bob."

"Likewise, Gunny," Escher replied. Turning to me, he said, "What's up?" I told him about the guy who asked to shoot with him. His eyes lit up. "See, I knew it. There *is* a God." He laughed. "Told you he'd show up. That him?" I nodded. "Invite him over."

I told the man that Escher would like to meet him. He picked up his drag bag and followed me back.

"Bob Lee," he said, laying his bag on the ground. "It's a pleasure to meet you. Loved your movie." He laughed, and offered his hand.

Escher shook it. "And you are?" he asked.

"Mosby," the man said. "Thaddeus Mosby. But everyone calls me Tad."

"To what do I owe the pleasure, Tad?"

"Just wanted to meet a fellow Marine sniper." He reached inside his collar and pulled out a leather cord. "A

HOG," he said, proudly displaying the hog tooth that hung from the cord.

"A 'Hunter of Gunmen,'" Escher said. "Me, too." He pulled out his own hog tooth.

"2nd Battalion; 1st Marines. Got shot up pretty bad at Fallujah in '04. Ended my career, unfortunately. At the time, I considered myself one of the best. But seeing you today, not so sure anymore." He pointed to his drag bag. "Brought my M40A5 with me," he said. "I'd like to try myself out against you. See if I've lost anything."

"You here for the CAS event?" Escher asked. "Or did you just happen to be in the neighborhood and hear about a sniper contest?"

Mosby laughed. "No. I'm a member of Cowboy Action Shooting," he replied. "Wouldn't have missed it for the world. Just heard yesterday about the Sniper Challenge, though. Couldn't resist."

"You're late," Escher said. "Sniper Challenge is officially over."

"Did that on purpose," Mosby said. "Hoping I could go up against just you. Not that the others weren't worthy, but you had the pedigree, and I like to test myself against the best. Just like Quantico. At sniper school. You know – one-on-one."

"Who do we check with to see if it would be okay to stay a little longer?" Escher asked me, carrying out the charade.

"I'm sure no one would mind," I said, playing along, "but I'll go check. In the meantime, why don't you two go to the firing line and get ready. Good thing we left the targets up."

I walked back and told Cartwright what had occurred. "Want me to *off* the son-of-a-bitch?" he asked. "I could do it right here and now. No witnesses."

I smiled. "I'd have to arrest you for homicide," I said.

"Yeah, sure. Then I'd have to *off* you, too." He laughed and then said, "Go back and tell them they have my permission, but they have to be out of here by seven thirty. That will make it sound official."

I returned to the firing line just as Escher was handing Mosby his rifle. "Never fired one of these," Mosby said. "Nice weapon. Not Marine issue, but it'll do in a pinch." He laughed, turning the rifle over in his hands. "This is the new special ops weapon, right? Came out a few years back? Mind if I fire off a few rounds?"

"Be my guest," Escher said.

Mosby went prone and brought the rifle up to his shoulder. Looking through the scope, he asked Escher, "BZO?"

"Nine hundred meters to the first target," Escher answered.

Mosby nodded, checked the scope, breathed slowly in and out, and fired off a round. *Ping.* He stood and gave the weapon back to Escher. "Nice rifle, but I think I'll use mine."

"You're good to go, gentlemen," I said. "Head guy gave you an hour."

"Plenty of time," Escher said. "Thanks, Mac."

Mosby looked at me, and then at my nametag. "Sorry," he said. "I've been calling you Thomas."

"No problem," I said. "Thomas is my name. So is Mac." I put out my hand. "I go by either. Nice to meet you."

CHAPTER 56

What the fuck! Mosby thought. *Mac? Tom Mac? Tom McGuire? The cop?*

"Likewise," he said, making sure he kept his voice even. He shook McGuire's hand. *I knew there was something going on here. Just knew it. This is a fucking set-up.*

He looked over at Escher and smiled. *Look who's caught in the trap now, you dumb shit. You blinked first. This is gonna be sweet.*

"Hey … Bob Lee. I know Tom's name. How 'bout you? What's your real name?"

Escher looked at him. "Bob Lee Swagger."

Mosby smiled and nodded. *Go ahead asshole. Be a dick. Your time is coming.* "Let's start shooting," he said, as he unsheathed his M40A5 and put two cartridges in the magazine. "Habit," he said when he noticed Escher looking at him oddly. "My baby here likes two in the box instead of five."

Escher nodded in acknowledgment. "What are you firing?" he asked.

"300 Win Mag. Best cartridge around, for my money," Mosby answered.

"We'll see," Escher said.

"I already hit the first target. Can I just move on to the second?"

"Suit yourself," Escher replied. "Want me to spot for you?"

"Nah. Let's go bareback." He lined up the shot and fired. *Ping.* "Got the second bullet already chambered.

Might as well just take the next target, okay?" Not waiting for a response, Mosby took a deep breath, let it out, and fired. *Ping.* "Your turn," he said, standing.

"Next target is at twelve hundred meters," Escher said. "Your A5 is going to start running short, I think. When the time comes, feel free to use my rifle. I have a longer barrel, plus I'm shooting the .338 Lapua Magnum. Better cartridge."

"We'll see," Mosby replied, looking back at Escher. Sparring with him. "As to *running short?* You're right. The *published* effective range for this rifle is one thousand meters. But I've made kills at twelve hundred. In Fallujah. Experience tells you that if you're over a thousand meters, hitting your target is dicey." *At the Bighorn, I took your friend out at five hundred. Nothing more than a nine-iron chip shot. But that was open range. Like here. When I come after you, Bob Lee, or whatever your name is, we'll be in Fallujah conditions. Urban. My environment. That's where I'm gonna take your ass down.*

"Still," Escher said, "my baby here has a listed effective range of sixteen hundred meters. Don't know about you, but personally I'd rather have an effective range of sixteen hundred than a thousand. No matter what environment."

Keep thinking that way, asshole, Mosby thought, but said, "To each his own. Tell you what. If I miss those shots, we'll chalk it up to the rifle, not me." He smiled.

Mosby hit the next target at twelve hundred yards, but missed the last two completely. Escher hit the last two, but it took him four shots.

"As of now, consider us even," Escher said. "We've got six more targets." He motioned to his right. "At varying distances, but none more than a thousand meters. Put your zero at three hundred meters. Have to make quick adjustments after that. Have to take them down in two minutes."

"Thanks," Mosby said. "Let's add to the challenge here. Let's pretend it's an urban environment. That you have to catch your own brass."

"Seems like a waste to me," Escher said.

"In Iraq we were taught to catch our own brass. Bad guys would pick them up and use them as part of their IEDs."

"No bad guys here."

"You never know," Mosby said with a forced smile. "In the CAS contests just now? We were shooting with lever action rifles. Man, those casings came flying out. According to the rules, you police your own brass. So there we were afterwards looking all over for our brass. Found all but one of mine." Mosby chuckled.

Hope they have fun with that one, he thought. *I can just hear 'em when I'm gone: "What's up with him catching his brass and finding all but one? Was that a reference to the Little Bighorn? Is he our shooter? Toying with us? Nah, can't be."*

"Up to you. I'm just going to acquire and shoot."

"I think I'll catch my brass and still beat your time."

Escher smiled. "You're on, Tad."

"I really don't like to put five in the box and one in the chamber," Mosby said. "But for our little contest, that's what I'll do. You first?"

"Sure," Escher said. He adjusted his BZO to three hundred meters. "Hey, Mac. Give us the *go* shout, and then time us, okay?"

"You got it," I said. "On the count of five."

Escher fired off shot one. *Ping.* Chambered the second round. Took his time. Fired. *Ping.* It went that way for all six of his shots.

"Time," Escher yelled.

"One minute, forty-eight seconds," I yelled back.

"Slow. Must be getting tired," Escher said with a chuckle.

"Ready, Tad?" I asked. Mosby nodded, his rifle tucked firmly into his shoulder. "On the count of five."

He fired. *Ping*. He worked the bolt action with his left hand, pulling the slide back slowly enough that he could pick the casing out with his index finger and thumb before it tumbled out. That sequence brought the heel of his right hand back far enough to catch the bolt, which he then slammed home. It took him no time to acquire the target and fire. *Ping*. He did it six times. And six times hit the target.

"Time," Mosby yelled.

"Incredible," I replied. "One minute, forty-eight seconds. You guys tied."

"I'd say Tad here won," said Escher, helping Mosby to his feet. "That was some damn fine shooting. And catching your brass? I'm impressed."

He's patronizing me, Mosby thought. *Fuck 'em. I'll be on McGuire the minute he lands in D.C.*

Mosby took Escher's hand and pulled himself up. Brushing off, he looked at Escher and thought – *then you'll be next.*

"Thanks, Bob Lee," Mosby said. "Appreciate it. I practiced that maneuver enough in Iraq to choke a horse. It became second nature to me."

"Winner of this Sniper Shootout was supposed to win a trophy. Give me your address. I'll have it made and sent to you. Something to show your grandchildren."

"I usually don't have much use for trophies," he said. "You from down here?"

"Nah," Escher said. "D.C. area."

"Damn. So am I," Mosby said. "Maybe we can get together sometime up there? I know some great ranges where we could shoot."

"Tell you what," Escher said. "Let's exchange phone numbers. When I get back home, I'll give you a call."

"Do that. I'll look forward to it." *More than you'll ever know,* he thought.

CHAPTER 57

"That's him," Escher said. "No doubt in my mind."

It was half an hour later and the four of us were riding back to the hotel. Escher came close to convincing me, but the cop in me still resisted. "Before we go running ourselves off a cliff," I said, "let me call Katelyn. See if the guy shows up on her networks."

"You still talking to her, dude?" Delgado asked.

"If I have to, I will. She's the only person I know that has all that data at her disposal."

Delgado shrugged. "Whatever, Bro."

"So let's assume this guy's our shooter?" Escher asked. "How do we play him?"

"Theoretically, he's probably mine to deal with now that he is the *numero uno* suspect in a homicide investigation. But I'll take suggestions."

"You open an investigation on him, he'll know he's been made," Escher said.

"But not by whom," I said.

"Don't kid yourself. He's seen you before. Planted one right next to your ear a few days ago, remember? May not have recognized you today as that guy from Montana, but as soon as he runs your name by his employers, he will. Conroy's pal."

"Shit. That means he'll make all of us," Delgado said.

"We have his phone number," I said. "Let me run it by Katelyn. If it's real, we'll get an address and pay him a visit."

"Thing that worries me most," Kincaid said to me from the back seat, "is that you might be in way over your head. Don't underestimate this guy. In your career as a police officer, you've never faced a guy like this. He's a pro. A hell of a shooter. And if he was in Fallujah, as he maintains, he learned his craft under the most stressful conditions imaginable."

"I hear you," I said. "But he's still my one and only suspect. I ain't giving him up."

"Don't worry about Mac, Rob," Delgado said. "I got his six. Ain't nuthin' happenin' to him on my watch."

"Since he deployed to Iraq in 2004," Kincaid said, "let me see if I can get a bead on him from my contacts in JSOC. Now that there's *another* professional sniper in the mix, this just became my op, too. If you don't mind," he said to Escher, "you and I can work that street."

"Not at all," Escher said. "I think we'd make a good team."

We got to the hotel and packed. I called Katelyn and asked if she could look up a Thaddeus Mosby in her database.

"I can do that," she said. "How fast would you need it? Won't be able to access it until tomorrow morning at the earliest."

"We'll be flying into D.C. tonight. Late tomorrow afternoon work?"

"Sure. Dinner?"

My head said *no*, but my heart, and other parts of me if I was being truthful, said *yes*. "Where and what time?"

CHAPTER 58

Cleburne, Texas

Mosby stayed in Cleburne that Sunday night, hitting the bars with his newfound cowboy friends. The next morning the chirping of his cell phone awakened him. He glanced at the clock beside the bed. Ten forty-five. If this hadn't been his business phone, he would have just let it ring and gone back to sleep.

The voice told him a package was waiting at the concierge desk. Then it disconnected. *Another one of these,* he thought. He called the desk and asked if that package could be delivered. It was a standard manila envelope addressed to him at the hotel. He ripped it open, and out fell a City Guide for San Antonio. *Who the hell comes up with shit like this?* He wondered. *It's that damn machine, I know it.* He leafed casually through the Guide and smiled. He hadn't expected to find any hidden messages, and he wasn't disappointed.

An hour later the hotel phone rang. The same disembodied voice told him to write down ten numbers in order. He did, and the phone disconnected. *More games,* he thought. *Let's see – numbers and a City Guide. What could they have in common? Duh! Page numbers, perhaps?*

He picked up the City Guide and compared the first number he had been given to the corresponding City Guide page. The phone number of one of the store ads on that page had been highlighted. He wrote that number down. He checked the second number and found the corresponding page. A restaurant ad on that page also had their phone number highlighted. Going back and forth in that manner, he ended up with a string of ten *10-digit* phone numbers. They were to act as his PINs whenever prompted. The original ten numbers used to look up the pages would be the phone number he was to call on his VOIP app.

A smile creased his lips as the machine asked him to identify himself. He did as instructed.

"Welcome, Tad. I am going to give you a new mission."

"We have to stop meeting like this," Mosby said. He couldn't help but mess with the machine's brain. It took a minute for it run through all the possibilities and then classify Mosby's response as nonsense.

"Please respond in the correct manner, Tad."

Again, Mosby smiled. Being scolded by a machine. *Who woulda thunk*? If he had told his eighth grade teacher such things would be happening in the not-too-distant future, Sister Bernard would have rapped his knuckles with a ruler for being a smart-ass.

"A new mission. Yes. Please proceed," Mosby responded, the penitent asking forgiveness.

"This is classified as urgent. You are to fly tomorrow to New York." The machine proceeded to give him the mission's parameters: the who, what, where, and why. Sometimes they gave him the why, sometimes not. This time it underscored the mission's importance. He was also given a time frame. Leaving nothing to chance.

Mosby wrote it all down. "What about the cop?" he asked. "I was supposed to do him next. Where does he now fit in my schedule?" While he waited for a reply, Mosby reflected on the hornet's nest that had been turned over by killing Conroy and his wife. *And now this.* A shiver went down his back. *Shouldn't be doing this damn many hits. One right after another.* He'd been at this long enough to know these kinds of reactive operations were *not* recipes for a long, jail-free, life.

"He is your next assignment. But maybe not your last."

Mosby hung up and sat back in the chair. *I'll take care of this mission,* he thought. *And then do McGuire and his Marine friend. But after that, I'm going on a long vacation. Someplace where hopefully I can't be found.*

CHAPTER 59

It was seven-thirty when I walked into the downtown D.C. restaurant that Katelyn had chosen. The dinner rush had not yet materialized, and I easily spotted her seated along the back wall. As I started toward her, my cell chirped. Rachel Skinner, Conroy's assistant-slash-girlfriend.

"Oh," she said, tripping over her words as they tumbled quickly out over the phone. "I'm so glad I got you. You'll never guess what happened."

"Whoa, slow down," I said. "Let's start over. Hi Rachel, it's me Tom McGuire. Sorry I didn't answer sooner. Didn't recognize the phone number."

She laughed. "Sorry, Thomas. I know it's you. Sorry for just rambling on without the proper preamble. Just excited, is all. And yes, this isn't my phone. I'm out with a girlfriend for dinner. I'm on her phone.

"Anyway, I had visitors this morning. They were looking for Matthew. I told them he wasn't here. They had French accents, said it was important they talked to him."

"What did you tell them?"

"I told them he had died. They were visibly shaken. The older of the two men said he had mailed Matthew the Custer papers. From France."

"I'll be damned," I said, dodging people and tables as I made my way toward Katelyn. "Did you get their names?"

"Yes, but they were reluctant. A father and son. Jonathan and James. They didn't give me their last names. They said they lived upstate. They didn't tell me where.

But listen to this – they left another carton that they say contains the remaining material pertaining to the family's secret. Carried it from France."

"You have the box with you now?"

"Not with me. It's at the house. I put them in the underground vault in the backyard. You remember where that is, don't you?"

"Yes," I replied. "I even remember the combination."

"Good. I left the package there so you could pick it up in case I'm not home. I wrote down their names on a piece of paper and left it in the box."

I finally reached Katelyn's table and sat. *Be off in a minute*, I mouthed. To Rachel, I said, "I could come up right away. Tonight if you want, and get them." Katelyn looked at me and frowned.

"Can you come up tomorrow morning, instead?" Rachel asked. "I have to be at the office tomorrow, so call when you get to New York and I'll meet you at my house."

"Absolutely." I smiled at Katelyn and gave her a thumbs-up. "I'll leave here at eight in the morning. Be there about noon. Will that work?"

"Perfect," she said. "Just call me when you arrive."

I hung up and looked at Katelyn, saying with all the neutrality I could muster, "Good to see you."

"Likewise," she responded with a smile. "Who was that?"

"Rachel Skinner," I said. "The woman Conroy had as an assistant. She was visited today by some guys from France." I felt bad, but I wasn't yet prepared to spill any secrets. "Matt had given them her name in case they ever visited the States and wanted to contact him. She was calling to let me know what they had said to her. That's all."

"And she wanted you to come to New York to tell you? She couldn't have told you over the phone?"

"She was out to dinner, and couldn't talk." I knew it was lame, but the best I could do on short notice. Katelyn wasn't having any of it.

"If you're going to New York to see her, I want to be there, too. I can't go in the morning, though."

"Okay. We can talk about it later." She was about to respond when thankfully the waitress interrupted. After ordering drinks, the conversation changed.

"Did you get your fill of shooting over the weekend?" Katelyn asked.

"Got my fill of shooting *and* fake cowboys," I said with a chuckle. Back to the small talk. Chewing around the dotted lines. Nothing serious and yet everything serious.

I gave her a quick summary of what we did. Then, with nothing else to say without getting into things personal, I went back to business. "And what did you find out about my friend Tad Mosby?" I asked.

"You've found yourself an exceptionally interesting person," she said. "First off, you already know about him being a Marine sniper." I nodded. "I figured you had. I'm also sure you've already made the connection that this guy might be your shooter."

"I have. But with the caveat that there's no evidence whatsoever to place him there." I paused, then said, "That's why I called you." Her mouth twitched and she cocked an eyebrow at me. *Who am I trying to kid*, I thought. *She's a freaking female. You can't fool 'em about relationships. She knows exactly why I called.* "I need as much information as I can get on the guy."

An all-too-knowing smile creased her lips. "Well, the most interesting thing about your Mr. Tad Mosby is," she said, "he's the grandson of George Hinrick."

"George Hinrick?" I said. "*The* George Hinrick?"

"The one and only." She laughed. "That obscenely wealthy fellow who gives bucketfuls of money to a variety of disparate political causes. The ordinary folk out there think he's a loon."

"How so?"

"Not sure if you'd know any of his causes," she said, "but he's known as a major funder for about every progressive cause known to man. And not just in this country."

"Out in California, where I come from, most of the people wouldn't consider that being a loon," I said with a chuckle.

"I know. I didn't mean to leave it like that. Turns out, if you dig a little deeper, you find that Hinrick is just as big a funder for conservative causes as he is for progressive ones. And, in the same way his progressive funding is for what most would call radical groups, his conservative funding goes mostly to the radicals' polar opposite. Hard right causes."

"Interesting," I said. "Is that well known? I've never heard of him being associated with conservative causes."

"It's not well known," she replied. "By design, we think. All his conservative donations are made through corporations he either owns or has interests in. They come from the corporate offices so his name never shows on the checks."

"He wants to keep it secret?" I said.

"It looks like it. The press could look into it if they had the stomach," Katelyn said, "but they don't. Since he is a huge contributor to the liberal media, our guess is he tells them not to look too hard into his finances. And the IRS surely knows. But no one says a word."

"Yeah. No side wants to derail the gravy train."

"Exactly," she replied. "And when he is directly asked, he spins it by saying he may not like them giving to conservative causes, but the Boards of his corporations make independent decisions as to who to fund."

"Sounds like bullshit to me," I said. "Where did he come from? Originally."

"The story is he's Romanian," she said. "Not much known about his father. He just shows up in the late twenties as managing director of the Romanian oil fields. Rumor had it that Hinrick was personal friends with Hitler."

"Romanian oil was the lifeblood of the German military all through World War II," I said. "If Hinrick's father controlled them, he would be a big time friend, maybe not of Hitler personally, but surely of the German General Staff."

"There's a counter story, though," Katelyn said. "Actually, more of a rumor than story. There's a guy named Hans Abrahamsohn who showed up in Romania at the end of World War I. From Germany. He was formerly the CEO of a company named Edmunds United Steel Trust. That's about all we know of him. He gets to be the manager of the oil fields. Then he disappears from the face of the earth. And Hinrick becomes general manager."

"Weird."

"Yes. One day Abrahamsohn is the manager of the oil field, and the next Hinrick is. Speculation has been that the Nazis murdered Abrahamsohn and his family. And Hinrick, who was a friend of Hitler's, took over the fields. But the fact is there are no records left from either Romania or Germany that corroborate any of this."

"But by '44, the good times came to an end," I said. "Germany had been so weakened that the Russians invaded Romania, kicked the crap out of the Germans and captured the oil fields. The country then got itself locked behind the Iron Curtain for over half a century. How did the Hinricks survive?"

"I'm impressed," Katelyn said. "Forgot you were a high school history teacher."

I smiled. Starting to feel comfortable again in her presence. But still wary. "What happened to the family?" I asked again.

"No one really knows because the only story we have is from Hinrick himself," Katelyn replied. "As he tells it, he was fifteen years old when the Russians conquered the country. They killed his mother and carted his father off to the Gulag. George contends he never saw or heard from him again."

"How did George supposedly make it out of there?"

"He says he hid in the home of a family named Hess. They were related to his mother's side of the family. Together, they all fled to Italy."

"Lucky to get out. The Soviets weren't all that gracious to those who tried to escape. Maybe the family knew the Russians as well?"

Katelyn nodded. "Some people have said that, yes. In any case, he made it. Lived in Venice for three years, then emigrated to the States. Enrolled in Columbia. Discovered he had a flair for finance. Manipulating currencies. That's how he made his fortune."

"And my guy Mosby is Hinrick's grandson?"

"Yeah. It's a convoluted story. From an early age, George had a checkered past with women. His first girlfriend got pregnant. A baby girl named Maria. Maria's birth certificate says 'father unknown.' Hinrick had juice even then.

"I've never read or heard any of this about Hinrick."

"No one but the CIA knows what I just told you, but again, even what we *know* are from documents no one can verify." Katelyn answered. "And now you know. And I'm sure Tad Mosby knows. Anyway, when Maria turned twenty, she marries James Mosby. In nineteen seventy-two they have a boy they name Thaddeus. James Mosby turns out to be a real loser. Is found one early morning in an alley in Harlem with his throat slit. The official police report classifies it as a drug hit."

"How old was Thaddeus when this happened?"

"Thirteen," Katelyn answered. "Three years later, he enlists in the Marine Corp."

"At sixteen?"

"His birth certificate had been altered," she said. "But get this? They knew it and let him in anyway."

"Shit!" I said. "What kind of friends does Hinrick have?"

"Powerful," Katelyn answered.

"And now," I said, "Tad's rather unusual skills can be used by those powerful people. By the way, does anyone know George Hinrick even has a grandson?"

"No official record anywhere. But it's clear to us that Tad knows."

"The stuff I've read about Hinrick is he has no children. Correct?"

"He's been officially married three times, and *officially* has no heirs."

"So who *is* Tad Mosby?"

"Guess there could be a question as to *who* he is. But we already know *what* he is. An efficient, military trained assassin."

CHAPTER 60

It was an awkward moment. Dinner had finished. And so, unfortunately, had our "business." As we left the booth, I reached for my wallet.

Katelyn grabbed my arm and shook her head. "The government will pay for this," she said. "You work for us now."

I smiled and nodded my head. "Thanks for all the information on Mosby and his grandfather," I said. "I know who I'll come to when I need help in the future."

"Where are you headed now?"

"I thought I'd go back to my hotel. I've got to be up early tomorrow. Long-ass drive. Otherwise I'd take you out on my dime for a drink. But maybe some other time."

The look on her face was either one of disappointment or annoyance. I couldn't tell. But finally she smiled and said, "I'd like to come with you to New York. Now that we're on the same side, we should be able to work together. I can go tomorrow, but not in the morning. Too short a notice. I can finish up pressing issues at work and be ready by, say, one."

I didn't know how to respond. My hesitation caused the smile to melt from her face.

I'd have loved her to come along, but didn't think I could handle four solid hours alone with her in a car. There were still far too many conflicting emotions roiling around inside me. I was having a hard time finding the balance between *I'd love to be friends with you, and maybe more,* and *you treated me like shit.*

My pride got the best of me. "I'm gonna have to go up in the morning. I told her I'd be there by mid-day, and I think I should keep to that schedule." I could see the hurt in her eyes. "I promise I'll call you when I get there. If she received any more material, I promise I won't read the material before I get back."

She looked at me with an expression that revealed nothing. "Suit yourself," she said. After paying the bill, she shook my hand, and left.

CHAPTER 61

After casing the neighborhood for anything that looked even remotely out of place, Tad Mosby parked in front of the house. The machine he had talked to the night before described it perfectly. Modest with cutesy little flowers lining the path to the front door. *No Marine lives here*, he thought, a smile crossing his lips. *This is chickville all the way.*

Mosby looked at his watch. Seven forty-five. It was a cloudy morning. The crisp, cold air made him wonder whether snow was on the way. *Unusual for this time of year in New York. Oh, well, at least I'll be indoors.* He rang the bell, hoping she hadn't already left for work. He didn't want to come back tonight. *I'll just get this over with,* he thought, *so I can get on with McGuire and Escher.*

It hadn't been hard unmasking Bob Lee Swagger, aka Kyle Escher. Not when Mosby could use his grandfather's name and contacts in the Department of Defense to give him access to confidential records. He had kept the short biography the CAS people published on Bob Lee Swagger. It hadn't been difficult for him to follow the paper trail. Marine sniper. 1st Battalion, 8th Marines. Beirut, Lebanon. 1983. Led right to Kyle Escher. Mosby had been impressed with what he found out. Escher had a distinguished career. *Didn't have the battle experience I did*, Mosby thought with pride, but he did have a number of confirmed combat kills. And he was a HOG. Hadn't lied about that. Mosby's take-away? *He's a worthy foe. Don't take the SOB for granted.*

Mosby heard footsteps approaching the door and straightened up. A large carton at his feet and a hand held electronic signature pad in his right hand made him look like your normal everyday UPS delivery man. The door opened as far as the internal chain would allow. The woman who peeked through saw Mosby, the package at his feet and the pad he held in his hand. What she didn't see was the Glock 17 stuffed in the hollow of his back, nor the Osprey suppressor in his front pant pocket.

Mosby looked down at his electronic pad. "Rachel Skinner?" he asked as if reading her name. She nodded. "Special delivery," he said, motioning with his head to the carton at his feet.

"Can you leave it? I'm just getting dressed to go to work."

"Sorry, ma'am. Signature and ID required." He held up his pad. He could see the look of resignation on her face.

"Okay. Hold on a minute," she said. "I'll be right back." She closed the door. Mosby picked up the carton and waited. A few moments later, the door opened wide.

"Where can I put this for you, ma'am. It's heavy. From France."

At the word *France*, Rachel Skinner beamed. "Put the package over there," she said in an excited voice.

Mosby did as she directed. As Skinner bent down to read the label, he pulled the Glock from the back of his pants.

"Wait," Skinner said, standing up and turning toward Mosby. "I thought you said … " That's as far as she got. Mosby clubbed her on the side of the head with the Glock. She went straight down without making a sound.

"Good hit, old man," Mosby said to himself in a congratulatory tone as he screwed the Osprey suppressor to the Glock's barrel.

CHAPTER 62

I'd been on the road close to three hours when it started to rain. *Good time for a pit stop*, I thought, pulling off at East Windsor and following the signs to Woodbridge Center Mall. A ride down memory lane. I'd been to this mall with Maureen years ago. Driving from New York to Philly. She'd been pregnant with TJ, and looking for a bathroom. Now it was my turn. Twenty-one years later.

After taking care of business, I spent the next half hour wandering around the mall. Last time I was here, Woodbridge Center Mall had been filled with families looking for ways to spend money on things they really didn't need. Now it was filled with teenage girls looking for ways to spend money on things they really didn't need, and teenage boys hangin' out looking at the girls. I smiled. Some things never change.

By the time I left the mall, the rain was coming down in sheets. Halfway to the expressway, I noticed a car behind me. Not directly behind me, but behind the one directly behind me. Funny how things stick in your memory. I remember walking through the mall lot and noticing a green Chevy parked a row over from me. Wouldn't have even registered seeing it if it hadn't been for the damaged front headlight. I took another quick look in my rearview mirror. Green Chevy. Damaged headlight. Coincidence? Could be. Probably just being paranoid what with all the snipers I'd been around these past few days. Then I flashed back on Delgado and how he had made Randolph following us. Being aware of your surroundings wasn't paranoid. Just smart. Assured a longer life. Hopefully.

Driving as normally as I could, I kept an eye on the Chevy. Still two cars back. Still driving normally as far as I could tell. Maybe just me being paranoid. *But let's make sure,* I thought, unholstering my P7 and holding it on my lap.

There was a light-controlled intersection about a quarter mile ahead. I put on my right-hand turn signal and looked in my rearview mirror. The green car's right-hand turn signal started to blink. I felt the adrenaline rush.

"Okay, asshole," I whispered to myself, "let's see how good you are."

I had a car in front of me. We were stopped for the red light. As soon as it turned green, he went forward across the intersection. I started to turn right, but then changed direction and went straight through. As luck would have it, the car directly behind me turned right, leaving the green Chevy with a decision to make. It followed me.

"Now what?" I asked myself rhetorically. But before I could formulate a plan, the green car sped up and started to pass me on the left. I raised my P7 and rested it on my left arm, pointing out the window. Prepared to shoot at the slightest provocation.

Didn't get that far. As the green car came up beside me, the passenger window came down. Katelyn motioned me to pull over.

I drove a block to a side street, pulled over and was out of the car before she came to a full stop.

"What the fuck?" I said as she rolled her window down. "What the hell are you doing here?" I holstered the gun.

"Hey," she said. "Take it easy."

"Take it easy? You're damn lucky I didn't blow your head off back there."

"You want to get in?" she asked. "Or stand in the rain and get soaked?"

I nodded. As I started to walk around her car, I noticed a small U-Haul van turn the corner. It drove straight toward us. I moved in front of her bumper and pulled the P-7.

The van stopped opposite me. The driver window came down. "Dude," Vinnie Delgado yelled out the opening. "You guys need any help?" I could do nothing but laugh out loud. A good way of releasing stored up tension.

"Might as well join us in the car, Vinnie," I said, nodding to Katelyn's vehicle while again holstering my weapon. "Hell, everyone else has."

I purposely sat in the back seat. She passed me a towel to dry my face and head. "I'm glad you didn't shoot me – or him for that matter," she said, her smile hypnotic, as usual. And having its desired effect upon me. I felt myself start to relax. A minute later Delgado let himself in the passenger side door.

"Looks like the cats and kittens are all here," he said, looking back at me with a toothy grin.

"I'm surprised as hell you are here," I said. "I know Kincaid said he'd have you come up and watch my back, but I didn't expect you here so soon."

"Yeah. Sorry for coming at you like that. I've been on the road since you talked to Kincaid. Only caught up with you five or six miles back. Followed you into the Mall parking lot. Thought I'd get to you there, but then I noticed the Divine Ms. K here. Surprised the hell out of me. Didn't know if you two were there to get a room, or to shoot each other." He laughed. Neither Katelyn nor I joined him. "Thought I'd lay low to see what unfolded." He turned around and looked at me. "Saw your clever little maneuver back there at the light. Making Katelyn have to decide what to do. I've seen people get killed doing that same maneuver, by the way, so I sped up. Unfortunately, I got stopped at the light. Glad you didn't shoot her."

"Gotta tell you, took great restraint when I didn't know it was her, and likewise took great restraint when I did know." They both turned to look at me. "Just kidding. Just kidding." Looking at her, I said, "Sorry for my initial reaction. Jumping on you like I did. But damn, lady ..." I left it there.

"I know. I apologize," she said. "I thought I could make it all the way to New York before you saw me. I wasn't prepared for what happened."

"Okay, let's forget it." I said. "We probably should get going. Don't want to make Rachel nervous wondering where the hell I am. I'm thinking you should leave your car here," I said to Katelyn. "No use having three of them in New York. You can go with Vinnie or me. Your choice."

"I came up following you. I'll stick with you if you don't mind." *Not in the least*, I thought. Turning to Vinnie, I said, "Before we roll, you got to tell me what's up with the U-Haul?"

"Dude. That's L-T all the way. I sure didn't want it. Those damn things shake like crazy and are noisy as hell. But he thought it would be good to have a non-descript vehicle up here in case we get in a jam. And there's nothing more nondescript than a freaking U-Haul bobtail."

As Delgado made a u-turn, Katelyn locked her car and got in mine.

"How long have you been following me?" I asked, as we followed Delgado to the expressway.

"From the beginning. I drove that car back to the restaurant last night. A clunker on loan from the AFF's fake garage." She laughed.

"Can I ask why you're bothering?"

"Sure," she said. "I watched the way you did a crime scene. You're good at it. I wanted to learn from you."

"Crime scene? First of all, you've never seen me work a crime scene. And the one in New York I screwed up royally. You were right to call me on it."

"I'll give you a pass on that," she said. "Everyone makes mistakes. I saw enough to know you are good at what you do. That's all I needed."

I had to admit this woman had a gift. She could beat you up; be an arrogant, backstabbing bitch, and then make you feel special. And I wasn't about to complain.

"Second," I said, "didn't you tell me you couldn't make it this morning?"

"Would it have made a difference to you if I said I could make it?"

"No," I said.

"QED," she said. "In any case, would you believe I called in sick?"

"Probably not," I said.

She laughed softly. "I didn't think you would. You have a lot to learn about me. I did call in sick, and I'm here. I wanted to be here. And I did what I had to do to be here."

I didn't quite know what to say to that. What I felt like doing was taking her in my arms and kissing her. Feel her warmth next to me. Instead, I took her hand and said, "Here's the deal. Do you think it's possible for us to put aside everything that happened between us? To start from square one and work together?"

"It's possible if we let it be possible," she said.

"Can we?"

"I can if you can," she said.

I pulled to the side of the road. Screw following Delgado. We could catch up later. I put my arm around Katelyn and pulled her to me. Our lips met over the car's console. Something I'd remember to point out if and when we ever had a discussion about who would lead our team.

"That's a good start," she said.

"A new start," I said with a hopeful smile.

The rain had lessened somewhat by the time we hit the expressway. I could see Delgado a quarter mile ahead of us. I sped up. "There's something I think I should tell you," she said. "To let you know I'm serious about entering into this relationship." She looked out the side window and went silent. I waited. "You know," she began, "when we were explaining the Dark Net to you and your colleagues?" I nodded. "And we said that we first heard Conroy's name mentioned in conversations being had by a *person of interest*?" I nodded again. "And we were monitoring that person of interest?" Another nod. "That person is George Hinrick."

"Son-of-a-bitch," I said, the connection with Mosby and Conroy's murder now crystal clear.

She went silent again, her hands clenched in her lap. I looked over at her. "There's more," she said, her voice suddenly icy. "I have a *personal* interest in George Hinrick." She took my hand into her lap and held it tightly between both of hers. "George Hinrick killed my father."

CHAPTER 63

"Dammit, Katelyn, you can't be serious," I said. "How'd you ever come to that conclusion?" She remained silent for nearly a minute. "You don't want to talk about it?"

"No. I do want to talk about it," she said. "Partly because it will help explain to you why I'm so interested in the Custer Papers."

"You can put Hinrick and Conroy together?" I said.

"I can, but let me start at the beginning. Matt Conroy first heard about the "Custer Secret" in the Dark Web. Not sure why he came to the Dark Web in the first place. Maybe because someone had told him about the *Custer is not Dead* sites. I can tell you from experience that there are many sites devoted to the rumor that Custer didn't die at the Little Bighorn. We supposed those sites were put up by the crazies who get hard-ons talking to each other about conspiracy theories. In any case, Conroy roamed around in there."

"How long ago are we talking about?" I interrupted.

"Over a year now," Katelyn said.

"Shit, Katelyn," I said. "You told me you broke into the Dark Web just a few months ago. Now you're telling me you broke their code over a year ago? Do you ever get tired of lying to people? To me?"

"Hey, just stop it, okay?" Her voice on the edge of anger. "I don't get tired of lying to people in general – that's what I have to do. But I'm tired of lying to you. That's why we're having this conversation, in case you haven't noticed. Be aware I'm dealing with national security issues here. I could go to jail because of what I just told you. What I'm about to tell you.

"In case you haven't realized it yet, we aren't, like, married. I still don't know you all that well, for God's sake. I'm putting a hell of a lot of trust in you. Going on straight female intuition." I didn't know what to say, so just kept silent. "You've been on juries, right?" She didn't wait for me to answer. "Don't you swear before a judge not to talk to anyone about the case, not even your spouse, until the case is decided and the verdict is in? If the damn government can fine you, and throw your ass in jail for divulging *to your wife* deliberations surrounding some idiot who stole a fucking car, what do you think they'd do to me if they found out I talked to you about the top secret shit I do?"

"Come on. Nobody pays any attention to that fucking courtroom deliberation nonsense," I said. "Hell, everyone knows you're going to talk about it at home, or to someone close to you."

"Not me. I actually pay attention to that *fucking* rule. Talk at home? I wouldn't know. I've never had *a home*." She stopped and put her hand out like a stop sign. That's exactly how she meant it, too.

"What say we don't rehash all this shit again, okay?" I nodded, admitting to myself she was right. "I misspoke back there," she continued. "Hinrick wasn't the one who actually shot my father. He ordered it done. How do I know that? Remember I told you about confronting Hassen Al I'man?"

"Of course."

"His words – *funding came mostly from the Infidels. From your own country. People high up. People who take no sides* – have haunted me ever since I heard them. Every day for the past nine years."

"*People high up?*" I said. "That narrows your list down to only about, say, one hundred thousand or so possibilities."

"That's exactly what I thought, too," she answered with a slight smile. "But something kept nagging at me. I was missing something. Had to be."

She stopped talking and turned to gaze out the side window, streaky with rain. I felt a shiver travel through her and into me.

"And?" I said, hoping to break the spell.

She looked over, staring at me with a blank expression. Then, slowly, life came back into her eyes. "Sorry," she said. "I zone out sometimes just thinking of that day." I reached over and held her hand. "I tried. I really tried," she said, "to make sense out of that senseless killing. And many more since then, too." I could see the beginning of tears forming in her eyes. "I just wasn't making any headway. I knew I wasn't going to find the person responsible. I decided to bag it all. To turn in my resignation to Langley. Do something less stressful with my life. Something that would turn off this – I don't know what you'd even call it. This pathological obsession that I had to find – a phantom.

"Then, one night in a deep sleep – I swear, a deep sleep. I heard a voice saying to me, *People high up. People who take no sides.* I woke instantly knowing what I had missed. The second sentence. It was the second sentence I had missed all these years. The years I had chased the *people high up* sentence, when I should have paid attention to the sentence that followed. *People who take no sides.*

"How did you get from there to Hinrick?" I asked.

"He'd been on our radar screen for a while. Nothing serious. Mostly curiosity. Because of all the crazy donations he hands out. We put it down as a sure sign of senility. Except we knew it wasn't senility because he'd done the same balancing act for years. Decades really. As far back as we had records."

"Before I lose something in the translation," I said, "let me recap. Hinrick is known for giving donations to left-wing groups, but it's not widely known that he also gives equal amounts to right-wing groups. Is that about right?"

"*He's the man who takes no sides*," Katelyn said.

"And that is what put you on to him?"

"Not at first. While it looked odd for him to be giving equally to both sides of the political divide, it certainly wasn't illegal. And except for stupidity, it certainly didn't hit a high enough threshold to open up a ticket on him."

"So what happened to lower the threshold?" I asked.

"September 11, 2001, happened. Iraq and Afghanistan happened. America lowered that threshold. In other words, took its head out of the sand. The rise of radical Islam had been happening for the past twenty or thirty years, but it took 9-11 for us to finally take it seriously. When we took it seriously, we started to notice things."

"Like?"

"Like he makes most of his money through his bank. A lot of funny things go on there. But he is so politically well-connected, no one wanted to touch him. Then there occurs a large international transfer of funds from his bank to another and then another. In the old days, no one would have noticed or even cared. In this case, though, the DHS noticed the amount of the second transfer was less than the original. Then another transfer was made. Again less than the original amount. And so on. Thirteen times. Ten banks, thirteen transfers. And each time the amount coming out was less than went in."

"And what is suspicious about that?" I asked.

"Most bank transfers on that scale are done *gratis*. But this transfer wasn't. It looked like the banks were actually charging a transfer fee. Smacked of a business transaction, not an ordinary transfer. Coupled with the fact that three of the banks double-dipped, the whole transfer looked a lot like money laundering. But what really caught our attention was the money ended up in a bank in Libya. A week later, next door neighbor Tunisia exploded. The Tunisian Revolution. The start of the so-called Arab Spring."

"Is that what got him put on your *person of interest* list?" I asked. "Seems kind of flimsy."

"I started going back through his banking records to see if this formed a pattern. It seemed he had been up to his eyeballs in funding the various factions in the Middle East. And on both sides of the divide. Strange bedfellows. Helping out both Hamas and the Jewish Defense Forces. But the one that hit me in the gut was his interest in Hezbollah. When my father was in Lebanon, he told me he convinced Hezbollah leadership to lay down their arms and work for peace. The last letter I got from him was one of hope. That at last cooler heads were taking over. Then he was assassinated. Hassen Al I'man said the money came from – *the man who takes no sides*. George Hinrick was a major player in funding Hezbollah."

"But why?" I said. "I don't understand why he would do that. Or even *how* he could do that?"

"I'm not sure, either. That's what I'm hoping to find in the Custer Papers."

CHAPTER 64

We were a mile from the George Washington Bridge when I looked at my watch. Since the rain and traffic worsened as we approached New York, the trip took longer than I anticipated. I called Rachel at home. No answer. I tried her office.

"I called her a number of times this morning," the receptionist told me. "But she didn't answer. Probably at a meeting with another attorney and just forgot to tell us. It happens. I'm sure she'll be back after lunch." She took my name and number and said she'd have Rachel call me.

Delgado was right behind me in the U-Haul. I called him. "Vinnie, Rachel doesn't answer her phone. Her office hasn't heard from her all morning. What do you think?"

"I think we better get our asses over to her place pronto, Bro."

Twenty-five minutes later the three of us were standing, guns drawn, on Rachel Skinner's doorstep ringing her bell. No response. I tried looking through the glass panes, but the curtains were too opaque.

"Stay here in case she answers," I said to Katelyn. "She could be in the bathroom sick, or something. Vinnie, follow me."

We ran down the driveway toward the back of the house. I stopped at the back door, remembering from the last time I was here that it opened into the kitchen. Vinnie ran to the cabin in the back, the one Rachel had built for Conroy. The one where she had installed the underground safe, and where she hopefully had stored the new delivery.

I pressed myself against the outside wall of the house and peeked around the corner. The back door had windows similar to those on the front door, but unlike the front door, these curtains were pulled back and kept open by ribbons fastened to the door frame. I inched forward and looked through the windows. What I saw made me sick. Rachel Skinner was tied to a chair in the middle of the room, her chin resting on her chest. Blood had matted the hair on the top of her head. More blood splattered the wall behind her.

I quickly ran to Vinnie. He had flattened out against the wall of the cabin. I could see the cabin's front door slightly ajar. When he looked my way, I pointed my finger at the kitchen, and then ran it across my throat. He raised his hand and nodded. I clenched my fist, signaling him to stay put until I got back. Again, he nodded.

I ran to the front of the house and told Katelyn to call 9-1-1 and get a police unit out here immediately. We had a homicide. I sprinted back to Vinnie.

I could tell from the condition of Rachel's body that Mosby – I caught myself simply assuming it had been him – killed her well over an hour ago. I figured the odds were small that he was still on the property. Still, Vinnie and I approached the cabin door cautiously. Whoever had to breach that door ran a big risk. In my business, we called door frames *vertical coffins*. The first person through the door had a high probability of being shot. And likely killed.

I told Vinnie I'd go in first. He nodded and switched places with me, kicking open the door. I barreled through, the P7 sweeping the room. No shot rang out. I took a deep breath, thanking God that I'd be walking and breathing for at least another day.

Mosby had been in this room looking for the box. The bed's mattress and box spring were propped up against the back wall, both sliced open with something sharp. Rachel's antique five-drawer dresser lay face down in the middle of the room, its back broken and pieces of its drawers scattered around it.

"We're golden," I told Delgado with a smile. "Mosby threw this shit all over the room in anger. This ..." my hand swept the room, "this was an act of frustration. He didn't find anything."

"Let's make sure, Bro," Vinnie said.

I heard sirens in the distance. "We got maybe five minutes before they're here, Vinnie. Let's rock and roll. Whatever you do, though, don't touch anything. Finger-prints at a murder scene never lead to anything good."

I carry a pair of latex gloves tucked into the wallet that holds my badge. I put them on and pulled back the Persian rug from the wall. I then began tapping the floor with my foot. It didn't take long to find the hollow space.

I knelt, found the finger-holds, and pulled. Just like be-fore, the four hardwood floor planks pulled up and re-vealed the steel safe below. I lifted it out, dialed the com-bination, and opened its top. Inside was the cardboard box Rachel received from her French visitors.

The sirens told me the police were less than two blocks away. Had to hurry. I gave the box to Vinnie and told him to put it in the U-Haul and cover it with one of their moving blankets. In the meantime, I cleaned the cab-in up as best I could.

I had the plastic gloves in my pocket and my SFPD badge high above my head as the two police cars bumped their way up Rachel's driveway.

CHAPTER 65

The three of us spent the next two hours with the cops and the medical examiner who arrived about thirty minutes after them. I showed my identification and explained that my association with Rachel Skinner was through a murder investigation being worked out of California. They were not pleased. Operating in someone else's territory without permission is a no-no. I apologized, making up a story about having just arrived last evening. That I had scheduled this appointment with Ms. Skinner a week ago. That I had every intention of stopping by their headquarters and introducing myself, but when I got here early and she never answered my calls, I got spooked. Total bullshit, of course, and they knew it. I'll give 'em kudos, though. They were classy enough to let it slide. Probably had something to do with Katelyn being here. No cop wants to look like a petty shit in the presence of a pretty woman. It also didn't hurt that I introduced her as an employee of the Central Intelligence Agency.

I told them only as much as I wanted them to know about Skinner and her association with Matt Conroy. The medical examiner told us that Rachel Skinner had been badly beaten before being shot. I bowed my head to her in silent admiration. She had proven to be one tough lady. Gave up her life protecting Matt and his secret. I felt badly not being able tell these cops about Rachel's heroism. Instead, I told them I had another appointment in upstate New York, also related to the murder case, and had to get going. I told them I'd for sure check in with them before I left the area.

Katelyn and I signed our crime scene statements and left the house. Even though the rain had stopped, the sky still remained heavy with low gray clouds stretching to the horizon. "Okay. Okay," she said excitedly as we got in our car. "Tell me what you got."

"A small box." I said. "Vinnie's got it in his truck. I never opened it. Never looked inside. Didn't want a certain someone to think she had to steal it to keep some bumbling police department Inspector from contaminating evidence." I looked over at her with a playful smile. She stuck her tongue out at me.

"Where can we go?" she asked. "I'd at least like to see what's in the box."

"Escher lives somewhere around here, doesn't he?" I said. "If he's home, we could go there."

"Yeah. Stony Brook," she said. "Hold on. I have his information on my phone. Let me call him." He answered. "We have the next installment of the Custer Papers," she told him. "Want to read 'em with us? We're in Manhasset."

"Well, hell yeah I want to read them," he replied. "You're about forty miles away. This time of day? Take you an hour and fifteen minutes to get here."

I asked Katelyn to call Delgado and tell him to follow us. We got on I-495 East and sixty-five minutes later were parking in Escher's driveway.

I carried the box into his house. He led the three of us back to his man cave. It still smelled of gun oil, but at least the heads of three trophy animals were gone. I was surprised.

"Have you seen this place before?" I asked Katelyn.

"Many times," she answered. "Kyle's graciously let me stay here whenever I needed a place to bunk down – or a place to shoot." She smiled.

"Katelyn," said Escher, "why not do us the pleasure of opening the carton?" He looked at me. "You don't mind, do you?" I shook my head.

Katelyn used her penknife to slit the carton open. Her eyes shone with excitement as she carefully reached in and removed the box's contents, placing them on Escher's desk. No one moved. The four of us gathered around and looked at the pile of papers in awe. I reached over Katelyn's left shoulder and took the modern envelope sitting on top of a stack of one hundred-year-old manuscripts.

"It's for me," I said, waving it in the air. "Rachel told me she'd put it in the box for safekeeping." I held it up to the light to ascertain the dimensions of the paper inside. Satisfied, I slit open the side of the envelope. "The names of the people who delivered the box," I said as I pulled the 5 x 7 note paper from its home. "Names: Jonathan and James," I said. "No last name given. Father and son. Dual citizens of the U.S. and Canada. Living in New York. Up near Albany. No phone number, and no address." I laid the paper on the desk. "Rachel told me they wouldn't give last names or any other information of worth. They were extraordinarily cautious and, she told me, scared."

"Conroy went to visit a person in France named Arnaud," Escher said. "Wonder if there's a connection? Hold on." He walked to his desk, pulled open the file drawer, and leafed through some hanging files. "Ah, here it is," he said with a satisfied sigh.

"These are notes I took from my first meeting with Conroy. In this room, actually." He quickly perused the file. "Hmmm. *Arnaud*." He bent closer and turned the paper to catch more light. "I can hardly read my own writing," he said, looking at his notes. "Okay, says here Arnaud owned a winery in France. Conroy visited him because he heard from a colleague that Arnaud was the great, great, grandson of Armstrong Custer." Escher paused and with a sideways grin, said, "That'll be General George

Armstrong Custer to the uninitiated. Okay, pushing on. Arnaud denied it vehemently, but Conroy didn't believe him. Thought he was covering up the truth."

Escher closed his notes and returned them to the drawer. "After all that's happened, I think Conroy had it right."

"Let's see why they wanted to kill him, shall we?" Katelyn said. She took a seat at the table and started leafing through the papers one page at a time. She waved us away when we tried to help her get through the pile. "Got to do this myself," she said.

"As long as you got anything good to drink, Bro, I think we should let her." Vinnie said.

"I do," Escher replied. "Let's go to the dining room down the hall and let this lady do her work in peace."

It was seven-and-a-half hours later, at fifteen minutes past midnight, when Katelyn called us to come back. While we seated ourselves, she straightened up the papers in front of her, leaned back in the chair, and closed her eyes.

"I've figured it out," she said.

CHAPTER 66

"Phone call, sir," the butler said as he placed his hand on the man's bony shoulder and gave it a light shake. George Hinrick's eyes blinked open, and his head jerked forward with a spasmodic tremor. It took more than a few seconds before the butler saw the light of recognition settle into the old man's eyes.

"Wha – what is it?" he said, accepting the butler's handkerchief to dab away the spittle that had formed on his lips.

"The phone, sir. The one in the back study." That caught Hinrick's full attention. He nodded and pushed his skinny frame up and out of the chair, squinting against the glare of the late afternoon sun as it reflected off the mirror on the far wall. Once standing, he tucked in his shirt and attempted to smooth the wrinkles in his pants. George Hinrick made it a priority to be neatly dressed when conducting business. And he knew this was business because it came in on the secure line. Hinrick steadied himself, reached for his three-footed cane, and trudged his way to the study.

Walking the length of his twelve-thousand-square-foot house took him the better part of twenty minutes. The people with access to this number would gladly allow him that time, and more if necessary. His eighty-five years on this earth demanded that kind of courtesy. That plus the fact that he was the twenty-eighth richest man in the world.

"Good afternoon, Mr. Hinrick," the voice said. "Hope I didn't disturb you."

"Not at all, Joe." Hinrick recognized the voice of Joseph Parkman, the Under Secretary of the Department of Defense. "Walked from up near the front of the house. Thanks for waiting."

"I never mind waiting for you, Mr. Hinrick," replied Parkman. "You've got such great music playing through the phone. I don't think in all the times I've called I've ever heard the same song twice. At least back-to-back. And I've been on hold, as you know, almost as long as God's been alive." Hinrick chuckled.

He liked Joe Parkman. Pleasant fellow. Followed orders. Bought and paid for by one of his corporations. One thing Hinrick had learned early on about governments. There was no position that couldn't be purchased. Fortunately for him, to most corporate types bidding for beltway influence, the Under Secretary of Defense was just a low level cabinet position. Hardly on anyone's radar screen. But to Hinrick, that particular cabinet position was numero uno on his list. And for good reason.

The Under Secretary of Defense was the only cabinet officer that interfaced directly with both the CIA and NSA.

"What did I do to deserve this call, Joe?" Hinrick asked. "You don't need more money, do you?"

"No, nothing like that, Mr. Hinrick," Parkman said with a laugh. "Wanted to bring you up to speed on a few outstanding issues. I'd like to know how you want me to handle them." Parkman paused briefly, giving Hinrick a chance to respond. He didn't, so Parkman continued. "First of all, then, Tad Mosby didn't get the papers."

"Oh, shit. Don't tell me that Conroy's girlfriend met with the CIA?"

"Nothing that bad," Parkman said. "Tad took care of the girl, but he didn't find the papers."

"You're sure she had them?"

"As you know, sir," Parkman said, "we had a tap on that woman's phone. Yesterday she received a call from those French people who dropped off our radar screen. We traced the call to a pay phone outside a 7-11 in Albany. Of course, they were gone by the time we sent a crew there. They told Ms. Skinner they had the rest of the Custer files and were going to deliver them to her. They thought it would be better if she had them. We got a team mobilized as soon as we could. But we were either too late, or they never showed up. We don't know for sure which. But I trust Mosby. He's an excellent interrogator. No matter what he did to her, she didn't break. Didn't know anything. I take that as a sure sign those men never arrived."

"Dammit, Joe," Hinrick said. "You know I don't like unanswered questions. We can't afford to have those papers in the wrong hands. Being read by the wrong people."

"That SF cop must have thought she either had them or at least expected them," Parkman said. "He went up there this morning. And the Murray woman followed him. They left her car in a town along the way called East Windsor. It's in New Jersey."

"Don't patronize me, Joe. I know where East Windsor is. Why would she meet him there?"

"I have no idea. We only found her because we have a tracking device on the car she drives. She left this morning a little after eight. We figured maybe she made arrangements to meet Rachel Skinner. But then the car stopped around eleven in East Windsor. Just sat there on a side street off Woodbridge Center Drive for over three hours. We thought maybe something had happened to her, so we asked the local police department for assistance. They checked it out and reported back that the car looked abandoned. No sign of foul play. We asked if they would check with police departments in the wider area. See if her name surfaced anywhere. Got a hit from the Manhasset Sheriff's Department. Murray and McGuire called in a homicide at one-ten today. The Skinner woman."

"Where are they now? On their way back?" Hinrick asked.

"No. They're now material witnesses in a homicide investigation. Witnesses aren't allowed out-of-area for at least twenty-four hours. Murray could have pulled out her CIA identification and claimed immunity, which she didn't or I'd have been told. So they're still there."

"So where is *there*?" Hinrick asked.

"They told the Manhasset sheriff they would be staying tonight at the house of a fellow named Kyle Escher," Parkman replied. "Escher, as luck would have it, is one of our contract employees. Lives in Stony Brook."

"Damn," Hinrick said. "That's only an hour from here. Maybe I should have someone pay them a visit."

"Probably not a good idea, sir. If they all got whacked, there would be way too many questions asked. We wouldn't be able to contain the firestorm. I have a better idea. The Murray woman will have to pick up her car tomorrow and get back to work. The twenty-four-hour time limit put on by the Manhasset police runs out at three tomorrow. I'm guessing that McGuire and Escher will drive her back to her car and then head back to Stony Brook while she drives back to D.C."

"And what time would that be?" asked Hinrick.

"I'm guessing no later than two," Parkman answered. "I'm thinking we can get a police unit to pull her over for speeding or something. While looking in the car, they just might find a kilo of cocaine under the front seat. They'd arrest her for possession and impound the car. They could search for the papers while the car is impounded. If she has them, by the time she's released, they will no longer be in her possession. Never to be seen or heard from again. If she doesn't, we hold her overnight while we go after McGuire and Escher."

"That's brilliant, Joe," Hinrick said. "Let me take care of that."

"Are you sure, sir? We have the resources."

"No. That's an operation way below your pay-grade. I can get it done. No worries."

"Up to you, Mr. Hinrick. Make contact if you change your mind or need anything else."

As soon as they disconnected, Hinrick called a number in Chicago on the secure line. "Alex, this is George. Need you to do me a favor."

CHAPTER 67

"*Got it figured out* has to be the best four words in the English language," I said as the three of us gathered around Katelyn's chair, careful not to disturb the piles of newspapers and loose letters stacked in piles around it. I sat, starting to feel the stress and fatigue of the past eighteen hours melt away.

"I think I have your motive," she said to me with a satisfied smile.

"Does that deserve a drink first?" Escher asked. "Or should we imbibe after you've told us?"

"Better have it now," Katelyn replied. "We may all be asleep before I finish."

"Done," said Escher, walking to the bar at the back of his man cave and pulling down a silk lined box. "Johnny Walker Blue," he announced, with a wide grin. "Unopened. Been savin' it for just such a moment." He gently took the bottle into his hands, holding it like he would a newborn baby. "Who will join me?"

Katelyn raised her hand. "You sold me," she said. "Just ice."

"Well, of course, just ice, darlin'," Escher responded. "You think I'm a troglodyte?" He looked over at me.

"Count me in, too," I said.

"And you, Vinnie?" Escher asked.

"Dude. Are you kidding me? Hell, yeah, I want one. Oh, with just ice."

"Cute," Escher said with a smirk.

While he was pouring the drinks, Katelyn leaned her head back in the chair, closed her eyes and rubbed them with her knuckles. I understood. We were all running on fumes.

Escher placed the scotch on the table next to her, served Vinnie and me, then raised his glass in tribute to Katelyn's hoped-for breakthrough. "The floor's all yours," he said with a deep bow.

"Thank you," she said, raising her glass back at him "I know we're all tired, but stay with me, okay? This might take a while."

And take a while it did.

"Remember last week when we were at Gaithersburg?" She looked over at me and smiled. A peace offering. I smiled back my acceptance. "I said they were using Custer as a guinea pig? That wasn't my assessment. That was Custer's. He had figured it out. This is his proof." She swept her arms over the stacked piles before her.

"Custer's death was going to prove, one way or another, whether determined and ruthless men could manipulate world events. And through that manipulation, become wealthy on a scale never before imagined."

CHAPTER 68

A lex Rhodes had been a force in Chicago politics since he was a young man making his bones on Mayor Richard M. Daley's staff back in the late eighties. The *Machine*, they called it. A hold-over from the days of Mayor Richard J. Daley, Richard M's father. And a Machine it was. Well oiled and perfectly ordered.

Things were so much better back then, Rhodes thought as he looked out at Lake Michigan from his fiftieth floor condo in Lake Point Tower. *The pay's a hell of a lot better nowadays, but everything is just too damn complicated.*

Rhodes' career spanned close to thirty years, culminating in becoming the personal advisor to the last president, also a man spawned from the Daley Machine. It was in those advisory years that he met George Hinrick. When Rhodes' friend termed out, Hinrick came knocking. He needed someone he could count on with influence in the wider political community. Now Alex Rhodes worked solely for him.

Rhodes picked up the phone and called a number in Albany, New York. "Governor's Office," a cheerful female voice answered.

"Hi Dianne. Alex Rhodes. I've missed you. I'll bet you're still as beautiful as you are cheerful."

"Hi Alex. You've been hanging around that Daley crowd again," she said with a laugh. "The Blarney is just bubbling forth from your mouth. What can I do for you?" Before he could answer, she said, "The Governor isn't here, by the way. At a highway ribbon-cutting over in Syracuse."

"Thanks, Dianne. I'm not looking for the Governor. Can you connect me with Billy Donovan? I need a quick word with him."

"You've got another one of those, huh? Hold on. I'll ring his office.

One of those was the euphemism for *you got a problem that needs fixing. Back channel.* "Alex, you old horse's ass," Billy Donovan said. "It's been a while. What can I do you out of?"

The two bullshitted a few minutes about old times, then Rhodes told Donovan what he needed. "East Windsor is actually in New Jersey. But not to worry. I'll call a friend in Trenton, and ..."

"I don't think you understand, Billy. We don't want real cops. We need stand-ins. My boss wants to meet this woman."

"Shit, Alex," Donovan said. "We can't get ourselves in anything illegal. If we get caught ..."

"When have I ever let you down, Billy? You're going to get a large payday for this simple job. Hire the contractors for whatever the going rate is. Make sure they have official police uniforms. The person I represent will pay whatever it takes. You bring this off with no complications, I'm authorized to offer you fifty large."

"Okay," he said hesitantly. "I'm sure you could have gotten it done through someone else, so I should take this as a compliment. That you trust me to do it."

"I know you can do it, Billy. Or I wouldn't have called in the first place." *And trust you, you dumb fart?* Rhodes thought. *Has nothing to do with trust. After today, we'll own your ass, Billy Donovan. From today forward, you'll be our little bitch.*

"Where's the car located?" Donovan asked. "What time do you want my people there? And what's her final destination?"

Rhodes looked at his notes from Hinrick. He gave Donovan the car's present location, its plate number in case she got there early and took off before the contractors arrived, and the place where they wanted her and her vehicle dropped off. "Have your people come at noon. We think she'll be there sometime after that. Maybe one o'clock. But no later. Be sure to let her get on the highway before they pull her over. Don't want to do this in town."

"It will get done," said Donovan.

CHAPTER 69

We awakened early the next morning and gathered at Escher's dining room table as he served us coffee and put out cereal and milk. Delgado and I sat next to each other reading the Custer material that Katelyn had already put in plastic sleeves. She was on the phone talking to her AFF people.

"Hey, Bro. What the hell is Esperanto?" he asked, passing me one of the sleeves. "In fact, tell me what this whole damn sentence means?" He leaned over and pointed to a particular passage from the Custer Papers – *The first Esperanto worldwide congress was held in Neutral Moresnet in 1908. I attended.*

"Your lucky day," I said with a smile. My mind wandered back to my youth. Dad telling me about writers and other artists who spoke in a secret and private language. I was ten years old. God – a gazillion years ago. But I remembered. *Esperanto.* Just the name mesmerized me. As a kid I thought how cool it would be to learn it. "It's a language." I told Delgado. "One that's made up. There are people today who speak it, but not many. It's not really secret. Exclusive would be a better word. Like the Pig Latin we-kay oosed-kay as ids-kay."

Delgado laughed. "I can relate," he said. "In grade school, Pig Latin was an *exclusive* language. You're looking at the third-grade champ."

"Esperanto's a little more complicated than Pig Latin," Katelyn whispered over to us, her cell cupped in her hand, obviously on hold and obviously eavesdropping. "I'm pretty sure it's classified as a legitimate language. But one *somebody* made up." She smiled.

"See," I said. "Corroborated by our resident expert." I winked at her.

"Okay, resident expert. Explain to me what the hell is *Neutral Moresnet?*"

I looked at Katelyn, pointing at myself in a *do you want me to answer that question*. She nodded, then went back to her phone call.

"This is the history teacher in me speaking," I said. "Otherwise I wouldn't have known the answer either." I took a sip of coffee and said *yes* when Escher offered me more. "Neutral Moresnet was this small spit of land – one square mile small – stuffed between Belgium and Germany. We're talking somewhere in the early 1800s. Both Germany and Belgium claimed it as theirs. But instead of going to war over such an inconsequential piece of property, they made it a neutral country. It was the joke of the ages, but it lasted well over a hundred years. Mostly because citizens of Neutral Moresnet were exempt from military service, and they didn't want to lose that perk."

"God, can you imagine the kind of wusses who lived there?" Delgado said.

"The other claim-to-fame Neutral Moresnet had is mentioned in this paper." I pointed to the section again. A little below where Delgado had finished. "The Esperantists wanted to make Esperanto the official language of Neutral Moresnet."

"Shit, dude. Why the hell would they want that?"

"According to Custer, every arms merchant and manufacturer in the world attended their conference." Katelyn interrupted, having hung up and now fully engaged in our conversation. "In fact, the armament industry *sponsored* the damn thing. They all spoke Esperanto. Custer got in because he spoke Esperanto. He says in this journal that he personally overheard them, speaking in Esperanto, conspiring to work together as business partners to keep prices high while they played the individual countries against one another."

Delgado turned to me. "Do you really believe all this conspiracy nonsense?"

"I'm beginning to," I said.

~~~~

Later that morning, we carefully repacked all the Custer material in the cartons and loaded them into Delgado's U-Haul. The plan was for me to stay the night with Escher to work out a strategy for dealing with Mosby. Delgado would take Katelyn to her car on his way back to D.C., but she insisted I drive her. How could I refuse? With a roll of his eyes, Delgado got into the U-Haul. Escher said his goodbye to Katelyn, and we all drove away.

Just before the George Washington Bridge, my cell rang. Vinnie telling me he had to stop for gas. That he'd see me back in D.C. tomorrow or the next day.

I turned to Katelyn. "We're all alone," I said with a smile.

"Damn," she said, with a laugh. "I thought he'd never leave." Reaching over she took my hand. I never got it back until I let her out an hour later in East Windsor.

We kissed, said our expected *I'll miss you* goodbyes, and she drove away. I put the car in gear and followed her to the expressway. She waved and headed south. I waved back and headed north.

No doubt I had fallen down the proverbial rabbit hole over this woman. Pleasurable and scary at the same time. Pleasurable because the actual fall had been fun. Scary because the landing was still unknown. Might be nothing but pain and sorrow. *Screw it,* I thought as I entered the highway back to Escher's. *The fall has been delightful. I'll deal with the landing if and when it happens.*

Fifteen minutes later my cell chirped. It was Delgado. "Where are you, dude?" he asked.

I looked around, getting my bearings. "About twenty minutes south of the GW Bridge. Why?"

"At next exit, turn around," he said. "I'll wait for you at the Chevron station at the bottom of exit 53A. They have Katelyn."

CHAPTER 70

Katelyn awoke in the back of the van, a hood over her head and her hands and feet bound. Every time the van turned, she tumbled from one side to the other. She thought of the "rough ride" the cops supposedly gave criminals in the back of their vans. If it was anything close to what she was experiencing, the criminals had a legitimate bitch.

She waited for her mind to un-fog before she started to process what had happened. She had no idea how long she'd been out. Not more than ten minutes from waving goodbye to McGuire and entering the highway, a patrol car pulled in behind her, lights flashing and siren wailing. She instinctively looked down at her speedometer. Well within the speed limit, she remembered noting to herself.

Dutifully pulling over, she rolled down her window, not bothering to turn off the engine. Both cops got out of their cruiser and approached her car, one on the driver's side, the other stopping at the passenger side rear light. Classic cop procedure when dealing with a suspected violent encounter. She saw in her side mirror that he had his gun drawn. They weren't playing around. She started to worry.

The cop on her side asked her to get out of the car. "What's this all about?" she asked, opening her door and stepping out.

"Please step behind our vehicle, ma'am," pointing to the patrol car's back door.

"I'm not moving until you tell me what this is all about. I have my license in the car. And my ID. I'm a federal employee."

By that time, the second officer had joined them, standing behind her. "Please do as we ask. Stand over by our car." He went to grab her by the elbow, but she yanked it away. As she prepared herself to fight, she felt the searing jolt of the taser in her back, and simply collapsed. Vaguely aware of being placed in the back seat of their car, her hands were bound by plasticuffs. She also felt the pin prick of the needle into her upper arm. That was all she remembered until waking up in the back of the van.

Those ten months of training in the Adirondacks plus the twice-yearly refresher courses started to kick in. *Focus*, she told herself. First a physical assessment. All over ache – check. No broken bones – check. Fingers and toes working reasonably well – check. She twisted her arms and legs against the cuffs. Bindings on hands and feet secure – check.

The van made a series of turns, slow enough this time not to cause her to roll around in the back. A few minutes later it stopped. The back doors opened. Someone grabbed her under her arms, pulled her out and forced her to stand. Four hands, two on each side, held her upright. *My police captors are still with me*, she thought. Be aware of your surroundings, her instructors had drilled into her over the years. She couldn't see the ground because the hood over her head had a drawstring that closed around her throat. But she was standing on a hard surface. It wasn't sticky, so not asphalt. Probably cement. Her hands felt a hot breeze. *Still afternoon*, she thought. Loud noises around her. Not right next to her, but in the distance. *Be aware of your surroundings.* She listened for a few seconds more. *Ah, shit*, she thought. *This is not good. We're at an airport.*

Teterboro? Probably not. Katelyn was no stranger to aircraft. She had a pilot's license since she was thirteen years old. Her dad insisted on it. The CIA was so impressed, they let her co-pilot some of their aircraft from time to time. From long experience, she knew this was a small private airport. Planes flying in and out of here were all piston, all single engine. But she was in Jersey. She hadn't been in the van long enough to be anywhere else.

The sudden *whoop-whoop-whoop* of blades turning startled her. *A helicopter*, she thought, breathing a sigh of relief. At least they weren't going far. When she first thought airport, her mind conjured up being taken to Iran or Syria.

Just as the pressure of the blades' downdraft threatened to knock her over, she was picked up bodily and deposited on the helicopter's metal cabin floor. From there, another pair of hands dragged her to the back and lifted her into a seat. She heard other seats near her being occupied and seat belts being snapped shut.

Five minutes later they were airborne.

CHAPTER 71

"I was in the far lane and almost past," Delgado said, "when I noticed her car leaving the highway – a highway patrol car with their lights flashing on her tail. If they hadn't had them on, I'd never have seen her car. I couldn't swerve in time, so I got off at the next exit and circled back. Dude, the next exit on this damn highway is five miles down. Took me close to fifteen minutes to get back here. By the time I did, no car. I'm really sorry, Mac."

"Not your fault, Vinnie," I replied. "You said on the phone *they have Katelyn*. How'd you know that?"

"Before I called you, I called her. No answer," he said, "Then I called the highway patrol. The squad car I saw wasn't theirs. So I called every damn police department and sheriff's office within a fifty-mile radius. None of their personnel reported any activity on this highway in either direction for the past five hours."

"Son-of-a-bitch," I shouted, pounding my hand on the dash of the U-Haul hard enough to cause a small tear in the rubberized fabric. "Her car's gone, so they took it with them." I was in full police mode now. "I'd bet anything they've already ditched it. Ditto the cop car. Those two vehicles have to be someplace close. Question is where?"

"Hate to bring this up, Mac," Delgado said, "but this could have been a straight hit. Maybe no change of vehicles necessary."

"Yeah. I've thought of that," I replied, keeping my emotions in check. "If it were nothing but a hit, they could have done it right there on the highway. Would have been some time before anyone stopped to check out a car parked on the side of a highway. Even if the hit took place away from here, they'd still have to dump the police car."

"Unless it was a police hit."

"Yeah, you're right. But my instincts, as well as my heart, say no. Both those cars won't be far. I'll guarantee you."

"Maybe I should look up some local storage units. Places with units big enough to store cars."

"Good idea. While you're doing that, I'll call Sullivan at AFF. Katelyn told me the car she drove up here belonged to them. Maybe they can trace it."

Five minutes later I told Vinnie to hang up. "Katelyn's car is two and a half miles from here."

Sullivan's CIA tracking device took us to the Auto Auction Nation parking lot. Had to be five or six hundred automobiles in this lot waiting to be auctioned. We found the police car first. Thirty minutes later we found Katelyn's.

While I talked a good game with Vinnie, fear and trepidation gripped me as I approached her car. I prayed to God her body wasn't in the back seat or stuffed in the trunk. I purposely let Delgado take the lead. As he moved around the car, I could tell by his body language that God had heard my prayer.

We called the local police department and stayed while they dusted both cars for prints. Nothing. Both had been wiped clean.

It was seven o'clock when the police finally released us. Vinnie called Kincaid and gave him a report on what had transpired. At the same time, I received a call from Escher asking if we wanted to spend the night at his place. I declined, saying I'd like to get back to D.C. tonight so we could use AFF's database to help in the search. He told me he would drive down in the morning and meet us at AFF headquarters about noon.

"I'm bringing my safari van," he said. "It's fully equipped."

"For what?" I asked.

"For hunting," he replied.

CHAPTER 72

Mosby drove around the corner and saw the balloons on the mailbox gently moving in the light breeze. He smiled. Right where Facebook Events said they'd be. It made the clown costume he wore appropriate – making him virtually invisible. Good thing, too. This particular clown was packing a HK 9mmViper in his baggy pants.

Mosby pulled to the side of the road and rolled down his window. Even at this distance, he could hear the laughter of the children at the party. It was a sound he'd always enjoyed. *Should have been a teacher*, he mused. Then he felt the HK in his pocket and smiled. *Ummm. Maybe not.*

The laughter died soon thereafter, however, drowned out by the sound of a live band playing *Sweet Child O' Mine* by Guns N' Roses. *Perfect timing*, Mosby thought. His own *cover* band. Congressman Perry lived five houses down. The noise generated by the band would *cover* whatever might occur in the next half hour at the Congressman's home.

He pulled into Perry's driveway, knowing from Google Earth that if you took the driveway all the way to the back of the house, his car couldn't be seen from the street. He did exactly that. As he walked to the back door, it opened. A woman stood there. Young. Good looking, though in a cheap sort of way. White short-shorts and a blue sleeveless top. Blonde hair piled on top of her head and held with a silver clip. She walked down the stairs to meet him. The baubles that adorned her wrists made a distinct noise as she walked. He shook his head at the image of her being interviewed by the FBI.

"You must have the wrong house," the woman said, frowning as she looked at the clown outfit. "The birthday party is up the street." She pointed.

"Are you Mrs. Perry?" Mosby asked.

"Yes. And who are you?"

"Just a clown," Mosby said with a laugh. She didn't crack a smile. "Sorry. I'm here to see you and the Congressman. But you first."

Mosby pulled the Viper from his front pocket. Before she could scream, he shot her twice in the chest. Even if the band hadn't been playing, no one would have heard the shots. Fitted with the Gemtech Tundra suppressor, the only noise emitted was a faint *pop*.

Mosby pulled the body out of the drive and onto the back steps, careful not to get any blood on himself. He'd burn the clown outfit when he got home, but in the meantime he didn't want to leave anything the authorities could find and analyze. No fibers, no nothing. *They had chemicals now so focused and powerful,* he thought, *they probably could get my sperm count through my fingerprint. No way little guys like me can compete anymore.* He rubbed the Viper reassuringly on his back pant leg. *Except for this puppy*, he thought with a smile.

Carefully opening the back door, he walked in. He found himself in the laundry room. A big dryer in the corner spun with an annoying clunk. Resisting the temptation to open the dryer to stop the noise, he walked through the room and quietly eased the entry door open a few inches. Listening before he peeked out. Wanting to make sure Perry didn't have guests. That would have made for an awkward moment. A mass murder wouldn't have pleased the boss.

He silently made his way through the bottom floor of the house. Room-by-room. No Perry. As he neared the stairs, he heard the sound from a television on the second floor. Quietly ascending the stairs, he followed the noise. A football game. He saw the open door at the end of the hall, and made his way toward it. Looking in, he saw Perry in a large leather recliner, beer bottle in hand, watching the Redskins game. He walked in.

Perry sensed another body in the room. Without looking back, he held up his beer bottle and said, "Darby, can you get me another beer?"

"What's the score, Mitch?" Mosby asked.

Perry jolted upright and jerked his head toward the strange voice, confusion masking his face as he stared at the man dressed like a clown. "Shit. Who the hell are you?" he shouted, jumping out of the chair. "What are you doing here? Get the hell out of my house before I call the police."

"Now, Mitchell, I'm surprised you don't recognize an old friend," Mosby said, having fun with him.

"A friend, my ass." He started to walk toward Mosby.

"Uh-uh," Mosby said, raising the Viper he'd been hiding behind his right leg. "Don't be stupid, Congressman."

Perry saw the gun and stopped, fear bubbling up in his eyes. Putting his hands in front of him, he took a step backward. "Please. Who are you? I'll give you anything you want. I'm a United States Congressman. Don't hurt me."

"Downstairs," Mosby said, motioning with the gun that Perry should lead. "Let's sit in your office, shall we?" Mosby said as they reached the main floor.

"My office?" Perry said. "Who the hell are you?"

"I'm surprised you haven't guessed yet. Hell, we sat together for an hour in the Botanic Garden just last week."

"Tad Mosby?" he said, beads of sweat appearing on his upper lip. "What are you doing here? Why the clown outfit?"

"Just fitting into the neighborhood in case you have nosey neighbors, Mitch. I want them to think I belong to that kid's birthday party up the street."

"Why the hell are you here?" Perry asked again.

"You know those burner phones you keep here?" Mosby said as they reached Perry's office. "I need them."

"Sure. Whatever you want," Perry said. *What a little pussy*, Mosby thought. *Not even a tiny push back.* "Want me to get them for you?" As soon as Mosby nodded his head, Perry jumped out of his seat and ran to the desk. Unlocking one of the drawers, he placed four phones on the desktop. "You want me to bring them over?"

"That all you have?" Perry nodded. "Then, no. You can leave them there. I'll get them when I leave. But I'll tell you what you can get me. The password to your home security system."

"The password? What do you need the password for?"

What a dumbshit, Mosby thought. "Well, duh! Because I want to erase a certain clown from ever being in your house. I can hack my way into the system, but it would save me a lot of time if you just gave me the password. If you do that, I just may let you live."

Perry hesitated less than two seconds before he opened another drawer in the desk and pulled out a folder. "It's in here, Tad," he said, handing him the folder. Mosby smiled. *The Stockholm Syndrome at work,* he thought. People naturally want to cooperate with their captors, hoping that cooperation would soften the captors' hearts. *Fat chance.*

Perry sat back on the sofa. "You know my wife is home," he said. "She'll be looking for me."

"She's in the back yard," Mosby replied. "I can tell you for a fact she won't be joining us."

"Oh, please, no," Perry moaned, realizing the meaning of Mosby's words. He leaned forward and covered his face with his hands. "You're not going to kill me, are you?"

"I warned you," Mosby said. "You didn't listen."

"I couldn't do anything about it. She wouldn't listen to me. You have to believe me. It wasn't my fault. Please." Crying now.

"You're weak," Mosby said.

"I've been a loyal soldier," Perry pleaded. "I did everything asked of me."

"Don't tell *me* about being a *soldier*, you little prick," Mosby spit out. "You never served. You're not only weak, you're a fucking coward." Mosby enjoyed watching Perry losing his dignity as he begged for his life. "My grandfather thinks it's time to pull the weeds from the garden," he said. "He uses me as his personal *Agent Orange.*" Saying that, he raised his gun.

"Wait," Perry shouted, turning his head to the side and putting his hands out in front of him. "You said if I got you the system's password, you'd let me live."

"I lied," Mosby said, and shot him in the forehead.

He spent the next fifteen minutes dismantling the security system. Pocketing the system's chip and Perry's burner phones, he walked out the back door. Stepping over the body of Perry's wife, he got in his car and drove off.

Finally, he thought with a smile as he turned right on the main road and headed out of town. *Now only McGuire and Escher –* and *then a well-deserved vacation.*

CHAPTER 73

According to Katelyn's calculations, they were airborne for close to three thousand seconds. Since they left her alone on the flight, she thought what better use of my time and helplessness than counting the number of seconds between take-off and landing. She smiled inwardly thinking how much more anal she had become while working for the CIA. A good kind of anal, though. A potentially life-saving anal. Doing the math, she calculated they had been in the air close to fifty minutes. Coupling that with what the CIA had taught her about helicopter speed capabilities, she calculated they had traveled somewhere close to one hundred miles. One hundred miles from an airport near Teterboro considerably reduced the possibilities of where they were taking her. She thought for a minute. One hundred miles could place her in Hartford or Danbury, Connecticut. For sure the outer edge of Long Island. Somewhere east, like Scranton, Pennsylvania. Possibly even Philly. She wasn't sure what good this knowledge would do her, but even the little things could give her an edge. You never knew. If anything, her training had emphasized that little things could save your life.

The helicopter flared and settled to the ground. The engine didn't shut down, so Katelyn knew it was only there to drop her off. Potentially a good sign, she thought as the cabin door opened.

She felt someone grab her feet, and felt the bindings being removed. She was yanked roughly to her feet and shoved forward. Her legs didn't respond quickly enough and she fell, forcing her body to roll so her left arm and shoulder would take the brunt of the fall. She didn't want to meet her captor with a broken nose.

Someone picked her up and guided her to the doorway. "Stairs," said a male voice. "Down." An Indian accent. *Little things*. He held her elbow as she negotiated each step. When they reached the ground, he helped her walk forward through the downdraft. She had this crazy thought about what a mess her hair would be when they took off the hood. She shook her head. *Get a grip, girl*, she thought. *It's life or death, not hair.* She had taken ten steps when she heard the helo's door click shut. Four steps later, it lifted off.

Even though she couldn't see through the hood, her other senses were hyperactive. The sun's warmth on her skin. The air heavy with humidity. No doubt close to the ocean. She thought she could faintly hear the sound of waves as they broke on a nearby shoreline. She could taste the sea air on her tongue. Salty. Like tears. *Scratch Hartford and Scranton from my list,* she thought. *Philly, too.* Either Long Island or somewhere on the Jersey shore. If she had to bet, it would have been the former.

A hand on either elbow escorted her from the helipad across a wide expanse of lawn. Spongy. Newly mowed. Then a hard surface. She was memorizing every step. *Be aware of your surroundings*.

They stopped. The sound of keys. A door opened. She was jerked through the opening into an air-conditioned interior. Her captor on the left let go of her elbow. "Stairs," he said. "Down." Katelyn carefully slid her foot forward until she found the step. The right-hand captor still held her elbow and helped guide her down. Katelyn counted ten steps. *Be aware. The little things.* Then the sound of a door opening in front of her. They led her into a room and planted her in a chair. Another person was present. She could feel him. Smell him. Someone grabbed the top of her hood and yanked it off. The sudden brightness temporarily blinded her. She bowed her head, allowing her eyes to become accustomed to the light. When she finally dared to look up, she saw an old man standing in front of her. He wore a blue blazer over a striped blue and white shirt, a blue and gray tie and tan slacks.

"Good afternoon Ms. Murray. My name is George Hinrick. I believe we have some business to conduct."

CHAPTER 74

"We heard from her an hour ago," Sullivan said. "By phone. And no, we couldn't trace it. A burner. Their stock in trade, as we know."

Delgado, Rob Kincaid and I were sitting with David Sullivan in AFF's underground bunker in Gaithersburg. I called Kincaid on the way and gave him the short version of what happened.

"She didn't know where she was being held or who her captors were. At least that's what they instructed her to say."

"Oh, bullshit," I said. "Hinrick has her. You know it, and I know it."

"How do you know so much about him?" Sullivan asked.

"Katelyn told me."

"She shouldn't have."

"Yeah," I said. "That's exactly what she said you'd say. So let's cut the crap. Tell us what you got on Hinrick, and let's go get his ass."

"It's a lot more difficult than you think," Sullivan said.

"What's so difficult?" Kincaid said. "Either you get a local SWAT team to go in, or I can call Admiral Thompson at JSOC and get a TEAM in there. It would take ten minutes to take him down."

"And get Katelyn out alive? I'm not trying to be difficult, but I'm not even sure that a SEAL team could pull that off." Sullivan paused, looked around the room, and then sighed. "Look – we've had Hinrick in our crosshairs for some time now. The more we learn about him, the more I can say he's one bad *MFer*. Trouble is he's a rich, bad *MFer*. And even worse, a *MFer* that's well connected politically."

"Okay," I said. "We'll get back to Hinrick in a minute. Tell us what else Katelyn said."

"She said she hadn't been harmed. That they'd call back later with a demand. She said don't try to find her, or they promised they would kill her. And then the phone went dead."

"Did she tell you when they would call back?" I asked.

"No."

"Then what are we supposed to do? Just sit here all night, waiting? Fuck that."

"You got a better idea?" Sullivan shot back.

I didn't have a better idea, but then again, it turned out I didn't need one. Katelyn called five minutes later. Sullivan put her on speaker.

"They will swap me for the Custer Papers," she said. "They want them all. In return, they will release me."

Just then, Escher walked into Sullivan's office. I quickly put my index finger to my lips. *Quiet*, I mouthed, gesturing for him to take a seat.

I leaned closer to the speaker. "Can they hear this conversation?" I asked.

"Yes."

"Then put them on," I said. "I want to ask a question."

There was silence, and then, "You've got exactly one minute and one question," a male voice said.

"What assurances can you give us that if we deliver the papers, you will release Ms. Murray?"

"I'll give you one assurance," the voice intoned. "If you do not deliver those papers to us by noon tomorrow, you will begin finding parts of your agent floating in the Potomac. Got that? Okay, time's up."

"Wait. Hold on. What if we give you half …"

"No more questions," the voice interrupted. "We will call you back in four hours. At exactly 9 p.m. your time." The voice paused, then added, "and you, Inspector McGuire. We know you've handled kidnapping situations before. Remember Beverly Garland, Inspector?"

Everyone in the room looked over at me. I felt a cold hand wrap around my heart. And squeeze. My breath came out in short spurts. I leaned back in my chair and didn't reply.

"You didn't meet the kidnappers' demands," the voice continued, "and poor Beverly didn't live to see the next sunrise. That was on you, Inspector. Bringing in outside resources to effect Ms. Murray's rescue will bring about her death, just as it did Beverly Garland's. No police. No FBI. No CIA. No military. Just you. And Escher. We want the two of you. You've been warned." Then the phone went dead.

~~~~

George Hinrick hung up, satisfied with the conversation. Enough of a show of power to let them know who they were dealing with, without being so over-the-top that they would think he was exaggerating. He smiled and picked up his phone again.

"You want to come to a real turkey shoot?" he asked the person who answered. "Guaranteed two for the price of one. Bring your finest weapon."

"I'd be honored, Grandfather," Tad Mosby said. "Tell me the time and the place."

CHAPTER 75

"**S**hit!" Kincaid said.

"Ditto that for me, too, Bro," Delgado said. He turned and put his hand on my shoulder. "You okay, dude?"

"Jesus!" I said after taking a few deep breaths. "Garland was five years ago. I took a two-month sabbatical after that incident. Where the fuck did they get that information?" Looking at Kincaid, I patted my chest and said, "And my bad, Rob. You were right about them having made us."

"Can there be any doubt now, David, that this has to be a Hinrick operation?" Kincaid asked. "Who else would even know McGuire's an SFPD homicide inspector? Who else would be able to get access to his classified medical files?"

"And, dude – Escher," Delgado said, looking over at him. "Wanting the both of you there. What's up with that?"

"They're bringing in Mosby, obviously," Escher said. "Probably to sniper us both. When we're planning this operation, let's keep Mosby's whereabouts in mind, okay?"

"Tell us what you got on Hinrick," I said. "We're not playing around any more."

Sullivan sat quietly for a few minutes, then said, "George Hinrick is a big cog in a big wheel. He's not an enemy you want to have."

"We didn't ask for this fight, David," Kincaid said. "But now that we're in it …" He left the rest to our imagination.

"So, tell us what makes Hinrick so dangerous," I said.

"We've been following him for a year now," Sullivan said. "Like I said before, he's rich and well-connected politically. Those two assets have made him virtually bulletproof."

"Why are the Custer papers so important to him?" I asked. "He's spending a hell of a lot of time and effort, to say nothing of political capital, keeping whatever's in those papers quiet."

"If I'm not mistaken, you found out quite a bit of the *why* last night," Sullivan replied. "At least on the general level." Seeing the surprise on our faces, he continued. "Katelyn called me last night. Well, early this morning to be exact. I don't know about you, but to contend there are men – and we're not talking here about elected officials, but rather *men* no one has ever heard of – powerful enough to manipulate world events is a pretty astounding assertion."

"It's not a completely new theory though," I said. "Conspiracy theories abound. Most people don't take them seriously."

"Maybe Hinrick thinks the Custer papers are so explosive that they will convince people that some conspiracies are real. At least the one about evil people manipulating world events for their own purposes. In any case, we hope to have an answer to that later tonight or tomorrow morning. We just got the papers from you a few hours ago. I tasked Holmquist and Ms. Wyatt with analyzing them until they find out what's so important in them."

He sat down. "Have you heard the term *peso brokers*?"

"Drug term," Escher said.

"Correct, Kyle," Sullivan said with a smile. "Forgot you worked with us. Anyway, that's what George Hinrick is essentially – a *peso broker*. The phrase, as Kyle said, is a drug term. Comes out of the drug wars. It's a name the DEA originally gave to the Mexican cartels' money launderers. You wanna take it from here, Kyle?"

Escher nodded. "Because the drug trade is an all cash business, you must have a way of turning the cash into pesos. Enter the *peso brokers*. They take the cash and buy goods from the United States, China, Russia, wherever – for Mexican importers. The importers then sell the goods in-country for pesos. Now all this goes on under the radar. After keeping a percentage of sales, the importers give the pesos back to the *peso broker* who in turn passes the profits back to the cartels. After, of course, taking his cut."

"You're not saying Hinrick is a *peso broker*, are you?" I asked.

"In a manner of speaking, he is," Sullivan said. "And as such, he lives right on the edge of the law. But his donations to various causes on both sides of the intellectual and cultural divide, plus the money he feeds to politicians, keep him immune. Bulletproof, as I said before."

"I guess I'm not as smart as the rest of you," I said, "but I see a *peso broker* as the bottom of the food chain. Not a place for a George Hinrick."

"On the contrary. Drugs, arms, human trafficking, you name it – couldn't exist without someone laundering the profits. Because he can do that, Hinrick is right at the top of the food chain. His money and his contacts make him the ultimate *peso broker*."

"Katelyn explained to me how he works. And how you finally traced a flow of money through his banks that financed the Arab Spring."

"And just recently – the terrorist attacks in Paris a few months ago. And the one in California. We think he was involved there, too."

"And even closer to home," I said. "Conroy and his wife, Rachel and now Katelyn." I looked at Sullivan. "You said Hinrick was immune from the rules of civilized society. That he was bulletproof. Maybe before. But not now. I'm going to get the son-of-a-bitch. He may not know it yet, but George Hinrick just bit the wrong wolf."

CHAPTER 76

During the early evening, Kincaid made arrangements with Admiral Thompson to use assets under his command to overfly Hinrick's house on Long Island, mapping the terrain and pinpointing heat signatures from the house. Thompson also offered to make available ST6's Red Squadron, Kincaid's old team, as a backup.

It wasn't to be. At exactly nine o'clock that evening, Hinrick called. We put him on speaker.

"You have disregarded everything I told you," he said evenly. "You will pay dearly for that."

"This is Inspector McGuire," I said. "We did exactly as you told us."

"That is not true, Inspector. I've learned you've discussed my private affairs as a legitimate businessman. Twisting them as a means of taking me down. You have engaged the military to send spy satellites over my dwelling." I looked over at Kincaid. His jaw muscles were twitching and his eyes hooded. "You can't hide from me."

Kincaid leaned close to the speaker, at the same time gently pushing me back. "This is Robert Kincaid speaking. Am I talking to Mr. Hinrick?" No reply came. "Well, in any case," Kincaid continued, "let me be clear. I had the military assets brought in. I did it without Inspector McGuire even being aware. I apologize and will cancel my request from JSOC. I should have better respected Inspector McGuire's case. You can deal directly with him from now on. His only concern is not losing the hostage. Everything else is negotiable."

"You are wrong, Mr. Kincaid," the voice said, again in his business-like way. "*Nothing* is negotiable. You will do exactly as I say. I'll wait to hear that your military assets, as you call them, Stand-Down. You have one hour. If I have not heard by then that you cancelled your arrangements, then the consequences will be on your head. You will have lost another hostage, Inspector."

"Wait," I said. "We don't have any way of contacting you. How can we let you know we've done what you asked?"

I heard a dismissive chortle. "We have ways."

~~~~

"Son-of-a-bitch," Kincaid said. "We have a leak." He looked accusingly at Sullivan. "On your staff!"

"Not mine," he said, a touch of anger in his voice. "Hell, my staff hasn't even been here today. They have no clue what's been happening in this room. No – this is higher up."

"Has to be," I said. "They know about Thompson and JSOC."

"I hear you about Thompson," Kincaid said. "But what about Hinrick or whoever we spoke to saying he knew we were discussing his *private affairs as a legitimate businessman*. Those are things that were discussed inside this office. Today."

"Shit!" Sullivan cursed. He put his index finger on his pursed lips to quiet us. "You know," he said, "I think this is all getting to us. We're not thinking straight. Let's take a break for fifteen minutes or so. I'm gonna go topside. Get some fresh air. Anyone wanna join me?" He motioned for us all to come with him.

When we had reached ground level, he led us out of AFF's garage. "Sorry, gentlemen. I forgot. Everything we say in that office is taped. Every keystroke we make is logged. Standard operating procedure. All sent back to Langley. Supposedly archived. Someone at Langley is listening to our conversations in real time!"

"Who the hell would have clearance?" Delgado asked.

The five of us looked at each other. We knew.

"Son-of-a-bitch," Kincaid said as he pulled out his cell. "I gotta call Thompson."

He stayed connected for twelve minutes. Sullivan started to get antsy. "Hinrick is going to be calling any minute. We've got to get back."

As if he heard, Kincaid hung up and joined us. "Okay. From everything I told him, Thompson thinks Hinrick's insider has to be the Under Secretary of Defense, a guy named Parkman."

"Joseph Parkman," Sullivan said. "The boss of my boss. I'm stunned. To think that all we've worked on these past few years has been compromised." He shook his head in disbelief and sadness.

"He'll be taken care of in due time," Kincaid said. "Thompson will see to that. In the meantime, I'll tell you what's happening. We're getting our oversight of Hinrick's place. Not with a satellite, but the next best thing. A Navy drone. Launched from the USS California, a submarine homeported in Groton, Connecticut, currently conducting training exercises thirty miles southeast of Montauk. Strictly for US Naval intelligence, of course."

"Of course," Sullivan mimicked.

"Does Hinrick have active radar? Could it pick up the drone?" Escher asked.

"Only if it has military grade electronics," Kincaid replied. "Which I seriously doubt."

"When will it be launched?" Delgado asked.

"2330 hours," Kincaid said looking at his watch. "A little over an hour and a half from now. This puppy travels up to three thousand miles an hour at an altitude of five miles. And it has heat sensors."

"Excellent," Delgado said, smiling. "We're in business."

~~~~

We were back in the office only fifteen minutes when Hinrick called. "A change of plans," he said. "It turns out I'll be leaving the country for a while. The temperature here has changed, and it doesn't agree with me."

"What about Ms. Murray?" I asked.

"Ah – your hostage, Inspector," he said. "Unfortunately for you, I'll be taking her along. A precaution. I don't trust that you will let me leave in peace. I will, of course, release her when I arrive at my destination."

"And where might that be?"

"No need for you to know now. I'm sure your country will keep close watch on me the entire trip. But enough of this. I still want the Custer Papers in their entirety. If you don't bring them, or if you only bring part of them, I promise I'll throw her out of the airplane right before I land."

"What's to prevent you from doing that anyway? Even if we do give you the papers?"

"Nothing. You'll just have to trust me." He laughed, a piercing cackle. "Now, on to more serious matters. We'll take off tomorrow afternoon at five."

"From LaGuardia?" Kincaid asked leaning over my shoulder.

"Of course not. You haven't seen my grounds, I guess. I have my own runway."

"And a plane, I hope," Kincaid said.

"Of course," he answered. "I even have a bed that I may share with the delightful Ms. Murray."

I felt myself getting pissed, but Kincaid patted me on the shoulder. "He's playing with you," he whispered in my ear. "Trying to keep you from thinking straight. Just keep a level head."

"We'll be in the air for over twelve hours," Hinrick continued. "With nothing better to do." Again, that cackle. "I want you here at three-thirty, Inspector. You and that Escher fellow. The both of you."

"And you know my name," Escher said. "I'm impressed."

"I didn't know you were there," Hinrick said. "You've been so quiet. How many others do you have in the room?"

"Just the usual. How did you know my name?"

"My grandson met you. You're a naughty boy, though. You gave him a phony name. Didn't take me long to find your real one, though."

"Do you want us to drive?" I asked. "I'm not even sure where you live. I'm from the other coast."

"Ask Mr. Escher to guide you. He lives near me. When you come onto the property, one of my guards will meet you. He will direct you where to go. Be there, Inspector. If not, you will find the pretty Ms. Murray splattered in some field in a far-away country."

As the call ended, Kincaid turned to me, and said, "Let's get out of here. We've got a shitload of things to do by tomorrow afternoon."

CHAPTER 77

Montauk

Two and a half hours after we left Sullivan at AFF headquarters in Gaithersburg, we made our descent into Long Island's Montauk airfield. The small, private airport was located at the northeastern edge of the Island, just three and a half miles from the Hinrick estate.

On the drive from Gaithersburg to Reagan National, Kincaid had made arrangements for Escher to meet Admiral Thompson around midnight at the Naval Academy in Annapolis. They were to work out the logistics for getting Escher onto the beach fronting Hinrick's compound undetected. We shook hands and wished him luck.

Fifteen minutes after taking off in Kincaid's Legacy 650, the computers on our seats came alive with pictures of Hinrick's property taken by the submarine's drone.

After studying it for a few minutes, Kincaid said, "Twenty heat signatures." He pointed them out. "About what I expected. Too many for us to take out."

"You were thinking of making a raid tonight?" I asked.

"Thought about it, yeah," he replied. "Would have made tomorrow's operation a whole hell of a lot easier. If it weren't for Katelyn's safety, we probably would have tried it. Vinnie and I have done this before. Against better armed and better trained adversaries. And *we're* still here." He smiled.

"As it is," Delgado said, "we'll do a recon on the property tonight."

"Tonight?"

"Dude. You'll thank us tomorrow when your ass is hanging out there transferring the Custer Papers to Hinrick."

"Don't know if you caught what I did earlier tonight with Hinrick," Kincaid said. I cocked my head, looking at him quizzically. "Remember I interrupted your conversation with him? Tried to goad him into supplying us with info? Well, we got him to confirm he had a plane on the property."

"I missed that. Probably because all I could think about was what I'd do to the prick when I got my hands on him."

"I'll bet." Kincaid laughed, then said, "Did you catch the part about the plane being airborne for twelve hours? Means he's probably going to Russia. If he makes it there, we'll never get him back. And once he's there, he'll have no use for Katelyn. If she's not killed outright, she'll disappear into the Gulag and never be heard from again."

"That intel, Bro," said Delgado, "also told us that for his plane to stay airborne that long it has to be at least as big as this one. The size of his aircraft means it has lots of cargo space aft. We're going to leave a gift for him in that space. Actually, two gifts."

"Come aft," Kincaid said, starting toward the rear of the aircraft. "I'll show you what we have in mind."

~~~~

After they left, I tried to sleep. No go. I ended up pacing – and thinking. This all started two weeks ago. *Two weeks*, I thought. *Son-of-a-bitch. Seemed like freaking forever*. And I knew if Kincaid's plan went south, it *would* be forever.

CHAPTER 78

Delgado shook me awake. Sunlight was streaming through the plane's windows. I looked at my watch. Nine-forty.

"Come, get up," he said. "Sullivan's on the phone. You gotta hear this."

I pushed the button to bring the chair to its full upright position. The last thing I remembered was looking at my watch as the chair started to recline. Five-fifteen, it said. I'd been asleep over four hours. "When did you guys get back?" I asked, finally able to stand.

"Five forty-five, or so. You were asleep. Didn't want to disturb you."

"You get any sleep?" I asked.

"A few hours. Plenty for us. Come on. Sullivan's on the phone with news about Hinrick."

We walked aft where Kincaid was waiting. His phone on speaker. "Continue, David," he said. "Mac is here with us now."

"Hi, Inspector. I just asked your colleagues whether Katelyn told you about the Esperanto conferences Custer attended in 1908 and 1910. They said she had."

"Correct," I answered.

"Then you know those conferences were nothing more than an excuse to get the world's leading arms dealers and manufacturers together. Great cover. No one made the connection. Except, of course, George Custer."

"And he couldn't say anything for fear of blowing *his* cover," Kincaid said.

"Exactly," Sullivan replied. "And by that time, those guys knew they could manipulate world events. Because they already had. A lesson they learned at Custer's expense."

"So how does Hinrick fit in?" I asked, impatient for the punch line.

"At the conference, Custer meets and gets to know pretty well a fellow named Max Gutnick."

"A relative of Hinrick?" I asked.

"That's what we're working on now," Sullivan said. "Possibly his grandfather. The Custer Papers are pointing us in that direction. We just have to piece it together."

"How could it be his grandfather?" I asked. "Hinrick's bio contends he's Romanian."

"He made it all made up, we think," Sullivan said. "To hide his family tree. The Gutnick that Custer met was German. This was the guy who founded an international arms trust he called Edmunds United Steel in 1910. The members of that Trust were the major arms dealers from – get this – Britain, Germany, France, Italy, Austria, Russia and the United States. Associate members – Argentina, Brazil, Mexico, Canada and China.

"Custer said Gutnick told everyone at the Esperanto conference that he made up a fictitious Jewish person by the name of Abrahamsohn to be the founder of that Trust. Gutnick disappeared at the start of World War I. Supposedly killed in the battle for Paris. His body burned beyond recognition. Convenient. No DNA tests in those days. We now think that Gutnick turned into Abrahamsohn and ran the arms cabal from Romania. Remember, the arms manufacturers in the Trust were non-state actors. Had no allegiances to any country. So when the Nazis came calling on Abrahamsohn, you'd think that being Jewish would be reason to take him to the camps. But no. All they asked him to do was change his name. Hitler couldn't be seen doing business with a Jewish interest. So Abrahamsohn became Hinrick. At least we think."

"Son-of-a-bitch," Kincaid whispered.

"Yeah," Sullivan said. "You can see why he can't let the Custer Papers become public. They could be a roadmap showing Hinrick's family as the glue holding together this cabal of arms manufacturers. That Custer's reported death taught them that a group of determined men could make themselves fabulously wealthy by simply keeping the world at war with itself."

Just then Kincaid heard the beep of a call waiting. He looked. Admiral Thompson. "David, gotta go. Remember – not a word back to Langley. Parkman can't know what's going on here."

"Got that," Sullivan said and disconnected.

CHAPTER 79

Montauk

At the same time McGuire, Delgado and Kincaid were talking to Sullivan, Tad Mosby arrived at the Hinrick compound. He was immediately ushered into the study. It had been over a year since Mosby had last seen his grandfather. What he saw shocked him. Impeccably dressed, as usual, Hinrick's skinny frame barely made a dent in the ebony-black leather chair in which he sat. *Son-of-a-bitch*, Mosby thought with a twinge of sorrow, *something is eating the old man from the inside-out.*

Hinrick made a feeble attempt to stand. "Don't, Grandfather. I'll come to you." Mosby walked over and embraced him.

"Glad you're here, my boy," he said in what Mosby considered a strong voice given his physical appearance. "I wanted you here because I've made a momentous decision. As you can see, I'm not the man I used to be." Mosby attempted to interrupt, but Hinrick held out his hand. "No need to reply. The doctors have assured me it's not terminal." He smiled. "They think I should just back off working so hard for a while. That the stress is getting to me. That's why I look like a skeleton. So, I've decided to take their advice."

"Good for you, Grandfather. You deserve it."

"I'm going on hiatus for a while. In fact, I'll be flying out tonight. To Sevastopol. Seaside R & R."

"The Crimea?" Mosby said, his eyes widening in surprise. "That's Russian territory."

"I know. That's no problem, though. I've made many Russian friends over the years. But that's not important. What's important is I need someone to run the Northern Hemisphere operations while I'm gone. Maybe for a year or two. And I'd like it to be you."

Mosby remained silent for a few moments as he digested what he just heard. Then his face dissolved into a happy grin. "I'm honored, Grandfather. I really am. Do you think I'm cut out to lead the Corporation?"

"You were in the military. You learned how to lead men."

"True, Grandfather. But the real truth is I'm just a Marine who acquired special skills while in the Corps. Skills not related to running your Corporation."

"Take my word for it. The skills you bring are precisely those it takes to run this business," Hinrick said. "I've been doing it long enough. I should know."

"Again, I'm honored. I'll start right after I take care of the task at hand."

"Of course," Hinrick said with a proud smile. "I'll be delighted when those pricks are no longer around to bother us."

Mosby unloaded his car and carried his gear into the room assigned him. Instead of unwrapping his weapons, he went out and started walking the property.

It was warm. The rain of the past few days left the air heavy with moisture. *Something to account for when setting my A5's dope*, he thought.

He remembered being here as a child, but still had to look online to remember some of the details. The compound had a total of thirty-three acres, bordered on two sides by the Atlantic Ocean. The house, in front of which he now stood, was on the eastern section of the property, about five hundred yards from the Atlantic Ocean. The distance from the house to the ocean had no relevance to him. He would be shooting towards the house from the copse of trees behind him.

McGuire and Escher would arrive by car up the long, narrow road that came out of those trees and ended just about where he was standing. He imagined the unfolding scenario. Both getting out. Grandfather coming out of the house and walking toward them. Maybe he'd have the woman in tow, maybe not. As long as she didn't get in his firing lane, it made no difference to him either way. Mosby took out his range finder and zeroed in on the trees. Picking out one in particular, he lasered it. Slightly more than one thousand yards. *Perfect*, he thought.

CHAPTER 80

Montauk

As Tad Mosby walked from the house to the tree line, Kyle Escher was eyeballing him through the Mk 21's scope. He'd waited the entire day for this opportunity. *Got you asshole*, he thought, his mouth forming a satisfied grin. *I could kill you so easily right now. But, dammit, orders are orders. Not until McGuire gets here and they get Katelyn out.*

~~~~

Escher met with Admiral Thompson at the Naval Academy for a couple of hours the night before. Thompson had already ordered the *USS California* to send a drone over Hinrick's property. The drone's aerial footage now allowed them to formulate a plan.

The plan had Escher being flown by helicopter to the *California*. From there, he would be carried on a Mark-11 SDV, an acronym for SEAL Delivery Vehicle, from the submarine to the Montauk shoreline.

It went as planned. Once on the sub, he changed into scuba gear, strapped on a breathing cylinder, secured his Mk 21 rifle to his back and climbed into the Mark-11. The SDV dropped him a quarter mile from the beach.

He made shore a half-mile south of Hinrick's compound just as the sun crept over the eastern horizon. The five-foot high stone seawall protected him from prying eyes as he made his way to Hinrick's property. Once there, he set up a camouflaged hide where he could rest his rifle on the seawall and survey the landscape through his scope.

From the drone aerials, he had a pretty good idea of what he'd see. Thankfully, there were no surprises. He set his scope's dope at a thousand yards. He'd make the necessary adjustments later when he got a clearer picture of where Mosby's hide would be. Pulling his cap low on his head, he took out his water bottles and placed them in a row on the seawall.

It was going to be a long day.

CHAPTER 81

"Admiral," Kincaid said into his cell phone after hanging up with Sullivan, "I've got Vinnie and Tom McGuire here with me. I'm going to put you on speaker."

"Good. Hello gentlemen," Admiral Thompson said. "I'm calling with an update on the plans. But so you know, if events don't go as planned, you're on your own."

"Understood, sir," Kincaid said. Noticing my quizzical look, he put his hand up in a *hold on, I'll fill you in later* gesture.

"Escher has checked in," Thompson said. "He's on the property. Hidden. Mosby's there already. I'm sure he thinks Kyle is going to be with you, Inspector. He'll be disappointed."

"What are Kyle's orders, sir?" I asked, hoping to hear that Escher would shoot Mosby before Mosby shot me.

"Escher is cleared to take Mosby down before he can fire a shot. But in cases like this you never know. A lot will depend on what happens where you are. Probably up near the house. And how Hinrick plays his hand. And, of course, if Escher can even acquire him as a target."

"Swell," I said.

"Don't worry," Thompson said. "I'm sending a Molle for you to wear."

I looked at Kincaid for a translation. He leaned over to me and whispered, "A bulletproof vest."

"Better be a good one," I whispered back. He smiled and nodded his head.

"How about your men, Rob?" Thompson asked. "You all set?"

"Good to go, sir. They should be here any minute." We heard a car approaching the plane. "In fact, I think they just arrived."

"I'll check," Delgado said. He picked up the M-4 that was propped on the seat in front of him and walked to the front of the aircraft. He came back a few seconds later and gave Rob the *thumbs-up*.

"It's them, sir," Kincaid said into the phone.

"Good luck, Rob. Anything else comes up you call me immediately. Otherwise, we'll just hope for the best tonight. Godspeed."

"My guys. From RSSA," Kincaid said by way of explaining where Vinnie had gone. "There are five of us altogether. All former teammates in Team 6. Good men."

"And why are they here?" I asked.

"Vinnie and I spoke with Thompson this morning when we got back from our recon of the Hinrick property. You were still asleep. We all thought that bringing my guys in as perimeter security beat the hell out of tasking it out to the FBI or local police. That would cause way too much publicity. Unwanted publicity."

"And if the shooting starts," I said, "you five are going to take down all his personnel? All twenty of them?"

"When."

"Pardon me?" I said.

"When," Kincaid said. "*When* the shooting starts. You said *if*. The shooting *will* start, Coach. No doubt about that. Either Mosby will start it by shooting you, or Escher will start by shooting Mosby. His guys will pinpoint where Escher is by his shot, and go after him. Then the battle begins."

"Son-of-a-bitch," I said. "No! No battle. You can't let that happen, Rob. They'll kill Katelyn. First thing."

"We don't think so. Hinrick isn't going to want her dead. He just wants to get away, and she's his exit visa. He'll protect her at all costs. As long as he doesn't get shot in the mêlée, nothing will happen to her. If he gets shot, though, she'll die for sure. So we're letting him go. He'll recognize that's our purpose, too. Protect her even more."

"And his men?" I asked.

"They'll dutifully die for the cause, or give up. In either scenario, Hinrick will get in that airplane and *adios*."

"So you're gonna let him get away. And as soon as he doesn't need Katelyn anymore, he'll kill her." I stood up. "Rob, I can't let that happen. I *won't* let that happen."

"Sit down," he said. "Nothing like that is going to happen. You haven't heard the rest of the plan yet."

So I fell silent and listened intently as he rolled out the rest of the strategy. He was so calm and matter-of-fact about it, as I'm sure he had been many, many times before when lives hung in the balance. I was at once comforted by his expertise and thoroughness, while still being apprehensive about what I knew was going to be a fight for life. Katelyn's life.

~~~~

"All set?" Kincaid asked, as I opened the front door of the car. It was later that afternoon, and the show was about to begin. I had the dubious privilege of being the opening act. "You okay with everything? Understand now how it's all going down?"

I nodded and tapped the Molle vest hanging on my chest courtesy of Admiral Thompson. I did a pirouette. "Does this make me look fat?"

"Dude, you look great," Delgado said with a laugh. "I know how you feel, Bro. Been there, done that. But it'll all work out. Those ballistic plates will stop any cartridge up to a .50 caliber. That peashooter Mosby uses won't come close to penetrating it. And no one's going to notice you're wearing it under your pretty new XL shirt." He laughed again.

"What if he shoots for my head? Like he did Conroy?" I asked.

"Well, that's a different story," Delgado said. "At least you won't feel anything."

With those comforting words, I got in the car and drove away.

CHAPTER 82

I drove three miles until I hit the intersection that led to Hinrick's compound. I stopped and leaned back against the headrest. The Molle vest pressed hot against my skin. *Keep me safe today, Lord*, I prayed. *If for no other reason than I'd like to be there to watch TJ grow into manhood.*

I thought of Katelyn. About how much we'd been through together in such a short time. My feelings having gone from the penthouse to the doghouse and back again. Maybe not yet back to the top, but getting there. Did I love her? I wasn't prepared to say that out loud yet. *But then why are you sitting here, dummy? Alone in a car on a road leading to – to life or death.* I smiled. *Come on McGuire. Time to face the obvious.* I rolled down the window and yelled into the wind, "I love you, Katelyn. I'm coming to get you." Then I put the car in gear, turned left and started down the road.

~~~~

Mosby set up directly in front of where he expected McGuire and Escher to stop. He saw it all happen in his mind. Both men would get out, and the passenger would walk around to the driver's side. At that time, they would both be facing him. The orientation wouldn't change much when his grandfather and the woman came up from the house. One of his grandfather's men would get the Custer Papers from the car. As soon as his grandfather had the papers in hand and nodded, Mosby would fire. He'd shot two people standing side-by-side before, and found the second man's panic and indecision delicious. It's what made his job so enjoyable.

He set his dope for one thousand meters. No wind. The air was still heavy with moisture from yesterday's rain, but he didn't think it would do much to disturb the bullet's path. Maybe adjust his reticle up just a hair, but no more.

He noticed some activity near the house. Men running in different directions. *McGuire and Escher's car must be near,* he thought as he swiveled his A5 completely around to face the entry road. Through his scope he could see the car approaching in the distance.

He toyed with the idea of shooting the one in the passenger seat before the car even reached the house. If he were fast enough chambering the next round, he could also shoot the driver before the guy realized what had just happened to his partner. But he dismissed the idea. Grandfather wouldn't be pleased. *No,* he thought, *patience is the better part of valor. At least in this case.*

He followed the car through his scope as it passed. Appearing close enough to touch. Then his eyes narrowed and his lips pinched together. McGuire. In the driver's seat. Alone.

What the hell? Where the fuck is Escher? His heart thumped as he crouched in his self-made rifle pit. Ever so slowly he swung his rifle through a one hundred eighty-degree sweep of the property. Nothing. Escher was here. He could feel him. Where? He slowly made the sweep again.

Wait! His eyes widened and his heart drummed a wicked beat as he froze the rifle's movement on a spot directly to his front. In the bushes on the far side of the house. He blinked and refocused. Is that a head I'm seeing, or just the thickness of a bush? He blinked again, refocusing his eyes on that one spot. His training all those years ago coming into play. Concentrate. Look at the leaves and branches around the area. Are they moving? Concentrate.

Is the suspected spot moving in sync with everything else around it, or simply stationary? Look for the rifle. The rifle barrel. Concentrate. A long black tube. Turned out he didn't need to concentrate so much. Escher moved.

Escher had his Mk 21 resting on the rock seawall. He felt exposed because there was nothing behind him except a hundred yards of open sand and the sea. A few hours before, he had walked the entire beach looking for an entry point off Hinrick's property. None there. Even though exposed, he knew he wasn't vulnerable.

The other problem he encountered was the hedgerow of trees and brush on the Hinrick side of the seawall. A man-made windbreak. While he loved the protection it provided him from prying eyeballs, it still took him forty-five minutes of careful pruning to clear a shooting corridor.

Escher stationed himself exactly four hundred and thirty-five meters southeast of the house. He chose this spot for tactical reasons. First, it afforded him a direct line of sight down the entry road, meaning he would be one of the first to see McGuire arrive. Second, and more importantly, his *hide* was directly across from Mosby's. He lasered Mosby's position and set his scope's *zero* at one thousand six hundred yards. *Picked the perfect spot*, he thought, giving himself an imaginary pat on the back. *Even if Mosby sees me, it's beyond the range of his freaking A5.* He grinned. *Thank you Cowboy Action Shooting.* Escher was a little surprised, though, that Mosby hadn't camouflaged his position as well as he should have. Any first year Marine sniper would have made him in an instant. Sloppy preparation. The kind that gets you killed.

Escher bent and eyeballed Mosby through his scope just as Mosby pivoted, rifle in hand, to look at something behind him. Escher tracked the area with his own scope and saw McGuire's car approaching. *It won't be long now.*

Escher sat down behind the seawall and made a mental video of how this operation would unfold. First, McGuire would drive toward him and then make the slight left toward the house. Before getting to the house, he would be met by one of Hinrick's lackeys and told to stop and get out. Upon exiting, McGuire would be facing Mosby front-on. His center mass exposed to the shooter. Escher had a hard time coming to grips with the part of the plan that allowed Mosby to kill McGuire before he could kill Mosby. Didn't make any sense. *I could nail the son-of-a-bitch right now, and be home by dinner.* He shook his head, dismissing all negative thoughts. *Focus on the job I'm here to do*, he told himself. *They're paying me to kill Mosby. Don't deviate.*

From his sitting position, he twisted around and got on his knees. Pressing his body against the seawall, he bent slightly from the waist, fitting his shoulder into the Mk 21's metal stock. Tilting his head forward, he looked through his scope at Mosby.

"Shit," Escher cursed, adrenaline spiking through him. He could just make out the smile on Mosby's face as he looked directly back at him.

CHAPTER 83

A mile from the intersection, the road came out of the woods and opened on a vast expanse of manicured lawn that fronted the biggest house I'd ever seen. Even though I saw the infrared photos taken by the drone, they didn't prepare me for the enormity and obvious opulence of the place. *This dude is pulling in some serious cash.*

I drove straight for a few hundred yards before the road curved slightly left. A man holding a short-barreled shotgun stood in the road. Leveling the weapon at me, he held up his hand to stop. I wasn't about to argue with the twelve gauge.

The guy came over, pulled open my door and took two steps backward, inviting me to get out. I did, feeling a bit awkward in the Molle vest, hoping it couldn't be seen under my oversized Hawaiian shirt.

I heard a noise. Turning to my right, I saw the front door of the house swing open. A second later, an old man shuffled through the opening wearing neatly pressed gray pants, white shirt, and a patterned black and brown sweater. George Hinrick. He cleared the door and yanked on the rope he had in his hand, pulling Katelyn Murray through after him.

She wore an oversized brown jump suit. Like pilots wear. Her wrists were tied in front of her. Her right eye swollen. Obviously from a blow to the side of her head. Her lower lip was split open. Even though it wasn't bleeding, it needed stitches. She looked at me and tried to smile, but then imperceptively shook her head. Warning me not to do anything foolish. I gave a short nod in reply.

"Mr. Hinrick," I said in the most polite and deferential tone I could muster. "I have come to escort Ms. Murray home. Her ransom, the Custer Papers, has been delivered into your custody." I motioned to the box I had taken from the front seat and placed on the ground in front of the car.

Hinrick told one of his bodyguards to fetch the box. Hinrick opened it, took out a few pages, smiled and returned them to the carton. "Can't wait to read the whole collection," he said, looking at me. "Are they worth the time?"

"Wouldn't know, sir," I said in a humble tone, hoping to convince him I was no threat. But he knew better. This guy had lived a lifetime with guys like me trying to suck up to him.

"You and I know that is not true, Inspector," he said, not buying my act. "Ms. Murray has already told me that *she* read them. And told others about their contents. You specifically."

"She may have told you that, sir," I replied, changing persona now. Being direct. Forceful, but not argumentative. *Hostage Negotiator Thomas McGuire at work.* "I can tell you for a fact none of us, her included, have read them. You have nothing to fear. You can keep the papers. I'm only here to bargain for her release."

"And what have you to offer in return, Inspector?"

"Me," I said. "Take me." Hinrick actually laughed at that. "No, seriously. I'm more valuable to you than she is. Her death wouldn't raise an eyebrow. State wouldn't care. Defense wouldn't care. And I suspect, with your contacts, you already know that, too. They'll wait until you're airborne, out over the Atlantic somewhere, and shoot the plane down with a missile. Your aircraft will just disappear from the radar screen. Malaysian Flight 370 all over again. No trace. The various agencies will say *what a mys-*

tery – a man like George Hinrick just disappearing like that. But you'll never know any of that because you'll be dead."

"And what makes you so valuable?" he asked.

"I'm a recognized police officer. Highly decorated." I hoped Hinrick wouldn't notice my nose growing. "Those agencies I just mentioned? They wouldn't want to cover for my death. I'm too well known. Too many questions would be asked."

"You're best known for Beverly Garland, the hostage you lost." He chuckled. I restrained myself from showing any emotion, even though I wanted to kill the SOB where he stood.

"Just bad luck," I finally said.

"Your bad luck is just beginning." Hinrick turned his head toward the woods and nodded.

CHAPTER 84

Mosby followed McGuire's car through the A5's scope until it stopped in front of the house. He moved the scope slightly to his right and put his reticle on Escher's *hideout*. He still couldn't make out Escher's shape through the dense foliage, but he was there. Mosby could *feel* him.

Having Escher as an active shooter in this drama complicated the equation somewhat. Mosby went over his options. He could get into a gun battle with Escher right now. *Would that be sweet, or what? The adrenaline rush when it's either him or me? Nothing even close.* Couldn't do it, though. An out-and-out gun battle might jeopardize Hinrick's safety, and he would do nothing to harm his grandfather. Besides, Escher could already have engaged him. But he hadn't. Why? Then it all made sense. *Escher will shoot me right after I shoot McGuire. As soon as he hears my shot, he'll fire. Well, screw that. When my grandfather gives me the nod, I'll take out McGuire. By the time Escher hears the shot and sees McGuire go down, I'll be on the ground rolling. If he gets a shot off at all, it won't be close.*

Mosby brought the scope to his eyes and reacquired McGuire in his reticle. When he saw his grandfather nod, he took his hand from the trigger guard, and flipped Escher off. With a satisfied smile, he shot McGuire.

Escher mirrored what Mosby had done. He followed McGuire's car as it made its way to Hinrick's mansion. He saw Hinrick, followed by a shackled Katelyn, leave the house. As soon as Hinrick engaged McGuire in conversation, Escher made sure the scope's crosshairs were on Mosby. He acknowledged Mosby's finger with an irritated grimace. When he saw Mosby's rifle recoil, he pulled the trigger on his Mk 21.

Mosby saw McGuire go down, but hesitated for a millisecond, wondering why he hadn't seen blood spatter from his chest. That hesitation was all it took for Escher's .338 Lapua Magnum to splatter Thaddeus Mosby's brains all over the trees behind him.

Escher smiled.

Then all hell broke loose.

~~~~

I lay flat on my back in front of the car with the sound of gunfire echoing all around me. *So much for my hostage rescue ability*. My chest hurt like a son-of-a-bitch, just like Delgado predicted. But also as he predicted, I was still alive.

I rolled over and tried to get up. I saw Hinrick standing exactly where he stood when I went down. This time, though, in a semi-daze. Confusion written all over his bony face. Katelyn saw me getting up and tried to come to me, but was restrained by one of the three guards now surrounding Hinrick. His protective phalanx.

"I told you," I yelled at Hinrick, hoping to be heard above the gun battle. "They're going to kill you." Just as scripted, bullets started hitting the ground around us. I smiled. Kincaid's shooters trying to get us moving.

Hinrick stared at me like I was a ghost. Then recognition slowly returned to his eyes. "They'll kill you," I yelled again. This time he reacted. "Take him," he said to one of his guards. "Take both of them to the plane."

One of his guards grabbed my arm and pulled me into the circle with Hinrick and Katelyn, walking as fast as

Hinrick's shuffle allowed. Which wasn't much. I struggled to put my arm around Katelyn, the burn in my chest not allowing me to pull her too close. "How you doing?" I whispered. "Looks like they gave you a hard time."

"Not that bad," she said, looking around to see if Hinrick's guards noticed their conversation. Satisfied they weren't, she quietly said, "How are you? I was so scared. A Molle vest? Ballistic plates?" I nodded. "Poor baby. You gotta be hurting."

"Hey, keep quiet, you two. And hurry up," one of the guards said, nudging us with the barrel of his rifle.

I stumbled forward, my chest barking at me. Letting me know it didn't appreciate my clumsiness.

"Can you tell me what's going down here?" she whispered as we fast-walked to the hangar.

"Kincaid's guys," I whispered back.

By this time, Hinrick had slowed down considerably. One of his guards picked him up in a fireman's carry and broke into a jog. We all followed suit. My chest rebelled, but I had no choice. *Suck it up, McGuire, or die.* Made for an easy decision.

Alerted by the gunfire, the pilot had the plane's jets screaming by the time we reached the hangar. Shots were still kicking at our heels. As we reached the plane's stairs, one of Hinrick's guards went down, hit in the upper leg. He dropped to the floor. I smiled, appreciative that Kincaid's men were thinning the herd.

The guard carrying Hinrick sprinted up the stairs and into the cabin. The other prodded Katelyn and me to move faster, not wanting to end up like his comrade. As soon as we were on board, the stairs were pulled up and the plane started to roll forward. Katelyn and I were led into the main cabin and told to sit. I welcomed the respite as my chest felt like someone had hit it with the broad side of a shovel.

Out the window, I saw Kincaid and his men standing by the house. In front of them, seated cross-legged with hands behind bowed heads, were six of Hinrick's palace guards. Kincaid's part of the battle had come to a close.

Ours had just begun.

CHAPTER 85

Hinrick walked over, motioning to one of the two sur-viving guards to stand behind me. "If he makes so much as a twitch, Antoine, put a bullet in his head." Then, looking down at me, he said, "You're wearing a vest?" I nodded. "Let me see."

"Hard to do while I'm sitting. Can I stand?"

He nodded and took a step back. "Same deal," he said to Antoine. "He makes any move not authorized by me, you kill him." He paused, looked at the other guard watching from the galley doorway, and pointed to Katelyn. "Same goes for her, Manny."

I unbuttoned my shirt and pulled it open. Just those movements made my chest feel like it was on fire. I looked down and saw where the bullet impacted the vest. Center breastbone. *Thank you Kincaid and Delgado*, I thought.

"Ah, a Molle." When I didn't react, he said, "Nice vest. Manufactured by a friend of mine. Norwegian fellow. Lives in Germany, but has manufacturing plants all over the world." He took a step closer. "And look where you were hit." He pointed to where the shell had torn into the mesh nylon fabric covering the ballistic plates. "My grand-son – he was a good boy." I could hear the pain in his voice. "And a good shot. If you weren't wearing the vest, he would have killed you."

"It's why I wore the damn thing. Because I didn't want to be dead. In fact, I wanted him dead. And he is." My mouth twisted into a cruel smile.

He didn't react to my taunt. Instead he stepped closer to me, again telling the guard to shoot me if I moved. "You must hurt." Not waiting for a reply, he said, "My grandson shoots a .300 Winchester Magnum. Great cartridge. I have another friend who manufactures that cartridge. In fact, has a virtual monopoly on it. 'Course he licenses it out. Last thing he wants, any of us wants for that matter, is government scrutiny.

"The combination of the mesh nylon and ballistic plates stopped that cartridge, dissipating the force of the impact over your entire chest. Take the Molle off. Let's see what it did to you."

I peeled the shirt off and then struggled through the pain to unclasp the fasteners holding the vest in place. Neither Hinrick nor the guards offered to help. As it came free, I looked down. A deep dark purple bruise ran across my chest from armpit to armpit, and from my collarbone to right above my belly button.

"My, my," Hinrick said, coming closer and bending down to inspect. "Looks like you may have a broken rib." With that, he hit me square in the chest with his bony fist.

I doubled over and fell back into the chair, gasping for air. I heard Katelyn cry out, and saw the second guard come across the cabin to restrain her movement toward me.

"That's for killing my grandson," Hinrick said, the spittle flying from his lips. "It's just a taste of what's in store for you once we land. And your girlfriend, too."

"Fuck you," I said through clenched teeth. "You're nothing but a low-life *peso broker*. I'll kill you with my bare hands before this flight lands."

"You better hope so," Hinrick said, taking a step back and jamming his hands in his coat pocket. "I do like your spirit, though, Inspector. Too bad we're on opposite sides of the playing field. But once this plane lands, no one will hear from you ever again. My Russian friends will see to that."

Seven miles behind them, and ten thousand feet below, Rob Kincaid was on the phone with Admiral Thompson. "Good going, Rob," Thompson said. "I'm glad it went as planned, at least so far. I'll alert my people that the plane is on its way."

Four minutes later, the aircraft carrier USS George H.W. Bush, at station in the Atlantic five hundred miles east of Montauk, confirmed they had radar contact with Hinrick's plane.

CHAPTER 86

"You were wrong about me, you know," Hinrick said with a wistful smile.

I looked at him quizzically. "Wrong?" I whispered. The pain roiling through my chest made it hard to breathe. "About what?"

"I'm not a *peso broker*."

"Well, that's what I heard."

He smiled. "You probably don't even know what that means – *peso broker*. They're low-level scum."

"And isn't that what you are?"

An unctuous smile broke the wrinkled lines of his face. "You'll have to do better than that, Inspector. I've jousted with the world's best for the past seventy years. You think a man spending his last day on earth can make me mad?" He looked down at me through rheumy eyes.

"*Peso brokers* are just money launderers," he said, the college professor explaining the facts of economic life to a recalcitrant student. "I'm an international financier. I only make deals with people I know and trust. I'm a one-stop shop for people needing *quiet* transactions."

"Quiet? Yeah, right. You mean secret. Non-traceable."

"My clients need privacy. I provide it. And they pay me handsomely for it."

"You're nothing but an arms dealer. A peso broker, like I said."

"Not true," he snapped. "But you wouldn't understand. I don't launder money. I complete an entire transaction, from finance to purchase. The manufacturers of goods and services deal with me only. Totally efficient."

"Like you learned from your grandfather?" Katelyn interjected.

His face twitched violently. A jerky, spasmodic movement. "*The Custer Papers*," he sputtered. "I *knew* something like that would be in there. That's why they have to be destroyed, and why you two are going to die."

"Your grandfather was Max Gutnick, wasn't he?" Katelyn continued. "Max – I'll use your word – *financed* the buying and selling of arms worldwide."

"So you think you made a connection between him and me. That's nothing new. For years, others have promulgated that filthy rumor, too. It's never gained any traction."

"But they didn't have the *Custer Papers,*" she said. "I've read those papers. George Custer knew your grandfather. Knew about his connection with the Edmunds United Steel Trust."

"Pure speculation. I can get a dozen world-renowned scholars who will swear the *Custer Papers* are a fraud."

"Then why are you going to all this trouble to stop them from going public?" she replied.

"You have no idea who you're dealing with here, do you?" Hinrick said, shaking his head. "This is so far above you. We're talking about a whole different level of authority. Of power. Worldwide power. Nothing short of a global shadow government."

"Don't you think you're giving yourself a wee bit more credit than you deserve?" I said.

He laughed. "Suit yourself. The fact remains that if these papers are allowed to go public, the way things are now with the Internet – let's just say we don't want to go through the aggravation of denying it over and over again. This will turn into a circus like the Kennedy assassination."

"What about Abrahamsohn?" Katelyn said.

"You see? That's exactly what I'm talking about. You bring up a name from the past. A name that's been buried for over a century. Another aggravation. Now people will start looking into connections. We're confident they won't find anything poisonous about that name, but why should we take the chance? Again, more aggravation. We're going to destroy those damn papers and be done with it."

"Well, the papers *are* out," Katelyn said. "Our people have been digging through them. It's clear that your grandfather, Max Gutnick, was *the founder* of the Edmunds United Steel Trust."

"So?" Hinrick answered. "Good historians already knew that. Not a big thing. But good historians don't know whether or not I'm related to him. Since we now have the original papers, we're going to keep it that way."

"Are you sure you have the originals?"

"Oh, no," Hinrick said in mock surprise. "You mean the papers you delivered weren't the originals?" He cackled again. "You people are such amateurs. In the world I come from, you'd be nothing more than a minor annoyance. To be swept under the rug at the first opportunity."

"Is that why you haven't killed us yet?" I asked.

"Brilliant deduction, Inspector. I have experts waiting for us in Sevastopol. If they determine the papers you gave me are indeed fake, then one of Ms. Murray's fingers will show up at your embassy every day until they are delivered."

"You're one sick puppy," I said.

"Only when I have to be. Maybe we'll intersperse your tongue with one of her fingers. Then I won't have to listen to you anymore."

"Since we don't have much time left in this world, could you just humor us for a minute?" Katelyn asked. "In the papers, Custer said at the 1910 Esperanto meeting he heard Gutnick telling people he was appointing one Hans

Abrahamsohn as CEO of the Trust. And you're saying that name was fictitious?"

"I didn't say fictitious. I said the name's been vetted and buried for a century."

"Not quite a century. Since 1927, to be exact. We researched Mr. Abrahamsohn. While doing so, we found your grandfather disappeared soon after World War I started."

"If you'd done your homework," Hinrick said, "you would have known my grandfather didn't just *disappear* as you say. He was killed defending Paris from the Germans in 1914."

"His body was never found," Katelyn responded. "After the war, a fellow named Abrahamsohn turned up in Romania. Manager of the oil fields. Oddly enough, where you say you are from."

"Talk about a coincidence," Hinrick said with a half smile.

"Yeah. But then in 1927, the Abrahamsohn clan disappears from the face of the earth. The official story is the Nazis executed them; the father, mother, a girl and boy. Convenient, because shortly after Abrahamsohn disappears, your family, Hinrick, surfaces. Also in the oil business. We connected the dots. We're betting the Hinricks are related to the Gutnicks who are related to the Abrahamsohns."

"Ridiculous."

"Want to bet a DNA test on that?"

He sat down opposite us and gave an exaggerated sigh. The professor showing off in front of his students. "Whether Gutnick was my grandfather or not, I'd be proud to be in his lineage. He was a genius. Before the start of World War I, he single-handedly convinced the world's arms manufacturers to be *a*-political. That their businesses would survive no matter who won the war. And he was right. Arms manufacturers survived World War I intact.

Ditto every other damn war, big and small, since then. Being *in* a nation-state but not *of* a nation-state is a principle my colleagues have lived by for the past hundred-some years. Since Custer's time."

"And you think that's a good thing?" I asked.

"I'm not into making moral judgments, Inspector. No, I'm just a humble businessman."

"A humble businessman that causes the deaths of millions of people worldwide every year," Katelyn said.

"I leave the question of *causality* to the philosophers. Let me say, though, that without someone pulling the trigger, our guns wouldn't kill anyone."

"You're a sick man," I said.

"No. I'm not sick. And my business doesn't make people sick. Society makes people sick. Mothers and fathers make their children sick. Drugs make people sick. If you want to be morally righteous and talk about causes, then go after what *causes* a sick society. I only make the toys that help sick people act out their sick fantasies."

"Give me a break," I said. "Your companies arm nations, not people."

"Keep it straight, Inspector. We don't arm anyone or any nation. I help finance the sale of merchandise. My help is strictly business. I don't take sides."

"*Don't take sides*," Katelyn said evenly. "I've heard that said of you somewhere before."

"You can't keep this going," I added.

"People have been saying that for decades. Too bad you won't be around to see how it all turns out."

"You're forgetting one thing," I said.

"What's that?"

"Ain't dead yet."

Hinrick laughed heartily, the spittle forming on the corners of his mouth. "You will be, my good man. You will be. You ain't gettin' no older than tomorrow."

CHAPTER 87

"I'm through with these tiresome people," Hinrick said, waving his hand contemptuously over Katelyn and me. "Manny, take a half hour break. Get a drink for yourself. It's going to be a long flight. I'll be with the pilot." He started to leave, but turned and said, "Antoine. Be sure there is no talking between the two of them. I don't want them hatching an escape plan." He laughed again and walked to the cockpit.

I looked at Katelyn. "Time to go," I whispered.

She smiled resignedly. "You're still in shock."

"No, God dammit. I mean it."

"Hey, you two. Knock off the talking. You heard what Mr. Hinrick said."

Katelyn looked over at him, then back at me. She nodded. "Then let's do it."

"Knock it off," Antoine said again, this time walking over in front of us.

"Come on," I said. "Don't be such a hard-ass. Was just telling my lady friend that I have to go take a dump." He scowled, like it was going to really inconvenience him. But he finally nodded and escorted me aft to the lavatory. "Leave the door open," he said.

"I don't think so," I replied. "I'm shy."

"Then you're going to have to hold it," he said, grabbing my arm to lead me back to the main cabin.

I yanked it free. "What? You think I'm going to try to escape by flushing myself down the crapper? Or are you just a pervert? Want to see my pecker? Maybe get on your knees?"

Antoine didn't appreciate my humor, but it had its de-sired effect. He pulled me roughly back and shoved me into the bathroom's door. "Don't fuck with me," he said. "Be quick."

I pushed the door open and entered. Dammit. I'd for-gotten how small these things were. I had to pretzel myself just to close the door. Once I had locked it, I looked to-ward the ceiling. The vent cover was right where Kincaid said it would be. On their recon mission early this morn-ing, Kincaid and Delgado had removed the fan from that vent. I was anxious to get my hands on what they left for me.

I stood on the toilet seat and put my fingernails under the vent cover's edges, slowly prying it off. It wasn't easy. To add to the degree of difficulty, it made a squeaky noise every time it moved. So much noise that Antoine banged on the door. "Hey, what the hell is going on in there," he said. "Open up. Now."

"Nothing's going on in here," I said. "Just trying to wash my hands. The damn faucet's stuck. Be right out." I knew I didn't have the luxury of time. I yanked as hard as I could. The vent came off, as did my foot from the toilet seat, causing me to fall backward into the door.

Antoine pounded on the door again. "Don't know what you're up to in there, but time's up," he said, trying to push the door open. My body weight against it kept it closed. "Come out right now, or I'll put a few rounds into you through the door. You'll die in a crapper." I could tell from his chuckle that it would be a story he would relish for years to come. Telling his cohorts how he took out a guy taking a dump.

"I'm coming. Hold on." I quickly stepped back on the toilet seat and put my hand into the vent. At first I didn't feel anything. *Shit. Where'd they put the son-of-a-bitch?* A jolt of fear coursed through me before the familiar grip of my P7 tickled my fingertips.

"You got 'til I count to three," Antoine said. "Then you die."

"Get your fat ass away from the door so I can open it," I said with feigned indignation, as if he were the reason I couldn't come out. I put the gun behind my right leg and opened the door.

"It's about..." was all he got out before I shoved the P7 hard under his left eye. His gun was still holstered, thank God. "Hands on your head, asshole," I breathed through clenched teeth. "You utter a single sound and it'll be your last. Understood?" He nodded, his eyes wide and radiating fear. *A punk*, I thought. I'd seen a hundred guys just like this. When they controlled the weapon and were able to bully you, they were the toughest guys on the block. Reverse the situation, and they became pussies. "Weapon?" He started to take his right hand down to get it for me. I pushed the P7 harder against his cheekbone and leaned in so close our noses touched. "I told you not to move, remember? Just whisper in my ear where I can find it."

"Under the jacket. Left side," he squeaked.

I reached down, found his gun and stuck it in my waistband. "Let's go see your boss, shall we?"

CHAPTER 88

I walked Antoine back into the main cabin. Thankfully, his sidekick hadn't yet come back from his break.

Katelyn looked at me with wondering eyes, then recognition at what had occurred, then that heartbreak smile. She jumped out of her seat and came to me. I handed her Antoine's Sig Sauer 9mm.

"Stay here with him," I said. "I've got something else to get. I won't be long. If his partner comes back, take him alive. We can't afford bullets flying around in this aircraft. Besides, we don't want to alert the pilot that something is going on. He'll freeze us out of the cockpit."

I went back to the lavatory, stood on the toilet seat and put my hand into the vent cavity. Kincaid and Delgado left one more package. With Antoine breathing down my neck, I didn't have time to it pull out. A baggie containing two-dozen heavy-duty plastic zip ties. The two-dozen was overkill, but when we were discussing the operation, they didn't know how many of Hinrick's people would be aboard.

Back in the main cabin, I whispered in Antoine's ear. "We're going to walk over to the galley doorway. You'll ask Manny to come join you. Tell him the prisoners are acting up. Got that?" He nodded as I walked him over to the doorway, the P7 pushing firmly against his skull. "You get creative, and your brains will be wallpaper. Understand?" He nodded again, swallowing hard. Scared. Good!

Antoine followed orders and soon we had Manny's wrists and ankles zip-tied to one of the cabin seats. "And now for the pilot," I said to Katelyn. "We've got to get him to put this plane on auto pilot."

"I don't think that will be a problem," she said. "I'll tell him real nice. He's got two choices. Either he does what we want, or we throw him out the door."

"I'm glad I brought you along," I said with a smile.

"But just between you and me? We really don't need him. I have a pilot's license. I can figure out how to engage the auto pilot." She smiled and gave me a quick kiss on the cheek. For just an instant, my chest stopped hurting.

When Antoine knocked on the cockpit door, Hinrick immediately came out. When he saw me, and then my gun, a wry smile crossed his lips. "I underestimated you, Inspector," he said. "But you've gone to a lot of trouble for nothing. The outcome will remain the same. It always does. Except for you and your girlfriend, maybe. You both probably will escape with your lives."

"Better than that, I think," I replied.

"We'll see."

A moment later, Katelyn came out of the cockpit with the pilot in tow. "Mission accomplished, sir," she said with a quick salute. "Autopilot set."

"What do you have in mind for me?" Hinrick asked as I zip-tied him and the others to their seats. I noticed the prick wasn't concerned about what would happen to his cohorts. He was only worried about the *me*.

"Not sure about you," I replied, "but Ms. Murray and myself have a rendezvous with a United States Navy aircraft carrier in exactly ..." I looked at my watch. "... one hour and eighteen minutes. It's waiting for us about twelve hundred miles due east of our present position."

"See, I told you, Inspector. With me, the outcomes never change." He pulled on his restraints. "So we'll land on a U.S. carrier, instead of Sevastopol. I'll be detained for a while. Maybe a day, but no more. With my connections,

I'll soon be a free man. Living among friends in the Crimea."

"You have that wrong, Mr. Hinrick. Wait here." I laughed, knowing he had no choice. "Ms. Murray and I have a surprise for you."

I took Katelyn's arm and guided her aft. "Kincaid told me you had graded-out third in your CIA parachute jump class."

"What does that have to do with anything?" she asked. "We're not going to jump from this plane, are we?"

I bent down and started pulling away Hinrick's luggage, revealing a large steamer trunk. I knelt down and opened it. "Take a look-see," I said with a smile.

"My God," she said, looking down at two parachutes, two sets of thermals to wear under the jumpsuits provided; two oxygen bottles attached to zip up vests, and helmets. "How the hell did they get all this gear aboard?"

"Rob and Vinnie brought them in last night. They found the plane unattended when they did their little recon mission. Hinrick's luggage was already in the plane so all they did was wedge this trunk in with it. Planted my P7 in the bathroom, along with this." I unfolded the cloth that contained the bomb.

Katelyn smiled and gave a slight whistle. "Those friends of yours are resourceful, I'll give 'em that," she said.

"It's got a timing fuse. After you pull this pin, you've got one hour. Do you want to do the honors?"

"God – you bet."

We put the jumpsuits over the thermals, and slipped on the vests with the oxygen bottles. We'd be jumping out of the plane at approximately thirty-thousand feet, opening our chutes four seconds after leaving the plane. Not much breathable air at that altitude, hence the oxygen bottles. We'd be gliding about twenty minutes, and – if we were lucky – make a spectacular landing right on the carrier's deck.

We strapped on the chutes and walked back into the main cabin. I carried the bomb. Their reactions were about what you'd have expected. Confusion. Disbelief. But most of all – fear. I watched Katelyn's expression change into a mixture of joy and relief. For her, justice was about to be served.

She walked over and stood in front of Hinrick. I knew what was coming, and I could tell how much she relished this moment. She bent at the waist, hands on her knees. She was inches from his face. "You're *the man who doesn't take sides*," she said.

He looked at her quizzically. "Is that a question?" he asked. "I don't understand."

"You don't, huh? Does the name Hassan Al-I'man ring a bell? He was the one who told me you were the man who didn't take sides."

"Am I supposed to know him?" Hinrick asked.

"You should. You paid him to kill my father. I've been waiting for this day for fourteen years. I was going to just shoot you. But this is much better. Give you a few minutes to think about what awaits you in the afterlife. Before your lungs burst from lack of oxygen."

"I'm sorry," he said, his voice feigning boredom. "Your name is Murray. I don't remember ordering anyone named Murray to be killed."

"How about Tucker? Does that name jog your memory?"

He was silent for a moment, then the light of recognition registered in his eyes. "Ah, yes. Now I remember. The station chief in Lebanon. Didn't know he had a daughter."

"Would it have made any difference?"

"No. It was strictly a business decision."

She stood and turned to the others. "Did you hear that? This man's business decisions have caused the deaths of millions of people around the world. And now yours."

"Please, Ms. Murray," pleaded Manny. "I have a wife and daughter. Spare me. I meant you no harm."

"Better you plead with your Maker than me," she said. "When you play with evil men, evil things happen. And Mr. Hinrick is evil." Katelyn turned and walked over to me.

"In a minute, I am going to open the cabin door," I said. "The cabin, of course, will instantly depressurize. You'll know because anything not tied down, and that includes Ms. Murray and myself, will be sucked out the door. Of course, we want to be sucked out the door. That's why we have on these parachutes."

"But you won't have to worry," Katelyn said in a cheerful voice, making eye contact with each man. "You won't be sucked out because you are already tied down."

"Don't forget to tell them about the oxygen," I said with a smile.

"I was just getting to that. When we open the door, not only will everything that is not tied down be sucked out the door, but so will all the oxygen in the cabin."

"There's a good news, bad news scenario to all this," I said. "The good news is that as soon as the oxygen is sucked out, the oxygen masks will be deployed from the ceiling there." All eyes went to the place where I was pointing. "The bad news is that with your wrists and legs bound like they are, you'll never be able to reach them."

I walked forward to the cockpit and got on the radio to the *Bush*. Wanted to make sure they knew we were coming, and were prepared to pick us up if we missed the flight deck. They were. Everything was ready.

As I came back into the cabin, I noticed Katelyn kneeling in front of Hinrick, talking in a low voice. I came closer, catching her words. "… watch you die," she said.

"But just knowing that you'll be flopping around like a fish out of water will sustain me for the rest of my life. You'll have three, maybe four minutes of agony before your soul rots forever in hell."

"Fuck you."

"Don't you wish."

She stood up. I tried to help her, but she pushed my hand away. "I'm okay. Give me the bomb."

"I've already put it in the cockpit and closed and locked the door so it won't fly out when we depressurize."

Katelyn turned back to the captives. "There's a bomb on board set to go off in one hour," she said. "It will explode when you are approximately nine hundred miles off the coast of Spain. You will all be long dead by then, of course, but I just wanted you to know. You will completely vanish from the face of the earth. No one will ever know what happened to you. Whatever parts of your body hit the water will quickly be eaten by sharks." I looked at her with a *what's up with that* expression. "Just letting them know what they can expect," she said.

"Nice of you – I guess."

With that, we put the oxygen breathing tubes in our mouths, opened the cabin door and jumped.

CHAPTER 89

Two Days Later

One thing I forgot about jumping out of an airplane at thirty thousand feet – it's really, really cold up there. Thankfully, Kincaid and Delgado supplied enough warm clothing to protect us for the twenty-minute glide to the *Bush*. I must admit, making a perfect landing on the deck of a moving U.S. aircraft carrier in the middle of the At-lantic Ocean was a pretty kick-ass feeling. Couldn't wait to tell TJ.

Katelyn and I stayed overnight on the carrier. Via the ship's radar, we followed the path of Hinrick's plane as it slid toward its inevitable rendezvous with the sea. It never made it. As it was descending through the five-thousand-foot level, it simply disappeared from the radar screen. One minute it was there, the next minute it wasn't. The bomb had done its job.

~~~~

The next day we flew to Ft. Bragg on the plane Admi-ral Thompson sent. His E-6 met us as we landed and es-corted us to Thompson's office.

"Come in," Thompson said as he walked around the conference table covering the back wall. He was a large man with brown eyes and a wide, friendly face. "At long last," he said, shaking Katelyn's hand and then mine. "Rob told me so much about you. He and Vin Delgado will be here later this evening. They're still cleaning up Hinrick's compound. Please, have a seat. We'll have dinner soon, but I did scrounge up some snacks in case you didn't have lunch. Hungry?"

I looked at Katelyn. She nodded. "Help yourself." We each took a croissant and coffee, and sat at the conference table.

"You're here, so the parachutes worked, obviously." He smiled.

"As did the Molle vest, sir," I said. "Still sore, though."

"And you will be for a while, I'm afraid. But it beats the hell out of the alternative." He paused to take a sip of his coffee. "The skipper of the carrier told me you made a perfect landing on his deck. Congrats. That's not easy to do."

"It's like riding a bike," Katelyn said. "You never forget the basics."

"Not sure you've seen this yet," Thompson said, pushing a copy of the *New York Times* across the table. "Page three. Below the fold."

I opened the paper and folded it back so Katelyn and I could both read it.

FINANCIER AND INDUSTRIALIST
GEORGE HINRICK FEARED LOST AT SEA.

Katelyn and I smiled at one another. "I'm surprised this didn't make the front page," she said.

"Yeah. Surprises me, too," said Thompson. "Another article that didn't make the front page was the death last night of the Under Secretary of Defense, Joe Parkman. In his office. He was working late. They found him this morning slumped over his desk. Heart attack. At least that's what we hear from the medical examiner."

"Another real shame," I said. "So what happens now, Admiral? With Hinrick gone, I mean."

"We expect there will be a lot of changes. Katelyn can tell you. Because Hinrick's family was present at the creation, *the cabal's* creation, they afforded him the primary place of honor. The glue, so to speak, that held the group together."

"But he's still only one guy," I said. "He's dead, but the cabal still lives."

"I don't know what Admiral Thompson thinks," Katelyn said, "but our group believes taking out Hinrick will create a power vacuum in their fraternity. Hoping that various members put up a fight to fill the vacuum. The net effect will be to destabilize the group. Getting them to go to war with each other."

"I guess we can only hope, huh? But to tell you the truth, this is all above my pay grade. I'm nothing but a poor homicide inspector from San Francisco. And I probably should start thinking of getting back." Katelyn kicked me under the table and gave me a stern look. I shrugged my shoulders. "I know," I said to her, "but I'm out of time. Lt. Bristow is going to throw a fit if I'm not back soon."

Thompson took note of our interaction and said, "Nonsense. You don't have to go back just yet. I can call your supervisor like I did a few weeks ago and extend your stay at least another few weeks. You earned it as far as I'm concerned."

Katelyn slapped the table. "See, McGuire? You've now got friends in high places. You're a free man."

"We'll see about that," I said. "But thanks, Admiral. I appreciate it. I want to call my son and tell him I'm all right, and could be here another few weeks. Can I do that?"

"You stay here and make that call," Thompson replied. "I'll take Katelyn for a short tour of the grounds. Make yourself comfortable. We'll be back in twenty minutes."

~~~~

I talked to TJ the whole twenty minutes. He hardly asked about what I'd been doing. Instead, he told me how much he loved police work, but, sadly, his internship had to be cancelled for budgetary reasons. Wanted to know when I'd be home. Maybe we could take that trip to the Little Bighorn. I told him I had a better idea – why not come east and spend the next two weeks traveling with his old man up and down the coast? I emphasized that it was an all-expense paid trip. It was the paid part that sold him. I hung up just as Katelyn walked in. Alone.

"What happened to Thompson?" I asked.

"His E-6 cornered him in the hallway. Something came up that required his immediate attention. He apologized. I guess you're stuck with me."

"Don't mind at all. Talked my son into coming out here. He jumped at the chance. He'll be here day after tomorrow. Staying two weeks. Would you like to meet him?"

"Of course I'd like to meet him."

"Think you can get off for the next two weeks?"

She flashed that heartbreak smile. "I thought you'd never ask."

###

EPILOGUE

In late September of this year, the CIA released a heavily redacted version of what has become known as The Custer Papers. The original was sent to the Smithsonian Institution for historians to study. Because of my involvement in finding the Papers, they sent me the first chapter. It details, in Custer's own words, how he managed to escape the Battle of the Little Bighorn and make his way to France. Respecting the wishes of Matt Conroy who died so that The Custer Papers could be made public, I'm including here what was given to me by the CIA.

September 6, 1914
Chinon, France

I pen this account on September 6, 1914. I am in frail health and fear that my beloved France, my adopted home for the past thirty-eight years, may soon be overrun by the German hordes now within fifty kilometers of Paris. Philippe, my son, enlisted in the French army in mid-August, just a few short days before his forty-fifth birthday. I tried to talk him out of it, but to no avail. I understand what drives him. All I can do now is pray God protects him. The day Philippe joined the army, I sent Amelie, his wife, and Francois, my twelve-year-old grandson, to neutral Spain. I do not want them touched by war... ever.

~~~~

My story essentially begins on March 20th, 1876. That day is etched in my memory because it was the beginning of the end of my life as Lt. Colonel George Armstrong Custer.

The 7th Cavalry's campaign against the hostiles had originally been scheduled to begin April 6th, but was postponed because I was subpoenaed to testify at a Congressional hearing in DC against President Grant's brother, Orville. The hearing was scheduled to start the next day, March 21st.

I arrived two days early and found myself on the 20th in the lobby of the Willard Hotel seated across from my friend and mentor, General Philip Sheridan. He had insisted on meeting prior to the hearing. I figured he was going to warn me that testifying against Grant's brother would almost certainly have deleterious consequences on my military career. I was prepared for that, and had an answer ready. What I wasn't prepared for was what he actually told me.

With a grim look on his face, he leaned forward and in a hushed tone told me that there were rich and powerful men plotting my death. In fact, it was to happen at the battle with the Sioux and Cheyenne that we all knew was imminent. I was, of course, startled at the news, but mostly mad. I asked him who these men were so I could shoot them through their cowardly black hearts.

No matter how much I pleaded, he wouldn't tell me. All he said was it wasn't personal. Sheridan said these men considered me pivotal to their plans because only my death could generate the anger sufficient to finally get the government to drive the Indians off the Plains. And once gotten rid of, all the land west of the Missouri River could be parceled and sold to the horde of expected settlers.

I didn't know what to say. My mind shot through the alternatives. It seemed I had only two choices. Either I accepted my fate and be remembered as a gallant soldier who bravely went to his death for his country, or I could refuse to go and be forever branded as a craven coward to live out my life as a societal outcast.

I would never have accepted the latter. So my fate was essentially sealed. But then Phil Sheridan provided me with a third choice. His final words to me that day, the last day I ever saw him, were, "Autie ...," he used the term of endearment Libbie reserved for me, "... someone named George Armstrong Custer has to die at that battle. It just doesn't have to be you."

~~~~

In the end, I accepted Sheridan's pact with the devil. And as I pen these memoirs almost forty years later, I will admit I've wondered everyday if I made the right choice. A decision that forever ordained that my life will end in my adopted France, not in the land of my birth.

In France, I am known for being a wine maker. In the United States, from all reports, I am still considered a hero. That amuses me given the fact that my last battle was a complete disaster. A massacre. I still feel the guilt for not being there to share the same fate as my brothers Tom and Boston; my brother-in-law, Lieutenant Jim Calhoun; my nephew Harry Reed (who shared my nickname Autie, and was only eighteen when he died); my regimental adjutant, Lieutenant Bill Cook; and my good friend Mark Kellogg, a reporter for the New York Herald. And, of course I regret what I did to **XXXX XXXXXX**.

But it couldn't be helped.

I am convinced the massacre would never have happened had I been leading the troop. Serious mistakes were made. Who made them? No one seems to know. My friend, Buffalo Bill Cody and I kept up a correspondence over the years. He even visited me here when he brought his wild west show to the Continent. His take was the military needs a villain for what happened there, and since I'm officially dead and can't defend myself, they can blame me.

While splitting the command was normal practice in those years, something I had done numerous times, I'm convinced had I seen with my own eyes the array of Indians in that valley, I would have withdrawn and waited for Crook and Gibbon to arrive.

But since everyone thought I was there, and was killed, history will forever place the blame for that defeat on me.

Rich and powerful men! As soon as Sheridan mentioned them, I was convinced that they had to be friends of President Grant. It took me thirty years to find out who these men were. Although I was wrong about his complicity, it doesn't change the fact that Ulysses S. Grant filled his administration with very corrupt people. Because I was honest to a fault, his dislike for me was common knowledge. The straw that broke the camel's back, however, was the Congressional hearings before which I was about to testify the day after my lunch with General Sheridan.

The Secretary of War, a Grant appointee named William Belknap, was on trial along with Grant's brother Orville for bilking the troops who lived in the army forts scattered across the western prairie. Belknap had issued an order requiring that soldiers purchase all their goods from the fort stores. Then he sold the trading post positions at the forts to his friends ... for kickbacks. The consequence of this despicable thievery was the troops, <u>my troops</u>, were charged double for what they would have paid for the same goods in Bismarck.

I was furious, and still am all these decades later. When the Congressional committee summoned me to testify, I was only too happy to accommodate them. My testi-

mony got the Secretary of War impeached and sent to jail. The same jail, thanks to my testimony, that Orville Grant was sent to for the next seven years.

President Grant, of course, was furious with me for helping convict his brother. He sent Sherman to tell me not to leave Washington without seeing him. I honored his request, asking three different times to see him, but all three times he refused to see me.

By now, it was March 30th. Libbie wanted to stay in DC and shop. I, however, needed to be in the company of people who had nothing to do with the army. Clever people who might come up with a solution to the conundrum Sheridan had put me in. I decided to go to New York. I knew a man there named Lawrence Barrett. He was a great Shakespearean actor I met in St. Louis more than a decade before We became great friends. I coerced Libbie to come along, and we took the train to New York.

Libbie and I had been fighting a lot in those years. She heard the rumors about me having an Indian squaw named Monahsetah. That I supposedly even had a child by her. She started in on me about Monahsetah the day we left Washington. To change the subject, I told her what Sheridan confided to me about the powerful people who wanted me dead. She cried and pouted, not because I was going to die, but because she was worried what would happen to her if and when I did. It was during this conversation on the train that I came up with a solution that solved both our problems. I knew a number of officers who had taken out life insurance policies that assured their wives would be taken care of if something were to happen to them. While in New York, I would buy her a life insurance policy that, in the case of my death, would keep her forever in the life to which she had become accustomed.

"Just my going away would make you rich," I remember saying to her. She immediately stopped her pout-

ing and looked at me with a most serene smile. Never said another word all the way to New York.

We arrived at Grand Central Depot the morning of March 31st. Lawrence Barrett met us at the station. Barrett was in the city staring as Cassius in Shakespeare's Julius Caesar at the Brooklyn Theater. Libbie hated Barrett. Looking back, it could very well have been Libbie's profound dislike for him that cemented his and my relationship. Over dinner that night, I mentioned to Lawrence that I was thinking of obtaining a life insurance policy on me making Libbie my beneficiary. He happened to know the President of the New York Life Insurance Company, a Mr. Henry Bogert, and the next morning he took us to meet him. After much discussion, we finalized a $5,000 policy on my life naming Elizabeth Bacon Custer the beneficiary.

*Two days later, I put Libbie on a train for Chicago where I would meet her in one month. Being free from her was like being released from jail. Lawrence and I went drinking every day and to the Theater every night. What really released me from my self-inflicted prison, however, was meeting a young actor named **XXXX XXXXXX**. He played Marc Anthony to Barrett's Cassius. **XXXX** was not a great actor, but didn't need to be since he and **XXXXXXXXX** owned the Brooklyn Theater ever since **XXXXXXXXXXXX** had died two years before.*

*Over cocktails one afternoon, **XXXXXX** gave me the solution to my dilemma. He was captured by the romance of my being in the cavalry, and told me he would do anything to be able to accompany the 7th on an expedition. I told him the 7th would probably be leaving Ft. Lincoln around mid-May to round up some hostiles in Montana. That maybe I could fix it for him to ride along. But only if he'd let me play his role as Marc Anthony for the rest of April. He countered by saying he'd agree to that as long as he could play me a few days during the expedition. Per-*

fect, I thought. He would become the fake George Custer that I would offer to the gods of war.

From that point on, everything fell into place. **XXXXXX** got Barrett's permission for me to play Marc Anthony. I officially became an actor, and a good one if I do say so myself. Unbeknownst to him, poor **XXXX XXXXXX** had just signed his death warrant. In hindsight, it was a terrible thing I did, and wished to God I hadn't. But at the time, I wanted to live, and this looked like my only chance. I told **XXXXXX** to let his hair grow long and grow a mustache. If he was going to play my character in this upcoming drama, he had to look the part.

We left New York by train on May 6th, and arrived in Chicago on the ninth. I knew General Sheridan would be there that day, and wired ahead that I'd like to with meet him. I introduced **XXXX** to Libbie and asked that she take him to lunch while I spoke with Sheridan.

Sheridan and I met at the Palmer House. I told him about finding **XXXX XXXXXX** and wanted to test his acting skills by playing General George Custer when the 7th went to Montana. Sheridan laughed and clapped me on the shoulder, but then peppered me with questions. Making sure I had all the contingencies covered. He told me the plotters had arranged with the Sioux that they would make camp in the Little Bighorn Valley in Montana. It was there the 7th would attack them. The Sioux said they would shoot me while trying to cross the river. There was a crossing known as Medicine Tail Coulee. The 7th's Arikara scouts would know where in the valley the coulee was located, and would lead the column to it. There would be many braves positioned in the bushes around the coulee whose job it would be to shoot the man with flowing blonde hair and wearing a white buckskin coat.

Sheridan knew that my brother Tom would be in charge, and I was to tell Tom that once the fake Custer was shot, the Cavalry had to retreat quickly, leaving the body there. Sheridan said the Indians would do to the body what they always do to bodies. Mutilate it beyond recognition.

Libbie, **XXXXX** and I took the late train to St. Paul, where we meet General Terry. From St. Paul, the four of us traveled to Bismarck and finally to Fort Abraham Lincoln.

The night before we left for Montana, I was in my bed and Libbie in hers. I told her I had this feeling I wouldn't be coming back from Montana. That I had a premonition that I would be killed. I never before had voiced a concern about dying in battle, so she took me seriously. I told her that if something did happen to me, the insurance policy would assure her a life free of want. She actually came over and kissed me on the lips for the first time in twenty years.

The next morning, May 17th, the 7th Cavalry saddled up and, with The Girl I Left Behind Me being played by the regimental band, rode out of Ft. Abraham Lincoln – and into history.

In the month it took us to get to the Little Bighorn Valley, **XXXXXX** had become a passable cavalry officer. Riding at the head of the column next to me and my brother Tom kept him away from most of the other troopers. He had grown a mustache like mine, but kept his now long blonde hair tucked securely under his hat.

We reached the Yellowstone River on June 17th where we boarded the Far West riverboat that was waiting with the provisions we would need for the battle. That night I privately told Tom, Boston and Autie what was about to happen and why. They sympathized with both **XXXXXX** and me, but understood the stakes. I cautioned them that as soon as **XXXXXX** went down, they had to get the troops out of there. They assured me they would.

Tom and Boston spent the next few days essentially giving **XXXXXX** stage direction on his new role. They assured me he played the part easily.

On the evening of June 23rd, I had Autie cut my hair. I was up a 3 a.m. and got dressed in civilian clothes. I left my buckskin jacket and hat for **XXXXXX** to wear. I shaved my mustache and did not wear a hat so the soldier on picket duty that early morning would testify, if necessary, that he was sure the man who rode out looked nothing like General Custer. To further muddy his testimony, I gave him a handwritten order from General Custer himself to saddle me a strong, fresh mount for my mission. I was out of the camp by three forty-five. At 4 a.m. I heard reveille, and at five, from a distance of eight miles away, saw the cloud of dust as the 7th Cavalry rode to their fate.

Before the campaign, I got word to Monahsetah to bring my son Yellow Swallow and meet me at the confluence of the Missouri and James Rivers on the 6th of July. A long ride lay ahead of me.

Monahsetah was a Southern Cheyenne woman taken captive after my 7th Cavalry attacked and destroyed her camp at the Washita River in Oklahoma in the winter of 1868.

As was our custom, captured women were divided among the troopers. I took Monahsetah as mine and kept her with me the entire winter. She was a stunning beauty. Couldn't have been more than eighteen years old. We had a saying back then – "Indian women were easy to rape." And rape her I did. One of the many things I'm not proud of looking back on my life.

That winter, she conceived and, in the late autumn of 1869, bore me a son. Inheriting my hair color, the Cheyenne named him Yellow Swallow.

Libbie and I had no children, primarily because Libbie refused to sleep with me. Never wanting to take the blame, she spread the foul rumor that she wouldn't lay with me *because I was rendered impotent by a venereal disease contracted while a cadet at West Point. A vicious lie, destroyed completely by my siring Yellow Swallow.*

I arranged for Monahsetah and Yellow Swallow, who was five years old at the time, to be admitted to the Grand River Indian Agency in the Dakota Territory. It was from that Agency that Monahsetah and my son started their journey south to meet me.

It was at the town of Yankton, just a few miles from my rendezvous point at the James River, that I first learned of the Massacre that had occurred at the Little Bighorn. A copy of the Helena Herald sat on a chair in the livery where I purchased a wagon and two horses for our trip to Chicago. I remember the headline word-for-word, as if it was sitting right here in front of me today:

"General Custar's (they misspelled my name) Command Annihilated. Custar killed, three hundred dead. General Custar's Two Brothers, a Nephew, Brother-in Law, and 17 Commissioned Officers Among Killed."

It was with heavy heart that I met Monahsetah and my son later that day at the James River. For the next three and a half weeks we made our way slowly across Iowa by wagon, arriving in Chicago on August 2nd. I wired Lawrence Barrett in New York asking if we could stay with him. After a week of train travel, we arrived in New York on August 10th.

We stayed with Lawrence for two months. At the beginning, I was consumed reading the reports of the battle and its aftermath. It was a self-inflicted nightmare, I now realize, fueled partly by my curiosity as to whether my deception had been discovered. But mostly fueled by the heavy guilt I carried for abandoning my beloved 7th Cavalry. I grieved for my brothers and for what I had done to **XXXXXX.**

But over time, mostly on account of the love I felt for Monahsetah and Yellow Swallow, my guilt flowered into thankfulness coupled with a searing resolve never to glory in war again.

In mid-October, as we were getting ready to board the ship that would take us to England, Mr. Barrett put his arm around my shoulder and told me I did the right thing. That the future was now, and was the only thing that mattered. He quoted Brutus' speech at the end of Julius Caesar: "There is a tide in the affairs of men, which, taken at the flood, leads to fortune ..." He told me to run with the current.

~~~~

That's exactly how I feel now. I'm running with the current. If Paris falls, the Huns will arrive in my beautiful Loire valley less than a week from now. I expect them to sweep away everything in their path in an orgy of death and destruction.

My life is full of ironies. Like the Sioux and the Cheyenne, I will stay here and defend the land that I love. The precious land where Monahsetah is buried.

~~~~

When we left New York, we took a ship to London and then to Paris. Monahsetah had a difficult time in this foreign environment, but she persevered and didn't complain. I loved her all the more for it. To assimilate, we learned French and changed our family name to Arnaud. I was Claude and Yellow Swallow became Philippe, after General Philip Sheridan. I bought property in Chinon in 1890. Soon after, Monahsetah came down with a sickness doctors couldn't name. Something she brought with her from America. She died in 1892.

Philippe and I planted grapes on our property, and prospered. Philippe met a town girl, Amelie, and they were married the first day of the new century. I let them have the family house and together we built a small one for me just fifty meters to the south. Two years later they had a son, François. My grandson.

And now war.

After all these years, I can't help but feel partly to blame. I should not have accepted Sheridan's pact with the devil. I should have spoken out. The battle in Montana was to be the proving ground, testing whether outside interests could manipulate public opinion for their own benefit. I should have been there.

My entire life had been touched by war. Consumed by war. But that day, June 25, 1876, taught me a truth that I take to my grave. Man's innate passion for war had been harnessed by people who have their own agenda.

How else could I explain the fact that just twenty-three years after my 7th Cavalry, was massacred firing single-shot Springfield rifles, the United States had an armada of ships showering 5-inch shells down on the Spanish fleet in the Philippines?

How do I explain to my grandson, Francois, a world run amok on building bigger and more destructive weapons? Or to my son Philippe, that ordinary soldiers like him will be ordered to advance against weapons that can spew forth death at four hundred rounds per minute.

Why did this happen? Who benefitted from the world rushing to war? Sheridan had it right. Rich and powerful men!

I had met them all. At the World Wide Esperanto Congress in 1910, held in Neutral Moresnet. An international cabal of arms dealers, who called themselves the Edmunds United Steel Trust, convened the Congress as a cover. They thought speaking in Esperanto, a secret language, would hide their purpose. Because I had learned Esperanto, I was taken into their confidence. The Trust was comprised solely of the major international arms dealers –

from Britain, Germany, France, Italy, Austria, Russia and the United States. They convened for one reason, and one reason only – to conspire as to how to keep the world at war with itself. These men had no country allegiance. They themselves and their businesses.

Rich and powerful men! The same men who used me and my beloved 7th Cavalry as their guinea pig. That by controlling certain events, they could convince countries they needed to go to war to right supposed wrongs. Wrongs that had been manipulated by them.

Manipulation on a grand scale.

How else could you explain a world now rushing toward the abyss because a nineteen-year-old anarchist shot and killed an Archduke and his wife? Who were the men who influenced the different rulers to enter into treaties obligating their countries to defend the honor of other countries? These were the men. The arms dealers.

Manipulation on a grand scale, indeed! Rich and powerful men, indeed! And the Battle of the Little Bighorn was their proving ground.

They won. The world lost.

I lost.

Acknowledgments

To **Kyle Garcia**, a HOG who served his country as a Marine sniper in Iraq and graciously gave of his time to instruct me on the art of how to hit your target at a thousand meters.

To **Patricia Leslie**, for her sharp eye and insightful comments.

To **Ed Addeo**, for his editing prowess and infectious smile. I owe you a beer.

To **Dave Almeida**, a great friend who shared with me his boatload of specialized knowledge.

To **Vivian Roubal**, for being the first to have faith in the book and review it in a mainstream newspaper.

To my **Naval Order of the United States** companions in the San Francisco Commandery, especially COL Allan C; CAPT Michele L; CAPT Ken H; CAPT Kris C; and RADM Tom B. Your overwhelming enthusiasm was much appreciated.

Thank you for purchasing this
Pen Books paperback.

Please remember to leave a review at
your favorite retailer.

DENNIS KOLLER is author of the popular Tom
McGuire suspense series including *The Oath*, *Kissed By
The Snow*, and *The Custer Conspiracy*. Mr. Koller and his
wife live in the San Francisco Bay Area.

Learn more about his work at
www.DennisKoller.com

Made in the USA
Middletown, DE
16 February 2017